Stellar Endorsements for Mary Mueller

Mary Mueller's *Mirror Images* is a story of despair and hope, brokenness and the yearning for restoration. Will Ryersen, a conflicted, confused yet tenderhearted teen, is the spitting image of his father, whether or not he wants to admit it. Warring with the feelings of inadequacy and teenage angst, Will wants nothing more than to establish himself as his own man in a world that sees him as his father's son. *Mirror Images* is often heartwarming, frequently heart-wrenching and always heart-centered. Will Ryersen's story is, after all, one about a heart searching for Home. Mary Mueller is at her absolute finest as she weaves a tale about a father's love for his son and a seeker's yearning to find Truth. This is a novel that stays with you long after you turn the last page.

> *– Josh Clark, author of "The McGurney*
> *Chronicles" series, the "Dakota Lester"*
> *books and the forthcoming novel, "The Streak". –*

Mary's style is very heartfelt, with a lot of raw emotion – enough to push the reader out of their comfort zone. She doesn't settle for cliche phrasing, and her characters are well-rendered. Their real-life, visceral experiences remind us that we could all be just one step away from desperate straits. The prose is refreshing, and Mary carefully depicts the book's locales with an economy of words. *The Redemption of Matthew Ryersen* and its sequel, *Mirror Images*, are perfectly titled novels that reveal the grace of God we all need. Both are sweeping in their ability to hold the reader's attention. Nicely paced, with an intimate feel for the supernatural, and each book features a memorable cast. Well done, Mary!"

> *– Steve Wilson, Author of*
> *"Red Sky at Morning" –*

This book should be carried by every Christian book store. In *Mirror Images* the continuing adventures of Matthew Ryersen flow like a cool mountain stream.

– J. Keith Jones
Author of "In Due Time" –

In *The Redemption of Matthew Ryersen"* Mary Mueller crafted a wonderfully realistic story about a man and his need for love and faith. It was a story that begged to be told and its message lingered long after the final paragraph was read. It left a yearning for more about this family and their struggles. We have to wait and anticipate no longer. *Mirror Images* has arrived! In this sequel, Mueller takes us on a journey with Matthew, Will and the others that leads to some perplexing and difficult questions. With her eye on the Lord and her feet grounded in the sometimes painful world in which we live, Mueller has crafted a fast-paced, relevant and engrossing sequel that meets some of the most challenging issues of our time head-on. You will want to read *Mirror Images*, and when you do, it will make you think long after you've closed the book.

– Bill Thomas, Author of
"From the Ashes" –

Mirror Images, the sequel to *The Redemption of Matthew Ryersen* flings you right back into the home of John and Carolyn Abbott, a place where four lonely souls have come to live, heal and find God. *Mirror Images*, by Mary Mueller is beautifully written and witty. It deals with addiction, suicide and bullying in an honest, yet surprisingly quiet voice... so well done, a welcome authenticity in the brassy, superficial culture of today."

– Kathy Frias, Author of
"Rumors of Eden" –

Mirror

Images

Mary

Mueller

Published by White Feather Press.
(www.whitefeatherpress.com)

ISBN 978-1-61808-041-7

Printed in the United States of America

Cover design created by Ron Bell of AdVision Design Group (www.advisiondesigngroup.com)

Interior wheat stalk photo ©iStockphoto.com/Matt Jeacock

All scripture quotations in this book are taken from the New International Version of the Holy Bible.

White Feather Press

Reaffirming Faith in God, Family, and Country!

Dedication

To my children,
grandchildren,
great-grandchildren –
by blood and by adoption –
all much loved

Acknowledgements

The God and Father of us all, in Whom all things are possible!

Friend and colleague Josh Clark, for plotting and unflagging encouragement. And for going on the hard parts of the journey without hesitation.

Publisher Skip Coryell and White Feather Press, for taking on not only the manuscript but also the author.

Artist Ron Bell, for another beautiful cover to make people want to peek inside.

Jodi, Will, the Writers' Forum, invaluable first readers.

Pastor Kent and the staff of Pettisville Missionary Church, for letting me write when the phone isn't ringing.

Author's Note

Dear Reader:

Thank you so much for choosing *Mirror Images*! I hope you are choosing this book because you have read the first book in the Ryersen Trilogy, *The Redemption of Matthew Ryersen*, and want more of the characters who captured you there.

The Redemption of Matthew Ryersen was never meant to be part of a trilogy. When it was finished, I heaved a huge sigh of relief that I had accomplished my goal, telling my spiritual journey (in what became extremely metaphorical terms!). Then my Faithful Readers (you know who you are) began to ask, "What happens next?" "What about Allison?" "What happens to Will?"

The temptation of Mary Mueller came in those questions and in the relentless prodding of my writing buddy Josh Clark, who insisted, "It's doable!" and wouldn't let me back off. He talked me through the plot-line for *Mirror Images* – and then we realized a third book is necessary to complete the circle of redemption. So he talked me through the plot-line for that! God willing, the final book will be published in 2013.

The heart of the story, in all three books, is the relationship between father and son, how it affects the relationship between Father-God, Abba-Daddy God, and His sons (and daughters!), and how only by grace can we come to healing of those relationships, both vertically and horizontally.

If I have done my job well, you will find yourself and your relationships with God and with people in this trilogy. I hope and pray for you that if you don't already have it, you will find for yourself rest in your Father's arms.

Blessings –

Mary

Mirror

Images

One

ATHER AND SON, PRACTICALLY MIRROR IMAGES, turned identical glares upon the pretty blond woman with the camera as they squinted against the glare of dozens of candles on what had to be the world's largest sheet-cake.

"Smile," she said. "This is a great occasion!"

"Yeah, right," they growled in unison, cracking themselves up. As they looked at each other, shaking with laughter, she snapped the picture – and another, for good measure.

"Perfect," she said.

"Blow out some of these candles, will ya?" the boy begged his father. "They're burning my retinas, and seventeen is too young to go blind."

Matthew Ryersen wiped a laugh-tear from his eye and looked at his son. "It's your name on the cake, so I figured you'd want to do it."

The boy flicked dirty-blond hair out of his eyes and surveyed the cake, where large red frosting letters spelled out "Will Ryersen."

"My name," Will said, "but it's your birthday."

Carolyn Abbott raised the camera again. "Maybe you could do it together," she suggested.

"A great photo-op," agreed her husband John from behind her, as he and his brother-in-law, Carolyn's brother Ted Seibenek, held back the four young Seibenek boys, who wanted cake, not ceremony.

Matthew and Will nodded to each other, matching sparks in matching slate-blue eyes, and bent to the task, taking several breaths each to finish it. Carolyn put the camera down and picked up a cake-knife the size of a small machete. As she began the stroke which would slice through the W in Will's name, Matthew said,

"Wait!"

Carolyn froze. "What?"

Matthew flushed and looked down at his feet. "I just – want to look at it a minute more," he said. He raised his eyes to look not at the cake, but at Will. "This is the best birthday present I've ever had – probably ever will have."

Will flushed in turn, the same delicate shading of ears and neck. "It was no big deal."

"It is to me," Matthew said. "I never hoped – never dreamed you'd want to change your name to mine."

"Oh, go ahead and hug the boy," Pearl said brusquely, her old voice quavering even more than usual.

Matthew tentatively reached for Will, taking nothing for granted, feeling tears rise as the boy stepped into his embrace and gave him some awkward back-pats as a bonus. Carolyn dropped the knife and took another picture.

"Cake!" yelled the Seibenek boys. "We're starving!"

The remains of the cake were wrapped in plastic wrap, half going home with Ted and Olivia and the boys, the other half sitting prominently on the kitchen counter for "the midnight raiders," as Carolyn referred to John, Will and – occasionally – Matthew. Dishes were washed, dried and put away; the floor had been vacuumed, the table wiped, the wrapping paper from Matthew's presents deposited in the burn barrel outside. Pearl had gone home across the road, taking Ed Yoder, the farmhand, another unofficially adopted Abbott family member who shared his house with her. The four remaining sat quietly on the front porch enjoying the mild June evening.

"I remember when I was little, getting a fruit jar from Mom and catching lightning bugs," Carolyn said as she gently shooed one from her arm. "Ted always caught more than I did, but if he was feeling nice, he shared."

"What'd you do with 'em?" Will asked from his perch on the top step.

"Oh, nothing, really. We'd poke holes in the lid with an ice-pick and put grass in the jar, thinking they would eat it. Then we'd put the jar on the table by the bed and just watch them light up the dark room. Mom usually made us let them go the next morning, because if you keep them trapped like that they die in a day or so."

"I get that," Will muttered, remembering his days in jail.

"Ted and I used to go camping down by the creek," John said. "We'd catch fish for supper and fry them up and eat them with stuff our moms had packed for us. Cookies, mostly, and baloney sandwiches." He grinned at Matthew, although it was too dark to see the expression on his face. "She never thought we'd catch enough fish to get by."

"Did you?" Will asked.

"Sometimes." John pushed with his foot to set the swing moving. "Sometimes not. It wasn't about the fish, though, as much as feeling like real men."

"How old were you?" Matthew asked, laughing just a little.

"Seven or eight when we started, I think. Kept on doing it, though, until we got our licenses. Then it was all about the girls."

"Don't go there," Carolyn warned, while Will and Matthew snickered.

"Speaking of girls," Will began casually, "can I borrow the car Friday night to take Tracy to the movies?"

"Fine with me if it's okay with your dad," John said.

Matthew didn't register for a moment that they were talking about him. He cleared his throat. "Sure, I guess so, as long as the chores are done."

"Thanks!" Will said, standing and stretching. "Guess I'll go call Tracy and then go up and read for a while." He moved with quick, light steps into the house.

Matthew cleared his throat. "Uh – John – about the car."

"What?"

"I don't like for Will to be borrowing your car all the time."

"Oh, I don't mind. He's young and likes to be out and doing things, and we're – not so young and usually stay home. So it's no problem."

"Well, that's nice of you and all, and you've been real generous with me and with Will, but it just seems like – like maybe we ought to be – you know – standing on our own feet more..."

"Don't you dare say anything about getting a place of your own!" Carolyn interrupted. "This is your home and we want you here!"

"I wasn't – not exactly. I just think maybe it's time I buy my own car or truck or something. Then Will can drive that when he needs to."

"Not a bad idea," John agreed easily. "Not that I care about letting you use the car and the truck whenever you need them, but there is something about owning your own vehicle." He caught Carolyn's hand as it attacked his ribs. "It's a guy thing, Caro, that's all." He turned his attention back to Matthew, keeping hold of Carolyn's hand. "Have any idea what you want?"

Matthew laughed. "Will's lusting after anything low and long with an eight-cylinder engine. New, with leather seats. I figure something used, probably a pick-up. Makes the most sense with all the hauling I do here. Also less likely to wrap my kid around a tree on some Fulton County curve."

After lunch the next day Matthew invited Will to go for a ride. The boy was not a big fan of farm work, although he did what he had to do well enough, so he jumped at the chance to get away.

"Where we going?"

"Into Lewiston."

"What for?"

"Get in the truck, okay?"

Will hopped into the old pick-up and belted himself in. "So why we going to Lewiston? I don't have a probation appointment 'til next week."

"I thought maybe I'd get me a birthday present," Matthew drawled.

"What you going to get?"

"You are worse than a three-year-old for asking questions!" Matthew said. "I'm sorry you never got to meet David; he was the master of questions." He was referring to the son of John and Carolyn, who at the age of three had stolen Matthew's damaged heart, when Matthew first came to the Abbots, and had broken it all over again when he had died of leukemia at the age of seven. Will listened carefully, because Matthew didn't often speak of David so openly.

"Little kids do that, huh?" Will said.

"Yeah, they do. His cousins did it, too. But David – he was curi-

4

ous about everything – how things worked and why God did things a certain way and – just everything." Matthew's voice thickened and he blinked hard several times.

Will gritted his teeth and told himself it was stupid to be jealous of a little dead kid. If his dad had been around when he was that little, he probably would have answered Will's questions. Except the big one was – Why *weren't* you there for me when I was three? He felt the old anger beginning to bubble inside him again and tried to push it out of the way. He turned on the radio and tuned it to a rock station.

"Not so loud!" Matthew yelled over the sudden explosion of sound.

Will turned the knob back one notch. It needed to be loud to block the stuff inside. But he couldn't tell that to Matthew. What if he decided he didn't like Will anymore and didn't want to have him around?

Matthew drove onto the lot of Lewiston Ford and parked the truck. "We're here," he said. "Let's look around."

"Huh?"

"I said, let's get out and look around." Matthew opened his door.

"For what?" Will asked.

Matthew laughed. "For my birthday present. I think it's time you and I had a vehicle of our own."

All Will's anger and fear washed away in a huge wave of delight. "You mean it? A new car?!" He leaped onto the asphalt and looked around wildly at dozens of cars and trucks with big stickers in their windows.

"I mean a something," Matthew said more cautiously as he joined Will. "Not sure what. Listen, Will, you gotta understand before we start looking – I can't afford a fancy brand-new sports car."

Will's face fell just a little, but he nodded. "Yeah, I get it. Not the right car for the farm, anyway. But something better than Ed's El Camino, right?"

"I promise."

They began to walk toward the back of the lot, where rows of trucks were parked. A middle-aged man in dress pants and a white shirt and tie came at a diagonal from the showroom to intercept them. "Afternoon!" he said, sticking out a well-manicured hand to

Matthew. "I'm Hal Stuckey. What can I do for you today?"

Matthew briefly shook the proffered hand, noting the lack of calluses. "We're looking for a truck, I think."

"Well, you've certainly come to the right place!" Hal said, waving his arm at the rows of gleaming vehicles. "Nothing better than a Ford truck!"

"Tracy's dad drives a Chevy," Will said before Matthew could shush him.

"Well, they make fine trucks, too," Hal agreed, "but not as good as ours. You know our slogan – 'Built Ford-tough.' Now here we have a real beauty, extended cab, standard air-conditioning, leather seats, tape player, stereo sound, automatic transmission, Michelin tires – all the best."

Will considered the maroon beauty, checking out the leather seats, but Matthew began to laugh.

"Hal, I gotta tell you: I am not in the market for anything like this. I'm looking for a little workhorse of a truck that will haul lumber in the back and pull a trailer and go through mud or water without bogging down. I don't care about leather seats and tape players. I want a reinforced chassis and a gooseneck hitch."

Hal stood quiet for several seconds, appraising Matthew and Will. "Well, I can see you're a farmer and you know what you need. But your boy, here, he looks like maybe he could use something that would make the girls sit up and take notice. So maybe we can look at a few things – let him drive a couple – and then see where we are."

Matthew looked at Will, who was carefully saying nothing. "What do you think, son?"

"Well, I'd sure like a Mustang, but I don't figure that's negotiable, right?"

"Right! I was thinking about something used, up to a hundred thousand miles, maybe, and not too much rust – "

Hal's face registered decidedly unprofessional horror, and Will's bore close resemblance. The boy looked at the supertruck with resignation and turned toward the used losers huddled off by themselves in the farthest corner of the lot. Matthew felt a pang of – something – and drew a deep breath.

"Okay. Let's look at the newer F-150's. You got any just a little bit used?"

"Right this way!" Hal said, leading them down the aisle at a rapid clip. "Our F-150s are all in this next section." He paused in front of a group of brand new trucks. "Here's the latest model, never been driven, and the sticker price is a real bargain compared to the supertrucks. You can still get your optional features, but without the leather seats, and they haul pretty good, I'm told."

"Used ones?" Matthew asked again, mildly.

Resigned, Hal led them to a much smaller group of trucks. Matthew could see that some were heavily used, rust, dings, one with a crumpled rear fender. But a couple of them were still shiny and undented. He went to a red one whose paint still gleamed in the afternoon sun and opened the driver's door.

"That one is a couple of years old," Hal said, "about sixty thousand miles on it. But the guy used it for vacation road-trips and only hauled a small travel-trailer. So it's in good shape. Not an automatic, though."

"We can drive a stick," Matthew said.

"Can we try it?" Will asked.

"Sure you can," Hal said. "I'll go inside and get the keys and you can take it for a spin."

While Hal was inside the dealership, Matthew said to Will, "Do you see any of these you like better? I never bought a vehicle before, but I surely think you're supposed to try more than one before buying."

"You never had a car?"

"Nope. Granddaddy had an old beater truck I learned to drive on, but when it died we never could afford to get another."

"You were really poor!"

"Yep. So what about that black one over there?"

"I like the red one. Here's Hal with the keys."

As a matter of principle, Matthew drove four different used trucks and one new F-150 before agreeing that the red one was the right one.

"This is a real deal," Hal said. "Not too many miles, tires pretty new, nice tape player for your boy, not a scratch on her..."

"Well, yeah, but it's more than I planned to spend," Matthew said. "I'm sorry, Will, but this would just about wipe me out."

"Oh, but you can get a thirty-six or forty-eight month loan with zero down and only ten percent interest – a great deal on the loan!" Hal said. "We can do in-house financing and get you approved before you leave the lot. Why, you can drive this beauty home today!"

"Sorry, Hal, but I don't believe in borrowing money. I plan to write a check for whatever I buy. Then I don't pay interest and no-body can take it from me later."

They grinned at Hal, who stood there sweating lightly in the af-ternoon sun, and made him the offer they hoped he couldn't refuse. One trip to the bank and several dozen papers later, Matthew let Will drive the red 150 off the lot into the stream of homegoing traffic.

"So is it cool or what?" Will asked Ed as the farmhand circled the truck.

Ed stifled a grin as he observed the boy's excitement; Will was not known for showing any emotion except anger. "Cool enough, I reckon," he allowed. "Nice color. How upset you gonna be the first time you get a ding in the fender or a scratch on the door?"

"Oh, no, I'm going to take real good care of it when Matt lets me drive it. And I'm going to wash it and wax it and shine up the chrome."

"Right," Ed agreed. "Nice looking truck, and Tracy's gonna like it. Kinda makes me think I shoulda got something other than another old El Camino..."

"You could still do that. It'd be cool."

"Nah, prob'ly not. We're kinda used to each other, the old girl and me."

"Aw, come on, Ed," Will teased. "You know you'd like one of those great big Ford 350s. Think of all that power!"

"*You'd* like me to have one of those great big Ford 350s, boy, so you could borrow it. Don't notice you ever ask to take Tracy out in the El Camino no more. Nope, we'll just let you and your daddy enjoy this one – after you finish choring. Let's go." He snagged the boy's elbow and steered him away from the truck toward the barn.

From the enclosed back porch utility room, Matthew watched his son interacting so comfortably with the farmhand and carefully, will-fully stifled a wave of jealousy. He wondered again whether he and Will would ever achieve that ongoing level of comfort and humor Ed had managed with the boy. *John and Carolyn have it, too. The only one he doesn't like or trust is me. Not that he had any reason to trust me in the beginning, but now – it ought to be better. What does he expect?*

Who are you kidding? Matthew heard inside his head. *You don't know how to be a father and you don't know how to love anybody but yourself. Why don't you just get out and let Ed raise the kid?*

Matthew almost staggered under the weight of condemnation before he caught himself. "No. I know who you are, and you aren't going to lie to me anymore. Shut up and leave me alone!" Almost at once peace came over him, and a different voice seemed to remind him, *I make all things new.*

Will came bouncing up the back steps, laughing over his shoulder at Ed. "Gotta get some nourishment before doing chores," he said to Matthew. "Might starve before supper." He rushed into the house to grab a huge handful of peanut butter cookies from the big nesting hen cookie-jar and handed one to Matthew as he went back out. "Here. You need it even more than I do." He gave Matthew a snarky smile and then paused. "Oh, and hey, thanks for buying the truck."

"You're welcome," Matthew breathed, fearful of disturbing the moment. Will dashed away toward the barn, stuffing cookies into his mouth as fast as he could, and Matthew stood there watching, absently taking a bite of his own cookie, delighting in the exchange.

Two

"**M**ATT!" WILL BELLOWED UP THE STAIRS. "Phone!" He turned to Carolyn, who stood at the sink finishing the dishes, which Will had reluctantly been drying. "It's some woman," he said, a touch of something in his tone.

"Oh," Carolyn said. "Here, dry this pot and we can call it a night."

Will applied his damp towel to the pot and put it away in a low cupboard. He was hanging up the towel as Matthew barreled down the stairs, thrusting his arms into a flannel shirt, to grab the phone. Carolyn took Will's arm and led him out of the room. "Phone calls are private," she said. Will grunted and wandered off.

"Hello?"

"Matthew?" The voice was tiny, husky, whispery and far away. "Matthew?"

"Yeah." Could it be? "Allison?"

"It's me, Matthew."

She's crying, he thought. "Allison, what's wrong?"

"Oh, Matthew!" she wailed.

His skin prickled. Something was terribly wrong. "Talk to me, Allie. Tell me what's going on." He kept his voice low and even to steady her.

"Oh, it hurts! And it's all your fault. I need you, Matthew, but you don't want me – "

"Are you at home?"

"Mm-hmmm..." He heard her snuffling, as if she needed but

didn't have a handkerchief.

"I'll come over. I can be there in fifteen minutes."

"No, don't hang up on me! Don't you hang up, Matthew!"

"Shh, Allie, just hold on. Wait. I'm not hanging up on you. Listen: I'm going to put on my shoes and get the truck and drive over to your house so we can talk in person. Do you understand, Allison? I'm coming to you."

"Really?"

"I promise. As soon as I put on my shoes."

"Hurry," she whispered and hung up with a loud click.

Matthew's heart was pounding the wall of his chest like a wrecking ball as he vaulted up the stairs, crammed his sockless feet into his sneakers and leaped recklessly back down the stairs.

"I have to go out," he called to John and Carolyn as he ran past the living room. "Don't know when I'll be back."

He buttoned his shirt inside his unzipped coat as he drove well over the speed limit to sleeping Lewiston, then slewed the truck into the parking space nearest Allison's townhouse and rushed up to lean on the bell.

Backlighted by every light in the place, swathed from neck to toe in a pale pink plush terrycloth robe, tiny bare feet peeking out, she was so beautiful she made Matthew's pounding heart stutter in his chest.

"What are you do-ing here?" she asked, enunciating very clearly.

"You called me," Matthew said, puzzled. "You asked me to hurry."

"Oh. Then I sup-pose you'd bet-ter come in." Allison stood aside to let Matthew enter, and he caught the familiar sick smell of Jack Daniels.

He noticed then that Allison's eyes were bloodshot, her skin pasty, her curly hair matted, a dark stain on the front of her robe. The living room into which he stepped would have been attractive, in a spare, modern way, but it was a mess – books, papers, dirty dishes everywhere, pillows and blankets trailing off the couch.

"Have a seat if you can find one," Allison gestured grandly. "Want a drink?"

"No, thanks." He stood still.

"Well, I do," she chirped gaily, heading for the kitchen at a slight

11

tilt.

"Allison, don't. You've had enough." As soon as the words were out of his mouth, Matthew remembered and knew he had made a mistake.

She turned on him, her eyes deadly. "Oh, no, I have *not* had enough. I may *never* have enough. There may not *be* enough – " Her face crumpled suddenly and she began to cry as a small child would, mouth wide open, arms limp at her sides.

Pushing past the smell, which still turned his stomach even after all these years, Matthew scooped up his tiny dragon-princess and carried her to the couch. Settling her into the crook of his arm, he held her and waited for the spasm of weeping to subside.

"Can you tell me now?" he finally asked. "What hurts? And why is it my fault?"

"Do you know how old I am?" Allison asked, only a faint slur marring her words.

"No. Twenty-five? Twenty-six?"

"You're so sweet! I'm thir-ty-two. Thir-ty-two. And I've never been married and I've never had a baby." She began to cry again.

"Aw, don't cry. You have lots of time."

"That's all you know!" The alcohol swung her mood almost faster than Matthew could follow.

"I'm sorry, honey." He stroked her matted hair. "Just tell me; I'll listen."

"When I was lit-tle, all I ever wanted to do was to have babies, losh – lots – of babies. But I did-n't meet the right guy in high shoo – school, so I thought I'd be a nursh – nurse – while I was wait-ing for Mr. Right, you know."

"Uh-huh."

"Only he did-n't come." Allison sniffed and wiped her nose on her sleeve. "And I had to work hard to put myself through sh – school – so when I got pregnant by some dip-o med sh – student – well, you know. I just got rid of it. No big deal, right? 'Cause I was gonna have losh – lots of babies later."

Matthew held her closer. "And then?"

"I don't want to tell you," she whispered into his collar. "You'll hate me." She was crying again.

"No, I won't hate you, honey," he promised, because he was pretty sure he already knew, and his heart was breaking for her.

"It was a guy named Ben. I was sure he want-ed to marry me, and I thought when I got preg-nant he'd be as hap-py as I was. But he slapped me, and he left me, and I just could-n't – so I did it again. I had two abortions then. Please don't hate me!" she wept.

"Shh, honey, I don't hate you. It's all right. You didn't know what else to do, did you?"

"No!" Allison wailed. "There was never any-body to take care of me but me!" She swallowed convulsively.

"You gonna be sick?" Matthew asked.

"Well, prob-ably," Allison said with sudden reasonableness. "I'm too small to drink that much." She gulped again.

Matthew carried his tiny drunk into the bathroom, which bore evidence of having been used for this purpose before, and held her until the heaving stopped. He was amazed to watch her brush her teeth and gargle mouthwash without gagging.

"I hate this part," Allison said, grimacing. "Now get out of here for a min-ute, okay?"

"You're not going to drink the mouthwash or anything, are you?"

"No, I promise. Just go."

Allison rejoined Matthew on the couch in a few minutes. She seemed more sober and self-possessed, but he knew that could be an illusion.

"You want to tell me the rest?" he asked.

"Where were we? Oh, yeah. You were being a wonderful Christian and forgiving me for being young and foolish." She pulled out of Matthew's arms and faced away from him. He decided silence was prudent as long as she felt defensive.

"Well, what do you know about it?" Allison challenged. "I was just getting my career under way in pediatric nursing. They might not have wanted an unwed mother nursing their kids. So I did it again, you hear me?"

"Uh-huh."

"It's no big deal, you know. Costs a lot, but I got a professional dis-count both times. Hurts, but what the heck – that's what pain meds are for. I mean, it's not as if they were real babies or anything. Only – only I felt so empty afterwards."

Allison began to cry again, tears leaving small, shallow dimples on the soft pink robe. "And I dreamed about my babies – I saw their little faces and their great big eyes – I heard little voices calling 'Mommy!' until I thought I'd go nuts. And I *swore* I'd never do that again!"

She whirled back to look Matthew in the eye, tears pouring down her face. "And then I met you. And you were so nice, so kind, so sweet, so sexy – I could have loved you, Matthew. But you didn't want me – "

"Allison – "

"No, don't interrupt me! 'Cause pretty soon I'll be too sober to say all this." She wiped her nose and eyes on her sleeve again and Matthew handed her his clean but crumpled blue bandana. She used it and kept it clutched in her hand as she continued, "I could have *really* loved you. I could have made you happy, if only you'd wanted me as much as I wanted you. But you went away and you never called back.

"And I was so lonely. And there are lots of men who do want me, at least for a little while. So I'd go out with one, and I'd pretend he was you – "

Please, God, make her stop now!

"And I tried to be careful. But one of those Matthews got me pregnant."

Please, God!

"So you know what I did, day before yesterday?"

Matthew nodded, tears flooding his own eyes.

"I did what I swore I'd never do again. And you know what my friend Doctor Jack told me?"

Matthew shook his head.

"He said, 'Allie,' he said, 'I hate to tell you this, but you'll probably never have another pregnancy, and you'll surely never carry one to term, because you're so scarred from those first two abortions and from an infection some time.'"

"Oh, honey, I'm so sorry," Matthew whispered, gathering her closer.

"My babies!" Allison sobbed. "All my beautiful babies. All I ever wanted – " Weeping wracked her, dragging up pain from so deep inside that Matthew feared she would break. He held her, and he prayed.

Finally, exhausted, the bedraggled little dragon-princess fell asleep in Matthew's arms. "I love you," Matthew told her sleeping form as the realization broke over him. "I've loved you for a long time, and I'm probably going to love you until the day I die, no matter what you've done, no matter what you ever do. I love you whether you can have babies or not, and I love you whether you love me or not. And somehow I'm going to have to convince you that God exists, and He forgives you, and He loves you even more than I do.

"You just sleep now, sweetheart. You're safe with me. You don't have to be alone any more. I'll be your family, and my family will be your family, and my God will be your God just as soon as you let Him."

Whenever Allison had a headache, she imagined a number of Disney's Seven Dwarfs busily at work inside her head with their sharp little picks and rock-hammers. This hangover was at least a five-dwarf headache. White light riveted her eyelids shut and a harsh bellows pumped painful, rhythmic noise into her left ear. Against her will, she moaned. Enter a sixth dwarf.

In the midst of her internal agony, Allison began to become aware of the world around her. Her left cheek pressed against soft, warm cloth; the rest of her pressed against –

"Matthew!"

Her own exclamation roared around insider her head and Allison clutched her temples. The sharp ridge of Matthew's pelvic bone cut into her hip, and his muscle-corded arm held her there. The harsh bellows had been his deep sleep-breathing in her ear. Now it hitched, lightened, as he woke beneath her. Sunlight flooded in to compete with the lamps she had turned on the night before, making her wince and squint to see the stubbled face inches from her own.

"Hi," he rumbled, sleep in his husky voice.

"Shh," Allison urged. "If one more dwarf shows up, I'm going to be sick." She carefully put her head back down on the blue plaid flannel covering Matthew's bony shoulder.

"Okay," Matthew whispered. Slowly, carefully, he shifted enough to raise his hand to her hair and began a slow, rhythmic, repeating caress.

Allison drifted awhile, until some of the dwarfs seemed to finish their shifts and go home. At last she was able, gingerly, to untangle herself from Matthew's embrace and to stand, more or less, on her own two feet. She was clear enough to read a look of relief on his face.

"You can have the bathroom first," Allison offered, "as long as you hurry."

He wasted no time on thanks and was gone before she could say more. *Poor guy. I wonder how long he waited for me to wake up. I wonder why he was holding me in the first place.*

And then the night before came back. Clearly. Allison sank back down onto the couch with another moan. *I can't believe I called him! I can't believe I told him everything – maybe I dreamed that part.*

The sound of the bathroom door interrupted Allison's reverie. She looked up from the puffy blue cushions at the man approaching her. Even unshaven and sleep-crumpled, dressed in a flannel shirt and worn Levis, he made her heart beat a little faster. Tall – but, then, everyone was tall compared with her own alleged five foot height – and far too thin, Matthew had a runner's long, tight muscles, working man's hands and the face of a fallen angel. Allison had never desired a man more. She almost seemed to need him – not just the pleasure of that rangy body, which he denied her, but something deeper she didn't understand.

"Your turn," he said, smiling down at her.

Detouring to the bedroom first for clean clothes, Allison treated herself to a look in the full-length mirror on the back of the closet door. She groaned softly at the matted curls, pasty skin, dark-circled eyes and dirty bathrobe. *You are so ugly*, she told her image. *He'll be out of here as soon as you hit the shower.*

She chose her plainest white cotton underwear, a penance for herself since Matthew would never see it anyway, old jeans and a soft pink oversized angora sweater. She stood in a cold shower until the pain receded further and the cobwebs cleared, in warm until she was relaxed and squeaky clean, from her chestnut curls to her tiny red-painted toenails. She brushed her teeth and discreetly gargled more mouthwash. After drying her hair into a fluffy cloud around her face, she applied a hint of blusher and lipstick with shaky hands.

Better, she mused. *Not great, but better. If I do a really good job, he'll just know I'm faking. He's probably long gone anyway.*

Trying not to hope, Allison returned to the living room. *I was right. He's gone.* Tears pressed against her eyelids, but she pressed back with cold fingertips. *No. I won't cry. He came when I called; he stayed until I was all right. He didn't have to do any of that. And he never criticized. He's one of the good guys. That's why he didn't stay, of course. One of the good guys. Way too good for someone like me.*

Allison gradually focused on the room and began to notice changes. Before he had left, Matthew had folded the sheets and blankets and stacked them, pillows on top, on the end of the couch. The books were neatly piled on the coffee table, newspapers and dirty dishes gone. Her grandmother's rust-and-navy afghan was draped neatly over the back of the couch. The lights were turned off.

Bemused, she wandered into the kitchen. The newspapers and a couple of old magazines were folded neatly and stacked by the back door beside a tightly tied bag of garbage. The dishes, she found, were loaded into the dishwasher, ready to run. The last drops of coffee ran down from the coffeemaker to fill the carafe, beside which sat her company cream-and-sugar set, the pitcher full of milk, and a large china mug beside them proclaiming, "Nurses do it with compassion." He had washed the table and counter-tops and hung up the dishcloth with its edges squared.

"The wife I've always needed!" Allison laughed out loud. Pouring half a mug of coffee and disguising it with all of the milk and three spoonfuls of sugar, she sat at her pretty glass-topped table and wondered, *What kind of man cleans your townhouse and makes you coffee before he dumps you?*

Then she saw the note, spiky handwriting on a paper napkin, "I'll be back by 1:00 with groceries. Please wait for me. Matthew."

Allison let the tears flow down her cheeks again as she carefully folded the napkin and tucked it inside her bra. She cried as she finished her coffee, as she loaded the rest of the dishes into the dishwasher and turned it on, as she scrubbed the bathroom, as she took out the trash, as she lugged out the vacuum that was nearly as big as she and then found she didn't have the energy to use it. She sank down on the ottoman next to the huge machine and bawled aloud.

There Matthew found her ten minutes later, as he shouldered his way through the front door with two large paper bags of groceries. He dumped them on the couch and rushed to kneel in front of her.

"Allie? Are you all right?" Matthew tried to lift her chin, but she turned away. "I could get used to this," he teased, scooping her up and settling her on his lap in the oversized easy chair.

"You came back!" she wailed against his shoulder.

"Sure I did. Didn't you find my note?"

Allison nodded, loving the feel of baby-soft flannel over unyielding bone against her face. She inhaled, as best her stuffy nose allowed, the special scent that was Matthew. *It must be the crying, because I'd swear he smells a little bit like Clorox! I didn't know I like the smell of Clorox. Or cheap shampoo. Oh, but I know I like the smell of Matthew!*

"Was that a giggle under all that bawling?" Matthew asked.

"No, of course not," Allison protested, giggling. She sat up and wiped her nose on her hand.

"Quit that! Use my handkerchief," Matthew ordered, placing another clean, unironed blue bandana in her hand.

"Thank you." Allison mopped and blew. "Honestly, I'm not usually a crybaby. It's just hormones – and – and – " The tears began again.

Matthew gathered her back and waited out the storm. When she quieted enough to sit up and look at him, Allison saw that his eyes were closed.

She took the opportunity to study him. He had showered and shaved, leaving his skin smooth and faintly gleaming. Even in winter he retained a trace of the golden tan of summer. His long dark-gold eyelashes were almost white at the tips and cast deep crescent shadows on his high cheekbones. As his hair was drying, it was feathering over his forehead. The bridge of his nose was narrow and elegant, his lips finely drawn and softened by a faint smile. His hands were beautiful, she realized, long, strong, fine-boned, tendons prominent, like an artist's or a musician's. And with a woman –

Allison swallowed hard against a dry throat. She was embarrassed by her lust and by knowing Matthew would know it. *Stop it,* she warned herself. *He just feels sorry for you. He made it clear a long time ago – he doesn't want you.*

Matthew opened his eyes and smiled.

"I'll put the groceries away," Allison blurted, jumping up from Matthew's lap. "You were sweet to clean up and to bring things. I'm really not this much of a slob any more than I am a crybaby, usually."

She knew she was babbling as she leaned down to scoop up the bags. He was there, hand on her shoulder, stopping her.

"I'll carry them; they're heavy. You can tell me where to put things."

What could she do but agree? "Okay." Trotting after his long, easy strides into the kitchen, Allison sat at the table and told Matthew where to put fresh and frozen fruit, vegetables, juices, cans of soup, chicken breasts, a loaf of obviously homemade bread, a huge plate of chocolate chip cookies.

"Put those cookies right here," she tapped the table in front of her. "Am I lucky enough that you brought milk, too?"

"Yes, ma'am," Matthew grinned. "I put the last you had in that pretty little pitcher before I left." He drew a glass bottle out of one of the bags. "This is our milk, Jersey, a whole lot better than store-bought."

Allison paled a little. "Uh – Matthew, I don't mean to be rude, but – is it, uh – well, I mean – " She flushed.

Matthew grinned again. "Relax. It's clean, it's safe, and if you want to ruin it by skimming, just put it in the fridge until the cream rises to the top. We drink it every day."

"Oh. Well. I didn't mean to be rude."

"It's okay," he said patiently. "You're just obviously a city girl." Finding two clean glasses, he filled one full and the other one about half-way and brought them to the table, keeping the smaller one for himself. "The cookies are homemade," he said. "Lucky for you, Carolyn was already baking when I got home. I had her add extra chips for you."

"You remembered," she breathed softly.

"I remember everything," he told her. "I remember the first day I met you. You were guarding the PICU like a tiny little fire-breathing dragon. I remember your tear on my sleeve when you asked me if I believed God could heal David. I remember your little tiny pink sneakers and Alice Campbell giving up her lunch hour so you could have lunch with me and how you told me your cookies were two from the chocolate group." He smiled tenderly.

"Then you remember taking me to the movies," she ventured.

His lovely, tender smile died. "Yeah."

"And refusing to have sex with me afterwards."

"Yeah." He could no longer meet her eyes. "You told me to go away."

"I wanted you to come after me!"

"Allie, I couldn't. If I had – "

"It would have been wonderful."

"It would have been wrong. It would have been sin. That would have made it ugly."

Allison sighed. "We can't talk about it, can we?" She pushed her chair away from the untouched cookies and milk. "I guess I'm not hungry after all. Maybe you'd better go. I need a nap." Her voice sounded dull and hollow in her own ears.

"Wait a minute," Matthew said firmly. "Last night, while you were drunk, you told me a lot of things. Do you remember? Do you remember telling me about the first two abortions? About how you got pregnant the third time pretending some other guy was me? Do you remember saying, 'I could have really loved you?' *Do* you remember, Allie?" His voice was intense; his eyes returned to force her gaze.

"Yes, I remember. And do you remember the kicker, Matthew? Third time's a charm. This abortion means no more babies ever." She stood. "Now go home. I need to rest. Thanks for the babysitting and the groceries; please lock the door on your way out."

She went into the bedroom and stood with her face against the closed door until she heard him leave. Then she crawled fully dressed into her dirty, unmade bed and wept again for all her losses and for the long, cold, empty winter of her future.

Under a remarkably blue summer sky, Matthew drove back to the Abbott farm. His mind spun in helpless circles until he felt like a bug being washed down the drain, leaving him actually dizzy. Once inside the farmhouse, he slipped unnoticed to the quiet sanctuary of his room and knelt at the side of his narrow white bed, burying his face in his hands. Slowly the whirlwind slowed and the battering images of Allison began to settle out like sticks and leaves and silt sinking to the bottom of the pond. Only the urgent claws in his gut remained.

Dear Lord, thank You for letting Allison call me. I wish she could have called before she did it. I would have married her and loved her baby even though it wasn't mine; I know I would have. You're teaching me how to love Will – I know You would do it again. But since that can't be, please show me how to help her. Because I do love her, and I do want her; and I know You do, too. Please forgive her and call her and heal her, Lord, please!

After a while the urgency of his prayer lessened and he began to confess his own sins, to praise God and then to be still before Him. Reaching for his worn old Bible, he opened it to the Book of Zephaniah. He turned to the third chapter and read:

> **The Lord your God is with you,**
> **He is mighty to save.**
> **He will take great delight in you,**
> **he will quiet you with his love,**
> **he will rejoice over you with singing.**

"That's for me. And that's for you, too, Allison. He will take great delight in us and quiet us with His love. God is mighty to save, and He wants to save you!"

Three

WHEN THE DISGUSTINGLY CHEERFUL GONG OF the doorbell forced her awake again, Allison's bedside clock told her six in bright red numbers.

"A.m or p.m.?" she mumbled, crawling out as wearily as she had crawled in. The bell summoned her again.

"Coming!" she croaked, stumbling to the door. The fisheye peephole distorted the image on the other side, but it was clearly Matthew. "Great," Allison grumbled. "The Good Samaritan returns." She opened the door, ready to attack.

All he did was smile.

Allison turned on her heel, leaving the door open, her heart actually fluttering. How embarrassing! *So what if he is drop-dead gorgeous,* she berated herself. *You're too smart to fall for another line.* She wheeled to face him.

Matthew smiled again, one step inside. "Hi."

She heard just a hint of Kentucky in his voice. "What do you want?"

The smile faded. "I came to bring supper for you. Carolyn sent some things." He gestured to the plate in his hand.

"Telling your good Christian buddies all about me?"

"No, Allie. I just told them you were sick and needed some lookin' after." Sadness filled his eyes. "I wouldn't break your confidence."

Allison realized she couldn't bear to be responsible for the pain in that beautiful face. "I'm sorry, Matthew, really. I know you're trying to help, and I appreciate it. I'm just – moody. It's not your fault.

C'mon, show me what's for dinner."

She was rewarded by another smile and a plate of beef stew with biscuits so fluffy they crumbled when she tried to break them open. At first she forced herself to eat to please Matthew, but the goodness and flavor of the meal soon led her to feel real hunger for the first time in days.

"This is great!" Allison said with her mouth full.

"Yeah, they're great cooks."

"They?"

"Carolyn and Pearl."

"Who's Pearl? For that matter, who are they all? You have a big family! Oh, but they're not your real family, are they?" Allison gulped some of the milk Matthew had set before her.

"They're my family now," he contradicted, handing her a napkin. "You look cute with that milk moustache, but I might have to kiss you later – " Realizing what he had said, he flushed and grinned sheepishly.

Allison experienced another brief episode of tachycardia. Did the man have any idea how adorable he was?

"Tell me about all these people," she urged.

"Well – John and Carolyn own the farm. It's been in John's family for generations, and he raises corn and wheat – some fodder crops – a real small Jersey dairy herd – "

"They're the parents of the boy who died."

"Yeah. David." Matthew paused, cleared his throat. "They lost a baby to SIDS before that. Haven't had any more. I don't know if they tried."

"How awful for them! If I could just –"

"Don't go there, Allie. Let me go on. Pearl is Pearl Gunderman, a widow, a retired school music teacher. I don't know for sure how long she's been around the family – before I came. She's old, somewhere in her eighties, but she won't tell." Matthew laughed. "And no one's gonna make her tell, either. No one messes with Pearl.

"Anyhow," he continued, "in November we moved her out to the farm because she needs to have someone around, just in case. Those biscuits are hers."

Allison acknowledged Pearl's skill. "But what about her own family?"

"All gone, I guess. She had a daughter who died, and her husband died. That's all I know."

"Go on," Allison said.

"Finish your milk, okay? There's Ed Yoder, John's right-hand man. Steadiest person I ever met. He owns the little white house and a few acres across the road. Pearl is staying with him until we can build on an apartment for her."

"That's going to a lot of trouble."

"Nah – we want her to be comfortable and happy."

"So where did Ed come from?"

"I don't know where he started, but he came here from Indianapolis, so drunk he doesn't remember the ride. John hired him and helped him sober up, and he found the Lord – and he's been here ever since, probably fifteen years or more."

"An alcoholic? What kind of do-gooder is your boss?"

"I don't think Ed's an alcoholic – not like my daddy was. He had some personal problems he drank over, and when he accepted Christ he just – "

"Stop it!" Allison jumped up and began to collect her dishes, not looking at Matthew. "I don't want a sermon, okay? Can't you talk about anything without turning it into a God thing?"

"I'm sorry," Matthew said. She saw the flush on his cheekbones again, and along the tops of his ears. "I'll go – "

"No! Don't go! Just be – careful, okay?" Allison sat down at the table again. "Go on."

Matthew settled back a little. "There's more. Down the road are John's sister Olivia – Livvie – and her husband, Ted Seibenek, who's Carolyn's brother. They have four boys. Nice people. John's folks are dead, and his brother Jim is – uh – he's in Ecuador."

"Whatever does he do in Ecuador?"

"Well..."

"What?"

"Well – he and his wife are missionaries. Now, you asked!"

"You're right," Allison laughed. "I did. And..."

"Let's see... Carolyn's father died a couple of years before I came. Her mother remarried to some dentist and they moved to Canada. Didn't come back for David's funeral, even. And she has two sisters in California. So we're all kind of alone, except John. And he has this thing about making a family. He collects us. We collected Will a while back."

"Who's Will?"

Matthew discovered something fascinating in the grain of the table. "He's my son."

"You have a son?"

"Yeah. He's seventeen now. I never met him until he was ten. His mother and I were just – it was just – you know – "

"A mistake?" she asked softly.

Matthew nodded. "We were just a couple of stupid kids. We didn't really even like each other much. A few beers, a truck – there's no excuse, but it just happened. His mother, she was one of those girls with a reputation, you know? I didn't believe her when she said the baby was mine. Even when she brought him to the farm I didn't believe it. But I was wrong. And after a few years of bein' a jerk about it, I agreed to take him in and try to be his daddy."

"How's that going for you?"

"So-so, I guess. We have good days and bad ones. I don't know how to be a father."

"But he means a lot to you, doesn't he?"

"Oh, yeah. Like a bad case of shingles."

"I don't believe that. You get a look when you talk about him, like the look you get when you talk about David."

"Oh. Is that bad?"

"No! I think it's sweet. You care a lot about kids." Allison paused, then took a deep breath. "Maybe you'd better go home now, Matthew. Thanks for dinner, and for telling me about your family."

Matthew captured her little hand between his own. She noted the warmth and callused strength of them and imagined them – *If only things could have been different. If only I could turn back the clock and do things differently. We would have made beautiful babies.* Tears spilled down her cheeks again.

Another blue bandana appeared in Allison's hand. "Honey, you can cry as much as you have to," Matthew said, "but don't run away from me every time kids come up. Let me help."

Allison sniffled, wiped her eyes and nose. "I'm going back to work on Sunday. Then I'm going to introduce you to my friend Leslie Brant. She's a nice little Presbyterian virgin – well, not little, really.

She's tall and willowy and has long black hair and green eyes. And she wants to marry a nice Christian guy and have lots of babies." She gave Matthew a wobbly smile.

Matthew's voice was deadly quiet. "Why introduce her to me?"

Allison deliberately brightened her smile. "Why, so you can date her! You'll be perfect for each other. You love children and you should have a bunch of them. And she wants lots of children."

"I have a son," Matthew said carefully. "I really don't need you to set me up at stud to fulfill my fathering urges."

"You're angry!" Allison was astonished. Little prickles of excitement flickered through her as she imagined the heat under the man's hard, flat control.

"You don't get it yet, but you will. I thank you, Miss Allison, but I'm not interested in your willowy friend, or in any other substitute you might think to offer." The Kentucky drawl was becoming clearer now. "Y'all just get some sleep and take care of yourself. I'll call in the mornin' and be back tomorrow evenin'."

He was almost to the front door before Allison collected herself to go after him. "Are you going to leave angry?"

Matthew turned and smiled at her. "No, ma'am," he said, drawing her into his arms, "but I reckon I am goin' to leave hungry."

He kissed her. And then he was gone.

"Oh, my!" Allison pressed her fingertips to her lips, then to her chest. Blood thundered wherever she touched. "Oh, my," she breathed again, " 'hungry' doesn't even begin to describe it!"

Four

WILL WAS WAITING IN AMBUSH WHEN MATTHEW returned from Allison's. He let his father take off his coat, but barely, before jumping in. "So where'd you go? What was all that about milk and cookies and 'see you when I get here'?"

Matthew looked at Will for a moment. "A friend in trouble," he said, turning away and heading for the stairs.

"Yeah?" Will persisted. "What friend? I didn't think you had any friends but us. You never go out, never have anybody over – a regular hermit. Besides, it was a woman. What are you doing being friends with a woman?"

"I don't guess that's any of your business," Matthew said, still turned away from his son.

"Right. I forgot. You and I, we don't have a relationship, do we, like real fathers and sons, like where a father would talk to his son about anything but cows and trucks." Will stalked away.

Matthew sighed and climbed the stairs to his room. *Will's right, as usual. I'm no father.* He hid away to think about Allison and to try to forget what Will had said, but neither was easy. They seemed to rub up against each other in a bad way, acid and metal, corroding his stomach. *Why can't I figure this out? Is Will jealous? Does he think I shouldn't ever be with another woman because of his mom? Not that Allison – well, Lord, what am I supposed to do!*

He heard Will come upstairs later, but he didn't attempt to talk with the boy. He told himself Will needed some time to calm down

– maybe to apologize for butting in where it wasn't any of his business. Wasn't even a father entitled to privacy? Of course he was! Will needed to grow up and not expect the world to revolve around him and what he wanted.

When I was his age –

When you were his age, you were makin' a baby in the back of your granddaddy's truck. And you were tellin' Dinah you didn't want anything to do with her or that baby, because it just didn't fit in with your plans for your life. So maybe at Will's age you kinda expected the world to revolve around you and what you wanted, huh?

Matthew considered cursing but discarded the option and prayed instead. Then he opened his door and went down the hall to knock on Will's door.

"Yeah?"

"It's Matthew. May I come in?"

Will came to the door and opened it part-way. "Not through telling me to mind my own business?"

"I want to apologize."

"So do it." Will didn't move.

Sighing, Matthew looked his son in the eye, almost on the same level now. "I'm sorry for being so nasty and for telling you my life is none of your business. Of course it's your business. I guess we're still not used to – you know."

"So?"

"I'll tell you the story if you really want to know it, but it'll take a while."

Will grudgingly backed up and allowed his father into the room. He turned off the radio and sat down on the bed, gesturing to the desk chair. "Have a seat."

"Thanks." Matthew sat backwards on the chair, linking his arms on top of the ladder-back. "I really am sorry, Will. None of this comes natural to me, and I – well, never mind. The woman on the phone was Allison West, a nurse I met when David was in the hospital. I liked her a lot, and I went out with her a couple of times back then..."

"So what happened?"

"We had some pretty serious differences of opinion on things. She's not a Christian."

"So?"

Matthew sighed. "It doesn't work well for a Christian and a non-Christian to get together. They have such different ideas about things."

Will snorted. "Yeah, I remember Tracy telling me that in the beginning. But, hey, she's with me now." He laughed. "So you could give this babe a Bible – "

"It doesn't work that way," Matthew said, studying the pattern in his shirt. "At least not for us. So I didn't go on seeing her, and I hadn't heard from her until last night. But she was in trouble and she asked for help."

Will's gaze bored into Matthew. "What kind of trouble?"

"That really is private," Matthew said, looking directly back at Will. "That's not mine to talk about. She needed me; I went."

"Must care a lot about her to go running out of here after all that time."

"I guess I do."

"You going to see her again?"

"Probably. If she's willing. If she'll agree to certain limits."

"Are you in love with her?"

The tide of color which cursed both Ryersens rose rapidly up his neck and ears. He looked away.

"You are!" Will said. "You love her!" He jumped up and flailed his arms in confusion. "How can you do that! You didn't love my mother, but you love some woman you hardly even know!"

"Will, please. Settle down. I – I was too young to love your mother, and she didn't love me, either. We would never have stayed together, never have made each other happy. I've told you before how it was."

"Yeah, sure. Okay, say you're right about Mom. Even so – how can you love some stranger, some woman, but you don't – " He cut himself off abruptly and charged out of the room, down the stairs.

Matthew followed, but by the time he reached the bottom, Will had bolted out the front door, leaving it open in his haste. His figure was dimly visible as he ran across the road to Ed's house, and Matthew heard the banging of his fist on the door even at that distance. He stood there to be sure Ed let Will in. Ed would know how to calm the boy and would help him to sort it out. For the millionth time, Matthew thought how much better a father Ed was to Will than he was. Closing the door, he remembered John's saying to him once that the generational curse of abusive fathers was broken because Matthew was a new creation in Christ. Times like this, it didn't seem likely.

Before he could go back upstairs, Matthew heard the phone ringing and raced to the kitchen to answer it. Ed was calling to say that Will would spend the night there if Matthew didn't mind.

"Why not? He's more at home with you and Pearl than here most of the time. He sure doesn't want to be around me right now."

"We'll talk some about what's eatin' the boy," Ed promised. "Don't fret none, this is just the way boys is."

Five

"YOU DIDN'T HAVE TO COME BACK SO SOON,"
Allison's supervisor chided. Tall and muscled like a
linebacker, Alice Campbell nearly made two of her
best PICU nurse. Her voice matched her size and could crack
like a whip over incompetence; now it was as low and gentle as
the bluff, hearty woman could make it.

"I'm fine. I'd rather work than sit around thinking about it."

"Sure," Alice agreed, "I understand. Just let me know if you need
to go home early, okay? Promise?"

"Yeah, yeah, I promise. Now give me a rundown and let me at
'em!"

Alice settled the elastic waistband of her white polyester uniform
pants more comfortably around her middle and began the patient
staffing. There were only four: eight year old Carey Adams, in for a
rejection scare with his transplanted heart; five year old Jenny Burns,
with asthma; a fourteen year old boy with closed head trauma from
a bicycle accident; and a premature infant readmitted for failure to
thrive.

"Leslie's on, too," Alice added, "and she's familiar with all four cases. Carey will probably be going home this afternoon, tomorrow at
the latest, and we've been over his meds adjustments with mom and
dad twice. Jenny needs another day of breathing treatments. Head
trauma's doing fine now, just a headache."

"What about the baby?"

Alice tightened her lips for a moment and looked down at the chart. "He's a real cutie. Name's Benjie Fry. But he's down to just under four pounds again and he won't suck much. Doesn't fight the bottle – just lies there. I wish he'd fight, show some spirit. They've done a lot of tests, but there doesn't seem to be anything wrong physically."

"How old is he?" Allison asked.

"Three months. Was home a couple of weeks after a couple of months in the NICU in Toledo before his mother brought him in to the e.r. He was dehydrated, running a little fever, limp and apathetic. Didn't cry when they did the blood sticks. Turns his head away from people."

"We know preemies are at high risk for abuse. Any bruises or anything?"

"Nope. Not some flighty teen mom, either. Nice young woman."

"Okay," Allison nodded briskly. "Got it." She headed onto the ward to lose herself in the needs and problems of other people's children.

Later, at the nurses' station, as Allison was charting, Leslie Brant slid into the chair beside her and flipped open a chart.

"Welcome back!" Leslie said with a smile.

"Thanks. Good to be back. How are you?"

Leslie's green eyes sparkled as she smiled again and said, "Couldn't be better."

Allison signed her name at the bottom of the page and took the next chart. "Hot date?"

"Nope!" Leslie looked up from her work. "Actually, I just dumped the guy for cheating on me."

"Why are you so cheerful?" Allison asked.

"Because I did a good thing for myself and I know it was what God wanted, because He never wants us to sell ourselves short and settle for an ungodly relationship. Now I'm free to meet the man He has lined up for me, and I can't wait!"

Allison all but gaped. "You're not humiliated or heart-broken or anything?"

Leslie shook her head, laughing. "I should be, shouldn't I? But no. I'm just thankful I figured it out and did the right thing. He wanted stuff I wasn't willing to do, and when I wouldn't – he found a girl who would. So obviously he didn't love me or respect me. I'm going to find Mr. Right, Allie, and you should be looking for him, too."

Allison let her hair fall across her cheek to hide her face as she bent over the chart. *I did find Mr. Right, Les. But he doesn't want me, even if he thinks he does.* She took a deep breath and arranged her face before turning back to Leslie. "You know, if you're really looking, I just might know the right guy."

"Really?"

"Yeah. I met him a couple of years ago, and we went out a few times. But he wasn't right for me."

"What's wrong with him?"

"Nothing, really. Just for me. He's good looking, in his early thirties, never married, from Kentucky. He's a farmer, doesn't smoke, doesn't drink much... The thing is, he's one of those born-again Christian people, goes to church every Sunday, all that stuff. So he'd be ideal for you!"

Leslie paused for several beats before saying, "Are you serious? You aren't interested?"

"You know I'm not into the God-stuff, Les. But you are, so I thought maybe..."

"Where does he go to church?"

"I don't know!" Allison snapped. "I don't know one church from another. His pastor looks like a stork, that's all I know."

Leslie laughed out loud. "I know exactly who you mean," she chuckled. "Pastor Corrigan. Well, I wouldn't mind being introduced."

Allison bit the inside of her cheek until she tasted blood. "I'll see what I can do," she said.

Six

"**S**O," WILL SAID, HIS MOUTH FULL OF CHOCOLATE chip cookies, "can I borrow the truck?"

Matthew, his own mouth full, held up one finger while he chewed and swallowed. "What's the occasion?"

Will made an elaborate display of unconcern, turning his milk glass in circles on the kitchen table where the two of them sat taking an afternoon break. Carolyn was stirring something savory on the stove and pretending not to listen. Matthew knew better.

"Tracy called and said there's this party Friday night for the youth group at some dude's pond. She thought I might like to go. We'll swim and eat hot dogs and have a campfire and all."

"Since when have you been hanging around with the youth group?" Matthew asked.

The Ryersen flush colored Will's neck and ears and cheekbones. He raised his head to glare at his father. "I do sometimes. What of it if I don't? I want to go *this* time. I want to take Tracy in the new truck."

"Got it," Matthew said. "When to when?"

"Need to pick her up at six, until whenever."

"No."

"*No*? Why not?"

"I need to know exactly where you're going, a number to call there, whether the parents will be home, and what time you will be parkin' that truck back in the driveway."

At the stove, Carolyn put her hand over her mouth to smother her laughter and let her shoulders shake silently. Will was not amused.

"You're kidding, right? I can't believe this! It's the church youth group, for Pete's sake!" He narrowed his eyes even more and clenched one fist on the table-top.

Matthew's glare was identical. "Not kidding. If you can't give me all that information, then I can't let you go. The last time you took the truck on a date – well, you know what happened."

Will jumped up, almost knocking over his chair. "You aren't ever gonna forget that, are you! Or forgive it! It's not the same now, you gotta know that. Oh, what's the use. Forget it." He stomped out of the room and up the stairs. Moments later they heard the muffled slam of his bedroom door.

Matthew said a nasty word and then apologized to Carolyn, who came over to sit in Will's chair opposite him. "I don't see what the problem is with letting us know where he is and who's with him. Why does he expect us to trust him after the way he behaved?"

"Oh, Matthew, try to remember when you were seventeen. His pride is insulted. I don't think he has any ulterior motives; he just wants to be with his girl and to have fun with a bunch of other kids. And he wants to show off the truck. Finish your cookie."

Matthew looked at the half-eaten cookie and felt the first half rise in his throat. He pushed the second half across the table so that he couldn't smell it. "You think I was unfair?"

"Well, no, not really," Carolyn temporized, pushing the cookie back. "I just think you were a little – well, heavy-handed. Will needs a light rein, I think."

"You're probably right. What do I know? I should have sent him to Ed."

"No," she denied, shaking her head, "you shouldn't send him to Ed – or to John or to me or to anybody else. You and he need to work these things out."

"Right. Every time I try to act like a father, he gets mad and walks out or starts a screaming match. He doesn't want me to be his dad."

"Of course he does! That whole thing of taking your name – that proves what he wants. But it takes time to get over feeling unloved and unwanted and abandoned. You know that. Now go to him and try to work it out."

Carolyn rose and went back to the stove; Matthew continued to sit there, pushing the cookie back and forth. He was amassing a large collection of crumbs and leaving chocolate stains on the wood, but it was better than facing the elephant in the living room.

When the phone rang a few minutes later, the "elephant" lunged into the room to grab it before Matthew was half-way out of his chair. "Hello!" Will gasped, out of breath. He paused. "Yeah." The excitement had drained out of his voice. "Who is this? That's what I figured. Just a minute." He turned to Matthew. "It's for you. That woman." He thrust the phone at Matthew and stamped out of the room, the swinging door flapping behind him.

Matthew put the receiver to his ear gingerly, as if it were hot from Will's temper. "Hello?"

"Hi, it's Allison."

"Hey. How are you?"

"Fine! I'm back to work now. I sort of thought you might call, but then I remembered I'm supposed to be the social director – "

Matthew took a deep breath. "I'm sorry. You're right; I should have called. I thought about you, but things here got – strange. Will – my son – he – "

"No, no, that's okay," Allison assured. "I know you have stuff to do, family things. But I thought maybe I could – well, I'd like to have you come to dinner so I can say thanks for taking care of me and all. I can cook, believe it or not. Maybe not as well as the lady there, but I'm not bad. Would you come Friday night?"

"I'd like that," Matthew said evenly, his tone belied by the grin splitting his face. "What time? And can I bring anything?"

"No, don't bring anything; I want to impress you with my skills! Come at six-thirty. That will give me time to clean up after work and get everything around."

"I'll be there. Are you sure you're up to this?"

"Absolutely!" she reassured. "See you Friday!"

Matthew hung up the receiver and turned to grin at Carolyn, who was making no pretense of ignoring the conversation. "I have a date."

"So I heard," she laughed. "And it seems like you're pretty excited about it. Isn't this the girl you felt you had to stay away from? Have things changed?"

"Yeah, things have changed. I realized my feelings for her aren't going away, and I think I need to try to share the Lord with her."

"And you really, really like her."

"That's for sure!"

Will came back through the swinging door, stopping it with his hand. His eyes were flinty and his jaw thrust out pugnaciously. "You're going out with her again."

Matthew sighed and tried to speak calmly. "Yes, I am."

"But I can't go out with Tracy."

Matthew sat down again at the table and looked up at Will. "I didn't say you can't go out with Tracy. I like Tracy. She seems like a real nice girl. I just said I need to know more details about where you're going and who you'll be with. That's not unreasonable, son."

"Don't think you're gonna soften me up by calling me 'son,'" Will snarled.

Matthew spread his hands helplessly and said nothing. *What's the use?*

"Are the kids going to the Rupps' pond?" Carolyn intervened.

Will spoke to her in much more civil tones. "Yeah. We're supposed to get there at six-thirty and stay until probably ten. We can swim and play volley-ball and we'll grill burgers and stuff, then have a campfire and sing later. Tracy says Pastor Miles and Penny will be there and do a lesson of some kind."

"Sounds like fun," Carolyn replied, taking off her apron and hanging it on its hook. "I hope you can go and have a good time." She left the two men alone in the kitchen.

"You could have said all that to me, instead of just in front of me," Matthew said. "It didn't seem to be too much when Carolyn asked."

"She doesn't try to pretend she's my mother. And she doesn't try to tell me what to do."

Matthew sighed. "I thought we agreed we were going to work on this father-son thing, Will. When I brought you home from Chicago – well, I had hope we'd find a way. Now it feels like we're almost back where we started. Are you sorry you took my name?"

Will turned his back. "Sometimes. Like, if we're really the same family, I don't know – you don't act like you care that much a lot of the time. It was cool getting the truck, but then you act like it's such a big deal if I drive it. I guess I can see why you don't trust me, after I ran off with Ed's El Camino and all, but – and that woman, she's not part of our family. Why would you want to bring her into it?

John and Carolyn don't know her, Ed doesn't know her, Pearl doesn't know her – *I* don't know her!"

"I don't get it," Matthew said, running his hands through his hair in frustration. "You think it's fine for you to have Tracy as your girlfriend, but it's not okay for me to date Allison? We're kinda in the same boat, don't you think?"

"No!" Will spun around to glare at Matthew. "I'm seventeen! I'm in high school, for Pete's sake! You're supposed to be a grown-up, a man, a father – not some kid like me!"

"Oh. So if I didn't manage to get married and stay that way, then I just have to be like Ed for the rest of my life?"

"You could do a lot worse!" Will replied and made a quick exit through the back door.

Before he went to bed, Matthew knocked on Will's bedroom door, hoping the boy was still awake. Will swung the door open almost immediately and glared at his father.

"What do you want?"

"I want to tell you it's all right for you to take Tracy to the youth group picnic. You can have the truck, and I'll be sure it has gas."

After a long, uncomfortable moment of silence, Will nodded. "Okay." After another long pause, he smiled and said, "Thanks."

"Sure," Matthew said. "I hope you have a good time."

Although Matthew would have denied being sneaky, he chose to see Allison while Will was trying his wings with the youth group. He saw no need to rub Will's nose in his relationship with her, since it produced an argument every time.

The only glitch was having to admit to John that he needed to borrow the old truck. John handed over the keys without a word, but he did give Matthew a measuring glance that raised the hairs on the back of Matthew's neck and made him feel the need to explain.

"I'm having dinner with Allison, and I told Will he can have my truck to take Tracy to the picnic-thing. It's just dinner..."

"I didn't say a word," John replied, hands in the air.

"No, but I know you think I ought to stay away from her, her not being a believer, but – John, I – "

"I get it," John said, briefly laying a hand on Matthew's shoulder. "Just be careful. We don't want to see you hurt."

"One thing – "

"Yes?"

"I'd rather not have anybody say anything in front of Will about this. He's real touchy about Allison."

"I'll be sure to tell Carolyn," John said, smiling. Then he sobered again. "You know, Matthew, sooner or later you'll have to tell him if you go on seeing her. That old saying about honesty being the best policy – probably true."

Matthew nodded, knowing the correctness of John's remark. *But just not yet. Next week, after Will has a good time at the picnic, after I see how it goes with Allison.*

Seven

SILENTLY ADMIRING HIS OWN RESTRAINT, MATTHEW handed over the keys to the truck without saying anything toWill except, "Have a good time."

"Hey, thanks!" As usual when he got his way, Will was cheerful and charming, a dimpled grin on his fresh-shaved face and a twinkle in his eyes. He had gelled his hair into little spikes, which he only bothered to do on special occasions, and wore an Ohio State tee-shirt with his standard jeans. His bathing trunks were rolled up in a huge towel Carolyn had unearthed from the back of the linen closet and he had looped a doubled plastic bag of two-liter soda bottles over his wrist, his contribution to the insatiable appetites of twenty or thirty teenagers. "I'll be home around eleven."

Before Matthew could hike up his gaping jaw to respond to the unexpected offering of information, the boy was out the door, whistling. Shaking his head, Matthew went back upstairs to complete his own preparations before the trip to Allison's home. *God, help me*, he prayed as he ran down the stairs. *Help me to not make a fool of myself. Help me to remember the boundaries. Help me to find a way to tell Allison about You.*

That prayer repeated inside his head more than once as he negotiated the uncrowded roads and parked John's truck in front of Allison's building. He noticed another car parked there, too, a silvery foreign two-door little thing that looked like it probably ran on twisted-up rubber bands, and smiled at it as he walked by.

Allison answered the door almost immediately in response to the bell, welcoming Matthew in with a hug and a waterfall of conversation. "I'm so glad you're here! It's great you could make it tonight, and I know you're going to like dinner, because I think it turned out really well. I have beer and stuff to make margaritas or rum and Coke and I have soft drinks if you don't want alcohol, because I know you're kind of touchy about that, and there are some snacks on the table in here to hold you until dinner's on the table – "

"Allie – slow down! I'm glad to be here, and I'd be happy to have a beer while you finish up in the kitchen. Let me help you in there." Matthew realized they hadn't moved from the front door and tried to ease Allison into the living room.

"No, thanks, I don't need any help," she said, backing away from him reluctantly. You sit down, and I'll bring you the beer."

He gave in gracefully, sitting on the couch, remembering sitting there with her. Allison disappeared into the kitchen, and just moments later he heard the door to the bedroom open and close. He swung around, surprised, because he knew Allison was in the kitchen, to see a tall, slender brunette in a yellow dress coming toward him. He noted that the dress was made of something soft and stretchy and draped around her gracefully but not too tightly. Trained by his grandmother in manners, he rose to his feet.

"Hello," the young woman said, smiling gently. "I'm Leslie Brant, and you must be Matt Ryersen. Allison's told me so much about you." She held out her hand as she approached, and Matthew shook it.

"Ma'am."

"Oh, please call me Leslie. I'm a nurse and I work with Allison." She sat on the couch and Matthew sat beside her.

"Pleased to meet you," Matthew managed. "I – uh – I didn't realize anyone else was coming to dinner. You just – uh – threw me off a little bit."

Leslie blushed, a pleasant rosy shade which emphasized her high cheekbones and broad forehead. Matthew couldn't help noticing that she was really lovely.

"Allison didn't tell you I was coming."

"No, ma'am. I mean, Leslie."

"I'm sorry, Matt. We've both been set up. But you know what? We're both here, and Allison's a great cook, so why don't we just enjoy dinner and ignore all her matchmaking plans?"

Matthew's face was burning, too, as he considered just leaving. But, no, it wasn't this nice woman's fault Allison was playing games, and he didn't want to embarrass her any further. "Okay. I know you didn't have anything to do with this, and I think I know where Allison's comin' from. Let's get through it."

"Get through what?" Allison asked, coming from the kitchen with Matthew's beer.

"Oh, nothing," Leslie chirped, picking up the drink she had left sitting on the table when she had gone into the bedroom.

Matthew didn't smell alcohol as Leslie raised the glass to her lips. *No, she probably doesn't drink. Some kind of Christian, Allie said.* "Thanks." He took the beer and sipped it gingerly.

"Have some snacks," Allison said, gesturing to a platter of cheese and crackers and cut-up vegetables surrounding some kind of dip. "Five or ten minutes to launch!" She seated herself in the chair across the table from them and scooped up a handful of crackers.

Silence reigned.

Allison looked back and forth at her two guests in some confusion. "I know I usually have to do the dialogue for Matthew," she said, "but I thought you would be able to carry your part, Les."

Matthew turned to Leslie and grinned. "So, tell me about yourself, Leslie," he teased.

"Well, Matt," she answered, "I'm an RN like Allison, and I love to work with little kids. I'm the oldest of six, two brothers, three sisters, and I attend the Lewiston First Presbyterian Church, where I teach fourth grade Sunday School. My favorite color is yellow, and my favorite food is strawberry ice cream. I want to have a big family and a golden retriever and a tire swing for my kids like I had growing up."

"What are you doing?" Allison asked, a dangerous sulfuric undertone to her voice.

Leslie batted her eyelashes at her friend and said as innocently as she could, "Why, I'm getting acquainted with Matt the way you wanted me to."

"His name is Matthew, not Matt," Allison hissed. "Come with me to the kitchen and help me put dinner on the table. Finish your beer, Matthew. Beer doesn't go with lasagna."

Smothering a grin, Matthew nodded and took a healthy swallow as he watched the two women go into the kitchen. They were a study in contrasts: tall and short, willowy and curvy, dark and light, gentle and gingery. Leslie really was a nice woman, and Matthew suspected he could have been interested in her if he had not met Allison first. But a kitten was far from as exciting as a dragon-princess, and he knew Allison's experiment wasn't going to work.

Dinner was even better than Allison had bragged it would be, and Matthew's always chancy appetite was fully engaged, to her delight. When he took a third oatmeal-raisin-chocolate chip cookie, she beamed with satisfaction. They all cleared the table and cleaned up the kitchen together, not too crowded in the small room, and then played a couple of rounds of Sequence, competing fiercely and laughing a lot.

"I have to go now," Leslie said as they finished the second round. "I have to work first shift tomorrow. Thanks so much for the great dinner, Allison, and for a fun evening. Matt, nice to meet you. God bless." She headed for the door.

"Let Matthew walk you out," Allison suggested. "It's dark, and you never know who might be on the street." She nudged Matthew. "Go on. Walk her to her car."

Matthew stood obediently, but Leslie shook her head at him. "No, thanks. I'm right out front, and there's a street light – and this is a safe neighborhood. See you at work, Allison." Hugging her friend, Leslie exited alone, leaving Matthew and Allison standing several arms' lengths apart with no buffer.

"So!" Allison said after a few moments. "This was a nice evening. Did you like the lasagna?"

"You know I did. You're a great cook, Allie. You're just not a very good liar."

"What!"

"You heard me. I told you I don't want to be set up with one of your friends. You let me think this evenin' would be just you and me, and then you sprung that poor girl on me without any warnin.' That wasn't nice to her or to me. She's a good person, and she likes you. That's no way to treat a friend. I'll be goin' now, too. Thanks for dinner." He let himself out without a backward glance and stomped down the steps to the sidewalk and the several yards to the truck.

"Genesis, Exodus, Leviticus, Numbers, Deuteronomy!" he swore, using Ed's pattern of substituting books of the Bible for real curse words. "What a mess! Lord, what are You doin' now!"

Allison stood at the front window, peeking between the blinds to watch Matthew leave. She saw how he stomped his feet and noted his ferocious frown in the light of the street lamp, but she couldn't see his lips moving as he cursed. She admired the way the light gilded his hair and created shadows that set off his rangy body. She kept looking until the truck pulled away and could no longer be seen on the street, replaying the evening in her mind.

Leslie had been so glad to come for dinner, glad to get out on a Friday night, glad to be with Allison, glad Allison was feeling up to entertaining. She had gleamed, Allison thought, just gleamed in that pretty yellow wrap dress. How could Matthew not be attracted to her? And they had seemed to hit it off, laughing together and sharing things about their lives – working well together in the kitchen, too, something not a lot of men were good at. Her heart had been breaking to see how well her plan was working, and then –

"I don't know why he was so mad. I know he liked her. He knows I'm not the right one for him, so why can't he just take my advice and be happy with Leslie? I want him to be happy. I do. I really – " The dialogue broke down as tears swamped her and flooded her cheeks. The truth was, she told herself as she used most of the box of Kleenex on the coffee table, that she loved Matthew and would probably just die from loving him and not being able to have him.

If that God he and Leslie think so much of were real, He'd have made my life different so I could marry Matthew and give him lots of babies. It's not fair! I could have been such a good wife and mother...

The truck had made it back to the farm on autopilot, Matthew thought, as he couldn't remember any of the drive. He had replayed the evening several times, growing angrier each time, until he was pounding the side of his fist on the steering wheel.

It's not fair! And don't tell me life isn't fair and it's not my business to question You, either!

Pulling the truck into its usual place at the back of the driveway, Matthew slipped in through the back door and hung the truck keys on their hook in the kitchen. John and Carolyn had apparently already gone to bed, as the only lights on were the back and front porch lights. He was glad he had made it home before Will, as had been his plan; now he could avoid the issue until some later date.

At 10:55 P.M. on the old alarm clock by his bed, Matthew heard the new truck pull in, followed by the closing of various doors and the sound of sneakers on the stairs and a light knock on his door.

"C'min," Matthew called.

"Hey, Matt! Here's the keys," Will said, handing them to his father.

"Have a good time?"

"Yeah, sure. Mostly." Will frowned a little, more in confusion than in displeasure, Matthew thought. The boy crossed the room uninvited and sat down on the ladderback chair. "It got kinda weird for a while..."

"Like what?"

"Pastor Miles gave this talk around the campfire, and he said weird stuff. It woulda creeped me out, but Tracy was cool with it, so I figured it was okay."

"You want to talk about it?" Matthew asked carefully, not wanting to close Will down.

Rubbing his hand over his head and destroying the spiky hairstyle completely, Will looked all around the room to avoid eyecontact with Matthew. "He was talking about worship. You know, how it isn't just singing on Sunday. He read out of Romans about being a living sacrifice, and – well, Paul made it sound like some kind of Aztec ritual or something! This church isn't into cannibalism or anything, is it?"

"No," Matthew laughed, "nothing like that. Didn't Miles explain himself?"

"Yeah, he did, kind of, but I just wanted to be sure. He talked about if you live for Jesus and do everything like you're doing it for him, that's worship."

Matthew nodded. "Makes sense to me."

Will looked relieved for a moment, until he schooled his face again. "So I guess I can keep going and not worry about being the main course."

Eight

IT WAS A CORN AND SOYBEAN SUMMER, AND MATTHEW almost missed the wheat. He still didn't like to drive the wagons full of corn and grew almost as nervy as John waiting out the long wet spell in August. "It's supposed to be hot and dry now," he complained to Ed as they slogged through mud from the barn to the house for a break. "This weather is going to ruin everything."

"Can't change it, can you?" Ed asked, slapping the side of his boot against the bottom step to dislodge the worst of the mud. "So might as well ask God for a dry spell and then let it go." He took after the other boot with vigor.

"You're right," Matthew sighed. "As usual. I'm not good at letting go of stuff." He scraped the bottom of his boot with a stick. "This stuff is like tar."

Finally they were able to go into the enclosed back porch to take off their rubber boots and slip their feet into battered old sneakers. Stepping into the kitchen, they found Will slumped at the table with a bowl of green beans, snapping them and tossing the ends into a wastebasket between his feet. His pout was worthy of a toddler, and he didn't bother to greet the two men as they entered.

"Hey," Matthew said anyway, as he made his way to the coffeemaker, where a full pot awaited them as usual. "Coffee, Ed, or iced tea?"

"Reckon it's more'n cold enough for coffee," Ed opined, bringing a large mug painted with cows to receive the libation as Matthew poured. "How you doing, boy?" he said to Will.

"How does it look?" Will returned, still not looking up. "Carolyn asked me to snap all these stupid beans. This is my third bowl of 'em. I think she's picking more right now. I hate being a farmer."

"Well," Ed drawled, sitting across from Will, "reckon you're more like a farm *wife* these days. Me and your dad and John don't have to snap beans, do we, Matthew?"

Matthew sat at the end of the table. "Nope. But I did last year. And you end up washing dishes half the time. So maybe we're all farm *persons*. Want some help with those?" he offered, reaching for the bowl.

"Nah. I'm almost done. Gonna head for the hills before Carolyn gets back."

"Too late," came her cheerful voice from the back doorway. "I have the last batch here, Will, and I'll help you with them." She came barefoot across the kitchen floor, lugging a bushel basket to the sink. Matthew snatched it up and deposited it on the counter for her. "Thank you! I'll just wash these off and we can get to snapping."

"Are you canning?" Ed asked.

"No, not this year. I'm freezing them. I think they have a better flavor when they're frozen – more like fresh."

"I think they have a better flavor when somebody else eats them," Will muttered, causing the men to smile and Carolyn to giggle.

"You all might like some donuts to go with your coffee," she said, letting the cold water run over the beans in the sink. "I brought home two dozen this morning. They're in the breadbox."

Will leaped from his chair to the breadbox with speed and grace, hauling out a large box of mixed goodies and making obscene sounds of delight over it.

"Just bring those over here, boy," Ed said, holding out his hand.

Carolyn found napkins and removed the green beans from the table to make more room for treats. Will surrendered the box but called dibs on the chocolate/chocolate-frosted pair. Ed went, as usual, for the powdered sugar, and Matthew bypassed the box to pour a glass of milk for Will. At the sink again, Carolyn finished washing the beans and let the water out of the sink. "I'll just save these until you're ready," she told Will.

"Thanks a lot," he mumbled around a mouthful of donut.

The three men applied themselves to food and drink, not talking much, ignoring Carolyn, as she didn't seem to have anything to say. Matthew could hear her snapping beans behind them as he sipped his coffee and considered whether he really wanted a donut. As he tentatively reached one hand toward a plain yeast roll, he heard a faint noise and a thud behind him.

Ed, who had been facing the sink, leaped up with a shout, and Will swiveled to see what had alarmed him. Matthew was on his feet without thinking about it and turned to see Carolyn lying in a heap on the floor.

The three looked at each other in horror and indecision for a moment before Ed moved to her side and felt her neck. "She's got a pulse, and her color's not too bad." He patted her face and called her name.

Carolyn stirred and opened her eyes, taking in the three anxious faces bending over her and her position on the floor. "I fainted?"

"Seems like," Ed said. "How you feeling now?"

"I... don't know. I feel kind of – well, kind of faint." She moved to sit up, but Ed put his hand on her shoulder.

"Better stay down there a minute so you don't do it again. Matthew, get on the phone to John and tell him to get on home."

"No!" Carolyn said, sitting up in spite of Ed's restraint. "No, don't call John. I'll be fine. I just – fainted. I don't have a brain tumor or anything."

"How do you know?" Will asked, panic all over his face.

"I just know, honey. I'll be fine. Sometimes these things just happen to women, and it's nothing to worry about." With Ed's assistance, she regained her feet. "I'll sit down at the table to finish the beans and I'll be perfectly all right." She followed words with action.

"I'll stay with you," Will said, his disgust over women's work forgotten. He went to the sink and loaded more beans into the bowl.

"Maybe we should call Dr. Hanna," Matthew said.

"Nonsense. I don't need a doctor. I just need to rest a bit."

"Maybe you should drink something," Will said. "Or eat something. Did you eat lunch?"

"Yes, I did," she smiled. "How about a glass of milk?"

Matthew rushed to provide one, and Carolyn sipped it slowly. The two men continued to linger by the table until she urged them out to do the milking.

"Should we leave her?" Matthew asked as they shooed the little Jerseys into their stanchions.

"Reckon she knows how she feels," Ed said, coupling cows to the machinery after Matthew had cleaned their udders. "Just ask the Lord to look after her and don't worry about it."

Matthew was remembering another illness, the frantic prayers of so many people, the blind faith that God would heal – and the death of the little boy despite it all. He didn't feel anything like the peace Ed seemed to walk in. *You're a hard master. It's not unfair, I guess, but it's hard. Please have mercy this time, and don't let anything happen to Carolyn. It would kill John.*

The supper table in the dining room was full, with Pearl and Ed and Will and Matthew as well as the Seibenek tribe seated around the extended sides, John and Carolyn presiding at the head and foot. If a table could really groan, this one would have under its load of ham, scalloped potatoes, fresh green beans, applesauce, corn and Pearl's homemade yeast rolls. Pretty glass dishes of butter and homemade strawberry and black raspberry jams filled in the gaps and conversation was limited as each person tucked in to whatever loaded his plate.

"What's the occasion?" Will muttered to Matthew with his mouth full.

"Don't know. Carolyn just called Livvie this afternoon and invited everyone. Chew with your mouth closed." He elbowed Will.

"Uh." Will chomped and swallowed noisily to make a point and gave himself another huge helping of potatoes from the bowl parked in front of him. "This stuff's really good."

"Thank you," Carolyn responded from her end of the table. She seemed to feel fine now, her cheeks lightly pink from working over the stove, her eyes shining. Matthew couldn't see anything to worry about, so he tried not to.

The Seibenek boys were evidently practicing being seen and not heard, following a bellowed threat from Ted before dinner as they ran from room to room yelling. Matthew remembered the first time he had ever seen them, years ago when some of them were still almost toddlers, singing "Row, Row, Row Your Boat" with David. The old sadness crawled across his heart again, scratching as it went, leaving him bleeding a little. He looked at his plate, with its dabs of food half-eaten, and felt a faint revulsion. *Oh, David!*

Matthew raised his eyes again to find John watching him intently. John leaned across Will to say, "It's okay," in a quiet voice. Matthew nodded and shoved his beans under his potatoes. He waited for Pearl to yell at him to clean his plate, but she merely raised one steel-gray eyebrow and primmed the corners of her mouth a little.

Oh, David.

"All right, kids," Livvie said briskly. "Let's clear the table for dessert. That means you, too, Will."

The Seibenek boys jumped up immediately and began to ferry things to the kitchen. Will shoveled a final bite of roll and strawberry jam into his mouth and slumped back in his chair. His attitude was not lost on anyone, but Matthew decided they were waiting for him to act.

"Go on, Will. Help Livvie and Carolyn with this."

The boy rose slowly, as if to prove he didn't have to, and gathered up his and Matthew's plates. Matthew felt as if a collective sigh was released as the teen followed the younger children in clearing the table. No unpleasantness was going to mar this family gathering.

"He's just being seventeen," Carolyn consoled Matthew as she placed a huge slice of three-layer chocolate cake in front of him.

"Remember when you were seventeen?" Livvie asked Ted, a smirk on her lips. "You were your mama's worst nightmare."

"Tough age for a guy," Ted defended. "And you were mean to me."

The children, catching this part of the conversation as they seated themselves, all laughed in appreciation of their father's wit. Matthew marveled for the – how many hundredth? – time at the easy relationship between the Seibenek parents and their children. He wished he could treat Will with the casual love and firmness Ted always seemed to manage.

Will's temper was vastly improved by chocolate cake, which he praised to Carolyn with genuine enthusiasm and no food in his mouth. Matthew cut a sliver from the front of his slice and offered the rest to Will.

"Heck, yeah!" Will said. "Thanks!" He managed to finish the sizeable second piece before Matthew had negotiated his sliver.

"Has everyone had enough?" Carolyn asked.

The boys were discouraged from asking for seconds by a stern look from Livvie, and for once Will seemed sated. Carolyn cleared her throat and took a drink of water. Matthew noticed she didn't have a cup of coffee.

"I want to tell you all something," Carolyn said, and the whole table fell silent immediately. "I wasn't sure before, but after this morning I did a little test. John, everybody – I'm pregnant! The baby's due in February."

Matthew felt his mouth hanging open and saw the same was true of everyone around the table except John. His jaw was clenched so hard the muscles quivered, and his skin had bleached out like clean laundry. The boys were giggling, and Livvie and Ted grinned from ear to ear.

"Congratulations, Sis!" Ted said, coming around the table to hug her. "You, too, John! This is great!"

Ted's outburst freed the others to speak, to stand, to hug Carolyn, to begin the questioning which naturally followed such an announcement. Even Will seemed excited. But Matthew stayed in his seat watching John.

John sat immobile for what seemed to Matthew to be several minutes before quietly getting to his feet and leaving the room. No one else seemed to notice for several minutes more, until Carolyn turned to him – and he wasn't there.

"Where's John?" she asked Matthew.

"Uh – I don't know. He just stepped out."

The revelers looked at one another, surprised. "Probably needed the facilities," Ted finally said, glossing it over. Reassured, everyone began talking again and the women cleared the table. Ted took the boys into the living room to watch a movie and came back to Ed and Matthew. "So what really happened?" he asked.

"I don't know," Matthew reiterated. "He sat there a minute, then he walked out. I don't know where he went. I didn't hear any doors, so my guess is he went upstairs."

"He was upset, wasn't he?"

"Looked like it."

"Well, what do you expect?" Ed asked. "Looked like maybe she didn't tell him first. None of my business, though, so I'm gonna watch movies with the kids until the dishes are done." He headed into the living room.

"He's got a point," Ted said. "I think movies sound good right about now. It's all hen talk in the kitchen, and I don't want to ruin my dainty hands with dishwater."

Matthew nodded, but he headed up the stairs instead.

John kicked off his shoes and laid down on top of the red and blue quilt covering the bed. His breathing was pretty much back to normal, and his heart had slowed to pretty much its normal rhythm, but he still felt the way a steer looked after a sledgehammer between the eyes. *I can't believe she didn't tell me first, before telling the whole family! I can't believe this is happening! How can we do this again, God?*

He dug the heels of his hands into his eye-sockets to prevent tears from welling up as he imagined all the things that could go wrong with the pregnancy, all the terrible things that could happen to Carolyn, to the baby, all the ways a child could grow up and then die along the way...

No, I can't stand it again. God, you have to fix this. Make it a false test. Make it her imagination. Make it go away!

And then he realized what he was asking.

I can't ask You to get rid of the baby. I know that's a sin, the baby is a real person already, it deserves its chance to live... Then give me grace to forgive Carolyn and to have faith in Your plans for us. Help me to be strong!

Matthew came across the hall and peered in at the bedroom door. John looked at him.

"You okay? They noticed you disappeared."

"Yes, I'm okay," John said, his voice steady. "Just kind of – over whelmed, I guess. Did you know about this?"

"No! I don't think anybody did. Honest."

John sat up and shoved his feet back into his shoes. "She probably figured if she told us all together I wouldn't be able to make a fuss about it. She probably figured I'd be upset, maybe mad – and she was right." He sighed. "No point in staying mad, though. It takes two to make a baby, as I recall."

"You don't want another one, though."

"No, I don't. It scares me to death to think of all the things that can go wrong. I've buried two sons, and I never want to do that again. And – well – I can't bear to think of anything happening to Carolyn, either. It could, so easily." He dropped his head into his hands. "Do you know how old Carolyn is?"

Matthew considered. "Uh – forty-something, right? Forty-three?"

John looked up, bleak and pale again. "She's forty-four. By the time this baby is born she'll be forty-five. That's old to have a baby. There's more chances of something being wrong with the baby, too, like Down Syndrome. There's more danger to the mother."

"Have you been researching all this?" Matthew wondered.

"Not lately. We went through it all when we were trying to have David. Of course, we never figured it would happen to us – any of it." John wiped his hands across his face and sighed again. "Guess I'd better go back downstairs."

Matthew smiled at him. "They think you were using the facilities. I won't say different."

Nine

"I CAN GO BY MYSELF IF YOU LET ME DRIVE," WILL told his father.

Matthew considered for a moment, then nodded. "No problem. I need you to come straight home afterward, though, to get your chores done before supper."

"Yeah, yeah," Will dismissed, snagging the truck keys from the key rack on the kitchen wall. "Dan doesn't keep me long, usually. I'm a good boy." He gave Matthew an exaggerated smile, and both of them laughed.

"See you later, then," Matthew said . He watched Will jump off the top step into the back yard and then jump into the truck. Soon only a rooster-tail of dust marked the boy's passing as the truck flew down the gravel driveway and turned onto the road. "Be careful..."

Will drove faster than he knew his father would approve, left arm soaking up sunshine on the open window edge, right smoothly steering down country roads to the highway, holding the wheel with his knee when he had to shift. *Yeah, I know,* he told the father in his head. *Be careful. Well, I am. I don't want to mess up this truck. But I'm a good driver.*

In less time than he should have taken, Will was parking next to the Lewiston courthouse, locking the truck and sliding the keys into his jeans pocket as he bounded up the steps. Inside, he trekked down the long first-floor hall, past the License Bureau and Tax and Title, to a suite of offices at the other end. "Juvenile Probation" read the sign by the door.

Will popped into the reception area with the easy familiarity of someone who had been doing so for a long time – which was true. He nodded to the redhead in the tight sweater, signed her clipboard and sat down opposite the counter so that he could appreciate her assets. For an older woman, Dee was hot.

"Dan will be with you in a few minutes," she told Will.

"No problem," he said and picked up an old, tattered edition of *Car and Driver.* He was engrossed in an article about the "new" Mustang when Dan's voice cut through his concentration.

"Hi, Will. C'mon back."

"Hi." Will followed the probation officer down a short hall into a small, messy office. The desk bore a cheap nameplate which read "Dan Winsler", a coffee mug full of cheap pens and two huge stacks of files. The chair behind it creaked as Dan dropped into it, his size-able, muscular frame really too much for it. Will sat on a molded green plastic chair in front of the desk and waited for the questions.

"How's it going?" Dan asked.

"Okay. No problems. Going to church, doing my chores at home, keeping curfew... Same old, same old." He grinned at Dan. "Got a new truck."

"No kidding! Yours?"

"No, my – dad's. But he lets me drive it. I drove here today."

Dan smiled. "You look pretty happy about that."

Will grinned back. "It's a sweet ride for a used truck. Tracy likes it."

"Oh, yeah, the girlfriend. Seeing much of her?"

"Not a lot. Her mom and dad aren't crazy about me. I see her in church on Sunday, talk on the phone – go to a movie or something once in a while." The grin had been replaced by a frown. "I think it's dumb for them to be so protective. I'm not gonna hurt her."

"No," Dan agreed. "But parents of teenage girls – they have a lot to worry about."

"Not with Tracy! She's a good person." Will forced himself to stay seated and not to clench his fists.

"Relax," Dan said. "I'm not questioning what kind of girl she is. Just saying how parents are. They'd be that way with any boy."

"Yeah, right." Will's frown deepened. "If I get saved, then I'll be better in their opinion, unless they know about my record. Then I'm toast."

"Well, they apparently don't know, and since you're staying clean they never will. Oh, speaking of staying clean, this is a good time for a test, okay?" He opened a desk drawer and drew out a urine specimen cup.

"Oh, joy," Will said dryly, taking the cup. "You gonna be my escort?"

After the specimen had been collected, sealed and labeled for the lab, they returned to Dan's office, where Dan set an appointment for a month later.

"A month! Man, that's cool!" Will exclaimed before he could stop himself.

"You're doing good," Dan said. "I want to get you off probation in a couple of months. Then I can spend my time with guys who really need it." He rose and offered his hand to Will across the desk. "Stay cool."

"Will do," the boy agreed, shaking hands briefly. He trusted Dan, but only so far.

As Dan was laboriously writing his notes from Will's session into the Ryersen file, his fellow juvenile probation officer, Aaron Rupp, stuck his head in.

"Hey, Aaron."

"Got a minute?" Aaron asked, stepping into the office. He assumed an affirmative before he got one, easing his almost three hundred pound frame onto the plastic chair. Aaron stood well over six feet tall and had been a tackle on his college football team, but some of the muscle had gone to flab and hung over his belt and stretched the thighs of his pants. Still, not one of his cases ever challenged Aaron; he looked like a man who could hurt a guy without trying. His son, Chance, was following in his father's footsteps as a football hero, leading the team in yardage and in touchdowns. Aaron was down-to-earth about everything until it came to Chance, whom he treated like a true hero.

Sometimes Dan grew a little weary of hearing about it. And he had to admit, in his heart of hearts, that he found the boy too entitled and demanding for his taste. But he liked Aaron, and they worked well together when a team was needed.

"Have a seat," Dan said, deadpan.

Aaron wanted to review a case he had inherited from another officer, a case Dan had seen but not worked on. They had spent a few minutes reviewing the particulars when a short knock on the doorframe caused them both to stop and look up.

"Hey, guys," Chance said, strolling into the crowded office as if he owned it. "Dad, I was going to your office, but Dee said you were in here. Hi, Dan."

"Hello, Chance." Dan watched as the boy sauntered a few steps more and planted his tight end on the corner of the desk, displacing a couple of files.

"Oh! Sorry!" Chance said. He stood and leaned over the desk to straighten the manila folders back into piles.

"Need something, son?" Aaron asked. "Or is this just a friendly visit?"

Chance grinned his most charming grin. "Always glad to see you, Dad, but in fact I need some cash. Got a date with Jenny Perkins, and I want to show her a good time."

Aaron nodded approvingly and, with considerable difficulty, hauled his wallet out of his back pocket. Chance took the wad of bills his father held out and headed out the door, calling over his shoulder, "Thanks, Dad."

"What a great kid!" Aaron enthused.

"Right," Dan said, trying to infuse enthusiasm into his voice. "Anything else about this case? 'Cause I still have notes to write up before I can go home."

"Nope, that's all," Aaron said, rising. "Thanks a lot. And, what the heck, Dan, it's quittin' time. Just leave that stuff for tomorrow." He left the office whistling.

Dan drained the last few swallows of cold coffee from his police academy mug and opened Will's file again. But the input of coffee had signaled the need for output, so he left the file and headed down the hall to the men's room. He noticed the light was already out in Aaron's office, and Dee was gone for the day.

Chance Rupp watched Dan head toward the restrooms and turned the other way down the hall. He entered Dan's office and made his way directly to the desk. No, he hadn't been mistaken: The file said, "Ryersen, Will." Only one of those! He looked over his shoulder and dropped his car keys on the floor close to the desk to provide an alibi if Dan came back too soon.

Chance noted the position of the pen on the page facing him and put it aside to pick up the papers from the folder. There were quite a few of them, but he was a lot smarter than football players were given credit for, and he was just about a speed reader. It didn't take him long to read through the pertinent facts about the short, unhappy life of Will Ryersen.

Finished, he put everything back the way it had been, rescued his keys and left the office. As he reached the courthouse door, he saw Dan coming back to the office, but it didn't appear that Dan saw him. He headed to his car, the adrenaline rush still buzzing as he thought about what he had read. He wondered whether Tracy knew all that. Or her mom. Or her dad! Must not, because they'd never let their precious daughter date a fag like Ryersen.

Ten

SUMMER FOOTBALL PRACTICE SUCKED. CHANCE AND his buddies were gung ho for the team and all, but it was just plain murder on an August day when the temp was ninety-eight and the humidity was a hundred and five. Sissy old Pete had fainted, and Coach Hopkins had called practice. Chance was secretly relieved, because puking had not been far in his future. Now they all stood as long as they could in cold showers, moping out one by one to try to dry off with damp towels. He thought he could see steam in the air, even though no one had turned on the hot water.

"Man!" Billy said, rubbing the towel over his buzzed head. "I can't remember it ever being this bad last year!"

"Nope," Chance agreed. "All I want is a cold beer and a long nap. In that order." He grinned at Billy, who was quick to agree, even though he himself didn't break the rule about drinking the way everyone knew Chance did. They sat side by side on a bench to put on their socks and shoes.

"You hear about Ryersen?" Chance asked, his voice just loud enough to be heard beyond the bench.

Billy stopped tying his left sneaker and looked at Chance. "Huh? Who?"

"Ryersen. You know, that kid from Kentucky who dates Tracy Showalter sometimes. The one who never joins in on anything."

"Sits with Kevin and Travis in the cafeteria? Sorta almost blond?"

"Yeah. Will Ryersen."

"So what about him?"

Chance considered carefully how to word it. "You know my dad's a probation officer, right?"

"Man, everybody knows that! Nobody wants to get caught by that dude doing anything bad."

"Yep, that's Dad. Well, anyway, he works with kids, not adults, and he's buds with this other p.o., guy named Dan Winsler. So I went to see my dad at his work, and he was in with this Dan guy talking. So I went in there, Dan's office, and I happened to see something."

"See what?"

"Well, Dan's desk had a lot of files on it. Like they keep each kid's record and stuff in one of those manila file folders, with the name on the tab. And one of the files on Dan's desk was for Will Ryersen."

Chance pretended not to notice that half a dozen other players had gathered around the bench as he was talking to Billy. He finished tying his sneakers and stood up as if to leave.

"Hey, wait!" Curtis said. "What about Ryersen? What did he do?"

"I probably shouldn't talk about it," Chance said.

"Come on, man," Billy said. "No fair. You brought it up."

The other boys nodded their agreement, as Chance knew they would.

"Okay, okay, but keep it quiet, right? Seems like quiet, minding-my-own-business Ryersen is a real bad-guy. Arrested a bunch of times – B&E, DUI, underage consumption and – get this – armed robbery. He did time in DYS before he came here."

"No s – !" Curtis yelped. "A felon! Anybody missing any money?" He looked around the circle.

Heads shook, but Billy said, "Hey! My locker's just down from his! I'd better watch what I leave in there."

Chance took control of the conversation. "I don't think he's dumb enough to steal from your locker, Billy. The school has to know about all this, and he'd be the first person they'd suspect. Thing is, though, you don't want to shower with him after PE."

"What!" Billy said in alarm. "You saying he's a homo or something?"

"I'm just saying to watch your back," Chance said, gathering up his wet gear and stuffing it into his bag. "Gotta go; see you guys tomorrow."

Eleven

FINALLY, ON LABOR DAY, THE RAIN STOPPED. THE sun was as warm and welcoming in the clear blue sky as if it had never abandoned the good people of Northwest Ohio, and the Abbott clan celebrated with a day at the Fulton County Fair.

"They say it's about the best county fair in the state," Ed remarked as he and Will and Matthew rode to the fairgrounds in his El Camino.

"Yeah, right," Will sneered. "That doesn't mean much if all the others are just cheesy."

Matthew sighed and leaned heavily against the door to gain a sliver of space. "At least you have a day off school. Maybe you'll meet up with some friends. Like Tracy."

Will crossed his arms and frowned. "Maybe."

"I'm aiming to see some livestock and get me some fair food," Ed said. "I'm thinking I'll have one of them smoked turkey legs this year. And a sausage sandwich. And a fair milkshake. And some greasy fries. And a whole box of them donuts. Nothing's as good as fresh fair donuts!" He smacked his lips and grinned as he cast a glance at Matthew, who looked a little green. "How 'bout you, Matthew? Greasy fries sound good? Then maybe a ride on the Tilt-a-Whirl?"

Matthew had to laugh, even though Ed's conversation was making him queasy. "Right!" he said. "And you be sure to sit right next to me on the ride!"

Now even Will had to laugh. "I'd *never* ride any of those things with you – not even the ferris wheel – not even the pony rides."

"Glad I could improve your mood," Matthew pretended to grouse, applying his elbow to Will's ribs, but gently. Then, as they approached the gate, he got serious. Fishing out his wallet, he said to Will, "I don't want you to have to spend all your own money or be short when you want to buy something for Tracy. Here." He handed Will a wad of bills.

"You're kidding! Hey, thanks, Matt!"

"You're welcome. Meet us at the grandstand at four, and don't get a tattoo or anything, okay?"

"Sure," Will agreed easily, stuffing his ticket and the extra money into his pocket as they began the long trek from the parking area to the action. A few minutes later they parted company, as the men headed for the barns and Will sprinted for the other end of the midway.

Ed stopped to close his eyes and inhale deeply. "Ah! Listen to it! Smell it!"

"I'm trying not to," Matthew said. The carousel music competed with the rumbling engines of tractors and rides and the whine of the golf-carts used to shuttle people from place to place, all of it struggling to be heard over the din of thousands of voices talking, laughing, yelling at once. He could smell the irritating, musky perfume of the huge woman in front of him, the sickly-sweet odor of cotton candy and candied apples, the spicy hot, feral smell from the taco wagon, and over it all the thick grease smell of dozens of fried-food wagons. Even the pickles were deep-fried – and it all smelled like last year's grease.

Swallowing hard, Matthew shoved Ed toward the barns. There were the familiar, pleasant odors of dust and hay and manure.

"Like home, sweet home, ain't it?" Ed smiled.

"Yeah. And not so many people."

They toured the livestock barns, admiring or devaluing steers and milk cows, goats and sheep. "Why doesn't John enter Suzy or Frieda?" Matthew asked. "They look a whole lot better than these cows."

"I dunno," Ed answered, standing back from a line of rabbit hutches. "I know he was figuring on having David show 'em for a 4-H project back when. You ever do 4-H?"

"No." Matthew paused to pet a large, lop-eared gray rabbit being held by its small, proud owner. "No, we didn't have 4-H in Rough

River. I just helped my granddaddy with the cow and the mule." He smiled at the little girl and moved on.

"About lunch-time," Ed noted. "All teasing aside, where do you want to eat?"

The thought of venturing back into that whirlwind of smells and sounds almost revolted Matthew. It certainly killed his appetite. "I'm not hungry. You go on, and I'll check out the horses. Meet you at the grandstand at four if I don't catch up to you before that."

"Pearl's gonna get on me when we get home if I tell her you didn't eat lunch."

"So don't tell her. I sure won't! Go on – find your greasy fries or fried pickles or whatever."

"All righty, then," Ed agreed and disappeared into the crowd.

Matthew ambled from stall to stall in the horse barns, enjoying the beauty and variety of the show horses – and their young riders. Every horse gleamed with hoof-shine and whatever the riders brushed into their coats, manes and tails. He enjoyed the absolute variety, from a piebald Shetland pony to a seventeen-hand black jumper of some kind whose perhaps-five-foot rider had to stand on a box to bridle him. When a horse was friendly and its owner was agreeable, Matthew stopped to pet and scratch and share breath with it. The huge black had taken a fancy to Matthew's hair, to his owner's embarrassment.

"No problem," Matthew laughed, accepting a towel from the girl to wipe the slobber from his head. "He just thought it was hay. Natural mistake, don't you think?"

The girl nodded and dropped her head to hide her flaming cheeks as she took back the slightly slimy towel. Matthew smiled and headed off down the barn's wide aisle.

As he exited the cool semi-dark of the barn, Matthew paused to let his eyes adjust to the light. Hearing a familiar laugh, he turned to catch a glimpse of bright blue and headed toward it, drawn like a nail to a magnet.

Allison, clad in denim short shorts and a bright blue tee-shirt, stood close to a laughing, dark-haired man as they consulted a program in his hand and looked at one of the harness horses. She looked up into his dark eyes, craning her neck to do so, letting her chestnut curls dangle down her back. Then she looked away and her gaze fell on Matthew.

It was absurdly like a cheap romance novel. They moved toward each other, navigating the crowd as if no one at all stood between them on the worn grass and gravel path, while the sun turned dust-motes to gold dust all around them and faint strains of "The Carousel Waltz" drifted down from the distant midway. When they met in the middle, he took her hands.

"I've missed you," he said.

"Me, too." Her eyes bored into him, huge and blue and full of shadows. "I thought I'd blown it – you know – with Leslie. I'm really sorry."

"It doesn't matter."

"I – well, I came today with a – a friend…" Allison gestured to the dark man, who stared at them, no longer laughing.

"Tell him to go home," Matthew said. "You need to be with me."

Allison nodded and turned back to the dark man. Matthew watched the question on the man's face turn to disbelief, then to anger, as Allison spoke, her tiny hands gesturing wildly. When she paused for a moment, the man took a step closer, looming over her, and Matthew found himself half a step behind Allison, his fists and his jaw clenched.

But the man just shook his head in disgust, spun on his heel and walked away with a stomping, ground-eating stride.

Allison turned around, not surprised to find herself within Matthew's grasp. She seemed a bit pale to Matthew, and she wasn't smiling as she said, "Well. That wasn't any fun. Ryan's a nice guy, and he didn't deserve to be embarrassed like that. You do strange things to me, Matthew. I've never dumped a guy in the middle of a date before."

Although he suspected he should feel guilty, Matthew couldn't seem to find any guilt. He put his arms around Allison and drew her against him. "Don't worry," he said, tipping her chin so she would see his face, "you won't ever have to do it again."

Ambling around the midway, Will took in the sights: ferris wheel, Tilt-a-Whirl, Space Ride, kiddie rides, haunted house, dozens and dozens of games of "chance" where the sucker was guaranteed a prize, food booths, food wagons, food tents – teeming with men in jeans and Stetsons or John Deere caps, women of many sizes in tight shorts and tighter tee-shirts, babies in strollers or backpacks – some sleeping, some screaming – toddlers tugging against their parents' hands, youngsters, geeky teenagers who hadn't yet grown into their hands and feet or bosoms, older teens more sleek and falsely sophisticated – pretending they didn't really care about the frenetic activity or the other teens around them.

Will watched what the other teens were eating and decided he could have the cheese fries and a Pepsi without losing face. Thus fortified, he kept walking, looking for friends, thinking he should have called someone.

"Hey. Ryersen!" someone shouted, and he saw two teens moving toward him.

"Hey, Travis. Kevin." They fell in together and chatted casually, one or other swiping Will's fries as they went. They had no destination, but nobody cared. It was enough to be free, to be together, to be moving. Will felt good. And all of a sudden, he felt better.

Tracy ran toward them, followed by Susan, winding her way through the crowd, and took her place at Will's side. "I thought my mom would never let me go! My little sister is showing her horse this afternoon, and we all had to 'show support,' whatever that means. I had to braid pink ribbons into Flyer's mane."

"My little brother's showing rabbits," Susan commiserated. "I had to help clean cages. Yuk."

"I have a steer again this year," Travis said, "but we don't show until Wednesday. Dad said I can have the afternoon off and then come back out after I feed this evening."

Thank God I'm not a country boy! Will thought. Seeing a trash barrel, he detoured to deposit the empty fries carton and returned wiping his hand on his jeans. As they walked on, he casually took Tracy's hand, as if it were nothing new, secretly relieved when she left her hand in his.

A red-haired, freckled older teen whose build and tight tee-shirt with the colors and logo of a rival school suggested he played football, slowed down as he came toward them in order to give Tracy the once-over. Will tensed, then let it go. It was *his* hand she was holding and *him* to whom she was chattering. Will looked at her pale green eyes and creamy skin, her honey-colored curls and the sleekness of her frame and decided he couldn't blame the poor loser for looking. Tracy was the prettiest girl in school, and the nicest.

"Time to win these girls some loot," Kevin said, and Travis agreed immediately. Kevin was the lead pitcher for the baseball team, so it was no surprise that he led the way to the baseballs and milk cans.

"Ah, those're fixed," Travis complained. "Nobody can knock 'em over."

"Bet me!" Kevin dared, buying two turns' worth.

"He always wins," Susan confided.

Will laughed. "Come on, Trav – what's a buck? Let's give it a try." He plunked down his dollar and took possession of three balls. "So, Trace, what prize are we aiming for?"

"The purple monkey," she said promptly. "Watch Kevin, then I know you can do it."

Travis just stood there shaking his head, hooting when Kevin missed with his first ball and only managed to knock over one can with the other two.

"You go, Will," Kevin said, whirling his pitching arm like a propeller. "I gotta warm up better before I go again."

He didn't mind so much losing the dollar, even with Tracy watching, and he lived through Travis's telling him he threw like a girl, but Will purely hated watching Kevin demolish the cans on his next turn and hand the purple monkey to Susan.

"It's okay," Tracy whispered. "I don't really like the monkey anyway." She took Will's arm as they walked on, and his heart swelled. Man, it was a beautiful day!

Like so many others around them, Will's small group worked the fair, eating randomly, spending almost an hour on the rides, only stopping when Kevin turned the color of raw clams and threatened to lose everything in him. Susan drew him aside to sit on a bench in the shade while Travis, Will and Tracy continued toward the big red-and-white-striped Merchants' Tent.

"Why go in there?" Travis whined. "The political guys are in there. The Culligan man is in there. The Gideons are giving away Bibles in there!"

"The Gideons won't hurt you," Tracy teased. "Just tell them you already have a Bible and they'll leave you alone."

Cultivating his look of disgust, Travis allowed himself to be led inside the huge tent, where, sure enough, the Gideons' representative was the first to greet them. Will thought the man looked like somebody's grandfather, and he politely explained that all three of them had – and used – Bibles.

The Culligan man and the Republicans and Democrats ignored this small group, who were clearly neither home-owners nor voters. Kevin and Susan rejoined them as Tracy was admiring a display of remarkably expensive jewelry. Travis dragged them to the Amish Bakery booth, where he purchased a frosted cinnamon roll as big as his face. Kevin blanched and looked away.

"Man, you can't eat that!" Will laughed.

"Watch me," Travis invited, taking a huge bite.

Will laughed again but was distracted by a booth on the other side of the aisle. A big white banner read "Meet the Authors!" Three people sat below it at a long, red-covered table piled with books. At the near end a tall, rangy gray-haired man who looked like a cowboy presided over three different western novels with intriguing horse-themed covers. He was chatting affably with an elderly man wearing a ball-cap proclaiming him an ex-navy vet. The older woman in the middle was fat and hump-backed, but she gave Will a smile that warmed him from the inside out. The two books in front of her looked girly to Will, but he smiled back anyway. To her right, a much younger man, not long out of his teens, Will guessed, reminded Will of someone...

Matt. That guy looks like my dad, only bigger, more muscles. Wonder if he lifts...

The books in front of the young man seemed to have scary covers. As the group of teens stepped closer, Will heard the young man describing his works as "action-adventure, with some time-travel – " and he reached out to pick one up –

Only to have his hand almost collide with a hand nearly identical to his.

Will looked into his father's face with surprise. Then he saw the face next to it, and his father's arm around the woman's waist.

Time froze.

Before the frozen moment shattered, Matthew had time to take in the mildly curious faces of the four teens with Will, the shiny pink fingernails of the hand Tracy had wrapped around Will's bicep, the sudden rough scratch of pen on paper as the fat lady at the table scribbled something in a thick spiral notebook. He saw Will's complexion blanch, his eyes go wide with shock and then narrow to angry slits. He registered Allison's shift to come face to face with Will.

"Hi," Allison said, breaking the stasis. "I'm Allison West, and I'll bet you're Will. I'd know you anywhere; you look just like your dad!"

Will didn't move.

"Dude," Travis said behind him, "is that your dad's girlfriend? Aren't you going to introduce us?"

"She's hot," Kevin murmured in a voice not meant to be heard.

Tracy's fingers bit into Will's arm. "Hi, I'm Will's friend Tracy," she said to Allison. "Hi, Mr. Ryersen."

"Tracy," Matthew acknowledged, only about half a beat off. "Hey, y'all."

"I'm so glad to meet you!" Allison enthused, her smile genuine and her curls bobbing. "Your dad has told me all about you."

"Thanks, *Dad*," Will snarled, yanking his arm away from Tracy. "Enjoy the fair." He spun away from them all and shoved his way through the crowded aisle as fast as he could. ·

"Dude's seriously cheesed," Kevin said.

Susan poked his ribs. "Shut up, fool." She reached for Tracy. "We'd better go, right?"

"Uh – yeah – I guess. Nice to see you," Tracy said in the general direction of Matthew and Allison. "Come on, Trav."

The old woman's pen continued to scratch in the sudden void. "It's all material," she said to the young man beside her.

Twelve

OWING ALLISON, MATTHEW LEFT THE TENT IN THE same direction Will had gone. Outside, he stood like a rock in the flowing river of fair-goers, looking for his son.

"What happened?" Allison asked, tugging his arm to get his attention.

"Will didn't know I'm still seein' you," Matthew said. "He was really torqued when he thought we were dating, then we didn't see each other for a while, you know, and I guess he figured... I didn't tell him when I went to dinner at your place."

"Whyever not! Are you ashamed of me?"

"No! Of course not!" *I don't have time for this! Where's Will?* "Allie, Will hates it that I didn't love his mother and didn't marry her. Sometimes he hates me. He had a hard life because I didn't take him in when Dinah dumped him and split. It's not you – it'd be any woman I liked."

"Oh." Allison moved closer to Matthew to escape being run over by a man in a motorized wheelchair. This time he didn't put his arm around her.

"I have to find Will," Matthew said. "The last time he got this mad at me he ended up in Chicago." An uneasy light dawned across his face. "You don't have a way home."

"No," Allison laughed, "you kind of took care of that. Let me help you look for Will. I can't see over the top of anybody, but I can bob and weave really fast. We can go in opposite directions and make a circle of the grounds."

Matthew looked at his shaking hands and stuffed them into his pockets. "Ah – I – Give me a minute, okay? I can't think." He closed his eyes and took a deep breath. *Lord, help me! Please keep Will safe and show me what to do.* He opened his eyes on a gusty exhale.

"I know what you were doing," Allison said, and Matthew couldn't tell whether or not she was teasing.

"You're right," he said. "It works. Stay with me, okay? I love Will – " *Yeah, I do, don't I!* " – but he's not goin' to run my life."

After an hour of shouldering his way through increasing throngs of people, straining his eyes for a glimpse of spiky blond hair or a brown tee-shirt with a huge white Chinese character on its back, repeatedly slowing his anxious pace to allow Allison to keep up, Matthew was beginning to panic again.

"The paper said they expect over seventy thousand people today," he said. "This is impossible."

Short of breath, Allison merely nodded. Then her face brightened. "Look! Isn't that your boss and his wife?"

John and Carolyn were ambling toward them, sharing a funnel-cake and laughing as the powdered sugar showered them. Carolyn's nose was sunburned to match her tee-shirt.

"Hello!" Carolyn called, urging John toward Matthew and Allison. As they met in front of a lawn and garden sales tent, they stepped onto its artificial side lawn to chat.

"This is Allison West," Matthew said. "John and Carolyn Abbott."

"Of course! The girl on the phone! I remember you came to visit when Matthew hurt his leg that Christmas," Carolyn said.

Matthew could see no hint of sadness as she remembered that first Christmas, just a few months after David's death.

"I'm looking for Will," Matthew said abruptly.

"There's a field behind the grandstand," John said. "The Lewiston Fire Department is having a fundraiser – ten bucks to take a sledge-hammer to an old car or truck. He's over there whaling on a Chevy."

Matthew felt his shoulders and his knees slump with relief.

"Something wrong?" John asked.

"He saw me with Allison. In front of his friends, too."

"Ah."

"Yeah. Thanks, we gotta go." Matthew began to move again, towing Allison.

"We'll pray for you," Carolyn told his departing back. "Nice to see you, Allison."

"Thank you," Allison called over her shoulder.

Will squinted against the sun and the sweat stinging his eyes and wiped his face on the shoulder of his shirt. The brown shirt was so sweat-soaked it looked black; his hands were blistered, his arms shaking from repeatedly swinging the ten-pound sledgehammer. Breathing hard, he fished another damp ten-dollar bill out of his jeans pocket and walked it over to the ticket-taker, a Lewiston Fire Department member wearing his yellow helmet as a sunshade with his khaki cargo shorts and LFD tee-shirt.

"Son," the man said, "we appreciate you trying to meet our goal all by yourself, but you're getting mighty hot out there. Why not take a break and go get yourself a drink, maybe try your hand on the midway?"

"You got a limit on turns?" Will snapped, thinking, *Don't call me son!*

"Nope," the firefighter said, taking the bill. "Knock yourself out. Not literally, okay?"

Will grunted and walked back to the wreckage, swinging the hammer next to his leg.

He didn't see Matthew and Allison standing behind him, watching as he pounded the remains of the Chevy until he couldn't lift the hammer any more. He leaned on it instead, gasping for air, unable to tell whether the water running down his face was sweat or tears, until a hand gently took the hammer from him and an arm came around his hunched shoulders.

"Let's get some water," Matthew said.

"I don't need you to take care of me!" Will yelled, pulling away and straightening, although he was swaying on his feet. "I don't need you, period!"

The firefighter walked over and shoved an opened bottle of water into Will's hand. "Son, you need to drink this and calm down. I don't want anybody passing out on my watch, and your dad's not gonna let you punch him, I don't think. Cool off."

Glaring at the man, Will took a long drink and poured some of the water over his head. "I'm fine."

"Good," Matthew said. "Then let's find some place to sit down and talk."

"I got nothing to say to you or her."

"I have something to say," Matthew persisted. "We can do it here in the middle of all these people, or we can find someplace quieter. Your call."

"There are some picnic tables and benches under the oaks near the main gate," Allison said. "Since it's past lunch-time, there might be some empty ones there."

"Good plan." Matthew herded his two charges in that direction, where they found several empty tables and little traffic.

"Sit," Matthew told Will, who plunked himself down on the opposite side of the table from Matthew and Allison. *Okay, Lord, here we go. Please give me the right words.* "Allison, I'm sorry you have to be in the middle of this. If you want to go for a walk and come back later, I'd understand that. But I'd kinda like you to hear what I have to say."

"Oh, I won't leave now unless you chase me off with a stick," she teased. Will looked like he might be considering it.

"Will, I told you before, your mama and I were a mistake from the beginning, and the only good thing that came out of that night for either one of us was you. It wasn't anybody's fault – we were just young and stupid. Dinah was a nice girl. Just not for me. And that was seventeen years ago. I'm not the boy I was then, and Dinah's gone, God rest her.

"You're my son, Will, and I love you. No matter how mad you get, no matter how far you run, no matter if you punch my lights out or steal my truck or whatever – I'm always gonna love you now that I've learned how.

"But loving you doesn't mean I don't have room to love somebody else without cheatin' you. I've had a thing for Allison since before you came back, and I think she kinda likes me, too." He turned to smile at Allison and was thrilled by the radiance of the smile she returned to him. "You feel that way about Tracy, and I respect that. It's good to care about somebody a lot and to have them care right back, isn't it?"

Will looked at the marred surface of the picnic table and said nothing, so Matthew soldiered on. "I'm ready to live a real life, son, not just be a hitchhiker on somebody else's. The Abbotts are family, and I'll always love them and think of them that way. But I want a wife and a home of my own now."

"So are you going to marry her?" Will asked, still communing with the table-top.

"We're not there yet," Matthew said. "We've just started – whatever it is we're doin'."

"Will," Allison said, "I don't want to come between you and your father. And I don't even think about replacing your mother. I know that's impossible. I like your father a lot, but there are some real obstacles in our relationship. We don't know how it will turn out. Can you just give us a chance to find out?"

"Like it's up to me."

"That's right," Matthew said. "It isn't. It's up to me and Allie. Your job is to stop actin' like a spoiled brat and accept that there's room for both of you in my heart."

"It's four o'clock," Will said, standing. "Can I go find Ed now?"

Matthew sighed. "Can I trust you to do that?"

"Yeah, yeah."

"Okay, then. Tell him we're right behind you."

As Will made himself scarce, Allison took Matthew's hand and stroked it. "I'm so glad I'm not a teenager anymore! I think you handled that pretty well, sir!"

"You think?"

"Well, he didn't punch you or cuss you out or cuss me out or run away... What more did you expect?"

Matthew closed his other hand over hers. "I guess every time I talk to him I hope it's goin' to be the time we – well, you know – we forgive each other and – oh, I don't know. I never had a dad who could be a friend and all."

"Don't beat yourself up," Allison urged. "We'll work on it until things get better. Now we'd better go find people, or we'll lose our ride."

When they got to the side entrance of the grandstand, Ed and Will were waiting for them.

"Howdy," Ed said to Allison. "You must be Matthew's girl."

"Hello," she smiled, "I'm Allison West. And you're..."

"Ed Yoder. Pleased to meet you. So what's the plan, folks?"

Matthew flushed a little, a change noted by all three of his companions. "I kinda stole Allison away from her – friend, and she needs a ride, too. I know we can't all fit in the El Camino. And I don't know who's ready to go home and who isn't..."

"What say, boy?" Ed asked Will.

The boy's flush matched his father's, which amused Allison. "Like I'd want to stay here after those guys saw – you know."

"Why don't you and Ed go home, then, and we'll find John and Carolyn again."

"They was going to watch sulky races," Ed said. "Supposed to start at five."

"Then they'll be here pretty soon," Matthew replied. "Okay with you to hang out a while longer, Allie?"

She beamed at him and nodded, a response duly noted by the sullen boy. He turned to Ed and jerked his head toward the gate.

"Guess we're leaving, then," Ed laughed. "Nice to meet you, Miss Allison. See you, Matthew. I'll get the milking done with Smiley there."

Breathing a sigh of relief, Matthew enveloped Allison in a hug. If round one was a draw, it had at least ended without bloodshed.

When John and Carolyn appeared, they decided quickly that the couples would go their separate ways and John or Ed would come back for Matthew and Allison a few hours later.

That fairy-tale, soap-opera thing was happening again, it seemed, as Matthew and Allison stood in the very center of moving streams of literally thousands of people and yet once John and Carolyn had gone he felt as if there were no one there with him but this one small, beautiful princess. He smiled at her, and if he had known the word "fatuously," he would have owned it.

"Do you think Will's all right?" Allison asked, effectively bringing Prince Charming back to earth.

"I hope so. I think he wore himself out enough to stay out of trouble for a while. Then he'll cool down. Doesn't mean he won't stay mad, but it does mean he probably won't do anything stupid." Matthew sighed. "So, in the meantime, here we are."

"I wish you looked happier when you said that," Allison told him.

"No! I *am* happy to be with you! I just can't help worryin' about

Will some. But I'll try, startin' right now." He took her hand and gave her his best smile, which wasn't hard to do when he looked into her eyes and saw his own feelings reflected there. "What would you like to do?"

"I'd like to ride the ferris wheel with you, but not until after dark. Why don't we see if you can win me one of those huge stuffed animals on the midway?"

"You're on."

"What's your specialty?" Allison asked as they stepped back into the bustle, holding hands to keep from being separated.

"Specialty?"

"Yes, you know, the game you always win."

Matthew's smile turned sheepish. "Allie, I've never been to a fair or a carnival or a circus before. My daddy wouldn't let us in Baltimore, and Rough River wasn't hardly even a town, just a few houses and a post office in Miss Evvie's house. Even the closest towns were too small for that stuff. And we were too poor to go, anyway."

"Oh, Matthew! I'm sorry! I didn't mean to bring up bad memories."

"You didn't. Until I came here a few years ago, I never knew what I was missin'. And after I got here, I wasn't all that interested – never came until today with Will. All I meant was I never tried any games." He squeezed her hand for reassurance and felt the tingle when she squeezed his in return.

"Well, then, let's walk around and see what kinds of games there are – and how people play them to win."

They rapidly lost count of all the ways a mark could be separated from his money, but there did seem to be one small ethic at work: the kiddie games always produced a winner.

"If you want a goldfish, I can probably do that one," Matthew offered.

"You're built like a pitcher," Allison said. "How about knocking over those milk cans and winning me that huge purple monkey?"

"I heard John say one time that Ed's really good at that one. Guess I can give it a try."

Trading his dollar for three balls, Matthew took aim and let fly at the pyramid of little cans. One hit, no falls. Again. Two hits, one fall. Again...

"Five dollars is enough," Allison laughed. "Let's let Ed be the master of this one."

"Fine," Matthew grinned. "My arm's gonna fall off pretty soon." He noticed another booth across the way. "Let's try that shooting gallery. I used to be pretty good at plonkin' squirrels with my granddaddy's twenty-two."

After a while, the carnie running the shooting gallery asked Matthew please to take his business elsewhere, paying tribute to Granddaddy's teaching with an overflowing armload of stuffed animals in improbable colors. The pink teddy bear was nearly as big as Allison.

"We can't take all these!" she said. "Let's give them to little kids going by."

Soon their arms were empty of everything but a rather pretty blue-and-white two-foot-tall giraffe. "I like this one best," Allison confided, hugging it to her, "because giraffes are tall."

Matthew snickered, earning himself a swat across the chest with said giraffe.

"I think it's time for dinner," Allison said, looking at her blue-banded nurse's watch. "Are you hungry?"

"Sure."

"Liar," she accused, wrapping one arm around his waist.

He returned the favor. "Well, okay, but I could eat – never had any lunch."

"Of course you didn't. Nobody was there to put it in front of you and make you eat it. You okay with trolling? I want some of this and some of that."

Trolling yielded Allison a corn dog, a paper basket of fries with vinegar, a slice of pizza so greasy the red grease dripped all over her shirt, a chocolate milkshake, an elephant ear whose cinnamon-sugar adhered to her mouth and to the grease on the front of her shirt, and a huge paper cone of poison-blue cotton candy. It yielded Matthew a bite or two of everything she ate and a surprising absence of nausea.

It must be love, he thought, laughing at himself, *because I could never eat all this stuff otherwise.*

While Allison was still licking cotton candy from her fingers, they ran into Ed.

"Ready for a ride home?" he asked, accepting a small pinch of cotton candy from Allison.

"Guess so," she mumbled through blue lips and teeth.

"You gonna kiss that?" Ed asked Matthew in a fake whisper.

Matthew blushed, but Allison laughed. "Of course he is!" She tossed the empty cone into an overflowing trash barrel and licked her fingers again.

"Let's go," Matthew said.

"Did ya?" Ed asked as he drove Matthew back to the farm from Allison's townhouse.

"Did I what?"

"Don't play coy, son. Did ya kiss her on those blue lips?" Ed was grinning like a fool as he teased Matthew.

"Well, now... My grandmother said a gentleman doesn't kiss and tell."

"No problem then. You ain't no gentleman."

Laughing in spite of himself, Matthew said, "All right. Yes, I did. She tasted like cotton candy, and I think that's goin' to be my new favorite flavor."

Thirteen

AFTER TRYING – AND FAILING – TO GET OUT OF going to school on Tuesday, Will resigned himself to being humiliated by his friends and dropped like a dirty sock by Tracy. They all knew that his mom had died, that Matthew was his real father. No one had made a big deal of his taking his father's name. After some easy teasing, they had accepted all those things.

Tracy's mom and dad had been a little slow to let him date their daughter, but he had won them over by going to church and youth group, ostentatiously carrying Matthew's Bible. He was a good student, which didn't hurt with them, either; and he lived with the Abbotts – extra points.

So his life had been cool from his friends' perspective and, more importantly, from Tracy's.

And now his stupid father had ruined it!

Bad enough Matt was a hired hand on the Abbott farm, without even his own little house like Ed, and hadn't had his own wheels until just a couple of months ago. Tracy's dad was a lawyer.

But how bad was it to have to see – and have your friends see – your own dad making out with some hot chick in public!

On the bus, Will's surly attitude made the younger kids around him give him a wide berth, while Travis and Kevin sat together and didn't even acknowledge him. In the school itself, the same people who always said hello to him still did, and the ones who thought they were too good for him didn't change. The test came in third period, when he walked into the math room where he and Tracy and the guys all had a calculus class. He walked to his assigned seat next to Travis's and sank down as low as he could. Moments later, the two guys came in together, laughing about something, freezing up when they looked at Will. Without saying anything, Kevin took his seat in the front row. Travis came to the back, greeting people along the way, and dropped his books on the desk next to Will's.

"Hey," Travis said.

"Hey."

"Tough homework," Travis said.

"Yeah."

"Listen, dude, what happened yesterday – forget it. Me and Kevin, we – I mean, families are, like, weird, y'know?"

"Yeah."

Will wanted to be more – something – to Travis, but he was bound in humiliation. And then Tracy walked in with Susan and several other girlfriends. Will muttered an obscenity under his breath.

"Dude!" Travis whispered urgently. "Chill out! She'll be cool."

Oh, God, Will prayed, *please let me get through this.* He almost laughed at himself for praying, since it wasn't his thing, but he was desperate.

Tracy waved and smiled as she and Susan sat down in the second row.

"See?" Travis whispered. "It's cool. Just walk her to her next class like you always do and it'll be fine."

And it might have been fine, if Will had been able to do it. Instead, he rushed out of the class, of which he had heard almost nothing, as if he were on fire and sought refuge in the boys' bathroom. He locked himself in a stall and stayed there through fourth period and through lunch before emerging for lit class.

In lit they were gearing up to study *Macbeth*, and Will didn't want to miss anything. It was his favorite class, secretly, although he complained about Mrs. Bender along with all the other guys.

Tracy was in this class, too, and she came right up to Will before it started. "Where'd you disappear to? I missed you! I thought we'd have lunch together, but you never came in."

Oh, great. Lie to Tracy. "I – uh – had an appointment."

"What?"

"Just – something I had to do."

Tracy's green eyes fixed him to the wall. "Don't do that, Will. Don't lie to me. If you don't want to have lunch with me or be with me, just say so." She looked hurt.

"Take your seats, students!" Mrs. Bender called from the front of the room. Seventeen young scholars stampeded to their desks – but quietly. No one tested Mrs. Bender's temper on purpose.

Will sat beside Tracy and tried to pay attention, but she was all he could think of. Finally he tore a corner from a page in his notebook and scribbled, "I'm sorry. For everything." He shoved it across his desk-top so she could ease it into her hand. Unfortunately, Mrs. Bender was calling on him at the time.

"Mr. Ryersen!" she said in her precise, clipped voice.

"Yes, ma'am?"

"Do you have something there you would like to share with the class?"

Will felt the Ryersen flush overtaking his ears, neck and face, abetted by the snickering around the room. He closed his hand over the note. "No, ma'am."

Mrs. Bender moved quickly to stand beside Will's desk, her posture perfect, her 1970's helmet of beige hair unmoving. She held out one perfectly manicured hand. "I will have that, please, Mr. Ryersen."

Will thought several obscenities, but he wasn't top of his class for nothing; he handed over the note. *Please, please don't let her read it out loud!*

"Thank you, Mr. Ryersen." She read the note to herself. "I see. Noble sentiments. I'm sure you will wish to address them verbally to the person for whom you have them at some time after class. I am sorry you found note-writing more important than our study of Mr. Shakespeare's language and its impact upon modern English, but you will have a chance to rectify that during detention this afternoon."

As Mrs. Bender quickly returned to her desk, a round of laughter and cat-calls cemented Will's humiliation. He hung his head and endured.

Then he realized he would have to call home to tell them he

wouldn't be on the bus and to ask for a ride. *A perfect ending to a perfect day. And it's all Matt's fault.*

Will had about four minutes from the last bell to call home and present himself in the library for detention. He had to go to the office and endure the further humiliation of making his phone call in front of the principal's secretary, who made no pretense of not listening.

"Yeah," he told Carolyn, "I have to stay late, so I won't be on the bus. Can somebody pick me up?"

"Of course we can. What time?"

"Four-thirty-five, I guess," he said. "Out front is fine."

After concluding his conversation and returning the phone to the secretary with perfunctory thanks, Will fled to the library, hoping not to run into any hall Nazis on his way.

I guess some prayers are answered, he thought, sliding into a vacant seat just before the teacher gigged him for being late. He spread his calculus book and notebook out before him and tried to make up what he had missed that morning.

Four-thirty-five finally came, and the teacher, a slight man with a bow tie and a nervous twitch in his left eye, dismissed the miscreants to their criminal futures. Will could almost see the relief in the teacher's eyes as the students, mostly large boys, filed out without causing any trouble. He joined the exodus and waited at the bottom of the front steps for an Abbott vehicle to appear.

No such luck.

Will dragged himself across the sidewalk to the F-150 and climbed in. He didn't look at Matthew or say anything, but he imagined a lot of things he would like to be saying.

"Hungry?" Matthew asked.

"What?"

"I thought you might like to stop for something to hold you over to supper. You didn't get a snack after school."

What is this? What's he trying to pull? "I'm fine."

"All right. Then we'll go straight home." Matthew pulled the truck away from the curb and into the flow of traffic. "Supper may be a little late, because Carolyn had a doctor's appointment."

Fear sliced through Will. "Is she all right?"

"She's fine. Pregnant women just have to go for check-ups a lot, especially if they're older, like Carolyn."

"How do you know so much about it? You weren't around when Mom was having me."

Matthew sighed. "No, I wasn't. I know because Carolyn told me when I panicked like you did. Now. You want to tell me what happened today?"

"No." *Like you care how I feel anyway.*

"Let me put it another way, then. I need you to tell me. It's not optional."

"Yeah, that's what I figured." Will slouched deeper into the seat. "I had detention."

"I know that," Matthew said as evenly as possible.

"I got caught passing a note to Tracy in lit class. Mrs. Bender's really strict. That's all."

"Okay."

Okay? You're not gonna chew me out or tell me what a jerk I am or anything? Not going to double my chores or say I can't see Tracy?

"I know yesterday was hard on you, Will. I'm sorry for that."

"Right." *Like when hell freezes over I'll talk to you about this.*

Will went straight to his room when they got home and didn't come out until he heard John call him for supper. He made clear his desire to be left alone by the family, and they politely ignored him, except for Carolyn's gentle caress of his hair once as she walked by. He wished she wouldn't do that, because it brought tears to his eyes. He couldn't remember ever receiving a loving touch like that from his mom, or his stepdad Jesse – sure not from Clete, that last boyfriend with the rodeo buckle on his belt! It made something inside him stretch toward it and it reminded him of when he came back from Chicago and his father held him. That hadn't happened again in a long time. It wasn't a guy thing. But even a strong guy needed – *Don't be a wimp. You don't need anybody. What do they say? Yeah – man up.* But he wished Carolyn would touch him again.

Allison hadn't been thrilled about meeting Matthew at Logan's Diner in Lewiston, but he was able to be immovable about it. *We need to go real slow. No parking in cars, no being alone in her living room. God, help me to remember what I'm supposed to be doing!*

When he arrived, Allison was already sitting in a booth drinking coffee from a thick white mug. She smiled and waved him over.

"Hi! I'm so glad to see you!"

"Hi. You, too." Matthew slid in across from her, filling his senses with her bright blue fuzzy sweater, her halo of curls, the scent of her shampoo. "I'm sorry I'm late."

"Oh, I don't think you're late. I came early to be sure I was on time." Allison smiled again. "I have trouble sometimes being on time. Which doesn't make sense, because I'm not one of those women who spends hours in front of a mirror or anything."

"You don't need to," Matthew said, feeling like a jerk as he said it. A middle-aged waitress whose muffin-top bulged over the top of her apron took his order and returned in moments with coffee. "Thanks," he told her.

"Sure you don't want some pie with that?" the waitress asked. "The apple and pumpkin are both good. Or we have a great chocolate cake…"

"Ding!" said Allison. "Two chocolate cakes, please." She grinned at Matthew. "I've only had three or four from the chocolate group today."

Matthew listened with pleasure as, between huge bites of cake, Allison told him about her day at the hospital. He occasionally placed a small bite on his own tongue and savored it a little, but when Allison finished her slice he shoved his across the table to her.

"Thank you, but you know what? You need to eat that yourself. At least half of it. You worry me sometimes, you're so skinny." She shoved the cake back at him.

"I had dinner," he protested. "I ate, really, chicken pot pie and a big salad – "

"Humor me, Matthew. Please."

Her winsome smile did him in and he began to force little bits of cake down his throat. It was good. Even better was the way this beautiful woman clearly cared about his well-being. Matthew felt his throat relax and began to actually enjoy the dessert.

"So how did your day go?" Allison asked.

Suddenly the cake was a lump of sawdust in Matthew's throat. He almost gagged and washed it down with a gulp of lukewarm coffee. "Not the best day ever. Will, he's pretty mad at me."

"About me, right?" She wasn't smiling now.

"Partly." Matthew wouldn't meet her eyes. "He's never gonna forgive me for not lovin' Dinah and not marryin' her. And he's so embarrassed about his friends seein' us together at the fair. I didn't think they seemed all that shook up about it, but Will – "

"I'm so sorry!"

"Not your fault. And I meant what I said about livin' my life now. Allie, I want to have a chance to see if you and I – if we're – I mean – "

Allison reached across the table and took Matthew's hand. "I know what you mean. I want that, too. I think if you give him some time, Will will get used to the idea. Especially if he sees that his friends just don't care. That little girlfriend of his was really friendly and nice, and she didn't seem upset at all."

Matthew was distracted by the warmth of Allison's hand but couldn't quite bring himself to break the contact. "Tracy's a nice girl, a good girl, and she seems to like Will in spite of everything. I know she won't give him a hard time. Those boys he was with are good guys, too, kids in his math class. It's more like a – a jealousy thing in Will. And a lack of trust." He laughed ruefully and ran his free hand through his hair. "But why should he trust me? I abandoned him twice."

Allison nodded. "But you came back and took him in. He's just not sure yet that you won't change your mind. And I guess I'm competition for your – ah – affections. He doesn't know enough about love to know it's bottomless."

"How'd you get so smart?"

"I thought maybe I'd go into psych nursing at one point, and I did extra course-work and some practicums with the psych department at the university."

Matthew felt ashamed of his Grayson County, Kentucky, high school education. What could she possibly see in him, so smart, so well-educated herself? He drew back his hand.

"Uh-oh!" Allison said. "What just happened?"

"Nothing. I didn't mean to complain about Will. It was frustrating, but we'll keep working at it."

"Good for you. I hope it doesn't take Will too long to figure out what a great dad he has." Allison finished her coffee and wiped her mouth on a paper napkin. "I know you're not going to finish that cake, and neither am I, so let's get out of here and go back to my place."

Oh, boy. Lord, help me. "You're right about the cake. It was good, though. Listen, Allie, I'm sorry, but I can't go back to your place."

"What do you mean?"

"Just that. I can't do it." *Please don't let her hate me!* "I've been over there a few times, I know, but it's – uh – it's a bad idea." He watched her wide-eyed smile become a squinty glare as she figured it out. "I like you so much," he said desperately, "and I can't trust myself to act like a gentleman if we're alone together like that."

"You know I don't want you to," she hissed, "so you're just making excuses. And don't start in on that God-thing again, either. I know plenty of people who go to bed together on Saturday and go to church on Sunday."

"Did you really think I was changing my mind about what I believe?" Matthew asked.

Allison paused for a long time, then shook her head. "No. I don't think you're fickle about anything, Matthew. I guess I was hoping, though. How can we see where the relationship is going if we're never alone and we never find out whether we're good together?"

"I don't have a lot of experience with relationships," Matthew said. "I guess I believe what John told me, that hanging out like this and doing things with other people will be enough."

"I have *never* had a relationship like this!" Allison said, caught between laughing and frowning. "I don't know what to say – or do."

"Say you'll go to a movie with me Saturday night."

Now she laughed. "Oh, you're getting bold, aren't you? I have to work Saturday until seven. It would have to be late."

"I don't mind. You're worth waitin' for."

"Maybe this will work after all," Allison chuckled, sliding out of the booth and dropping a kiss on Matthew's forehead as she passed. "I'll get the check and see you Saturday night."

Will looked up from his *Macbeth* text when he heard Matthew's truck pull into the driveway. He checked the clock – only nine-thirty. *Must not have been a score for dear ol' Dad, either.* He turned back to the book, in a mood for murder, but couldn't help hearing his father's footsteps coming up the stairs. *Don't stop here! Just go to bed and leave me alone.*

Alone suddenly seemed large and heavy, narrowing the walls of the room and pressing on Will from all sides. He felt the weight in his chest and behind his eyes, which were beginning to sting with the tears he hated. Will ground the heels of his hands into his eyelids and coughed to relieve the pressure in his chest. What was the point in getting all emotional about the sound of shoes going past the door? What did he care?

But it seemed he did.

I wish – What's wrong with me that nobody loves me enough to stay? God, if You're really out there, why did You make me like this? Why couldn't I be like Trav and Kevin? Their moms keep the house smelling like cookies, like Carolyn does, and their dads love their moms and come home for dinner every night and play ball with them and go to their games –

That's not fair, said a different voice in his head. *Your dad is here now. He'd go to your games if you had any. Is it his fault you don't get involved, or is that because you're afraid you won't be good enough?*

Will jammed his Walkman earphones over his ears and cranked the volume so high it leaked around the edges. Violent music split his brain and he mouthed the words. The tears he didn't want to acknowledge began their independent journey, falling in paper-crinkling blots onto the open text-book.

Because the music was so loud, he didn't hear the knock on the door, the opening of the door or the footsteps across the room to his desk. His first awareness he wasn't still alone came from the hands on his shoulders.

Startled, Will jerked away and spun around to face his father. He pulled the earphones off and threw them on the desk, saturating the room with noise.

Matthew stepped over to the Walkman and turned it off.

"Will – "

Will had turned his back so that Matthew couldn't see his face. Swiping a sleeve across his eyes, he muttered, "What?"

He felt his father's arm around his shoulders, turning him until they were face to face. Through the blur of his own tears, he thought he saw – no, couldn't be. Then he was drawn into Matthew's embrace and held fast, and he could feel the shaking that could only –

He's crying! What's going on!

"Daddy?" Will held on, afraid one of them was going to break apart if he didn't. "What's wrong!"

Matthew shook his head but couldn't seem to speak. Finally he wiped his face on his sleeve, still maintaining the embrace, and said, "Will, I can't stand bein' at odds with you all the time. I love you so much, and I want you to be happy more than anything else in the world. No matter what happens, no matter how you feel, I love you – and God loves you, so much. Your life matters, son, and it matters to me."

Holy – ! He means it!

Part of Will wanted more than anything to lean back into his father's embrace and hang on, to absorb the warmth and safety Matthew was offering, to believe it – and part of him wasn't ever going to be chumped again. Part of him felt sorry for the broken man before him, respected the humility that let him be so open – although Will wouldn't have known to call it humility – and part of him rejoiced that his father was suffering almost as much as he was. He took a couple of steps back. But he couldn't quite bring himself to deliver a crushing blow. He just turned away and, in a moment, heard the door close gently.

Fourteen

As Carolyn stretched to put the goose-decorated blue coffee mugs on the second shelf of the cupboard, Will noticed from his vantage point at the kitchen table a little bulge under her tee-shirt. His face scalded with embarrassment at this first tangible evidence of her pregnancy and he turned away – but not before she caught him looking.

"Just starting to show," she said easily, loading dry flatware into its drawer. "You're going to see a lot more belly before this is over, honey, so don't be embarrassed."

"Sorry," Will mumbled, face still averted. "I've never been around a – a lady I know who's – you know – before."

Carolyn laughed. "Pregnant, Will. It's okay to say pregnant."

"Ew!" he replied, immediately followed by another apology.

"Look at me," Carolyn said in the no-nonsense tone ordinarily used only by Pearl.

"Yes, ma'am," Will said reflexively, turning.

"That's better. See – it's still me. You guys have to get used to it, or it's going to be a really long winter."

"Yes, ma'am. It just – " He flushed again and tried to find a polite place to fix his gaze.

"Never mind now," she soothed. "Have you had enough cookies?"

"Ah maaght could force day-own a few more," Will teased in a gross exaggeration of his father's sometime Kentucky drawl. "But really what I'd like is to borrow Matt's truck for a while."

"Did you ask him?"

"No, they're out taking off beans in one of the north fields. Can't even see 'em from here. Do you think it'd be okay?"

Carolyn considered the logistics. "Will, is there any reason your dad might say no? If I okay it, am I going against anything he told you?"

"No, honest." Will gave her his best wide-eyed innocent look.

She fell for it. "Okay, then, I'll tell Matthew you took the truck with my permission. You'll be back by five-thirty for supper?"

"Uh – I might need a little longer. Let's say... eight. If I can't get here by supper, just eat without me. Oh, and tell Matt I only have some reading to do for homework, please."

Snatching the keys to Matthew's truck from the rack, Will escaped and drove swiftly away from the farm. He didn't want to risk anybody's trying to stop him; he had planned this caper too carefully to hit a snag at the last minute.

In town, stopped at the light, he drew a folded piece of paper from his jeans pocket and carefully studied the directions and address. Thirty minutes to Lewiston, maybe five minutes in the city itself – he might be early, but that would be okay.

It's Matt's fault I have to do this.

Half an hour later, Will parked the truck in front of the building and looked around. He saw the car he was looking for and exited the truck, making sure his hair was smoothed and his shirt tucked in. Suddenly his breath was constricted in his chest and he had to wipe his sweaty palms on his jeans.

Maybe this isn't such a good idea. Maybe I should go home. Then he thought about why he had come and straightened his spine. *You know what to do – now do it.*

Will climbed three steps and rang the bell. A voice called, "Coming!" and the door flew open a moment later.

"Will!" Allison said.

"Where's Will?" Matthew asked Ed as they set up the cows for milking. "He's supposed to help with this so you can stay on the combine."

"Well, Carolyn phoned John to say the boy wouldn't be here, so I come up. No problem." He coupled another cow, patting her encouragingly. "Seems he borrowed your truck to do some errand or something. Carolyn said he could."

"Oh." Matthew finished with his last cow. "He should have asked me."

"Prob'ly. But maybe it come up while we was in the field. Tracy, most likely, or some library project. He'll be home for supper."

However, when they went up to the house to join Pearl and the Abbotts, Will was not there.

"He said he might be as late as eight o'clock," Carolyn explained, "so we'll go ahead without him and I'll leave a plate in the fridge for him to microwave." She and Pearl carried a platter of fried chicken and a big dish of mashed potatoes to the table. "Matthew, please grab the gravy boat and the green beans," she said over her shoulder as she went through the swinging door.

"I hope he's all right," Matthew said, depositing his load on the table and waiting for Pearl and Carolyn to be seated.

"He's at that age," John said. "You remember – feels like a man and a kid at the same time and figures he can handle more freedom than he really can. I don't think he's going behind your back particularly. He's just asserting some independence." John held the platter for Carolyn to take some chicken and then passed it on. He heaped potatoes, beans and gravy on his plate and dug in with a contented groan of pleasure as Carolyn smiled.

"How are things going with that girl of yours?" Pearl asked Matthew. "Is she any closer to knowing the Lord?"

Matthew put down his fork, suddenly finding the potatoes and gravy disgusting. "She isn't, I don't think. She doesn't get mad any more if I say something, but she clams up. She won't even consider reading the Bible or watching a Christian movie." He sighed and pushed his plate away.

"Stop that!" Pearl said. "Eat your dinner. We just need to pray harder for the Lord to remove the blinders from her eyes. He wants that girl for Himself, you mark my words."

Matthew pulled the plate back and ate a green bean. He was too tired to go head-to-head with Pearl about anything.

"A funny thing happened this afternoon," Carolyn said, deftly changing the subject. "I was putting away dishes in the kitchen while Will was having his snack, and he noticed..." The story amused the family and turned the talk to babies, a happy topic for everyone at the table but John. Matthew watched him tense and grip his fork as if it were a weapon.

"Is what we're getting in those north fields as good a crop as you figured?" Matthew asked to distract John.

"Better," the farmer replied. "Great yield this year. I want to get in and out of those far fields early and put in the wheat."

"Right," Ed affirmed around a mouthful of chicken. Supposed to be a rough winter, so we best not let it wait too long."

"Funny thing," Matthew said with a wry grin, "but when the corn and beans are in, I wish it were wheat – and when the wheat's in – "

"Son, you're never satisfied," Ed laughed. "It's all God's blessing to me."

"Shut up, old man," Matthew teased. "Stop trying to be super-spiritual and make me look bad."

"You don't need no help, son," Ed said, scooping more potatoes onto his plate.

"Save room for dessert," Pearl advised. "We have a plum cobbler."

Matthew managed to eat the small chicken breast and half of the potatoes and beans before he was too full to manage another bite. Pearl forgave him his lack of appetite and dished up a generous serving of cobbler, still hot from the oven.

"I think I died and went to heaven," Ed said around a huge spoonful of dessert. "And I sure am glad we got dairy cows, because this cream makes it perfect."

John managed to eat his dessert and keep an easy grip on his spoon, but Matthew had a hard time getting beyond the second bite. "I wish Will would call."

"He'll be here by eight, you'll see," Carolyn said. "It will be fine."

"Do you want to come in?" Allison asked.

"Yeah."

She stepped back to allow Will to enter and closed the door behind him. He stood there for a minute taking in his surroundings, noting the comfortable couch and chair and the modern end tables and lamps. On the coffee-table in front of the couch sat a blue-and-white giraffe he recognized from the shooting gallery at the fair.

"Have a seat," Allison offered. "Can I get you a Coke or anything?"

"No, thank you." He sat on the couch.

"Well, I was just getting a cup of coffee, so if you don't mind..."

"Suit yourself."

"Ah, his father's son," Will heard Allison say under her breath as she went into the kitchen.

What the heck does that mean!

Mug in hand, Allison returned to the living room and sat in the chair across from Will. He noticed that her mug said, "Nurses Do It With Compassion."

"Will, when your dad comes, I usually have to get the conversation rolling, because he's kinda shy, you know? So I can do that for you, too. Or you can just tell me what brings you here. I know you weren't 'just in the neighborhood.'"

You can do this. Just say what's on your mind, idiot. "Uh – yeah – well – I wanted to know – you and Matt – my, uh, father – What's going on with you?"

"I don't mean to sound rude," Allison said carefully, "but is that really any of your business? I think your father would talk to you if he wanted you to know anything."

"We don't talk much." Will worried a button on his shirt which had a short thread sticking out of it. "But, frankly, I do think it's my business. If you're going to marry my father, I think I have a right to know."

Allison smiled. "I would love to marry your father. But he hasn't asked me. We're more than friends, I guess, but far from being engaged or married. We have a lot of differences to work out, and I'm not sure we can." Her smile disappeared and she buried her face in the coffee mug.

"You love him, don't you?"

"Yes," she whispered, still not looking at Will, "I do. I wish I didn't, but I do."

"So, if you really love him," Will persisted, "then you'd want what's best for him, right?"

"Right..."

Will stood up, as tall as he could. "Well, the way I see it, Matt doesn't need any complications in his life right now. He has a family and he needs to be with us, not with you. So if you love him like you say you do, then you should tell him not to come around anymore."

Allison gazed up, up, up at the tall, slender youth with her mouth open, a whole cascade of feelings pouring through her. Tears filled her bright blue eyes and hung suspended on her lashes. "Don't you think your father deserves happiness?" she asked.

No. Why should he be happy when Mom never was, and it's his fault? Will glared at Allison and refused to let himself be moved as one tear and then another fell onto her cheek and ran down toward her chin. *Bimbo. Cheap trick. Whore.*

"I think you should go now, Will. You've made your point. I hear you." She stood, also.

"Yeah, you hear me, but what are you going to do about it?"

Now some anger took over, and Allison also stood as tall as she could. "That really is none of your business, young man. Go home. You've overstayed your welcome." She marched past him to the door and held it open.

Fine. I've been kicked out before. Not like I want to hang around here. You got the point. Will forced himself to saunter to and through the door and down the steps. He didn't look back when he heard the door close behind him, but got into the truck and drove away, carefully maintaining the speed limit until he was back on country roads. Acting cool was everything when you weren't cool.

Before he came to his own road, though, Will came to a conclusion. He would rather not encounter the family around the supper table, and he would rather see Tracy. They might still be at supper, so he drove up one paved road and down a graveled other until seven, when he finally turned down the quarter-mile driveway to the Showalters' house. As he rang the bell, eyeballing the dried flowers in the wreath on the door, it occurred to him perhaps he should have called...

"Will Ryersen! What are you doing here?" Tracy's mother asked even before she had the door completely open.

"Evenin', ma'am. I was – uh – on an errand and thought I'd just see if Tracy could talk for a bit." Will had learned how effective his southern manners could be with his friends' mothers. More than one had asked her child, "Why can't you be as polite as that Ryersen boy?"

"Well, come on in." Mrs. Showalter stood aside to let him in. "Tracy! Will's here!" she called up the stairs. "Now, Will, she's doing homework, so don't stay too long."

"No, ma'am, I won't," he promised, watching Tracy come down the stairs. Her pale green eyes gleamed at the sight of him.

"Go on into the living room," Tracy's mother said. "Your dad and I will sit in the family room. Just remember your homework, Tracy."

"Yes, Mom," Tracy sighed, rolling her eyes just a little. She took Will's hand and led him to the couch. "I didn't expect you. What's up?"

Will flopped down and dragged Tracy down next to him. "Nothing! I was just out – thought I'd say hey."

"Are you sure?"

"Sure I'm sure!" He drew slightly away from her and looked around the room, at the cozy antique furniture and silver picture frames and expensive-looking paintings on the walls and over the fireplace. He knew Tracy's father had built this house some years ago, when Tracy was little and his law practice had taken off. It said "money" the same way the Abbott house said "comfort."

Trying to make conversation, Tracy asked, "Are you ready for the *Macbeth* quiz?"

What quiz? When? Tomorrow? "Of course. No problem."

They sat in uneasy silence for a few moments, then Tracy ventured, "Will, I'm worried about you. You've been so moody and distant lately, and we haven't really spent any time together. I know we're busy with school, but you used to call me and meet me for youth group... Will, if you don't want us to – to be together anymore, you need to tell me."

Panic seized him. *She's going to leave me, too!* "No! That's not what I want, honest!" How much to tell? How to not sound like a wimp or a jerk? He ran his fingers through his hair in a gesture he would have hated to know looked just like his father's, spoiling its carefully gelled spikes. "Tracy, please! You know how much I – I mean, you know – "

Tracy sighed. "I know you like me, maybe as much as I like you. But something's wrong and has been for a while. And it's getting worse. Will, I wasn't kidding when I first met you and I told you I couldn't date you because you weren't saved. Well, it's been a couple of years now, and I don't really know where you stand. Last year, when you came back from Chicago, I thought Jesus had really spoken to you. I thought you'd be – you know – like, giving a testimony and getting baptized and all. But instead, you seem to be getting farther and farther away from Him. I think – I think if you aren't ready to be a committed Christian, then maybe I need to – to not see you anymore."

"I can't believe this!" Will exclaimed, his tone just under a shout. "I come here because I think my girl will have some sympathy with all the crap going on in my life, and instead I get a 'come to Jesus' talk and a brush-off!" He jumped to his feet.

"Wait, Will," Tracy begged, standing beside him and trying to take his hand. "I don't want to brush you off – "

"You just did a good imitation," he countered, snatching his hand away. "I gotta go." He headed for the door. "Thanks for nothin'!" Yanking it open, he charged out and slammed the door behind him.

Tracy watched from the window as the furious youth stormed to the truck, jumped in and slammed the door and fishtailed down the driveway, spraying gravel all the way.

Matthew and Ed were out doing a last check on the stock before bedtime, but John and Carolyn heard the truck return, the door slam, the stomp of Will's feet up the back steps and into the kitchen.

"Uh-oh," John said. "Whatever that errand was, it didn't go the way he wanted."

"I'll just go see if he wants his supper," Carolyn replied, heading into the kitchen. She found Will slumped in his chair at the table. "Hi. I saved a plate for you; shall I warm it up?"

"I'm not hungry."

"Are you sure? It's fried chicken and mashed potatoes – and I won't tell if you don't eat the green beans. Pearl made plum cobbler for dessert, too."

"I said I'm not hungry," Will yelled.

"Oh." Carolyn's enthusiasm wilted and she backed up a bit. "I'm sorry."

"Forget it."

"Can I get anything else for you? Would you like to talk about anything?"

"Will you just shut up and leave me alone!" Will yelled, jumping up from the table and startling Carolyn so that she backed up against the sink.

Within seconds, John came through the swinging door, eyes

squinted and jaw clenched in anger. "Will!"

The youth looked at him, sullen and unyielding.

"Let me tell you," John said in a steely tone, "that I don't want this kind of behavior around Carolyn. And I don't want this kind of rudeness and disrespect *toward* Carolyn ever. Do you understand me?"

Will glowered and said nothing. He tried to push past John to leave the kitchen, but John didn't move.

"Come into the living room with me," John said in the voice which would brook no refusal.

Will made a silent snarl but followed John without comment.

"Now sit down."

Will sat on the couch.

"We need to talk about this," John said, "because you don't seem to get it. Carolyn's health and happiness is the most important thing to me now, and I don't expect that to change in the near future. I know you have things upsetting you, Will, and that's your business. But you don't have the right to take out your bad feelings on other people in this house. Do you understand me?"

Will just glared. Finally he said, "You're not my father. You don't get to tell me what to do."

John sighed and ran his hand over his eyes. "No, I'm not your father, but I am your friend. And this is my house. I do get to tell you what behavior is acceptable here and what isn't. And because I'm your friend, not your landlord, Will, I want to help. Will you let me?"

"I don't need any help. I'm sorry I upset Carolyn. I'll do better. Now may I be excused?" *Can I get out of here before I explode or start bawling like a baby?* Will heard the back door opening and Matthew and Ed speaking to Carolyn in the kitchen. *Oh, man! That's all I need!* "I gotta go!" His voice had gone from low and sullen to high and panicky, and he flushed with embarrassment as well as anger.

"I think so," John agreed. "Go on upstairs. But your dad will probably want to talk about where you went without asking him."

Without an answer, Will raced up the stairs and closed his door. He flung himself down at his desk and picked up *Macbeth*.

Matthew was looking at his truck keys on the rack and Ed was getting coffee when John walked back into the kitchen and sat down at the table.

"You want to tell me what's goin' on?" Matthew asked, sitting opposite John.

"I explained to him what just happened," Carolyn said, handing John a goose-figured mug full of fresh coffee.

"I had a chat with your son just now," John said, "and I think he understands that I will not tolerate his rudeness and threatening behavior to Carolyn. I told him you'll probably want to talk with him."

"I still don't understand what happened," Matthew pressed. "He went on some 'errand' or other, came back mad and – what? – yelled at Carolyn? Threatened her? I can't imagine...'

"He didn't threaten me," Carolyn said. "He just told me to shut up and leave him alone. He wasn't raising his fist to me or anything like that. He was just so – angry." She sat down next to John, shaking her head.

"He had you backed up all the way to the sink," John said. "I think that's threatening. And he was yelling. And disrespectful."

"I get that," Matthew said, feeling some irritation at John's insistence, or so it seemed, on making even more of the incident than had happened. It was bad enough as it was. "I'll go up and talk with him. At very least, he needs to apologize. But I want to know what's behind all this. If there's one person in the world Will loves and trusts, it's you, Carolyn."

"Maybe we ought to be praying first," Ed suggested, his first intrusion into the conversation. "Boy's got something eating at him, for sure. And he's that touchy about it any little thing could make it worse."

"You think I shouldn't talk with him?" Matthew asked. "You keep telling me I have to take responsibility as his father. That's all I'm trying to do."

"He ain't thinking straight, Matthew. I just wanta ask the good Lord to give you words to say that'll build bridges, not blow 'em up."

They bowed their heads to pray for wisdom and discernment to come to Matthew, for the right words and the right attitude – Matthew's prayer. After the hearty amens, he rose wearily and headed for the stairs.

God, please. Please let me do this right. I don't want to hurt Will, but I can't let him get away with havin' tantrums like a baby. He's almost a man grown now. In Kentucky, he'd be helpin' to run the farm and plannin' to get married in a year or two. He needs to get over his past and step up.

Yeah. Like I have. Forgive me, Lord. I don't know why I should think Will ought to be better at it than I am.

Taking a deep breath, Matthew knocked on Will's door.

"C'min," the boy called.

Matthew entered and stood just inside the door, taking in the room, neat and tidy as a teenager's room should not be, and the boy, hunched over a textbook. "May I sit down?"

"Why not? Take a load off." Will gestured to the bed.

"Thanks." Matthew sat on the edge of the bed and studied the red-and-blue quilt Carolyn had donated from her own bed the day they had remade the room from David's to Will's.

Will closed his book and sat backwards on the straight desk chair to look at his father. "So?"

"Soooo... I thought maybe you'd tell me. I don't understand what's going on to make you be nasty to Carolyn. John's really angry about that, and I can't say I blame him. But it puzzles me some, because you have never been short on manners with anyone but me that I've noticed." He observed that Will had the grace to look thoroughly ashamed, hanging his head and blushing far deeper than the Ryersen flush.

"I said I was sorry."

"So you did."

"So don't you believe me?"

"Sure I do. But I'm more concerned about what's going on to make you so upset."

Will began to jig his left leg up and down rapidly, the frown returning and deepening as he looked at Matthew. "Yeah, you're so concerned. You know I really don't want you to see that woman any more, but what do you care? You know how I feel."

Help! I can't do this. I want to hit him!

Matthew stood abruptly, stuffing his shaking hands into his pockets.

"Where you going?" Will asked. "Can't take hearing the truth or admitting it to yourself? You know how I feel, and you know how you feel. Don't start crying and making promises, because I don't buy any of it!"

Slatey eyes glowered into slatey eyes and two sets of fists clenched. Will stood, putting him just a fraction of an inch shorter than Matthew, and silently dared his father to strike him. If Matthew did, he would strike back.

"I'm going to go over to my room now and pray," Matthew said carefully. "I don't think we want to turn this into a brawl and upset the household any more than we already have. You might consider doing the same, son. It can't hurt, and it might help." He left the room, closing the door gently behind him.

Will dropped back into his chair and buried his head in his arms on the desk. The tears which had threatened earlier were gone now, and the heat which had suffused his face and his heart moments before was replaced by a thin, cold emptiness. He raised his head and looked at the scars on his wrists. He knew how to do it right now, running the cuts vertically instead of horizontally...

Matthew turned on the bedside lamp and closed his door. His hands were still shaking, but he didn't know whether that was from anger or from fear. *Maybe both. Am I going to turn into my daddy after all?*

He took his Bible from the table, put it on the bed and knelt down at the bedside, noting absently how much easier it was to kneel since Carolyn had placed a hand-braided rag rug there. He sometimes admired and tried to follow the blues and greens woven together, but mostly he just gave thanks when his feet didn't hit cold floor first in the morning or his knees didn't bruise from kneeling on the uncarpeted wood.

You can't distract yourself forever thinking about the rug, or whether it's time to paint this room or – whatever. Lord, Father, forgive me for this anger! I don't want it. I don't want to want to hit Will or yell at him or put him down. All this stuff comes into my mind, but I didn't send for it – You know that. Please take it away. Help me to love my boy the way You do.

"Right. As if." Matthew shook his head as if he could shake the stupid thoughts out of it.

As he reached for his Bible, he heard the phone, then footsteps on the stairs and a knock on his door. He rose and opened it.

"Phone call," John said, slightly out of breath. "Allison."

"Thanks." Matthew clattered down the stairs and to the kitchen, where the phone lay in wait on the countertop.

"Hello?"

"Hi, it's Allison."

"Good to hear your voice, Miss Allison. What's up?"

"I miss you, Matthew. I had hoped we'd get together again before now. Are you mad at me?"

Matthew smiled in the empty kitchen. "No, I'm not mad. I've been having some problems with Will, is all. I'm trying to walk a line here, see, to keep him reassured without just caving in to what he wants."

"I need to tell you something."

Uh-oh. The last time she said that, it was really bad. "Sure. Go ahead."

"Earlier this evening, I had a visitor..."

"Was it that guy from the fair tryin' to give you grief? If it was, I'll – "

He heard a slight giggle from the other end of the line. "No, of course not! He won't ever try again, Matthew. You scared him! No, it was Will."

Oh. That was the errand. To visit Allison. "And?"

"And he had a lot to say to me about us – you and me. He asked if you and I are getting married."

"Oh."

"Well, I told him you hadn't asked me. But he – uh – he asked me some more questions about our relationship, and then he basically told me that if I really – care about you – I'll stop seeing you. Because you need to focus on your family, not on some – well, he didn't call me anything but 'ma'am,' but he was sure thinking it pretty loud!"

Matthew collapsed into a chair at the table. "You've got to be kiddin' me!"

"I wish I were. He was really angry, but he acted like he had planned it all out in advance, you know? Pretty smooth, for a kid saying stuff like that."

"Then what happened?"

"Well, I was so hurt and angry I just told him to get out. He left and drove off in your truck like a crazy man. I'm sorry, Matthew. I tried to get along with him, but there was no reaching him."

"I know what you mean," Matthew said. "He had a tantrum here when Carolyn asked him what had happened, yelled at her and totally upset John. Then he flew upstairs to his room and had another fit when I tried to talk with him. I thought he was going to punch me. Trouble is, I thought I was going to punch him." Matthew sighed.

"Well, I – I just thought you ought to know," Allison said, her voice scarcely above a whisper. "I don't know what to do..."

"Yeah. Me, either. In the meantime – "

"I understand. I won't call again. Just know I miss you, okay?"

Matthew hung up the phone and just sat there in the dark kitchen, watching the eerie green glow of the stove clock. *It's worse than I thought. How could he be so hateful?* After a while, he slowly climbed the stairs back to his room and crawled into bed in his underwear. Sleep was slow in coming, but he had expected that. What he hadn't expected was the replay of so many scenes from his past.

There was his pretty little mother again, her blond curls and gray-blue eyes just like Matthew's, humming a sixties folk-song about dying rather than being a slave again – and his tall, broad, dark-haired father, still in his police uniform at the end of the day, slapping her across the mouth for making noise. His Kentucky grandparents in their tiny house, just more than a shack, really, on Rough River Ridge, showing him how things grow and how to cultivate them – and his daddy's huge, booted foot grinding flower starts into the ground because a boy who grows flowers is nothing but a sissy. His granddaddy, teaching him how to milk Posy, the gentle cow who never kicked over the bucket no matter how clumsy his little eight-year-old hands were – and his daddy, dumping the milk on the ground because a piece of straw had gotten into it, then catching Matthew across the back with the bucket. He hadn't been able to sleep on his back or his left side for over a week.

Then there was Dinah, slim and big- busted and coming on to him in the bar, buying him a drink he wasn't old enough to buy for himself. She promised him things no seventeen-year-old boy could resist – and she made good on her promises. But he knew before they had even parked the truck out there on the dam that the two of them were so different they couldn't ever even be friends. Of course, that hadn't stopped him from doing what they both wanted.

And then she was back a couple of months later, looking for him, finding him at the feed store where he worked after school, telling him he was going to be a daddy. He had grabbed her by the arm and dragged her out of the store into the alley behind the building, where maybe nobody would hear them, to tell her he knew it was a lie, that she probably ought to check her long list of other lovers to find a sucker, because he knew that baby wasn't his and he wasn't takin' somebody else's kid to raise...

Matthew groaned softly and threw his arm over his eyes. That didn't keep him from seeing Will that first day, when Dinah had dragged him into the farmhouse and told Matthew she was leaving him there. Will had been small and slight for his age, quiet and scared, trying to cling to the mother who didn't want him. The next day she had dumped him on the doorstep, freezing in just a sweatshirt in the November cold, clutching a letter to Matthew and a worn little back pack that contained everything he owned. Matthew remembered how the little boy had crumpled onto the couch crying – but sound-lessly, as if he had been trained not to disturb anyone with his feel-ings. Just what Matthew had learned from his own daddy: crying gets you beaten.

Abba-Father, You must be bringing all this back to me for a reason. John always says our history isn't our destiny, and I want that to be true! Please help me – save me! Don't let me become my daddy just because being Will's daddy is hard. I love him so much, and I want him to be happy. That's only going to happen when he understands about Jesus and accepts salvation and forgiveness and then learns to forgive. How are You going to do it? We've all tried – for over two years now – and he's just moving farther and farther away. Please, Father, don't let him go!

John and Carolyn turned off the television and carried their cof-fee mugs and ice cream bowls to the kitchen. John rinsed the dishes and put them into the dishwasher while Carolyn stood there smiling at him.

"I think I should get pregnant more often," she teased. "You're turning into a good wife."

John grinned back at her. "I'm embracing my feminine side. Saw on tv that real men need to do that."

"Does that mean I'm supposed to embrace my masculine side?"

"Definitely not!" John laughed, putting his arms around her. "That means you are supposed to embrace your masculine other half – me." He drew her closer and kissed her smiling mouth until they were both a bit breathless. "Let's go upstairs now."

They paused to lock the front door, leaving the back unlocked as usual, and went up to prepare for bed. John lay there after brushing his teeth and watched Carolyn change into her nightgown. He was both delighted and frightened at once to see the increasing curve of her belly.

"Are you feeling all right?" he asked.

She gave him a totally surprised look. "I'm fine. Why? Do I look bad?"

Oh, I'm not that stupid! "Honey, you look great! I just want to be sure you're okay."

"Just fine," she reiterated, climbing into bed next to him. "Everything is doing just what it's supposed to do. In a few more weeks you'll be able to feel the baby move."

John moved away just a little, which didn't go unnoticed.

"Don't you want to feel it move?"

Maybe I am that stupid. "Honey, I – it scares me. I'm afraid to get attached to it before it gets here. If something happens to it – "

"I think maybe we need to find out the sex of the baby after all," Carolyn said, rubbing John's back in soothing little circles. "As long as you keep referring to 'it' you won't feel close to the baby the way I do."

John flopped over on his back so he could look at her directly. "I don't think the father ever feels as close as the mother. I mean, it's growing inside you – there all the time. I don't remember – "

"Don't tell me you don't remember when I was expecting Johnny or David. You used to lie here like this every night and rub my tummy and talk to the baby so he'd know your voice. You were involved, John. This time – this time you're standoffish. I know you're scared, but this is really happening."

"I'm still trying to get used to it," John admitted. "Maybe it will be a good idea to learn what we're getting. We can – maybe we can pick out a name."

Carolyn threw her arm over his chest and hugged him. "I love you so much, John Abbott! You are going to do just fine, and you're going to be such a good daddy."

They were quiet for a few minutes, and then John said, "Daddy. I remember David calling me Daddy. And I remember Matthew talking about his 'daddy.' So different. And then Will – can't make up his mind whether Matthew is his daddy or his enemy. It's a magical word when it's used right. I could get used to hearing it again."

"That's good, because you'll hear it a lot over the next few years." She stroked her hand back and forth across his chest. "Do you think things are going to be all right with Matthew and Will? I don't exactly understand why it got so bad again all of a sudden. I don't mean just Allison, because I do understand how that's rocking Will's foundations. But before that – he stopped going to church, stopped going to youth group – "

"My theory – and it's just a theory – is that Will is so angry with his mother for abandoning him, and with his father for abandoning him, that he wants to lash out and hurt someone the way he's been hurt. Dinah's dead, but Matthew's right here. And he's also probably pretty terrified of being abandoned again, no matter how many times Matthew tells him that won't happen."

"What can we do? I hate to see them both suffering so."

"I think this is one only God can fix," John sighed.

Fifteen

WILL FOUND A MESSAGE ON HIS DESK WHEN HE went upstairs: "Dan called; please call back."

What the – What'd I do? He did a quick inventory of recent behavior but couldn't think of any probation violations. *Can't get me for thinking.*

Rather than postpone the distress, Will checked Dan's number, scrawled in the back of his calculus notebook, and headed to the kitchen to make the call. Halfway down the stairs he realized Carolyn and Pearl would be in the kitchen – and it was too late to call Dan today.

Man, what isn't screwed up? Like Ed says sometimes, can't win fer losin'. I wish I could call Tracy. But she's not even talking to me in school anymore. I wish I had a dog. He laughed aloud at that, standing there in the middle of the staircase. *How pathetic am I!*

Matthew appeared at the bottom of the stairs, headed up. They passed in the middle as Will pretended he was actually going down. "Sorry," Matthew said as they brushed by one another.

"No problem."

He heard Matthew sigh as he continued upward and echoed the sigh in his own heart. *He isn't such a bad guy all the time. He tries. He just doesn't get what I – want? Need? How can he, when I don't know myself. What a loser! I should never have been born. Then Mom would still be alive and Matt – Daddy – could have that woman and Tracy would be dating Kevin and – if I just wasn't here.*

You do know what to do about that, the other voice told him.

In the few moments between his breakfast and the school-bus the next morning, Will managed to be alone with the telephone to call Dan. Apparently, however, Dan didn't come in at seven, so Will left a message.

He was not thrilled, as he got off the bus that afternoon, to see Dan's old rattletrap parked in the Abbotts' driveway. He bit the bullet and walked into the living room, where Dan sat comfortably in John's chair.

"Hey," Will said.

"Sorry to drop in like this," Dan said, gesturing for Will to sit down. "I was just afraid we were going to play phone tag forever."

"Yeah." Will sat, dropping his book bag onto the couch beside him, shrugging out of his jean jacket and dropping it on top of the books. "So what'd I do?"

"I got a call from your dad, and we had a chat. Any idea what that was about?"

Crud. "He's just on me about stuff. Listen, man, I'm doing what I'm supposed to be doing! I'm clean, you know I am – I gotta have passed the pee test. I'm going to school and getting good grades; I do my work around here; I'm home by curfew – what do you expect?"

"I know you're doing the right things, Will," Dan said with a sigh. "It's your attitude we're all worried about. Matthew says you're so angry he can hear your detonator ticking, and he told me you tried to intimidate his girlfriend, that nurse – Allison. That's not exactly the kind of behavior the judge wants to hear about."

"So don't tell him. Matt says 'intimidate,' but it wasn't like that. That broad – I mean, woman – doesn't scare. I just wanted to talk to her, to tell her how it is. When she threw me out, I left without any argument." Will tried his innocent little boy face, but he could see Dan wasn't buying it. *Double crud.* "So what do I have to do?"

Dan shook his head and ran his hand over his buzz-cut hair. "Will, it isn't just about getting off probation. If you're careful, that's going to happen when you turn eighteen in February. But it's about being happy and having a good life after probation. It's about learning how to deal with feelings in responsible ways and how to use the resources you have to make a life you want to live. It's about learning to love and trust your dad and these other folks who are your family now."

Will felt both tears and anger rising behind his eyes and clenched his fists until his fingernails scored his palms. "You ought to try living with Matt," he said. "He doesn't really give a rip what happens to me once I'm outta here. He wants to play 'daddy' so he looks good, but he doesn't really c – " In spite of his efforts and bravado, Will's voice cracked, and he hung his head so Dan couldn't see his eyes.

The good thing about having PE first period was that it woke you up. The bad thing about having PE first period was that if you didn't want to go all day stinking like a goat, you had to shower. Will wasn't sure which was worse, but he figured stinking wasn't cool if he ran into Tracy, and it was only two days a week. *John would say I'm building character by facing my fears,* he told himself. *Right,* he answered. *Nothing to it. In and out fast, back to the wall – these guys hardly notice me anyway.*

Coach Hopkins warned everyone as they headed for the locker room, "Everybody in the showers! None of that sissy girl stuff about pretending to get your hair wet so it looks like you showered. And use soap; you guys smell like a pig farm!"

The swirl of naked boys around him boggled Will, but he stripped off and walked across the room toward the showers, not making eye contact with anyone. That was the way they did it, mostly, because everybody was embarrassed. It was just that most of them weren't afraid.

As Will reached the showers, a large hand shoved his shoulder. "Hey, Ryersen," a deep young voice said loudly, "get out of the way. No way I'm getting in there with a fag."

Will looked up into the face of Pete Coombs, one of the football players. Pete didn't look like he was joking. Will stepped aside.

As he stood against the wall waiting for Pete to come out of the shower, Will noticed several other guys eyeing him suspiciously. A couple of them made deliberate eye contact with his crotch and then smirked and whispered to each other. Will forced himself to stand there and not to cover himself. He didn't know why all of a sudden this was happening, but he did know acting afraid brought out the violent bully in some guys. He was mentally gearing up to fight if he had to, but he considered praying that wouldn't happen.

At last, minutes that had seemed an eternity, the showers were empty and Will could take his turn. He heard the bell and knew he was going to be late for second period. He considered saying he was sick and going home, but then his anger kicked in. *No way! I'm not going to let those guys push me around and get me in trouble. Maybe Pete just had a bad night or something. He's never even talked to me before.* Clean, reasonably dry, deodorized, Will went to the office for a tardy slip and tried to put the incident out of his mind.

"So how was your day?" Carolyn asked as she served Will peanut butter cookies and apple slices after school.

"Fine." He bent his head to his plate and ate as if he were really hungry.

"Really?"

Nuts. She was too perceptive. No way was he telling Carolyn about his locker room experience. "Really. Thanks for the snack, but I got a lot of homework. See ya later!"

Will made a strategic retreat to his room, where he could escape interrogation. He threw his book bag down by the desk and laid down on the bed, hands behind his head, shoes on the quilt.

Will opened his locker to swap out his chemistry book for his calculus book and stared in shock at the paper taped to the inside of the door. Torn from a standard spiral notebook, it featured a vulgar cartoon and, written in bloody swipes of broad-tipped permanent marker, the unmistakable message: "FAGS BURN IN HELL."

He ripped the paper from the door and crumpled it in his hand, leaning against the locker to keep his shaking knees from dropping him to the terrazzo floor. Embarrassment scalded his face, and then all the blood drained out, leaving little sparkles around the edges of his vision. *What's going on? Who's doing this – and why?* Mindful of the time, he stuffed the smashed paper into his jeans pocket, grabbed his calculus book and ran for his class, making it to his seat just as the bell rang.

Will really enjoyed calculus, although he went to some pains to disguise that fact from his teacher and schoolmates, but he wasn't able to focus on anything except the message in his locker and the previous episode in the showers. He began to get a clue at the end of the class, when Jenny Perkins, Chance Rupp's sometime girlfriend, said to Tracy, in a voice pretending to be quiet but actually pitched to carry, "You better be careful sitting next to Will. He steals things."

Tracy turned to look at Will, her eyes wide. She turned back to Jenny. "Don't be dumb." She dropped back to walk down the hall with Will. "Don't pay any attention to Jenny. She's just being stupid. I don't know why, but she is."

Will said nothing, but the worm of suspicion was beginning to gnaw in his brain.

Sixteen

"DON'T GET ALL UPSET," ALICE CAMPBELL warned, "but Benjie's back."

Allison dropped her purse under the nurses' station desk and her backside into a chair. "Same thing? Failure to thrive?"

"Looks like it," Alice nodded. "He's just all shriveled up like a little old monkey. Dr. Hanna was in twice yesterday and twice today, and he has a new treatment plan." She grinned at Allison.

"I smell a rat," Allison said. "What are you about to get me into?"

"A sling."

"What?!"

"Literally – a sling. Dr. Hanna thinks the baby needs to be carried all the time, next to somebody's body every minute. Like African and South American babies."

Allison gaped, then laughed. "This is a joke, right?"

"Nope," Alice said cheerfully, "not a joke at all. We're going to nurture Benjie and see if that brings him back. Leslie has him now, but you get him for your shift."

"How am I supposed to do my work with a baby lashed to my chest?" *And how will I stand it?*

"We'll cover for anything you can't do that way, but Leslie's finding she's pretty free to do most stuff; and we don't have any contagious kids on the floor right now, so the baby's safe. Actually, the other kids seem to get a kick out of seeing Benjie. They talk to him and want to touch him. Here comes Leslie now."

Allison looked up to see her friend walking toward them, a chart in one hand, the other cupped around the tiny bottom of an infant in a cotton sling across her chest. Her long, dark hair was pulled back in a ponytail to keep it off the baby, and her pretty face glowed with pleasure.

"Hi," Leslie said. "Oh, Allie, this is so much fun! He's such a cute little guy, and he never cries. I just had him in the nursery for a feeding for the last forty-five minutes, so he's good to go for another hour. You'll love carrying him!"

"Right. Okay, boss, I guess I'll become a monkey-mom. Help me on with the thing."

The transfer was easily made, although the sling had to be shortened considerably to accommodate Allison's much smaller, shorter frame. As she began her rounds, she noted how light Benjie was, almost as if he weren't there. And he kept his eyes closed even when she tried to rouse him and talk to him.

"Come on, baby," Allison encouraged as she walked down the hall.

The sling treatment continued day after day, as Allison, Leslie and several other nurses each took care of Benjie during her shift. Even Black Bob, the male nurse named for his heavy beard rather than for his race, took his turn on the late night shift. He claimed the baby made eye contact when Bob sang to him, but Leslie insisted that was only his way of asking Bob to stop.

At the end of a week, they were all surprised and thrilled to learn Benjie had gained several ounces. "I think it's working!" Allison enthused as she and Leslie made the swap.

"If he'd just interact with us," Leslie said. "He still won't look at me or make any noise. I wish he'd even cry."

"More time," Alice said. "He just needs more time."

Don't we all, Allison thought. She lived in terror of coming in one morning and learning that Benjie had died in the night. She lived in terror of the feelings she was developing for someone else's child. She had fantasies of adopting the little boy, whose single mother seemed to be proving unequal to the task of parenting him. She had fantasies of lying in bed with Matthew, with this little mite between them, peaceful and secure. She wished she could tell Matthew about Benjie, but she had promised not to call.

Driving into Lewiston, John kept one hand on the wheel and the other on his wife's hands, which were clenched together on her lap. They arrived at the medical building attached to Lewiston Medical Center with time to spare.

"You doing okay?" John asked.

"Fine! Really!" Carolyn said, not making eye contact, not unclenching her hands.

"It's all right to tell me you're scared," John said. "I always am."

"I don't really like getting the ultrasound. I know that's foolish – but I'm afraid they'll see something wrong. This way, as long as the baby moves and I don't see anything, then I'm sure he's all right." She took one hand from under John's to rub away a tear which was sneaking down her cheek.

John took both her hands in his and bowed his head. "Father, we ask You to help us to trust You better. We know You haven't made us to live in fear. Forgive us and grant us peace with whatever Your will is for our baby."

"Amen," Carolyn whispered. "Well, let's do it."

In Dr. Dana's office, the Abbotts settled in for a long wait, but this time they were ushered into an examining room within minutes.

"Doctor will be with you shortly, Mrs. Abbott," the nurse intoned. After taking Carolyn's vitals, she said, "Please change into the paper gown."

"Why?" Carolyn asked, fear edging her voice. "I didn't have to do that the last time."

The nurse, whose name tag read "Juanita," drew a deep breath. "It's just so she can do a more thorough exam, and then for the ultrasound. Nothing is wrong, Mrs. Abbott. In fact," Juanita joked, "I'm glad I took your blood pressure before I told you to change. It's perfect, and so's your heart rate - or was before you started to panic. Now just change and relax."

"Easy for her to say," Carolyn groused, changing into the pink paper flimsy which almost, but not quite, covered everything.

"That's not going to be the star of the fashion show," John teased, "but if anyone could make it look good, it would be you."

"Liar. But keep up the good work."

Half an hour later, Dr. Dana breezed into the room, long white coat and long brown ponytail flapping. She was pure cornfed Midwesterner, but she had married a man from Saudi Arabia with a long, unpronounceable last name, so everyone called her by her first name. Dr. Dana was a specialist in high-risk pregnancies and had seen the Abbotts through David's prenatal journey. They loved and trusted her as much as they could trust anyone with this.

After some preliminary questions and a fairly thorough physical exam, Dr. Dana smiled and said, "Everything still looks good from the outside. You measure just about right for this stage, and your cervix is holding just fine. You haven't had any problems, right?"

"Nothing but the occasional faint in the first couple of months," Carolyn said. "Not even morning sickness. That's been a blessing!"

"Well, we'll take a look-see now, but I don't expect any difficulties. Keep taking those prenatal horse pills and rest for at least an hour every afternoon – more often if you feel like it. Oh, and don't lift any refrigerators, as my friend Dr. Hanna says. See you in two weeks!" She breezed out as quickly as she had come in.

Juanita came to lead them down the hall to the ultrasound room, wrapping a light blanket around Carolyn for the walk. "Just hop up on the bed, and Susan will be with you in a minute."

Carolyn barely had time to settle the blanket over her lower body before Susan entered, chart in hand, her white lab coat decorated with a series of turtle pins, from large to small, and her long fingernails painted with tiny turtles to match.

"Hi, Carolyn! Hi, John!" she said, settling herself on the stool at the side of the bed. "How are you?"

"Fine," Carolyn said clearly. "How are you?"

"Oh, just great!" Susan replied, fiddling with the machine. "My kids are playing pee-wee football and my husband's building an NFL house of dreams. Okay, then... Let's just uncover your belly here and get ready to take a look."

"Susan, we'd like to know the baby's sex," Carolyn said.

"Really! All right! We'll see if we can tell this time." She squeezed on the cold gel and began to move the blunt-tipped wand around. John stood at the head of the bed gripping Carolyn's hand so hard it had turned white.

"Uh-huh," Susan said to herself. "Um-hmm... Looks good..." She turned the screen so both the Abbotts could see it. "Look! Full frontal! You have a daughter!"

Seventeen

"**W**HY'RE YOU LOOKING AT ME LIKE THAT?" Will challenged as he caught Matthew staring. "I wasn't doing anything."

Matthew flushed. "I know you weren't. I was just – just – "

"Well, quit it. You're making me self-conscious. It's creepy." He turned back to the Armor-All he was applying to the truck's dashboard. *He's freaking out. Looks at me like Celeste looks at a mousehole, just waiting... Every time I look up, there he is again, looking. Sick.* Will shuddered, a move not lost on Matthew.

"I'm sorry. I won't do it again. I'll go on inside, okay?"

"Yeah, sure." *And don't come back. Stay the heck away from me. I don't need you.*

Will avoided his father for the rest of the day, managing to do his Saturday chores when Matthew was occupied elsewhere or hanging out with Ed when they had to be near one another. He couldn't put his finger on what was happening, but it had that 'off' feel. *He better not be turning into a pervert! I can't live with that – I'd have to leave.*

Yeah, sure you would. Like, where would you go? You don't have enough money to go far, and Dan would have the cops after you even before Matt did. Crap.

Matthew sat on the edge of the bed to read Psalm 139 again. *"Where can I run from your Spirit...?"* He prayed for Will's salvation, and for Allison's, and wrestled down an urge to call her. He was free for the afternoon and had nothing he had to do. It would be so easy to go into Lewiston and meet her, unless she was working... No, he decided, not a good day to test Will like that. Will probably was cleaning the truck because he wanted to use it.

With a sigh, Matthew hauled the yellowed old pillowcase out from under his bed and laid the contents on top of it beside him. He hadn't carved anything in a long time, but he felt the urge to occupy his hands and mind with something exacting. The tools lay there, nestled in oily rags to keep them from rusting, all tucked into a cheap plastic tackle-box. There were only a couple of pieces of wood in the case, a block of white pine, easy to carve into tiny mice, and a remnant of Philippine mahogany, close-grained and softly red in the afternoon light shining in through the window.

Matthew turned the mahogany over and over in his hands, seeking the figure in the wood. It was big enough that he didn't want to waste a third of it by carving a mouse. Besides, no particular mouse was emerging in his mind. Maybe if he just started...

After taking out the chisels and knives and shining them up, Matthew left them lying out on the bed as he took up the wood again. This remnant was left over from carving the bust of Christ for John all those years ago, and he felt a kind of reverence for it. Not a thing to spoil or waste or profane. He put it down and picked up the pine. This was familiar territory. He could see a mama mouse and a baby mouse. He would give the mama Carolyn's face...

About an hour later, Will came galumphing up the stairs and paused to look in as he passed Matthew's door. "At it again, huh? Been a long time since I've seen you carving. Making mice for a change?"

"Nice sarcasm," Matthew acknowledged. "Yeah, mice for a change. I had another piece of wood, but I couldn't see anything in it."

"See. Right." Will fidgeted but didn't pass on.

"Want to come in?" Matthew offered.

"Why not? Nothing else to do." Will sauntered over to the desk chair and drew it closer to the bed. Matthew noted the closing distance and silently gave thanks. Every time Will let himself be in close quarters with a man it was a tribute to God's power to heal even the deepest wounds.

"I thought I'd do a mama and a baby this time," Matthew said. "For Carolyn and little Whoever."

"Doesn't look like much," Will said, rising to get a closer look.

"Well, I just started," Matthew laughed. "Gimme a break!"

Will looked at the block from several angles and shook his head. "You can really see stuff in there?"

"Usually." Matthew picked up a sharp knife and began to pare off thin slivers.

Will bent over and casually picked up one of the carving knives, juggling it in his hand.

"Hey, be careful!" Matthew said. "Those things are really sharp!"

"Yeah?" Will examined the blade and made to run his finger down it.

"Stop!" Matthew reached up and took the knife away from Will. "I'm serious about how sharp these are. They have to be razor-sharp to remove tiny bits of wood at a time, and that's the kind of sharp that can really hurt you." He held up his left thumb, where the thin white line of an old scar stood out clearly. "I cut that on that same knife you're holding years ago when I was making the first boat for David. Bled like a son-of-a-gun and took a long time to heal. Thing is, a blade that sharp – you don't even feel the cut. Doesn't hurt at all until later. You can get to the bone without even noticing." He put the knife back in its nest.

"No kidding." Will nodded to himself. "Well, good luck with it. See ya." He exited and went to his room, where the hard-rocking music he favored leaked under the door moments later.

Eighteen

ALICE CAMPBELL MIGHT BE A MIDWESTERN DRILL sergeant of a nurse, but she had sensibilities. The NICU nursery often filled with the soft strains of Mozart and Handel or the etudes of Chopin. She was convinced that this particular classical music was soothing to troubled babies, and to all appearances she was right. Although at almost subliminal volume, the music seemed to ease the tensions terribly sick newborns and preemies suffered in the hospital's high-tech environment. Alice had also demanded dimmer switches for the lights in NICU and PICU and kept them low as often as medical necessity permitted.

Allison sat in a padded rocker, Benjie out of the sling and cradled in her arm as she fed him his bottle. After weeks of Dr. Hanna's treatment, he had gained weight and was able to take four ounces of formula at a time. He no longer looked like a dying monkey, and he had begun to respond to the nurses with smiles and cooing sounds and good eye-contact.

"You are so cute!" Allison said, and the baby gave her a huge grin, milk leaking out of the corners of his mouth. She put him over her shoulder and patted until she received a loud but dry burp as her reward. "Yes, you are," she said, bringing him back to the crook of her arm, "just so cute!"

"Not getting too attached, are you?" came Alice's voice from behind her. The supervisor walked into the nursery and stood in front of Allison, a slight frown on her usually affable face.

"Of course not!" Allison denied. "But he is cute, isn't he?"

"Sure he is. And he's doing so well I imagine he'll be discharged by the end of the week."

"Oh. Of course. Back to his mother?"

"No, I don't think so. I think they were getting her to sign over custody to the state so they can place him for adoption. She kinda indicated she wants to do that."

"What if she changes her mind?"

"Well," Alice said, "I don't think they're going to let him go back to his mother no matter what, because there's too much evidence that she couldn't care for him. He'd end up in foster care for a long time, maybe until he's eighteen, if she wouldn't give up her rights. The state always tries to reunite families, but he's too little to take a chance on now."

Allison shifted the sleepy baby back into the sling. "I wish – "

"Don't go there," Alice said. "You can't take him."

"You're right." She looked down at the dark hair wisping over Benjie's head, the soft eyelids now closed in sleep, the milky drool at the corner of his relaxed little mouth. "No big deal."

On Friday morning, shortly after Allison had come on shift and taken Benjie from Leslie, Cathy Horvath and another woman from the children's services offices stepped off the elevator and approached the desk. The other woman carried a car seat and some baby clothes; Alice came around the desk to meet them.

"Good morning!" Alice said. "We have all Benjie's discharge paperwork done and ready for you, and he's had his first morning feeding. Allison," she called down the hall.

Allison turned and walked back to the nurses' station, cradling Benjie close to her.

"Allison, this is Cathy Horvath and Peg Slater. They're here to take Benjie to his new foster home."

"Hello," Allison said. "He's asleep."

"I'm sorry," Cathy said. "I guess we'll have to wake him to change his clothes and put him in the car seat." She looked sharply at Allison, then turned to Peg. "Why don't you give the clothes to Allison, Peg, and she can get the baby ready for us."

"Thank you," Allison whispered, taking the clothes. "I'll just take him into the nursery for a minute."

Cathy and Alice nodded, but Allison only had eyes for the baby.

She missed the sympathetic look the women exchanged.

In the nursery, Allison gently took Benjie out of the sling and laid him in his baby-basket. "I hate to do this, sweetheart, I really do," she said softly, removing Benjie's swaddled blanket.

Benjie woke up suddenly, as he often did, the startled wakening of a child unsure what was coming at him. He was poised to cry but began to smile as he recognized Allison. He waved his arms and kicked his skinny legs as she undressed him and changed his diaper.

"Oh, you're going to be a basketball player," Allison crooned as she fitted him into a onesie. "Look at those long, strong legs."

Benjie responded to the sound of her voice with gurgles and reached for her hair, a new trick he had taught himself in the last few days.

"And your new mommy is going to have such fun playing with you and teaching you how to do things. She's going to love you so much – " Huge tears welled over and splashed onto the baby until she scooped him up and held him close. "I'm going to miss you, sweetheart," she sobbed. "I wish I could have been your mommy. I would never, ever have hurt you or let you go."

Alice appeared in the doorway. "Time to go," she said gently. "Want me to take him out?"

"No." Allison straightened up and wiped her eyes with her hand. "I can do it." In the hallway she handed the baby to Peg, who took him impersonally, like a package, and wasted no time buckling him into the car seat.

"That's it, then," Cathy said. "Thank you – all of you – for saving Benjie's life and getting him ready for a good future."

"Will he have a good future?" Allison asked.

"What!" Peg said.

"I mean, will he go to a good home and be adopted and – and have brothers and sisters and enough to eat and – "

"Of course he will!" Peg snapped. "What kind of people do you think we are?"

"She's just concerned," Cathy said, easing the tension. "These nurses have been caring for Benjie for weeks and weeks, and they've gotten close to him. I promise he will go to a good home. He's so cute, everyone who sees him will want him." She smiled at Allison and signaled Peg to pick up the car seat. In moments the elevator door had closed behind them.

"Do you need to go home?" Alice asked.

"No, of course not. I'm fine. Plenty to do today." Allison gave an un-professional snuffle and headed away toward her next patient's room.

"Poor kid," Alice said to herself. "Glad I don't get attached like that." She looked around before wiping her eyes with the heels of her hands.

He always puts them under the bed.

Will got down on his hands and knees and lifted the edge of the white chenille bedspread. If a faint twinge of guilt ran through him, he suppressed it immediately. He knew what he wanted.

Nothing under the bed except the old pillowcase, not even dust bunnies. Will pulled it out. *In here.* He unfolded the top and pulled out the contents, setting aside several small blocks of various woods and the half-finished mouse with what seemed to be Carolyn's face. *Cute*, he acknowledged in spite of himself. *It must be nice to have a talent like that...* Will opened the old tackle-box and found nothing but the tools themselves, nestled carefully in greasy rags.

He looked at the carving knives and chisels for a long moment, trying to remember what Matthew had said. *Oh, yeah. So sharp it can cut to the bone and you don't even feel it. Yeah.*

Matthew rubbed his tired eyes and yawned until his jaw cracked. He was worn out after a long day wrestling with machinery and cows who didn't want to come in out of the late September sunshine, but his mind was going too fast to sleep. The cheap wind-up alarm clock on his bedside table told him in fluorescent numbers that it was two a.m. *Nehemiah, Ezra, Esther, Amos, Habakkuk,* he cursed under his breath. *Nearly time to get up, and I haven't slept more than an hour or two!*

Facing reality, he turned on the bedside lamp and sat up on the side of the bed. *Lord, I guess I have some sorting to do... What do You want me to do about Allison? How can I help Will with the stuff that's bothering him?* After a few more moments in prayer, he took the Bible from the table and read the account of King David and his rebellious son Absalom. He understood the heartcry, "O Absalom, my son!" That story didn't end well. Better to consider the prodigal son, dragging home in defeat and suffering, taken back without question by his father to be part of the family again. *That's what I want for Will, Lord, to come home to me and to come home to You, even though he doesn't realize he's gone.*

Putting the Bible aside, Matthew reached under the bed and drew out the old pillowcase. He might as well occupy his hands while he waited for the alarm to go off. Drawing out the little mouse-mama and her baby, he selected a knife and began to refine the lines of the mother. In a few strokes he saw the need for a finer, sharper tool and turned back to the box, meditating on which knife would give him the best control as the work grew more exacting. He had his favorites. But the one he wanted wasn't there.

What the – He searched through the toolbox, shaking out the oiled rags to make sure it wasn't under anything. He took out the top tray from the old tackle-box and looked in the bottom space, where things were jumbled together. He poked his finger painfully on an old tapestry needle, but he didn't find the knife.

Maybe it fell out, Matthew mused, going down on his knees to look under the bed. But there was nothing there.

Confused, he shrugged and chose another knife, almost as sharp, to continue the work until the alarm went off at three fifteen.

When Allison didn't show up for her shift on Thursday, Alice called her at home, only to receive no answer. Torn between anger and concern, she left a "call me" message and checked the emergency room, which had no record of Allison's having been there. Leslie was working on another floor, but Alice called her, too. No, she hadn't heard from Allison in several days.

Using her Sherlock skills, Alice figured out how to contact Matthew, and at eight o'clock she called the Abbott house, explaining to Carolyn who she was and that she needed to speak with Matthew, who came to the phone after a long wait, breathless and concerned.

"I'm sorry to bother you," Alice said, "but I'm worried about Allison." Briefly she explained the situation.

"I haven't seen her or talked with her lately," Matthew admitted. "We're kinda – my son isn't real happy about us, and we've been kind of cooling it. Look, maybe she was just in the shower or something."

"No," Alice said. "She never has a problem being on time for work, no matter what shift it is. She never forgets. If she's sick, she calls in."

"All right," Matthew said, "I'll go to her house and see if she's there.

121

I'll let you know, Miz Campbell."

"I couldn't help overhearing," Carolyn said. "I'll tell John and Ed you had to go."

"Thanks. I'll be back as fast as I can."

Matthew prayed his way into Lewiston, pushing the truck to seventy-five on the back-country roads and as fast as traffic allowed in town. When he came to Allison's townhouse, he saw her car in the parking lot almost all by itself.

His assault on the doorbell produced no results, so Matthew began heavy-fisted knocking. After five minutes or so, he heard something behind the door.

"Allie, open up! It's Matthew!" he hollered. No response.

"Allison, open the door! I'm not kiddin'! If you don't open it, I'm gonna have to break it down, and that's gonna hurt."

After a moment of fumbling, she opened the door and stood aside. Matthew eased his way in and looked her over. *Drinking again.* His heart sank.

"Alice is worried about you," he said.

"So what?"

Belligerent Allison. Nuts. "You need to call in and tell her you're okay. You didn't show up for work or answer your phone, and she got scared. She called me."

"And here – you are – rid-ing to the res-cue." Allison pulled the sash of her pink robe tighter around her and stuck out her chin. "Go away, Matthew."

"I don't think so, honey. Let's make some coffee and you can tell me what's the matter. After you call Alice."

"How dumb do you – think – I am? I can't call her!"

Matthew sighed and ran his hand through his hair. "Okay, then, I'll call her. I'll tell her you're sick."

Allison gave Matthew what he could only describe to himself as an evil grin. "Gonna lie for me, huh? Can you – shp-spell co-de-pen-dent?"

God help me! I hate bein' around a drunk! The smell of Jack Daniels wafted over him every time Allison spoke, bringing back the painful images of his drunken, brutal father like hammer-blows. He stepped around her to the phone in the kitchen and placed the call. As he told

Alice the lies, he heard glass clinking on glass in the living room.

"Can you tell me why you're doin' this?" he asked, frowning at the large glass tumbler half-full of whiskey. "You know it's gonna make you sick. You know it doesn't solve anything. What's really wrong, Allie?" He sat down beside her on the couch.

"Jus' go home, Matthew," she begged. "Go home an' leave – me alone. Call Leslie."

Anger flashed through his gut. "Leslie? I told you before I don't want to date your friend! I don't need for you to set me up with somebody else, I need for you to – ah, what's the use?" He stood abruptly. "I'm goin' home. Call me when you're sober, okay? I can't talk to you like this." *And I'm not goin' to.*

Without waiting to see whether his departure mattered to her, Matthew slammed his way out the front door and stamped his way back to the truck, not seeing Allison standing in the open doorway, glass in hand, tears streaming down her cheeks as he squealed out of the parking lot and headed home.

Instead of going directly home, Matthew detoured to the church, hoping Pastor Miles would be available for some sorting-talk. He recognized his own anger for the hangover from his past that it was, but he didn't feel able to shake it.

Miles was in his office, working on his sermon.

"Hi, come on in!" the pastor said, seeming genuinely glad to see Matthew. He unfolded his tall, skinny frame from the chair to walk around the desk and shake Matthew's hand. "Have a seat. What's up?"

Matthew sat on the couch, shoving aside half a dozen bright needle-point pillows to make room, and ran his hands through his hair. "I need to be sorted," he said ruefully. "I just came from Allison's house. She's drunk."

Miles sat in the adjoining armchair, stretching out his long legs in front of him and draping his long arms along the padded arms of the chair. "Allison – the girlfriend, right? The nurse?"

"Yeah."

The pastor waited.

"She didn't go in to work, and her supervisor couldn't raise her. She called me, so I went over and found her. She was in a mean mood, and she wouldn't tell me what's going on. She hasn't done this for a while

– that I know of, anyway – but she sure drinks like somebody with a problem."

"It's hard for you to be around a drunk, isn't it."

Matthew unconsciously rubbed his left knee, which had been badly injured by his father and healed a couple of years before as he came to terms with his past and forgave the man. "I think I'm over it all, and then the smell – it all comes back. Not maybe as bad as before…"

"Deliverance is a process, like 'most everything else," Miles said, "and we should expect to have these little relapses into old feelings. Doesn't mean you've screwed up, okay? Just means you need to ask God again to help you let go of it. I'm more interested in what's up with Allison. I thought you were seeing her again - kind of hoped to meet her some Sunday morning."

Matthew laughed, a bitter laugh. "Not likely. She doesn't believe in God, and she gets real prickly if He comes up. I keep praying for ways to share the gospel with her, but they don't turn up. I did believe that's what God wanted me to do – to keep on loving her and spending time with her and showing her God's love until I could tell her… But I can't do this!"

"A recovering priest I know says you can't talk to a drunk, because either they won't listen or they won't remember. So I guess it makes sense not to hang around. The trick is to catch her sober." Miles sat up and drew in his legs. "Let's pray about it, okay?"

"Sure, why not?"

Matthew sat forward and bowed his head over his knees as they prayed together. By the time they were finished he felt much calmer. "Thanks," he told Miles, "that helped. I'll go back to work now."

"Call or drop by again if you need me," Miles said, grinning as he walked Matthew out into the hall. "The Boss and I are always glad to see you."

As an afterthought, Miles said, "And I don't mean Bruce Springsteen."

Nineteen

CHANCE RUPP FLIPPED THE HAIR OUT OF HIS EYES and smiled at the two guys behind him in the lunch line. "Hey, Travis. Hey, Kevin."

They returned his greeting warily. They were popular enough not to have to sit at the losers' table, but they weren't part of the jock elite. Chance wasn't a buddy.

"How's it goin'?" Chance asked, putting two hamburgers on his tray.

"All right," Travis said. He took only one hamburger, but he doubled on the Tater Tots. Kevin took two of everything and eyed Chance from under his lashes.

"Where's Ryersen?" Chance asked.

The two friends looked at each other. Kevin shook his head. "I dunno. He has lunch this period..."

"Guess you guys are being kinda careful about being seen with him now, huh? Can't have people thinking you're like that. Of course, we – " he gestured toward Pete and the other football players, already seated at their table – "we know you guys are okay." Chance picked up two big chocolate chip cookies and three cartons of chocolate milk and waved his cafeteria pass at the beleaguered little stick-woman at the register. "See ya!" he told Travis and Kevin over his shoulder as he went to join his table.

"What was that all about?" Kevin asked as they took their trays to the table frequented by the semi-popular non-jocks.

"I don't know. I haven't heard anything about Will. I know he's been acting weird since we ran into his dad and that woman at the fair, and I know he and Tracy aren't together any more, but why wouldn't we want to be seen with him?"

As they inhaled hamburgers, Tater Tots, and Jell-o with suspicious bright-colored bits in it, Kevin and Travis listened to the conversations going on around them. Will's name came up several times in twenty minutes, always with that sense of innuendo but no concrete information.

"Listen," Kevin said as they headed for their next classes, "I don't get it, but sounds to me like somebody's trying to get Will in trouble of some kind. We better talk to him."

"I don't know," Travis answered. "He might not like it. Maybe he already knows and he's just ignoring it."

"But we don't know what 'it' is. He might be in real trouble. Will's a friend, man. We gotta help him out."

Travis and Kevin became aware as they got on the bus to go home that Will Ryersen had somehow attained pariah status. As he walked toward the back of the bus, smothered snickers and whispers followed him. When he tried to sit next to one of the guys from his calculus class, the boy said, "It's taken." Travis and Kevin watched Will shake his head and slide into an empty seat.

Undaunted, they walked back to him and sat, Kevin beside him and Travis behind. "Hey," Kevin said, "how's it going?"

"Fine."

"You busy today? Can we get together?" Travis asked.

"Homework," Will said shortly. "Chores." He didn't look at either of his friends.

"I'll help you with the chores," Travis said. "Then we can goof off for a while. I don't have anything I have to do except homework. How about it?"

"No, thanks."

"Will?" Kevin asked.

"What?"

"Are you okay?"

"Fine." Will stepped over Kevin to move to a seat farther back in the bus.

Travis moved up to sit with Kevin, and they stared at one another, bewildered.

"What do you expect from a guy like that?" asked a junior from across the aisle.

Will bypassed the kitchen to go directly to his room, sacrificing food for the safety of not having to face Carolyn, who seemed to be able to read him all too well. He dumped his book bag on the floor next to his desk and flopped down on the bed, feet hanging over the edge to avoid dirtying the red and blue quilt. His mind replayed every whispered insult and mocking look from the whole day. *Fag. Homo. Queer. Jailbird. Thief. Liar.* Those were just the tamer ones. He replayed being knocked into his locker by Pete and Chance, smacked on the back of the head by a heavy hand whose owner he didn't even see, given the stink-eye by Billy when they happened to open their adjacent lockers at the same time.

What did I do? Why is this happening all of a sudden? Nobody knew about this stuff except Dan and the family, and none of them would ever tell anyone. Would they?

He considered that for a minute, betrayal from inside, but he couldn't begin to believe it. They might not think he was the perfect kid or anything, but they didn't want to hurt him. Not even Matt. Not this way. *He doesn't think I'm gay. He knows I'm not. No way he'd say something like that to anyone. If he wants to get rid of me, he doesn't have to do that kind of stuff. All he has to do is tell that lady at the social services office he wants to give me back.*

Sighing, Will got up and hauled his book bag onto the desk. Might as well get started on his homework; he'd have chores after supper today. Plotting out what to do first, he drew his calculus book and a bunch of notebooks out of the bag, dropping them onto the desk. As he pulled them out, a handful of loose papers also slid out of the overpacked space, fluttering to the floor.

"Nuts!" he exclaimed, bending down to pick up the mess. Will didn't like his room untidy, willing to take John's teasing about not being a typical teen for the sake of having order around him. He had learned in his early years with Dinah, his mother, to create a tiny oasis of sanity in the midst of all kinds of chaos by keeping things neat.

Plopping down on the desk chair, Will looked at the papers in his hand: returned calculus test – A; Macbeth essay – A; history quiz – D... and a ragged sheet torn out of somebody's notebook and crammed into his bag when he wasn't looking.

Get out of this school or else, faggot. We don't need your kind here.

"Will!" Carolyn called up the stairs. "Come down and get your snack!"

Snack. Right. "I'm okay," he called back. "I'm not hungry." *Please leave me alone!*

No such luck. He heard her light footsteps coming up the stairs and barely had time to shove the note back into his book bag before she was standing in the doorway, a plate of cheese and crackers and apple slices in one hand, a glass of milk in the other.

"I know you must be hungry," Carolyn said, holding out the food. When Will didn't take it, she gave him a closer look. "Unless you're sick. Don't you feel well? You look kind of pale."

"I'm fine," Will said, taking the plate and glass from her and putting them on the desk. "I'll eat it."

"Well, good, then." Carolyn turned toward the door but then turned back again. "Will?"

"Yeah?"

"Is there anything I can – I mean, would you like to talk about anything?"

"No. I'm fine." Belatedly, he said, "Thanks."

"You know I love you," Carolyn persisted, "and I'm here for you if there's anything at all you need. You do know, don't you?"

"Yeah, sure. Thank you." *Now get out of here before you see me cry.*

He turned away and listened to Carolyn's footsteps receding down the stairs, wiping a few tears away with the heel of his hand. After what seemed to him a respectable interval, Will took the plate and glass into the bathroom and flushed away the contents.

I'm gonna turn into my father after all, he laughed bitterly to himself. *We'll have matching ribs.*

At dinner Will managed to eat enough to avoid comments and to nod or smile at the right places in the conversation. Carolyn was talking about names for a girl, and that led to a contest for most preposterous name. In the general merriment, Will's silence was unremarked, if not unnoticed.

"Chores now, boy," Ed said at the end of the meal. "Me and you is gonna leave your daddy and the boss with the dishes and go button things down for the night."

"Suits me," Will agreed quickly, following Ed through the kitchen and out the back door before anyone could naysay him.

"Did you grab the trash?" Ed asked.

"Took it just before supper. It's in the barrel. Figured to burn it tomorrow, when there's less wind."

"Good thinking. Okay, then. Make sure the chickens are in the coop and lock 'er up for the night. I'll do the barn."

"Do I need to gather eggs?" This was one of Will's least favorite chores.

"Nope. Done that this morning. You're off the hook. Now git! Join me in the barn when you're done."

Will went away without another word. He detested the stupid, smelly chickens, with their dirty ways and sharp beaks. Fortunately, he only had to herd two of them inside, and the rooster didn't bother to attack him during the process. Padlocking the door to foil raccoons, Will loped off to the barn to meet Ed, who was making sure the cows had water and hay for the night.

"You spoil these things," Will opened.

"Nah," Ed countered, "just like to keep 'em content. Better milk, and more of it."

"Whatever." Will moved to Ed's side, hoping to avoid a manure detail at this hour of the evening. No such luck.

"Git those stalls over there," Ed gestured. "Don't know why they been inside, warm as it's been, but them's the breaks."

"Aw, let Matt do it tomorrow," Will tried, not really holding out any hope. Sure enough, Ed just handed him the pitchfork and gestured toward the wheelbarrow.

At least there were only two stalls to muck out, Will rejoiced, and neither was too bad. He bent to his work, trying to imitate the easy rhythm Ed and Matt always had. There was some value in mindless, repetitive work for quieting the mind, if only Ed would be still. But tonight Ed had a mouthful to say, apparently.

"You been acting kinda funny since school started," he said, coming right to the point. "You and me, we've spent some time together, and I reckon I can tell. What's going on, son?"

"Nothing." Will flung a forkful of wet straw into the barrow.

"Don't," Ed said gently. "I know better. I been praying for you a lot lately, because the Lord's been bringing you to my mind so much. I know He only does that for a reason."

"I told you, nothing!" Will snapped. "Leave me alone." He scooped and flung again, nearly overshooting the wheelbarrow with the exaggerated snap of his arms.

"If you don't wanta talk to me," Ed persisted, "then talk to your daddy. He'll want to help you."

Sure he will. He'll be just so proud to know his son's the new jerk of Lewiston High.

"Right." He finished the work as fast as he could and pushed past Ed to take his load to the manure pile. Gagging, he dumped and scraped and toted everything back to its place in the barn. Ed had gone by then, so Will was able to slip back to the house without further confrontation.

But he found everyone in the living room when he came through from the kitchen.

"Come on in," John called. "We were just talking."

"I got homework," Will said, heading up the stairs before they could stop him. In his room, door carefully closed and locked, he stripped out of his clothes and gathered fresh things for his shower. He put on the heavy bathrobe he had convinced Matthew to buy for him and let himself out into the hall to slip across to the bathroom. There he locked the door again and stood for a long time under water as hot as he could stand it. He didn't look at himself in the mirror as he dried off and combed his wet hair, fearing the face he might see. Did he look like a jailbird? Did he look like a fag?

As he went back to his room, Will heard the steady hum of voices rising from the living room like a piece of quiet music. Pearl's tremulous soprano and Carolyn's gentle alto balanced against Ed's bass, John's baritone and Matthew's almost-tenor. They rose and fell over each other in steady rhythm, warming a cold place in Will's chest. He wished he could be there, just sitting in the midst of that music of family, easing away the chill and the pain, pretending he belonged. His room was cold and empty.

With a sigh he didn't notice, Will sat down at the desk, still wrapped in his bathrobe, and pulled the calculus book toward him. Sometimes the elegance of the formulas was soothing, too.

Chance humored his dad by catching really bad passes as his dad relieved his glory days on the football team. It didn't take much, because his dad could talk without interruption for at least a day and a half, and he couldn't really put much behind the throw any more. Chance had lured his dad out to the yard by offering to play, and now he was waiting for his moment. It came with an overthrown return which his dad couldn't move fast enough to snag.

"Let's take a break," Aaron Rupp panted. Chance nodded and joined his dad on the lawn chairs at the edge of the yard. After a few moments of companionable silence, Aaron unwittingly gave his son the opening. "What's new at school?" he asked.

"Not much," Chance said. Two-beat pause. "But there is one thing..."

"Yeah, what?"

"Dad, I know you're friends with that other p.o., Dan. I know you can't talk about your clients, but – I just wondered – some rumors are going around at school..."

"What kind of rumors?"

"Well, there's this guy – a senior – " Chance paused and studied his hands.

"Friend of yours?" Aaron asked.

"No! I hardly know the guy!" Chance projected agitation with his bouncing knee and furrowed brow. "But people are talking about him – about how he has a bad record, been in prison, maybe killed somebody. And – and they say he's a – you know, a – "

"A what, son?" Aaron looked almost alarmed when Chance sneaked a look at him.

Two-beat pause. "A – well, a queer. You know – a homo."

Aaron's face darkened and he seemed to swell up. "Has this kid come on to you?"

"No!" Chance said quickly. "Nothing like that! It's just what people are saying, especially around the locker room."

"Who is this kid?"

"His name's Ryersen. Will Ryersen. A transfer in from somewhere, but nobody knows where – except the prison thing. I thought maybe you'd know him, or Dan would. I mean, if it's true, then he'd have to be on parole or probation or something, right?"

"That would be right," Aaron agreed.

"I don't mean to make trouble for anybody," Chance said, widening his eyes and looking directly at his dad. "But if this guy is dangerous or something, well, people oughta know."

"Don't you worry, son," Aaron assured his boy. "I'll look into it. We won't let anyone hurt you or the other kids, I promise." He rose and flung a heavy arm around Chance's shoulders.

Together father and son headed indoors. Chance's face held a beatific smile in the waning twilight.

Twenty

"MATILDA," JOHN SUGGESTED. HE GRABBED Carolyn around her expanding waist and began to waltz her around the living room, humming "Waltzing Matilda" with a heavy downbeat as he went.

"Natasha," Matthew countered. "Moose and Squirrel like," he added in an atrocious pseudo-Russian accent.

"Hollyhock," Pearl contributed, "or Daffodil or – ah – Dahlia." Her dark eyes twinkled with amusement.

"She's gonna be a gem," Ed offered, "so how 'bout Ruby?"

"Topaz," John offered. "Carnelian. Beryl."

Will leaned back against the couch and grinned in spite of himself. "Ima," he said. "Like, I'm a Abbott."

Carolyn stopped dancing, a bit short of breath, smiling at all of her helpers. "I think we need to choose a name that shows how grateful to God we are for this baby." She sat down beside Will and patted his knee.

"Okay," John agreed, sitting on the other side of her. "We can call her Patience or Longsuffering or one of the other fruits or gifts of the Spirit."

"What kinda name is 'Longsuffering' for a little girl?" Will said, half-alarmed. "She won't be able to write it until she's in sixth grade!"

"Point taken," John said. "Well, we still have a while to figure it out, don't we? If you have any more great ideas, just submit them in writing to the little mother, okay?"

"Names are important," Carolyn said, sitting down and taking up some yarn and a crochet hook. She was making a lacy pale pink blanket in her sedentary moments. Pearl was knitting a little sweater in pink and white, with tiny owls knitted into the pattern across the front.

"Sure they're important," Ed agreed.

"David – " Carolyn hesitated only briefly before going on, "that means 'beloved.'"

"He was, too," Matthew said, the usual fleeting trace of sadness crossing his face, bringing the usual responsive frown to Will's.

"Exactly," Pearl agreed. "And that's why you will be so careful about this little one's name. The Bible is a good source for the names of godly women. There's Sarah and Deborah and Ruth and – "

"Excuse me," Will interrupted. "I have homework."

He took the stairs two at a time and made it into the safety of his room in a few more steps. His calculus book confronted him, its page of unsolved problems demanding attention.

"Names," Will muttered. "Baby stuff. You'd think this was the most important kid born since Jesus." He dropped into the desk chair and pulled the book toward him. In moments he was absorbed in the purity of mathematics, where he remained for half an hour or so, until a knock on the door startled him back to reality.

"What?" Will called.

"Phone call," Matthew said through the door.

"Coming!" Will hastened down the stairs to the kitchen and grabbed the receiver.

"Hello?"

"Listen, faggot," a voice said, "we don't want you in our school. Get out. Go hang with your own kind."

"Who is this?"

"Somebody who doesn't like homos and thieves and jailbirds. Take the hint, queer."

"Wait a – "

Before he could complete his sentence, the phone went to dial tone. Will carefully replaced the receiver with shaking hands and leaned against the counter trying to breathe. He wiped cold sweat from his forehead and shoved his hands into his pockets so no one would find them trembling.

What's going on? Who was that? He hadn't recognized the voice, except that it was male. It could have been any guy he knew – or any guy's father. *What am I going to do?*

Sneaking back upstairs to avoid running into any of the adults in the house, Will fell back into his chair again and stared unseeing at his unfinished homework. His hands were still shaking too hard to write, and his mind was stuck and spinning like a bald tire on ice.

I don't know what to do. I don't know who to talk to.

With the realization of just how alone he was, Will couldn't suppress the tears any more. He flopped face down on his bed and stifled his sobs in the pillow. What kind of a life was this, anyway, he wondered. And what was the use of trying to do better? It was going to end badly no matter how hard he tried.

Allison's headache was definitely a five-dwarf headache this time, but she couldn't call in sick again without getting into serious trouble. She medicated the pain with extra-strength over-the-counter pills and three cups of stand-a-spoon-in-it coffee, which did little for the incipient nausea haunting her but made her alert enough, she figured, to drive safely. She hid her red-veined eyes behind huge sun-glasses and braved the fall air. It bit her. Looking down at her panda-print scrubs, Allison realized she had forgotten a jacket.

"Too bad. I'm not going to walk up the steps and mess with the locks again just to get a coat," she said aloud, wincing at the sound of her own voice. The neighbor's boxer barked frantically as she passed 'his' townhouse, and she snarled at him, "Shut up, Avery!"

The little blue car's heater was working as well as it ever did, and by the time she arrived at the hospital, Allison was almost warm again. More coffee would do it, she thought as she took the elevator to the Peds ward.

Alice was waiting. "Where have you been this time?" she asked, no smile of welcome lightening her unusually stern tone.

"What do you mean? I was at home getting ready for work. Now I'm *at* work. Where else would I be on a Wednesday?"

"Frankly," Alice said, "you might be anyplace. It's nine-thirty, Allison, and you were due on at seven."

"No! That can't be right! I – " Allison looked at her Snoopy wristwatch and saw that Alice was correct. *How did that happen? I know*

135

the alarm went off, and I know I only hit the snooze once or twice...

"This has gotten out of hand, Allison," her supervisor said. "I called in Lori Wilson to cover your shift. I want you to come with me to Mr. Paulson's office."

Harold Paulson was the hospital administrator, the head honcho, as Alice always called him. Allison didn't really know the man, and she didn't care to. He was well over six feet tall, skinny and dried out as a winter stick. She had never seen him laugh, but he had a smile like a scalpel blade. Or a hatchet. Because he was, she knew, the hatchet man.

"Alice, I'm really sorry! My alarm must have gotten screwed up. I won't let it happen again, I promise! If you don't want me to work today, I'll go home and just come in tomorrow as scheduled, okay?"

"No," Alice said, "not okay. Come on." She shadowed Allison to the elevator and stepped in beside her. They rode in silence to the sixth floor.

"I haven't been up here since they remodeled," Allison said, trying to make normal conversation. "It looks like some huge corporate office building where all the best offices have great views."

"It is," Alice said, "and they do." She led the way into the reception area marked "Administration."

A gray-haired woman of probably sixty, dressed in a deliberately understated charcoal pinstripe suit and mid-heel black pumps, looked up from her glass desk as they entered the area. "Hello, Alice," she said in a carefully modulated Chicago accent. "Mr. Paulson is expecting you; go right in."

Like flotsam in the tide, Allison washed into a huge office and up against the front of a huge black granite-topped desk. Her first impression was of cold – pale gray walls, black furniture, brushed chrome and stainless accents, black-and-white photographs instead of art on the walls. She shivered and the little pandas danced on her scrubs.

Dancing pandas aren't exactly the way to dress to meet the head honcho, she thought. And she realized he was speaking to her.

"Good morning, Mr. Paulson," she responded.

"Sit down." She sat on a hard black chair in front of the desk.

"Your supervisor, Nurse Campbell, tells me we have a problem," Paulson stated in a voice as desiccated as the rest of him.

"No, sir," Allison said, "I don't think there's a problem."

"She says," he went on, "that you have been missing work, late for work, coming in smelling of alcohol – well, surely I need not go on. You appear to have a drinking problem, and it appears to be impacting your work. Therefore, under the terms of your contract with this hospital, you are required to undergo an evaluation for substance abuse and to enter such treatment as shall be recommended – or to resign your position immediately." He didn't bother to make eye-contact as he delivered this blow; he was already studying some documents on his desk and looking at his watch as if the time he was squandering on her had far exceeded his limit.

Allison remained seated. "Mr. Paulson, I'm a member of the nurses' union here, and I believe I am entitled to union representation in this."

He raised his eyes to meet hers this time. "Are you threatening me?"

"No, sir, merely pointing out my rights. I don't want to get into a big argument about all this. Yes, I have missed some work, but I'm not having problems on the job. I'm really good at what I do, and I love my work here. Alice can vouch for that!" She turned beseeching eyes on Alice, who seemed to reluctantly nod. "So what I propose is just that you let me do my job and not talk about this anymore. I promise – no more absences, no tardies."

"Ms. Campbell?" Paulson asked, one gray eyebrow quirked.

"Sir, I wish I could just agree," Alice said, wringing her hands like a silent movie heroine. "But – our patients are so little and so sick – one mistake could kill a child. Allison, I know you love the kids. You don't want to hurt anyone."

"Of course I don't! And have I, ever?"

Alice shook her head.

"It seems to me," Paulson said, "that if you don't have a drinking problem an evaluation would show that and remove any doubt. I don't want a fight with the union, but I do not intend to be held hostage in my own office. You may get the evaluation or bring in the union rep, as you prefer. That's all." He turned his back to make clear the force of the dismissal.

In the elevator Allison turned to Alice and glared. Matthew

would have recognized the look immediately – the sulphuric glare of the princess-dragon.

"How could you do this to me?" she asked.

"You know how," Alice said, an edge to her voice. "You know what's going on, and so do I. You're the best nurse I have when you're sober and not hung over, but the way you've been going since Benjie left, you're just a liability waiting to happen. I don't want you on my service anymore, Allison, not unless you get some help. My father was an alcoholic, and I watched him die by inches for twenty years. I saw the trail of destruction he left behind him, too. I know where this goes."

The elevator spat them out at the nurses' station. They stood there staring at one another until Alice said, "Go home. Think about what's been said and call me tomorrow to let me know what you want to do. Don't come in – just call. And, if you can, call sober." She turned her back and walked away.

Summer was clearly over. October was dry and cold, colder than normal by fifteen degrees most days, but the sky was so blue and the remaining leaves were so red, so yellow, the mums in flowerbeds around the county so lush with gold, purple and amber, that no one could seem to muster a complaint. The beans were almost in and the corn was coming; farmers were giving thanks for a bountiful harvest and plotting out the new year with hopeful hearts.

The Abbott farm, like all the others, was running on a dark-to-after-dark schedule, all three men harvesting by headlamp well into the night, sometimes only sleeping a few hours before rising to do the milking and begin the harvesting all over again.

"I never see John during this season," Carolyn complained to Pearl as they sat in the living room, Carolyn working on the pink blanket and Pearl knitting booties to match the pink and white sweater she had finished.

"I know," the old woman said, "but it's this way every year, and then comes the easy time for the winter. You and John will have plenty of time together before the baby comes." She smiled at the booties. "It will be so good to have a little one in the house again."

"October's a hard month is all," Carolyn said, looking off into the distance. "David's birthday, David's death..."

138

"Yes, it is," Pearl said. "And you've both handled it well this year. That's how it should be – time doesn't take it away, that kind of pain, but it does get easier."

"Do you want to say, 'I told you so'?" Carolyn laughed.

"Certainly not!" Pearl made a small sound which, in anyone else, might have been considered a snicker. "Although I did."

The phone rang. "I wonder who's calling in the middle of the afternoon," Carolyn said, rising and moving toward the kitchen. She wasn't quite as light on her feet as she had been, and the phone rang three times more before she got to it.

"Hello? Oh, hello, Allison! Matthew's not here right now; he's out in the fields. Harvest time, you know. Hmm? Oh, they'll be in for supper around seven or eight, I think. Yes, I'll tell him."

"What was that about?" Pearl asked when Carolyn came back. "You have a funny look on your face."

"That was Matthew's sometime girlfriend Allison, and she sounded strange. I don't know why she'd think Matthew would be in the house in the middle of the day. She knows he farms."

The men trooped in together at about eight-thirty, covered with dust and chaff, deep purple shadows under their eyes, and washed up at the kitchen sink without speaking. Carolyn had sent Pearl home half an hour before; she quietly set three plates on the kitchen table. The men sat down heavily, as if too tired to keep on standing, and bowed their heads in silent grace before beginning to shovel meat loaf and mashed potatoes into their mouths. Ed and John methodically ate their way through the peas and carrots, too, but Matthew pushed his to the side, too tired to fish out the carrots and leave the peas.

Carolyn refilled coffee cups and Matthew's milk glass and ventured, "How's it going?"

John looked up and smiled at his wife. "Really well. We're just a couple of fields from finished with the beans, and then – " He broke off to cough, then to cough again.

"You all right?" Ed asked, handing him a glass of water.

"Fine," John rasped, taking a sip. "Bean dust, I think. Well, let's get back at it. Maybe we can finish tonight and get to bed before midnight."

"What about dessert?" Carolyn asked. "There's blueberry pie."

A wistful look crossed Ed's face, but he stood up with the others. "Best save it for tomorrow," he said. "Unless Will gets to it."

"He didn't eat any," Carolyn said. "I'm afraid he's coming down with something."

"I'll check on him when we come in," Matthew said. "He always has a light under his door until after midnight."

"Oh, Matthew, I almost forgot! Allison called you this afternoon and wanted you to call her back. I told her it would be about this time before you took a break."

"Oh." Matthew stopped his progress to the back door. He inhaled deeply and exhaled loudly. "I don't have time to call her now."

"You can take time for a call if you want to," John said.

"No, not tonight," Matthew answered. "Let's get the job done."

Allison shifted around on the couch so her head was propped against the arm. In one hand she cradled the phone, in the other a half-full glass of whiskey. Why didn't he call? It was nine-thirty. It was ten o'clock. It was eleven...

At one o'clock John and Matthew trudged to the house and up the stairs to bed.

"Sleep in until five," John said. "Cows will be all right." He coughed. "Get some sleep."

"Thanks, I will." Matthew noted no light under Will's door now, not that he had expected one so late. He went into his own room and managed to throw off his work boots and clothes before he fell into bed. His body ached and seemed to have a leftover subliminal vibration from all those hours on the tractor. His eyes were gritty and weighted down and he closed them gratefully. Sleep seemed to be washing over him like a warm bath, and he slid into it willingly.

Until his eyes popped open.

All right, Lord. Who do You want me to pray for?

Allison came to mind, so he began to pray for her, not trying to figure out what he was praying or why, just going with the flow of it until he noticed he was crying. *God help her. She's in trouble, I know it, and I know it's her drinking. Please, please keep her from doing any-*

thing stupid! ... Am I supposed to go over there now?

Matthew sat up and tried to listen for an answer, wishing again that he were one of those who actually heard a Voice telling him what to do. After a few minutes, the sense of urgency went away, which seemed to mean he didn't have to rush off on a rescue mission, although he would have been willing. He lay down again, ready for sleep.

Until he found himself kneeling at the side of the bed, clutching the edge of the quilt, praying for Will with desperation.

After a time had passed, Matthew's fear raised him to his feet. He pulled on his dirty jeans and moved on soundless bare feet into the hall.

There was no sound from John and Carolyn's room, and none from Will's. Silently Matthew walked to Will's door and opened it.

Faint light came through the window-shade, just enough to show Will's form hunched under the covers. Matthew walked closer to the bed, praying no floorboard would creak and give away his presence. When he made it to the side of the bed, he could just make out the boy's features – and what appeared to be traces of tears on the boy's cheek.

Twenty-One

LEANING FORWARD OVER HIS DESK AS FAR AS HIS belly would allow, Aaron Rupp peered through his half-open office door and called, "Hey, Dan! Got a minute?"

Dan, on his way to his own office, stopped and stuck his head in. "What's up?"

Aaron motioned him in. "Shut the door, will ya? Have a seat."

Dan sat in one of the institutional molded plastic chairs, this one a sickly green not found in nature, and cocked his head. "Why the closed door?"

Leaning back, a more comfortable position for his body and a non-verbal suggestion of ease, Aaron said, "Need to ask about one of your clients."

"My client?" Dan frowned a little. He and Aaron didn't usually discuss one another's cases without prior request.

"Yeah. I been hearing rumors about one of your guys, and I want to check it out before I do anything."

Dan sat up straighter and ran one large hand through his short, dark hair. "Listen, Aaron, I don't discuss my clients directly without a release of information, you know that."

"Ah, don't go all bureaucratic on me," Aaron soothed. "I'll just tell you what I know and you can decide from there what to do about it."

Dan gave a short nod, clearly uncomfortable with the tenor of the exchange.

"There's rumors going around the school," Aaron said, "that one of the kids has been in a lotta trouble, big trouble. Robbery, DUI, assault, stuff like that. And they say it's that Scandahoovian kid of yours – Peterson? Anderson? Ryersen? – that's it, Ryersen."

"Scandahoovian?" Dan said, quirking one eyebrow.

"You know: Swedish, Danish, something like that. Anyhow, it's Ryersen. Rumor is, he's dangerous."

"Now, listen, Aaron, that's just b – "

"And that's not all. They're saying he's a homo and they're afraid to get in the showers with him. I can't have a kid like that preying on my son and the other kids, Dan. What the heck possessed you to put somebody like that in school with the normal guys?"

Dan stood up and carefully unclenched his fists. "I don't know who's spreading stinking nasty rumors like that, but *if* I have a client named Ryersen – or any other 'Scandahoovian' name – and *if* he has anything like that in his record, I can guarantee two things: one, there's two sides to every story and, two, I'd never put a client who is a danger to others back into the school system. You ought to know me better than that. Tell your rumor source he's full of it."

Dan turned on his heel and left the room, opening the door with enough force to slam it into the wall and rattle the frosted glass in its window. In his own office, door closed, mug of coffee steaming untouched in front of him, he slumped in his chair and tried to figure out what had happened. Obviously someone had read Will's file and drawn the worst possible conclusions from it. Obviously that someone wanted to make Will's life miserable, just out of meanness, because Dan knew Will hadn't been doing anything at school to cause trouble or get a bad rep.

For a moment he wondered whether Will knew about the rumors, but then he thought, *Of course he does. When that kind of bull starts going around, people just have to react to it. I wonder how long the word's been out. Will hasn't said anything to me. Guess we'd better talk about it when he comes in next week.*

It wasn't a very satisfying solution, but Dan didn't want to make more of it than it was by calling Will in for a special appointment. He documented the conversation with Aaron and put the notes into Will's file, wondering again how anyone outside could have gained the information to bully Will. He kept his files locked in the cabinet, locked in the office. He never went home without being sure all the files were safe and the door locked. Never. Didn't he?

"Son," Aaron told Chance after dinner that evening, as they bonded over the sports news on the network channel while Mom did the dishes, "I talked to Dan about that Ryersen kid today."

"Yeah?" Chance said, looking at his dad, "What did he say?"

"He didn't really say much. He can't talk about a client with me directly unless we jump through all kinds of government hoops first. But he didn't deny having Ryersen for a client, and he didn't exactly deny the kid's record. But he did kinda make it clear that *if* there is such a kid, he isn't dangerous."

"Right. Tell that to the guys in the shower room. Dad, it's not right for us to have to be afraid some queer's going to – you know." Chance managed to blush, a nice touch.

"Son, has this boy approached you, or anyone else you know of?"

"No, sir. It's just – it's a feeling, you know?"

"I'm afraid there isn't anything I can do unless something happens. If he tries to touch somebody, or if money goes missing or something, then the cops can step in. Until then, you just watch out and don't hang out with him."

Chance laughed. "No danger of that! Well, thanks for trying, Dad. Not your fault the system's screwed up."

Will was standing over the cookie jar shoveling in his father's favorite oatmeal-raisin-chocolate chip cookies when the phone rang. Since everyone else was in the living room, he answered the phone, choking down most of a large bite to clear his mouth.

"Ryersen, that you?" The voice was male and gruff, and again Will didn't recognize it. Immediately his mouth went dry and the remains of the cookie threatened to choke him.

"Yeah."

"Watch your back, homo. When you least expect it..."

"Who – who is this?"

"Not a friend, that's for sure. Get out or get what's coming to you, fag."

As before, the caller hung up, leaving Will hanging at the other end of the line, sweat running into his eyes and knees shaking too hard to hold him up. He sank to the floor and huddled there, shaking.

It's happening all over again. It wasn't true then, and it's not true now, and I don't know how to – I don't know what – what am I going to do!

The swinging door almost hit Will as John came into the kitchen, apparently to refill his coffee mug.

"I'm sorry, Will! Didn't see you there on – Will?" John stopped and squatted down beside the boy. "You all right? What's the matter?"

Will wanted to bluff his way out and say he was fine, but the worry and compassion in John's voice caught him in this weak moment, and the tears escaped in a huge sob.

John was no stranger to people in distress. Setting his mug on the table, he sat down on the floor and put an arm around Will's shoulders. Will was so distraught he didn't remember to be leery of the touch of another man; he leaned in to John's shoulder and cried, feeling like an idiot, feeling hopeless, feeling. John held him and waited.

Loser! Will berated himself, trying to bring the explosion of weeping under control. *Why couldn't you just keep it together and get to your room? Just suck it up.*

"If you want to talk about it," John said softly, "I'll be glad to listen. Or I can call your dad – "

"No!" Will sat up and began to palm the tears from his cheeks. John handed him a handkerchief to blow his nose, saying nothing, standing up slowly and extending his hand. Will bypassed the hand but stood also. "Thanks. I'm fine."

"Okay," John answered. "Just know I'm available. Sometimes your dad finds it helpful to sort things out with me; I know he or Ed or I would be glad to do the same for you."

"Yeah, thanks. I gotta go." Will fled past the living room and up the stairs to his room before anyone could catch him.

In his room, safe enough for the moment, Will sat at his desk and opened the lap drawer wide. Far in the back, buried under rubber bands and pencils and sticky notes and CDs was an unmarked envelope. He drew it out and weighed it in his hand. The weight was far too slight for the importance of the contents.

Making sure the door was closed, he slid the knife out of the envelope onto his palm. The handle was worn, as if many hands had held it, but the blade was bright and shiny in the light from the desk lamp, newly sharpened and thirsty for work.

Will turned the knife from side to side, making flashes of light across the desk. He put it on the cluttered surface and lifted his hands in the light. He could see the white scar-lines across both wrists, fine and faded, disappearing monuments to failure. He looked at his left wrist and traced the line of a large vein with the forefinger of his other hand. It wouldn't take much...

What else could he do? He couldn't get far if he ran away, he'd proved that in Chicago. He couldn't tell anyone what was going on. Why would they believe he hadn't done more bad things? He had a past, and if they knew all of it, about the men who had abused him, they might think it had been because he wanted it. What if he was a – what they called him, and he just didn't know it. There was stuff on t.v. and in the papers every day about guys who had just figured out they were – *why do they call it 'gay?' There's nothing happy about it. But how do I know I'm not just kidding myself? Why would they pick me if there wasn't something wrong with me? There are always plenty of choices.*

He picked up the knife again, drawing it in the air along the path of the vein. It wouldn't hurt, Matt said, almost like he was suggesting Will use it. That would make things easy for Matt, at least. No more trying to be a real daddy, no more hassles with the woman. Everybody would feel sorry for him, and in a week or two he'd go on with his life like Will had never happened – which was what he had wanted in the first place.

Blinking back new tears, Will brought the knife to his skin and pressed delicately. The sharp point of the blade punctured him pain-lessly and a big drop of dark red blood bloomed like a rose around the knife-tip. Will watched in fascination as the drop grew and grew un-til its surface tension broke and it began to trickle down his upraised arm toward his elbow.

Twenty-Two

WHEN THE AMBULANCE ARRIVED, LIGHTS FLASH-
ing red through the window, Alice Campbell gave a
sigh of relief and went to open the door. Within seconds, three paramedics, stretcher-bed and huge bags in tow,
were surrounding the couch where Allison lay unconscious.
Alice had turned her on her side in case she vomited, but that
hadn't happened since Alice had been there.

"Her name is Allison West," Alice told them, "and she's overdosed
on alcohol. I haven't found any other medication except Tylenol in
the house. I don't know whether she took that. Her pulse is thready
and she's unresponsive. She hasn't vomited since I've been here,
which hasn't been more than twenty minutes."

The paramedics recognized Alice from the hospital and asked
more questions as they did their exam, started an i.v. and wrapped
the unconscious woman for transport.

"I'll get her purse and follow you," Alice told them.

Allison stared at the e.r. ceiling, where the little perforations in
the tiles seemed to be dancing around and around. Her nose hurt
where the nasogastric tube had gone in, and she wiped away a slight
trickle of blood. Her throat hurt and the taste of vomit made her
stomach wobble again. She had helped perform gastric lavage several times, but this was the first time she had had her own stomach
pumped – and it needed to be the last. A five-dwarf headache had

settled in again, and she wished she could have something for the pain. Fat chance of that.

"Well, Allison! Back among the living!"

The overloud, overcheerful voice belonged to the emergency room doctor, Peter Tilloch. Allison wondered whether he was doing it deliberately to punish her, but then she remembered he always talked that way, as if patients couldn't hear him at normal volume.

"Little trouble with our drinking?" he asked.

She couldn't resist. "I don't know about your drinking, but there's no problem with mine."

"Not so funny, missy," the doctor chided, frowning and tugging with both hands on the stethoscope dangling around his neck. "Your B.A.C. was .38. That's about four times the legal limit, and it could be enough to kill you."

"Sorry, doc, but I'm still here. At least until I call somebody and go home."

Dr. Tilloch frowned again. He ran a hand through his short, graying hair. He tugged on the stethoscope again.

"What?"

"Well," he said slowly, "it's like this. Your B.A.C. was so high, and your liver enzymes are high, and your white count is low, and – the bottom line is, we need to admit you for a day or two to make sure you don't go into kidney or liver failure. We need to get some history on the other drugs you're using, too, to make sure we don't miss any interactions."

Allison pushed herself upright, holding her head on with both hands. "I'm fine! I don't use drugs! I'm going home." She swung her legs over the edge of the bed, getting ready to get up, but Dr. Tilloch stood right in front of her and put a gentle hand on her shoulder.

"Please don't do this," he said, in a nearly normal tone of voice. "Alice came in with you, and she told me about your drinking. I know you don't want to think it's a problem, but that's just a symptom of the disease. Let us help you now, while there's still time."

"Are you saying I'm an alcoholic!"

He paused for a moment, then nodded. "Yes," he said, "I am. And here's the thing, Allison: it takes one to know one. I'm a recovering alcoholic and drug addict, been clean and sober ten years now. I was just as full of denial as you, and I lost my license, my wife, my kids –

some of my liver – before I realized I'm powerless over alcohol. You're not there yet, but you're skating on the edge. I can get you some help before you fall in."

A sixth dwarf joined the chorus hammering in Allison's head as she stared at the doctor. He was probably the same age her father would have been, and she could see the signs now that he had told her – the bulbous nose with its faint tracery of broken capillaries, which would have been fiery red when he was drinking, the liver-disease-induced redness of his palms, and the kind sincerity in his muddy brown eyes.

"I'm going to order you some Seven-Up and see about a room upstairs for you. Lori Wilson will be in sometime to talk about rehab, and I want you to listen to her." He patted Allison's shoulder and left the cubicle.

Allison threw herself back on the hard cot and then grasped her head in both hands, moaning. *I need something for this pain – and they're not going to give me anything, because they think I'm an addict. What a mess! Why can't people mind their own business?*

"Hey," Alice said softly, slipping in through the curtained glass door. "How you doing now?"

"How do you think?" Allison snapped. "And what do you care?"

"Oh, Allie, come on," Alice said. "You must know I care about you. I want to see you well and happy again and back to work and hanging out with Matthew – "

Allison glared her most sulfuric glare. "You know none of that is going to happen. You've ratted me out to the administration and forced me in here to have my stomach pumped in my own e.r. – no way I'm going to be allowed to practice nursing ever again." Tears welled up and spilled over, but Allison dashed them away to continue glaring. "You must really hate me to ruin my whole life like this! Even Matthew – he hates drunks. No way he's going to stick with me after he finds out about this."

"It seems awful to you now," Alice said, "but it's not automatically the end of the world. When you talk to Lori, she'll explain your options and tell you how it works to get back to the job. Everyone knows Dr. Tilloch lost his license ten years ago, but now he's working full time and – "

"He's a doctor. You know the rules are different for them."

"Allie, he almost killed a patient. He almost died himself. It took five years to get his license back, but he did it, by staying clean and sober. There are some others here and in the area, too. Nurses. Listen to Lori, all right? And believe me – I do care about you, and I want you back on my service." Alice smiled, patted Allison's hand and left.

I don't believe it. But I guess what I believe doesn't matter now, because they're going to think what they think no matter what I say. I might as well be dead – and the way I feel, I wish I were!

"Pearl, will you get the phone?" Carolyn called from the dining room, where she was arranging apples in a wooden bowl on the table. She heard Pearl's heels click across the kitchen and the creaky old voice saying "hello."

Several minutes later, Pearl came through the swinging door into the dining room, a vague frown between her wise brown eyes.

"Who was it?" Carolyn asked, turning the bowl to admire her handiwork from all sides.

"Woman named Alice Campbell, from the hospital. Do you know her?"

"I don't think so... What did she want? Oh! Is it something about the baby?" Carolyn's hand protectively covered the increasing bump of little Longsuffering.

"No, no," Pearl hastened, "nothing like that. Odd, though. She was calling for Matthew. When I told her he wouldn't be available until this evening, she gave me a message for him."

"Let's sit down," Carolyn said, "and you can tell me."

They took adjacent chairs and admired the apples for a moment. Finally, Pearl said, "She told me she's Allison West's supervisor at the hospital. Allison's Matthew's – girl, I guess we'd say." Carolyn nodded. "Anyway, it seems Allison is in the hospital – as a patient – somewhere in Minnesota – "

"Minnesota!"

"It's not a regular hospital. It's a place that treats people with drug problems. And Miss Campbell seems to think Matthew should know about this."

Carolyn nodded, rubbing her belly gently as she thought. "He told us something about her drinking a while back... I knew they weren't seeing each other again... maybe that was why. He never said anything about drugs, though..."

"Alcohol *is* a drug," Pearl said, her acerbic tone cutting through Carolyn's musings. "The point is, we have to tell Matthew about this, and he's not going to take it well. So we'd best pray for him – and for her – before we do anything else."

Twenty-Three

SHE WAS CRYING. WILL DIDN'T KNOW WHAT TO DO, but he couldn't just stand there and watch the tears roll down her cheeks. He walked fearfully toward her, clammy sweat filling his palms as he wondered whether she would even let him approach, much less comfort her.

"Tracy, what's wrong?" he asked softly, still standing several feet away just in case.

The girl raised her tear-drenched green eyes to look at Will directly for the first time in over a month, and to his horror her lip wobbled even more. But she didn't turn away and she didn't step back, so he dared to come closer, wishing he had a handkerchief, even one of Ed's crumpled blue bandanas, to offer her.

"Please tell me. I hate to see you upset." He hoped she didn't hear the quiver of fear in his voice, fear that once again she would reject him. He had lied when he said he didn't care.

"Oh, Will," Tracy whispered, and then she began to sob, covering her face with her hands.

Will didn't care that they were standing outside the cafeteria, in one of the main hallways, that a bell would ring any minute and spill hundreds of teenagers into that hall. He closed the gap and took Tracy in his arms. "Please talk me!" he begged.

She held on, and it was the sweetest thing he had felt in forever. He had loved her from the first day he met her, several years before at church, and he figured maybe he was going to love her forever. An image of his father and that Allison woman flashed through his head, and for just a second Will allowed himself to think it might be this way for them, too. But he had to squash that, because less would be disloyal to his mother.

"Will," Tracy finally said, "I – heard something about you. I heard a lot of bad things, and I just – how could it – I mean, I didn't believe any of it! But they were so sure. And I wanted to tell you, to ask you, but I was afraid – "

Will's heart froze in his chest. He had to gasp several times to bring in enough air to clear his head. He also had to bite his lip to keep from making his first words the blistering string of filth that was running through his mind.

"Let's go outside," he said, "before anybody comes along."

They slipped out the nearest door, which spilled them into the parking lot. Will led Tracy to a low wall over by the bike racks, where no one was likely to see them or interrupt, and they sat down, side by side, but no longer touching. Will took another enormous breath.

"What did you hear?"

"I can't say it," Tracy said, blushing an unbecoming deep red. "It was horrible!"

"Okay, then, let me say it. You heard I'm a convicted felon, who might have killed somebody, who had a DUI, who's a thief. Right so far?"

She nodded.

He forced himself to finish. "And you heard that I'm – gay."

She nodded.

"And you're crying because you believe it and you think I'm going to hell."

Tracy began to cry again, waving her hands in the air and twitching her shoulders as if she didn't quite know what to do with all her feelings. She wouldn't look at Will, but in a moment she told him, "I can't imagine how any of it can be true! I thought I knew you, Will. Nothing you ever did would have made me think you're – like that. Bad, I mean. And we – you kissed me! How can you be gay?"

"I'm not! I don't know who started all this sh – talk, but it's all over the school now. Who told you?"

Tracy wiped her eyes on the sleeve of her sweater and snuffled mightily. Even that action didn't seem indelicate to Will when she did it. Still not looking at him, she whispered, "Kevin."

Will had thought his heart was frozen, but apparently not, because the pain went deep. He had allowed himself to make friends with Travis and Kevin, taking a chance he hadn't taken in a long time. He had believed it was real.

He must have made a sound, because Tracy suddenly looked up and put her hand on his arm. "I walked in on Kevin and Travis arguing about it. Travis said none of it can be true, and Kevin finally said he didn't believe it, either. They were just so shocked. Like me..." She cast her eyes down again and removed her hand, leaving a cold, lonely spot on his arm.

"Tracy, I swear – I am not gay. But the rest – I haven't told you much about my past. Before I came to the Abbotts' – to stay with my dad – I was in juvie. I did steal stuff, and I did do some drinking, some pot, you know – well, probably you don't know, but – I was part of a robbery and I did hit a guy in the head with a – well, shoot, it was a fake gun, not a real one! I never had a DUI; I wasn't even old enough to drive until last year. And I never, ever killed anybody. And things – things are different now. My – dad – tries and the Abbotts are good people and God – well, I know I'm not saved or good or anything, but –"

He had hung his head, afraid to watch her reaction. So he didn't see her coming. The next thing he knew, her arms were wrapped around him in a huge hug and she was kissing his face all over. He closed his eyes to savor the moment and didn't see what else was coming.

"Won't work, homo," came Pete's voice, followed by a heavy hand shoving his shoulder from behind, knocking him off-balance and pushing Tracy back. "You can't fake it by molesting some girl. Get away from her."

Will stood up and whirled to face his accuser, but Tracy was faster. She hopped up on the wall and met Pete face to face, her eyes flashing green fire and her little hands with their pale pink fingernails curled into miniature fists.

"Who do you think you are!" she challenged. "You ought to be ashamed of yourself, telling lies and bullying innocent people like this! You shut up and get out of here, Pete!"

"You really are a pansy, Ryersen, hiding behind a little bitty girl like that."

Will decided it would be worth getting expelled to kill Pete and quickly ran through his options for doing so. None of them looked too hopeful, but sometimes a guy had to do what he had to do. He vaulted over the wall and squared off with Pete, who looked at him with a grin and drew back one huge fist. Tracy screamed, the sound echoing in the deserted parking lot, startling Pete enough for Will to land the first blow, a deep fisting of the larger boy's midsection. Pete grunted and grabbed Will's fist, crunching the bones so hard Will heard as well as felt the snap. Pete's other fist landed on Will's jaw and threw him to the ground, which rose to meet the back of his head with a melon-splitting thunk.

"Don't bother to get up, faggot," Pete sneered, "or I'll break the other hand. Tracy, you better get away from this homo before somebody starts thinking you're a lesbo." He walked away across the parking lot, whistling the school fight song.

Tracy jumped down beside Will, but he shooed her away. "You better get somebody," he ground out between clenched teeth. "I think my head's busted. Go on. I'm gonna puke."

Which he did. Disgustingly. Loudly. Copiously. And blessedly alone, as Tracy ran back toward the building.

Matthew, Ed and John were just about to head out to separate fields again when they heard Carolyn screaming from the back of the house. They turned as one and ran toward her, Matthew ahead by virtue of age and weight, but John right on his heels. It became clear within a few yards that she was screaming Matthew's name.

He skidded to a stop at the foot of the back stairs, Ed at his shoulder while John leaped up the steps in one bound to put his arm around Carolyn.

"Thank God I caught you," she said. "Matthew, the school called – Will was in some kind of accident and they're taking him to the hospital in Lewiston. They said he has a head injury and you should come right away."

Ed's hand gripped Matthew's shoulder like a vise. "I'll drive. Get your wallet."

"Where is it?" John asked. "We'll get it."

"Bedroom," Matthew said between dry lips. "Table." He turned toward the truck, but Ed steered him across the yard, heading for home and the El Camino.

"I'll get his wallet," John said, "and we'll follow. What about Pearl?"

"She said she'll stay here and pray and call Miles."

Ed continued to hang onto Matthew by brute force as they faced the admissions clerk, who wanted only insurance information. "You'll get it," Ed promised. "John Abbott's bringing it. Now let this man see his son."

Moments later they stood outside the e.r. cubicle, staring through the glass as several people bent over the body on the cart. Ed still held on. "Wait for it. Just a minute more. God's got him in His hand now, so you can let Him do His job." He felt the muscles flex under his hand and patted gently. "Let's just pray right now, okay?"

Matthew nodded, basically a reflex, and bowed his head. He heard Ed's slow, steady voice but couldn't make sense of the words through the spinning terror inside his head. His prayer was probably just a supplication, but he didn't even know. All he knew was the body on the bed wasn't moving.

A woman in surgical scrubs came out of the cubicle and addressed Ed: "Mr. Ryersen?"

Ed directed her to Matthew. "He's Matthew Ryersen, Will's dad."

"Sorry," the woman said briefly, not sounding sorry or even concerned. "Mr. Ryersen," addressing Matthew this time, "I'm Dr. Gray. I'm the e.r. doctor on call today. We're taking your son for x-rays and a CT scan of his head. He has a broken right hand and what looks like a pretty severe concussion. You can wait out there." She gestured to the double doors, which led to a waiting area.

"I need to see my son," Matthew said.

"Later."

"No. I need to see him now," Matthew told her, and he suited actions to words, entering the cubicle before either the doctor or Ed could stop him.

He approached the bed and shooed the nurse and orderly away. Something in his face must have convinced them to move, because they didn't even look to the doctor for permission. Fear like an iceberg inside him, he stepped to the head of the bed and looked down at his son.

"Oh, Will," he whispered. "What happened to you?"

The boy on the bed was a shade of white so pale it seemed tinged with green, and his hair was matted with blood, as were his tee-shirt and the pillow under his head. His right hand was flattened and tied to a board of some kind, and i.v. and oxygen lines were putting things into his still body. Vomit was caked around his mouth and on his shirt. A machine was charting his blood pressure and heart rate, but Matthew didn't know what the numbers meant. He put his hand on Will's forehead and smoothed back the pale hair, remembering another day in the e.r. with Will and the violence with which he had treated his son then.

Will's eyes fluttered and opened. He stared blankly, blinked again and tried to focus. "Daddy?"

"I'm here," Matthew said, tightening every muscle in his body to keep from crying or gathering the youth into his arms. "I'm here. What happened, son?"

Will frowned, trying to concentrate. "I... I don't know." Alarm crossed his features and he began to try to sit up.

"Lie still!" Matthew said, holding his shoulders down. "You hurt your head, and you shouldn't move around. They're going to take you for some x-rays, and I'll be right here when you get back, I promise."

"Oh." He sounded like a small child to Matthew. "Daddy, my head hurts. Bad." His color was even more green, and he seemed to swallow hard. Before Matthew could do anything, Will began to vomit again, retching dryly over and over, moaning.

Matthew found himself displaced by a nurse with a basin who held onto Will and murmured soothingly as the boy suffered. She turned to Matthew and said, "This is typical with a head injury, so don't be too alarmed by it. We need to take him now, so please wait with your friend in the waiting room. My name's Pam, and I'll come for you as soon as he's back, I promise." Her smile did as much as her words to convince Matthew she meant it, so he tentatively touched Will once more and left the room, joining Ed in another plastic waiting area, noting in some part of his disordered mind that they all looked alike.

"Set down," Ed said, indicating the chair at right angles to himself. "I'll find coffee."

"No coffee. I can't – "

"One Ryersen puking I can handle," Ed said, "but not two. Forget the coffee, then. How's the boy?"

Matthew sank into the chair as far as its unforgiving cushions would allow and ran a hand through his hair. "He's a bloody mess, in a lot of pain – and he said he didn't know what happened to him. Somebody must know! His hand is broken, too."

"I know waiting's the hardest part," Ed soothed, "but it's gonna be all right. We'll get to talk to the doctor or somebody pretty soon. They'll know."

"I don't even know where he was, or who was with him or anything!"

Matthew jumped up and began to pace around the small room, to the disconcertment of a middle-aged couple sitting in the opposite corner. He heard the door behind him whoosh open and turned to see John, Carolyn and several teenagers moving toward him. He recognized Tracy, Kevin and Travis.

"Oh, Mr. Ryersen!" Tracy cried, rushing up to him. "How is Will? I was so scared!"

"How'd you know about this?" Matthew asked.

Tracy's lovely pale green eyes gleamed with unshed tears, and her lips quivered. "I was there when it happened. It was awful!" The first tears fell, followed quickly by others.

Matthew automatically handed her his clean but rumpled blue bandana. "Tell me what happened, please. I don't know anything about what happened!

"That big jerk Pete Coombs!" Travis said, clenching his fists and turning red as he spoke.

"What?"

"Well, sir," Tracy began, giving the boys a quelling look, "Will and I were sitting on the wall by the back parking lot at school talking, and – well – Pete came along and said some really awful things to Will, trying to provoke him. And then – then I got in Pete's face and told him to leave Will alone – but that only made it worse!" she wailed, burying her face in the bandana.

"So – ?"

"So," Travis said, "Will had to fight him. He had to. Pete was gonna cream him. That guy is huge! Will got in the first punch, but Pete just crushed his fist. And then he pushed him down and his head hit the concrete... It was awful!"

"You were there?" Matthew asked Travis.

"No," Kevin said, "me and Trav were in the building when Tracy came running in screaming for an ambulance. She told us, though. Trav told it right, didn't he, Tracy?"

"Yes," Tracy agreed, her response muffled by the bandana.

"A bully hurt my son," Matthew said in a very soft voice. "Will wasn't doing anything to provoke him, and he came after Will on purpose."

"Yes, sir," Tracy whispered, looking at him with wide eyes.

"So where is this boy now?"

"We don't know," Kevin said. "We didn't see him in the school after that; he probably went home. The principal was looking for him. *He* was *really* mad!"

"And where does he live?" Matthew asked, his voice still almost inaudible.

Travis and Kevin looked at one another with a uniquely adolescent mixture of avidity and trepidation. "I don't know," Travis said, elbowing Kevin. "He doesn't, either."

"I imagine there aren't too many Coombses in the phone book," Matthew said.

Twenty-Four

ALLISON ACKNOWLEDGED THAT THE TREATMENT center was a nice building in a really beautiful setting. She had heard Minnesota called "the land of ten thousand lakes" before, and now she understood why. Several – not just one, but several! – of those lakes were part of the grounds, and the patients (*Inmates,* she thought. *Prisoners.*) were allowed to wander around during their few hours of free time to enjoy the amazing scenery. Although it was still early fall in northwest Ohio, the season was far advanced here. The leaves were mostly fallen, and the pines had taken on a deep blackish-green hue. Ducks still swam around the lakes, but not as many as she was told were there in the summers. She had been there several weeks, and in that time the average temperature had dropped considerably. Natives assured her they were having a mild winter, as snow was usually a foot deep on the ground by now, but Allison wasn't sure whether or not to believe them.

Now she scuffled her way back to the main building through a thick layer of dead leaves, burnished bronze of oak and yellow, orange and red of maple, plus others she didn't recognize. She still had some time before group and thought she might finally call Matthew. It was on her list of goals to accomplish before she left treatment, and the counselors were all reminding her of that several times a day.

"Hey, Allison!" called a small, skinny man whose thin gray hair and heavily lined face suggested he was in his late fifties. He loped across the lawn to join her as she came to the building.

"Hi, Jerry." She smiled sympathetically. The man was, in fact, thirty-four, estranged from his wife and three daughters by his drinking, praying for his liver to regenerate itself so he wouldn't need a transplant. He lived each day in fear and guilt, which his counselor assured him would guarantee a relapse as soon as he hit the streets.

Thank God I'm not that bad! As fast as Allison thought that, she remembered saying it at an AA meeting a couple of nights before and being rapidly corrected by a very pregnant recovering alcoholic named Marian, who had simply said, "Yet." "Yet" was Marian's favorite word. "I haven't lost a job" would garner "Yet." "I've never had a DUI" would earn "Yet."

"Dang. She's right."

"Huh?" Jerry asked from beside her. "Who's right?"

"Oh!" Allison blushed a little. "I was just – just thinking out loud, I guess. I was remembering Marian telling everybody, 'Yet.' You know – like, I've never been in jail – 'yet.'"

Jerry laughed, a laugh which sounded as if it hadn't been used much in a long time. "Oh, yeah. I'm afraid she's right. It's all out there waiting for us." He held the door for Allison as they entered, and she smiled her thanks. He nodded, ducking his head, awkward with women as with much of life, as far as she could tell.

"Uh – would you – uh – like to get some coffee?" he asked.

"I'm sorry," Allison replied, "but I have some stuff to do before group. See you there."

In the room she shared with a jumpy meth user named Sophie, Allison flopped down on the bed, grateful that her roommate was off somewhere, probably talking someone's ear off. It was a symptom of her withdrawal, Allison understood, to talk compulsively and bite her nails and pull out her hair a few hairs at a time, to lie down, bounce up, lie down again all night sometimes. But understanding didn't make her any easier to live with. *I want to go home! I want my own bed and my own bathroom that I don't have to share with anybody. I want to lie around in my pajamas if I feel like it and eat chocolate at midnight and watch bad movies on t.v. and – whatever I want, when I want to.*

And what else do you want? she asked herself. *Do you want to be clean and sober? Do you want to keep on nursing? Do you want to get married? Do you want Matthew?*

Matthew. Of course she wanted Matthew. She had wanted him for a long time, with the same kind of hopeless longing she had had for a Madame Alexander doll when she was five. Her mother had explained over and over that they couldn't afford the doll, it was too expensive, it was too fancy, she'd have more fun with a rubber baby-doll she could dress and undress – but it hadn't mattered. She hadn't ever quite gotten over the yearning for that doll. And she suspected she would probably never quite get over her yearning for Matthew Ryersen.

Stopping in her room for her pre-paid phone card, she trekked down the hall to the public phone patients were only allowed to use at certain times. This wasn't one of them, but she had special permission because Matthew was usually at or near the house at this time of the afternoon. *Here goes nothing.* She pushed several combinations of numbers until the phone on the other end began to ring.

"This is Allison West, calling for Matthew," she told the voice on the other end, a voice she had not heard before. She listened... "Oh, Mrs. Gunderman, I'm so sorry! Do you know how he is? ... Of course I understand. Will you just tell Matthew I called, and – well, I'll be thinking good thoughts for him and for Will." She replaced the receiver and stuffed the card into the pocket of her jeans. Almost time for group.

"I tried," she told her counselor. "He's at the hospital. His son was hurt. I'll try again in a couple of days, maybe." *If I can hold out that long. Poor Matthew! Poor Will. I wish I did believe in praying; there's nothing else to do so far away.*

Twenty-Five

"HE HAS A SUBDURAL HEMATOMA," DR. GRAY told Will's anxious family. "A slight bleed on the surface of his brain. If it doesn't get any worse, it should just resolve by itself over the next few days. If there's more swelling, then we'll have to operate. I'm giving him some steroids for the swelling and medication to relieve the nausea and let him sleep lightly. We'll keep checking him throughout the night. You can go now; we'll call you if we need you."

Matthew stood directly in front of the doctor. "Thank you for your help with Will. Where is he?"

Dr. Gray looked up a few inches into implacable slate-blue eyes. "He's in a room in ICU on the fourth floor. You can't visit there more than ten minutes on the hour, and only immediate family, and no more than two per visit. Go on home, Mr. Ryersen."

"No, ma'am, I won't be going home without my son. I'm going to ICU now. John, Carolyn, Ed – you decide who visits besides me." He turned toward the door, only to be stopped by the doctor's hand on his sleeve.

"Mr. Ryersen, you can't do anything for Will except get in the way. He needs to rest. He needs to have expert nursing care."

"Let go," Matthew said, and Carolyn flinched at the edge in his voice.

"I think," John said to Dr. Gray, "that if that were my son, I'd be there, whether he knew it or not. He won't bother you. And there is something he can do – he can pray."

"Come on," Ed said, taking Matthew's other arm, "let's see where this ICU thing is." He ushered Matthew out of the waiting area to the nearest elevator while the doctor stood there with her mouth slightly agape.

Every time Will struggled through the fog and pain to conscious-ness he imagined he saw his father standing or sitting beside the hospital bed, sometimes holding his hand. But he couldn't seem to keep his eyes open or his mind clear enough to speak. When the pain surged over him like a huge wave and he groaned, he thought he felt his father's hand smoothing his forehead and his father's voice say-ing softly something he couldn't understand. That hand, that voice, were the only safe points in his mind. Everything else was loud and bright and sharp and threatening, but if he tried to get away the pain increased and another set of hands held him roughly to the bed. He tried to say "Daddy," but the word wouldn't come out.

"We call it aphasia," the nurse at the ICU desk explained. "The part of his brain which processes speech is under pressure from the hematoma right now, and he can think the words, but he can't speak. And, of course, he's under sedation, too."

"Is it permanent?" Matthew asked.

"Not – not necessarily," she told him, hesitating just long enough to plant doubt. "Often, when the swelling goes down the speech is fine."

"Often. That means not always."

"Yes, I'm afraid so. But really, Mr. Ryersen, it's far too soon to think that way. Will has only been here twenty-four hours, and the swelling seems to be going down. Dr. Alvarez, the neurologist, seems pleased with Will's progress. I'm guessing he'll be fine."

"Guessing."

The nurse shook her head, taking a deep breath and holding onto her patience. "I can't promise you anything, and you don't want me to lie to you, I know you don't. It must be really hard for you, just waiting, but please hang on."

Matthew hung his head and grimaced in disgust. "I'm sorry. You're right, I wouldn't want you to lie to me. And I know none of this is your fault or anything. I'll try harder to be patient. Excuse me." He turned away and headed back to Will's cubicle.

They had quickly given up on enforcing the ten-minute-per-hour rule, both because Matthew clearly was not going to do it and because his presence did seem to calm Will rather than agitate him. Will was beginning to be more alert now, and his inability to speak clearly frightened him.

Matthew took his post at the side of Will's bed and continued the dialogue he had been having with his God ever since the phone call had come yesterday. It was interrupted by this and that, but it was never actually over. Matthew wanted to be sure God was paying attention to Will every single moment.

A soft sound interrupted the dialogue again, and Matthew looked toward the door to see Pastor Miles Corrigan entering. He was not pleased to see that Miles was wearing the serious black suit which Matthew always associated with David's funeral.

"How's it going?" Miles asked, coming to stand beside Matthew.

"I don't know. He sleeps – he wakes up – he falls asleep again. He's having trouble with his speech. His right hand is broken, too." He gestured toward the cast.

"I'm pretty sure he's going to be all right," Miles said, resting one hand on Matthew's shoulder. "We've all been praying for him, and for you and the rest of the family, of course, and I think God's not finished with Will yet."

"I hope you're right," Matthew said, his voice breaking.

"Is it all right if I pray for Will now?"

Matthew considered. "I don't see why not. He's used to people praying at home, even though he never seems to join in."

"Okay, then," Miles said, folding his long, skinny frame onto his knees by the side of the bed. He placed one hand on Will's arm and the other on Matthew's knee.

Matthew bowed his head and closed his eyes to join his prayer with the pastor's. *Please. Please let him be okay. Please.*

It was a long prayer, and it flowed over Matthew like syrup, soothing, calming, carrying him beyond his panic. He was almost reluctant to open his eyes after the 'amen.'

Rising in stages to his feet, Miles smiled at Matthew and at the sleeping youth on the bed. "Is there anything I can do for you?"

"No, not really. Just keep praying. I don't know what I'd do – how I'd – I mean, if anything happens to Will – "

Miles returned his hand to Matthew's shoulder, patting gently. "I'm available if you need to sort things out, and we'll all keep praying. Don't go back, Matthew. Look to the future and how you want things to be with Will from now on. You *are* a new creation, and you *can* do all things through Christ, Who strengthens you. I'll be back tomorrow, or sooner if you need me."

Will began to moan and move around in the bed, and Matthew stepped quickly to him.

"It's okay, Will. Take it easy." He laid his hand on the boy's chest to still him.

"Dad – dy – "

"I'm right here." Matthew gently turned Will's head to face him. "Right here. I'm not goin' anywhere, son."

Will lay still, eyes locked on his father's. "Dad – dy – "

"Easy. Your head is hurt pretty bad, and if you get upset it's gonna hurt worse." He sat down again beside the bed, keeping a hand on Will's arm. "Just take it easy. Easy."

Will frowned and started to shake his head, then thought better of it. "No. Daddy. I remember. Tracy – "

Matthew smiled a little, for the first time in days. "I know what happened, son. Tracy and Kevin and Travis were here, and they told me. Tracy is fine, except for bein' scared, and I'll let her know you're better. Don't worry about any of this."

Will's eyes filled with tears. "The school – I'll be in trouble. I – hit him – first."

"I know. Don't worry about it, son. I'm goin' to take care of it, I promise. When you feel up to it, you're goin' to tell me all about this, and I'm goin' to talk with your principal, among other people. You just concentrate on feelin' better now, okay?"

Matthew watched Will's eyes close, which squeezed the tears onto his cheeks. Taking a tissue, Matthew blotted the sparse moisture from the pale face and leaned in to kiss the wrinkled forehead. "Just sleep some more," he said, stroking back the boy's hair. "It'll be all right soon."

As Will's breathing settled into the deeper rhythm of real sleep,

Matthew slumped back in the chair, exhausted but rejoicing. Will could speak! Will could remember! God had been merciful to them again, and he was going to trust God to help him bring justice to the youth who had been fool enough to lay hands on his son.

Twenty-Six

"**Y**OU DON'T UNDERSTAND," ALLISON TRIED TO explain to the counselor and the psychiatrist. "I did call him. And I found out his son had been hurt – was in ICU – and of course he was there with Will. Of course he was. I know it was a week ago, but so what? He isn't going to have time for me while Will is recovering. I hope he's recovering…"

"How do you feel about that?" the counselor asked.

"Oh, please!" Allison fidgeted in the confines of the too-large, overstuffed brown chair, her feet unable to reach the floor, her jeans sticking on the microfiber.

"Allison," the psychiatrist said in the condescending tone she hated, "you know part of your recovery is to deal with this unhealthy relationship while you're still here, in a safe place, where we can help you to deal with your feelings. You do want to go home, don't you? To go back to work?"

She hung her head. "Yes, I want to go back to work – if they'll have me."

The counselor jumped in quickly, "You know they're willing to take you back on probation for a year if you successfully complete treatment. And that means fulfilling all the goals of your treatment plan, including talking things over with Matthew."

"All right. All right! I'll try to call again tonight."

"Why not call now?" the counselor urged.

"Because if he isn't at the hospital with Will, he'll be at work! You think he's just sitting by the phone waiting for me to call? Fat chance! He's a farmer; he'll be out in a field somewhere doing – whatever farmers do in fields."

"I think that's enough for now," the psychiatrist said. "You may rejoin your group, Allison, and we'll meet tomorrow morning at ten to hear the results of your phone call."

That was fun, Allison told herself as she retreated toward her room, hoping her roommate was out somewhere. *They think Matthew is the problem, but they don't get it.* Passing by the chapel, she peered in. No one was there, and pale sunlight was streaming through the stained glass windows, making warm splotches of light in the little room. Hesitating only for a moment, Allison went in and made her way to the second pew from the front. *I'll just stay a minute,* she thought, sitting gingerly on the dark blue cushions, looking around for someone to tell her she didn't belong there.

What am I supposed to do now? Matthew would pray. Pray. That would be nice, but I think you have to believe in God to pray to Him... I could say the Serenity Prayer, though. It's allowed for everybody.

Slowly Allison whispered her way through the short prayer of surrender always used in Alcoholics Anonymous meetings, asking for "serenity to accept the things I cannot change, courage to change the things I can, and wisdom to know the difference." To her surprise, she did feel a calm come over her, different from the flat emptiness from alcohol and pills just before she passed out, different from the intense focus when she was working, different from the fizzy buzz of being in Matthew's arms.

What happened?

As she sat there wondering, Allison found herself talking inside her head, as if there really were someone listening. Every time she stopped, the calm restored itself; every time she began again, she had that sense of someone listening, hearing her. *Whoever you are, whatever you are, thank you.*

"I'm fine!" Will snarled, trying to get out of bed against the restraining hand of his father. "I feel fine! I want to put on real clothes and go – go outside."

"You've only been home a day," Matthew protested. "They said you need to take it easy for the rest of the week. Lie down, Will."

Huffing a huge sigh, Will flopped back on the pillow, wincing as the forceful movement sent a shimmer of pain through his head.

"That hurt, didn't it?" Matthew said, and Will could hear the "I told you so" in his voice.

"Yeah, all right, it hurt. But it doesn't hurt to walk to the bathroom, so why would it hurt to walk downstairs and go out in the yard?"

"You're whining," came a voice from outside Will's room, followed a moment later by the slightly red face and short, stout body of Pearl, who came bearing gifts.

"You shouldn't have carried all that up the stairs," Will protested, reaching eagerly for the covered plate and glass of milk she offered. "I could have come down to the kitchen – "

"No, you couldn't," she replied, fixing him with a stern frown. "You are going to stay in this room and do as you are told until Dr. Hanna says otherwise. Your father and the rest of us have been worried enough for one lifetime, young man."

Will surrendered and sank down into his pillows, reaching a languid hand for cookies from the plate which now resided on his nightstand.

"You just eat those and relax," Pearl ordered, coming to stand beside Will, stroking his hair briefly. "You're going to be just fine in another day or two, and then you can be up and around and worrying your father again." She gave him a wink and left him there among the crumbs.

"She really loves you," Matthew said, a faint smile curling the corner of his mouth. "I've never seen her wink at anybody before, and she sure doesn't touch people very often."

"Yeah, she's cool," Will said. "Want a cookie?"

"What kind?"

"Man, you sure are picky! Peanut butter, okay? With some kind of nuts or something in 'em. Go on. I know you haven't been eating like you're supposed to."

Matthew grimaced and took a cookie. "How do you know so much?"

Grinning, Will lowered his voice so only Matthew could hear if there chanced to be someone lurking in the hall. "I fake being asleep and listen. Duh."

"Duh, is right." Matthew took a cautious bite and chewed carefully before swallowing. Will watched with interest. "Not bad," Matthew said. "Can you reach your milk?"

"Yes, Dad," Will sighed. The smother factor was rising.

"I have an appointment tomorrow with your principal," Matthew said around another mouthful. "It's time to get to the bottom of all this. I'm just telling you so you don't find out by accident and get surprised. You don't have to do anything or talk to anybody."

Will washed the last of his cookie down with a swallow of milk and put the glass back on the nightstand. He could feel the food rumbling in his stomach. "I don't want you to do that, okay? It won't help anything. I have to go back to school, and if you make trouble for Pete, it's going to make things worse for me."

"That boy nearly killed you," Matthew said, "and I don't intend to let him get away with it. Tracy was a witness, and he's going to be punished one way or another."

"You don't understand," Will tried. "He's not the only one who's – you know, who hates me and wants to hurt me. If you stir things up, they'll find a way to make me pay for it." His eyes filled with tears, so he turned his face away.

"That's what bullies count on," Matthew said, "that people will be too scared to call them on it. That kid didn't just badmouth you, Will. He darn' near killed you."

"Now he will kill me," Will muttered, hiding his face in the pillow.

Allison took a deep breath and punched in the long string of numbers to call Matthew. *Please let this work,* she asked the something she had been talking to in the chapel. *Please.*

The phone rang four or five times before a familiar voice said, "Hello?"

It's him! Oh, now what!

"Hello?"

"Matthew – it's Allison."

Long pause, then – "Allie, hi!"

"I hope I'm not bothering you, calling like this, but I – "

"No! I'm glad you called. Alice told me – well, she told me where you are and all, but she said I couldn't contact you, nobody could, so

I – well, how are you?"

"I'm fine! It's a good program, I guess, and I haven't had a drink in thirty-eight days, and – well – the reason I'm calling, my counselor says I have to talk to you before I can go home."

"That's great! What can I do?"

Allison imagined Matthew, in jeans and a blue plaid flannel shirt or a plain white tee-shirt, barefoot, as he had told her he liked to be indoors, his wheat-blond hair just long enough to muss as he ran his fingers through it, his eyes made bluer by the shirt... How could she tell him what they wanted her to tell him?

"Matthew – " *I love you! I want to marry you and be with you forever, but I can't say that...* "Matthew, I – I miss you. I know we've had such a rocky relationship, and I won't blame you if you don't want to see me anymore, but – "

"Easy," he said, as if he were gentling a horse. She didn't hold it against him. "Allie, I told you before: I love you. If we can be together without it making you drink and get messed up, that's what I want. We can work it out, if you want to."

Despite her best intentions, tears began to run down her cheeks. "I do want that, I do! The counselor thinks you're bad for me, and nothing I say convinces him it's the other way around. I try to explain and he just gives me lines out of a Psych 102 textbook. They want me to say I talked to you and told you it's over between us."

Another long pause. "Is that what they think you need to make you well?"

"Yes – but that's not what I think! Except for the babies. Matthew, I really can't have babies. They did all kinds of exams here, too, and it's a million to one that I could conceive or carry a child."

"Let me say it one more time, honey: I don't care. If you want a baby, we can adopt one. I don't care whether it's biologically ours or not. And if you don't want to adopt – well, we have Will." He laughed a little. "I know that's probably not the best incentive for you to be with me, after the way he treated you, but – well – he is my son, and he'd be yours, too."

"I can't say it," Allison finally admitted. "I can't tell you to get out of my life. I want to be with you, and I think I can stay sober even so. That's what I'm going to tell them tomorrow morning."

"Is that the best way?" he asked. "Can you stay sober if we're together? Will they let you go home if you tell them that?"

"I'm not here on a court order," Allison said. "I can leave any time I want. It's better for my job if I 'graduate,' but they have to let me go. Don't worry about it. Talking with you has let me see what I need to do, and I'll call you again soon, I promise."

"I'll look forward to it. I'm praying for you, honey. I love you."

"I love you, too." *You have no idea how much!* "Good night, Matthew."

"That looked like a tough call," Jerry said, coming up beside Allison. "How about a cup of coffee in the dayroom before we turn in?"

"Thanks, Jerry, but I need to talk to someone. Maybe another time."

Allison left Jerry and made her way to the chapel, where a dim light over the altar was the only illumination in the room. Making her way to the same pew she had tried before, she sank down and closed her eyes. "Are you still here?" she whispered.

"Allison! Wake up!"

Dragging herself out of a deep sleep, Allison opened her eyes to find the night nurse leaning over her, shaking her shoulder. "Hi, Andi. I must have fallen asleep. What time is it?"

"After midnight," Andi said, her pretty mouth pruning with disapproval. "Your roommate came out to the nurses' station to tell us you never came back to your room."

"No. I made my phone call and thought I'd come in here for a few minutes before bed. I must have fallen asleep." She rubbed a stiff spot in her neck and grimaced. "Must have been here over an hour; my neck's all cricked up."

"Anything else I should know about?" Andi asked.

"No, I'm fine." Allison rose and started back down the aisle to the door. "Sorry I worried you, but I was right here all the time, honest. In good company, don't you think?"

Andi either snorted or laughed, or some of both – Allison wasn't sure. "Right. Okay, go to bed. You still have to be up at six."

Twenty-Seven

MR. HOWARD'S OFFICE LOOKED PRETTY MUCH like principals' offices everywhere, Matthew thought. It was painted institutional green and had old, scarred oak furniture. Three unpadded straight chairs faced the desk – just enough for father, mother and unruly child, Matthew figured. Mr. Howard's diplomas hung on the wall behind him and a sickly African violet huddled on top of a putty-colored four-drawer file.

Mr. Howard, on the other hand, was the very picture of Midwest chic. His abstract-patterned tie was clearly a silk designer number, and his shirt was so crisply starched it would probably crack apart if he bent over. No danger of that, though. His posture was impeccable. His brown hair, with just an elegant touch of gray at the temples, was sprayed into place, and his fingernails were buffed to a high gloss. When he smiled at Matthew, he revealed snowy porcelain caps.

Matthew felt more like a bumpkin than usual in his jeans, work boots and chambray work shirt. He sat in the straight, hard chair Mr. Howard indicated and took a deep breath.

Mr. Howard preempted the conversation, saying, "I'm glad you're here, Mr. Ryersen, so I can express my sympathies over what Will has gone through and tell you Lewiston is not that kind of school, normally. Our students are well-behaved and courteous and do not discriminate against anyone, no matter what the situation. So I'm sure you can appreciate our surprise to learn that one of our football players was involved in an altercation with your son. I have spoken with Pete and with Mr. and Mrs. Coombs, and I know the situation. I am going to let Will off with no more than two weeks' in-school suspension, because I understand he was provoked."

Matthew stared at the dapper, confident man across the desk. He needed a moment to comprehend what he had just heard.

"Let me be sure I understand you," Matthew said slowly. "You're goin' to give Will in-school suspension for two weeks because Pete Coombs tried to kill him."

"No, no, no, Mr. Ryersen! Will gets in-school suspension for brawling. He struck the first blow, after all, in direct violation of school rules."

"Did Pete tell you what was going on? Did you talk to Tracy?"

Mr. Howard smoothed his face into a friendly smile. "Of course, I talked with both of them. Since she and Will are – close – I have to take that into account when evaluating what Tracy has to say. Pete admits he was teasing and maybe pushed it a little. He only shoved Will in self-defense, though."

"Football team's doin' well this season, isn't it?" Matthew asked. "And Pete Coombs is one of the most important members of the team."

Mr. Howard allowed a frown. "What are you insinuating, Mr. Ryersen?"

"I'm not insinuatin' anything. I'm sayin' straight out that you don't want to have to suspend one of your star players from the foot-ball team when you might be lookin' at a league championship. By blamin' Will, who's the new guy and doesn't do sports, you let Pete off the hook so he can still play ball."

"Now just a minute!"

"No, sir, I think you've said all you need to say. Now you need to let me say what I came to say. My son almost died. He has been accused of all kinds of things that aren't true, shoved around, threat-ened and finally beat up, and I can't let that go on. I don't much like dealin' with the police, Mr. Howard, but that'll be where I'm goin' next, to press charges against Pete Coombs for harmin' my boy. And while I'm at it, I just may press charges against the school for allowin' this kind of bullyin' to go on, and against you for not doin' your job."

Matthew rose and went through the door, immune to the sputtering protests rising behind him.

Although he made it quickly to the truck, before he could get in he heard a man's voice calling his name and turned to see a short, rather portly middle-aged man whose white shirt strained its buttons across his belly, whose flag-striped tie flapped in the breeze of his hustling walk toward the truck. Matthew thought the man would probably have been running if he were able.

"Yeah?" Matthew said as the man pulled up beside him, puffing a little.

"Mr. Ryersen, I'm Ed Lewis, the superintendant for the Lewiston Schools system. I understand you had a bit of a set-to with Mr. Howard a moment ago, and I wonder whether we might talk about it."

"I don't see there's much to talk about, Mr. Lewis. My son is bein' treated unfairly and punished for what is not his fault. My boy almost died, Mr. Lewis, and I aim to have some justice for that. I'm on my way to the police department now."

Mr. Lewis very gently touched Matthew's arm, a conciliatory gesture, and wary. "Please, won't you come to my office for a few minutes so we can talk this through some more? Mr. Howard can be a bit – precise – sometimes, and – well – I believe we can reach a better solution."

Still lusting for blood, Matthew prayed for peace, eyes closed. He didn't particularly care what the superintendant thought of that, either. Finally he opened his eyes and looked directly at Mr. Lewis. "I'll come in if you can guarantee it won't just be a rehash. Because if it is, I don't have time. I need to get back to work after I see the police."

Mr. Lewis's ruddy cheeks blanched at the p-word, and he shook his head vigorously. "I guarantee we will work things out," he said.

Matthew nodded and followed the little man back into the building. A bell had rung, and the halls were filled with students, many of whom glanced curiously at Matthew as they passed. He saw Kevin and Travis coming, and they waved as they went by.

The superintendant's office, at the far end of the administrative hall, was much nicer than the principal's office. To begin, it was wallpapered in a masculine stripe, with crown molding and an ornate frame around the large window. The desk was a deep real wood, and the chairs were upholstered in dark green leather.

Job must pay pretty well, Matthew thought. He sat in one of the soft leather side-chairs in the conversation area by the window as Mr. Lewis took the couch.

"Now, then," Mr. Lewis said. "Would you care for coffee before we get started?"

"No, thank you. This isn't a social visit, sir, and I don't have all day. Are you familiar with my son's situation?"

Mr. Lewis frowned slightly at Matthew's refusal to observe the amenities, but he offered, "I am aware that your son and Pete Coombs were involved in an altercation on school property and your son sustained some injuries requiring hospitalization. I understand that Tracy Showalter was with your son – Will, isn't it? Yes. And it seems Will struck the first blow. Am I getting it right?"

"Almost," Matthew said. "Let me tell you the rest." For several minutes he went over all he had learned about the bullying, the lies, the threatening phone calls, the disgusting notes in Will's locker. "My son did commit some crimes when he was younger, before he came here. He was in juvenile detention for a while, and he is on probation. But he hasn't been in any trouble here. He's a good student, he hangs out with a couple of nice boys, he's keepin' company with Tracy, a good church-goin' girl from a fine family – Will's not a trouble-maker, not a fighter... Somebody found out about his past, apparently includin' the fact he was – sexually abused, and they decided to use it against him. I don't know why, and neither does Will.

"The Coombs boy is one of the football team members who started all this and have kept it goin' since the beginnin' of the year. He's twice Will's size, and he was shovin' Will *and* Tracy around. Yeah, Will took a swing at him, to keep Tracy safe. He grabbed Will's hand and squeezed it until he heard the bones break, and then he slammed him down on the concrete and busted his head. Big as he is, he didn't need to do any of that. He could just have walked away, and Will wouldn't have done anything."

"I gather Pete tells it a little differently."

"I gather he's valuable to the football team, and Will's nobody. So Will takes the blame and Pete plays ball. That's not justice, Mr. Lewis. I believe I need to file a police report and find me a good attorney. I'm goin' to sue the school for allowin' bullying and not givin' justice to my son, and I'm goin' to sue the Coombs family to cover all my son's medical bills and I'm goin' to see that kid in jail for what he did."

Matthew stood up. Mr. Lewis did, too, reaching his hand out again.

"Please, Mr. Ryersen, sit down. Let me – well, I want to – "

"You want to talk me out of it so the school doesn't look bad. You want the football team to have another winnin' season and the Coombs family not to get upset. Are they big contributors or somethin'?"

"Mr. Ryersen, you're doing me an injustice, too. Please. Sit down."

Matthew could glimpse why this man was superintendant. He grudgingly sat on the edge of the soft chair, indicating he didn't intend to stay long.

Mr. Lewis eased back on the couch. "Thank you. Now, let me say first of all that I believe you. I know Will's friends, their families, their church attendance – all fine families. I know Will's school records – good attendance, excellent grades, although he did seem to be slipping before this happened. Of course, now we can see why.

"Let me also say the Lewiston Schools system has a zero-tolerance policy for bullying and for fighting."

"Not enforced too well, is it?"

Lewis sighed. "Not always. It's hard to enforce, because the child being bullied often refuses to report or even admit the situation. But that is the policy. Since we now know for a fact that bullying is happening to Will, we can enforce it. All Will has to do is report to me who the bullies are – in addition to Pete – and we will deal with them."

"What does that mean – 'deal with them?'"

"It means they will each receive ten days' out-of-school suspension, without ability to make up the work, and they and their parents will be called in for discussion of the situation and their word that it will never happen again. If appropriate, apologies will be issued. Children and their families will have to attend three sessions of education about bullying."

"And Will? What about him?"

Mr. Lewis steepled his fingers and stared at them for a moment. He sighed. "I know you don't want to hear this, but a zero-tolerance for fighting policy means that any student who strikes another student must be punished. In Will's case there are mitigating circumstances, but he will still have to serve the in-school suspension. However, I believe we can reduce it to five days without any backlash from anyone."

"So you're goin' to call in the Coombses and lay this all on them. What about football?"

"According to our policy, he will be suspended from twenty percent of the season, which would be two games."

"Two games for nearly killin' my son."

"It's not a perfect system, Mr. Ryersen. I'm sorry for that. And, let me say, I'm truly sorry about Will. I wish for his sake and yours as well as mine that none of this had ever happened. If I could change things, I would." His affable face was creased with little lines around his eyes; Matthew believed him.

"All right," Matthew said. "I'm willin' to take you at your word and see how things go."

"Excellent! I'll keep you posted myself. When is Will scheduled to come back?"

"Next week, I think. He's still got a headache and gets kinda dizzy. Dr. Hanna has to clear him."

"Well, be sure he brings in a note from the doctor. If you want his work sent home in the meantime, so he doesn't fall any farther behind, I'll have that done. And if you let me know the day he's returning, we'll begin the suspension then and get it over with."

Matthew allowed himself to be shuttled out the door and back into the hallway. As he oriented himself to the closest way to his truck, a couple of tall boys came toward him down the hall. He recognized Chance Rupp and Pete Coombs.

"Hey, Mr. Ryersen," Chance said with a grin as they came abreast.

"Chance."

Pete said nothing, but glared at Matthew, who glared back.

"Gotta go," Chance said to Pete. "Come on!" He dragged Pete by the elbow until they were past Matthew, who heard them snickering as they went on down the hall.

God help me, I thought I was goin' to grab that kid by the throat! Lord, what am I goin' to do? Killin's too good for him, but it's sure temptin'!

"Storm front coming," John said from the barn door. "It's warm enough to be a bad one. Let's keep the cows inside after you finish

179

milking." He stared at the sky, where masses of white clouds were pushing up into mountains in the late afternoon sun. "How'd it go with the principal?"

Matthew shoved the last cow out into the alleyway with deliberate gentleness. "He's a dumb – jerk – and doesn't give a – care – about Will. He just wants to put all the blame on Will so the Coombs kid can play football." Matthew slammed his fist into the metal stanchion and winced. "Hosea, Joel, Amos, Ezra, Nehemiah – Ezekiel!"

"Must hurt a lot for a six-book swear," John teased. Undeterred by Matthew's snarl, he offered, "Want to talk about it out here where Will can't hear you?"

"No. Yes." Matthew wandered over to the hay bales and plunked down, wiping his hands on a blue bandana. "I told Mr. Howard I was goin' to the police, goin' to sue the school and all – he sure wasn't happy about that!" He smiled a little, remembering the man's discomfort. "Before I could get to the truck, the superintendant was huffin' and puffin' after me to save the day." Now he grinned. "He's a pretty good guy, I think, for a bigwig. Sure has a fancy office!"

John sat beside Matthew, leaving one bale between them. "So he had a better offer?"

"Yeah, actually, he did. There's a 'zero-tolerance' policy about bullying and fighting, and he said he'll enforce it as best he can. He'll lay it on Coombs, and he'll get two weeks out-of-school suspension and have to sit out two games. He wants Will to give him the names of the other kids involved in the bullying and then they'll get it, too. But Will – he has to serve five days of in-school suspension for fighting." Matthew shook his head, frowning, then looked directly at John. "That's not right!"

"He did hit Pete first, right?"

"Yeah, after the kid pushed him and Tracy!"

"If the policy is zero tolerance, then Mr. Lewis doesn't have any choice. I'm sorry, Matthew, but – well, you can see – "

Matthew hung his head and studied his manure-caked work shoes. A lot of things were stinking at the present time. "I don't want to see; that's the truth. I want revenge. I want to beat that kid's face to a pulp and stomp on his hand 'til the bones crumble and hit him so hard in the gut he can't breathe – " He dropped his head into his hands.

"I imagine I'd feel like that if it were David," John said softly. "But I'm not in your shoes, so I can be a little bit more objective. Let's think about Jesus and His Father."

"Oh, please," Matthew groaned, not looking up.

"No, seriously," John insisted. "God turned His Son over to the bullies and allowed Him to be battered and slandered and killed. He loved Jesus as a father loves his son, yet He stood back and let it happen. He didn't strike down the priests or the soldiers or the people who were calling Jesus horrible names and yelling for His blood. So He knows how you feel, and He knows what's right."

"You're pushing it," Matthew said, leveling his gaze on John at last. "God the Father and His Son did that because it was the only way to bring salvation to us. Don't try to tell me Will is like Jesus and I have to sacrifice him. Don't go there, John!"

"No, I'm not trying to take the comparison that far. It's more like seeing that even when things are horrible, revenge isn't God's way. Love is."

"We've had a lot of talks sitting on these hay-bales," Matthew said. "And I reckon it usually turns out you're right. I remember when you wanted me to forgive my father – talk about a bully! You were right that freedom comes from forgiveness. So I'm gonna pray about forgiving Pete Coombs and all the other kids who hurt my son. But in the meantime, they'd better keep clear of me. Because I just might not be as Christian as I'm supposed to be!" He got up and stalked out of the barn, leaving John to sit there and commend him to the Lord – again.

Twenty-Eight

"YOU LOOK GOOD!" ALICE SAID WITH A WIDE smile as Allison dragged her huge suitcase through the gate and met her boss with a big hug.

"I am so glad to see you!" Allison cried, letting go and allowing Alice to see her from every side. "I *am* good! And I'm so glad to be home."

"Well, let's go, then." Alice hefted the suitcase into the back of her SUV and popped the lock for Allison to leap up onto the front seat. As they headed away from Toledo Airport toward Lewiston, she looked over at the tiny woman beside her. "Nervous?"

"No. Should I be?"

"Well, I don't know. I mean, you've been gone a long time, and things were pretty tough for you before – and maybe while you were there – and now you're going to have to do things you didn't have to do before, not just at work, but in your real life, too."

"Keep your eyes on the road," Allison laughed, "and don't worry. I'm sober, I'm drug-free, and I know what I have to do. I'm prepared to eat crow to get back to work, and to pee in a cup as long as I have to."

"About the work thing," Alice said. "You know there's going to be at least a year's probation, right?"

"Right. They explained all that to me in the conference call. Work the day shift, under close supervision, no dealing with any controlled substances. Can't dispense meds, can't adjust morphine i.v.s, et cetera." She turned to face Alice. "I'm okay with all that, Alice, honest,

I am. I want to be back with the kids, that's all. If I have to be an aide instead of an RN – I don't care."

"You may not feel that way after a while. Or being around – stuff – may be hard. You gotta promise to let me know what's going on with you."

Allison laughed again. "I promise. Alice, you're my supervisor, and about the best boss a girl can have. I love you and I respect you. I'll play by the rules, and I'll tell you if something is getting to me. But one thing you can't be is my mother, and another is my sponsor."

Alice's hands tightened on the wheel. "I don't mean to intrude," she said. "I just want to help."

"You are helping! But I have to take responsibility for myself. That's part of working the program. I'll go to meetings and find a sponsor and say the Serenity Prayer as often as I need to – and it'll be fine."

They finished the trip to Lewiston with hospital gossip, nothing of substance, until they turned onto Allison's street.

"So," Alice said, "what about Matthew?"

"What about him?"

"Oh, come on. You can tell me. Are you gonna keep seeing him, or did they make you give him up as part of your treatment?"

Allison fixed the dragon-eye on her boss; Matthew would have said a faint hint of sulfuric acid could be detected. "They tried. I told them to stuff it. Shall I tell you that, too?"

"Just checking," Alice chuckled. "Does he know he's still on the radar?"

Allison relaxed into the seat again and said, "Yes, he does. I'll call him tomorrow and set up a time to get together. Right after I call the Clinic and get an AA meeting schedule. Oh, look! Home sweet home!"

Alice pulled the SUV to a stop at the curb in front of Allison's townhouse. "Uh, before you go in, I need to tell you something..."

"What?"

"I – uh – took the liberty of cleaning the place up for you. I mean, I had the key and all, and it was pretty nasty. I did the laundry and cleaned out the fridge and stuff. I picked up some groceries for you this morning, too. I hope you don't mind."

"Mind! I think it's great! Thank you so much for taking such good care of me. I know I didn't deserve any of it, Alice, and there's no way to repay you for being such a good friend. But from now on, things are going to be different, I promise!"

Alice squirmed uncomfortably in her seat. "Let's not make promises, okay? Let's just take one day at a time and let you ease back into things. No stress. No pressure."

"Look, I don't need the kid-gloves treatment. *My* responsibility, remember? Pop that hatchback and let me get my suitcase, then you can get on home. It's really late, and I'll bet you're working tomorrow morning."

Inside the front door, the two women hugged again and Alice handed over the keys. Allison stood in the open door until the taillights of the SUV disappeared, then locked the door and dropped the keys on the console table.

Home sweet home for sure! she delighted as she dragged her suitcase into the bedroom and heaved it up onto the neatly made bed. *No curfew, no wake-up call, nobody telling me when to shower and when to eat and when to go to this meeting or that meeting – I love being home!*

In short order she was unpacked, clean things put away, dirty clothes in the hamper, AA Big Book on her nightstand. As she changed into her nightgown, Allison realized how tired she was, almost dizzy with fatigue. She crawled into bed and lay there in the dark trying to imagine Matthew's face, until she fell asleep imagining the smell of sunshine and Clorox.

"Allison came home last night," Matthew informed the Abbott family as they sat around the dinner table. "She'll probably be calling tonight." He looked suspiciously at the platter of – something – Carolyn passed to him and began to hand it on to Will.

"Stop that!" Carolyn said. "Take a piece and eat it. What kind of an example are you going to be for the baby if you won't try new things?"

"Yeah, well, I don't guess she's noticing too much right now, is she? And what is that, anyway? It smells funny."

Will hid his guffaw in his napkin; Ed chuckled. Pearl put her lips together until they disappeared, but her dark eyes were twinkling.

"It's salmon filets," Carolyn said, forcing herself to glare.

"Like – fish?" Matthew asked.

"Yes, like fish. It is fish, silly."

"It has stuff all over it."

"Panko bread crumbs and Dijon mustard," Carolyn said.

"Somebody's been watching the Food Network," Will laughed.

Matthew sighed and studied the platter until he found the smallest piece of fish. He filled his plate with oven-roasted red potatoes and a few green beans. The others pretended to ignore his choices and he pretended to eat. The salmon wasn't too bad, actually; he managed half of it.

"Celeste is gonna love you," Will teased. "She *likes* fish. I kinda like this, too," he said, taking another piece. "How come we never had this before?"

"John's not a big fish-eater, either," Carolyn said. "But Dr. Dana said I should eat fish once or twice a week, and I saw this recipe – well, yes, it was on Food Network."

"It's good and all," Ed agreed, "but what's wrong with bass outa our own pond?"

"Nothing," John said. "But this is supposed to be good for us. I guess."

"I hope you saved room for dessert," Pearl told them all. "We have apple pie with cheddar cheese. And, Ed, they are our apples, the Granny Smiths."

Matthew was much more enthusiastic about the pie and managed to eat the whole piece with no effort as he dropped out of the conversation, now focused on something about church, to think about Allison. She had told him her arrival time, so he hadn't expected her to call last night. He had hung around after breakfast hoping she might call, but had decided she had probably slept in. He had hurried back to the house after the afternoon milking, lurking in the kitchen by the phone until Pearl put him to work paring apples, but the phone had only rung once, to confirm Carolyn's next doctor's appointment. Now he was nearly twitching with the need to hear her voice.

"You might want to answer the phone," Will said, jabbing him in the ribs. He hadn't even heard it ringing.

"So, like what did she say?" Will asked when Matthew came out of the kitchen, where he had barricaded himself by sitting against the swinging door.

"She said hello. She said she's glad to be home. She asked to be remembered to you."

"Yeah, right." Will's face darkened and his eyes turned the color of autumn rain. "So, you going over to see her?"

"Yes, I am, unless you need for me to stay here."

Will turned his back. "No. I'm fine. Go see your girlfriend. I know it's been a long time. I'll go upstairs and – and read some history or something."

"Will, honest, I don't have to go."

"I know. Thanks. See you tomorrow." Will clomped up the steps without looking at his father again.

Too dispirited to turn on the radio or reach for his Walkman, Will flopped down on his bed, careless of his shoes on the quilt. *What did I expect? The minute she calls, there he goes. He isn't going to have any time for me now.* He sighed and pressed his eyelids against the tears of self-pity gathering there. *Tracy hasn't called me, either. I guess she thinks I'm not worth the trouble. Kevin and Trav, too. Nobody wants to risk hanging around with a real loser. Maybe they believe what Pete and those other guys were saying, but good little church kids are too polite to say so. I have to go back to school Monday. How can I? Maybe I should just have died when I hit my head. Then I wouldn't care about anything.*

Now I'm home, Allison thought, burrowing into the circle of Matthew's arms. *Now everything will be all right.*

"Let's sit down, Miss Allison," Matthew drawled, breaking the embrace with a smile. "I can't be doin' too much of that without gettin' in trouble."

"Yeah, yeah," she teased. "I get it. Okay, do you want some coffee?"

Matthew carefully sat in the side-chair rather than on the couch. "No, thanks. I can't stay long, because Will's still kinda messed up. I just couldn't wait any longer to see you."

He smiled, and Allison's blood went fizzy, like soda. "Oh, I'm glad! I couldn't, either."

"So – what do you have to do now that you're home?"

Allison plunked herself down on the couch and tucked her bare feet under her, holding a pillow to her chest. "Well, I go back to work tomorrow. That means I fill out a lot of paperwork and sign some kind of oath or something about staying clean and sober and submit-

186

Mary Mueller

ting to drug tests whenever they feel like it, for as long as they feel like
it – a year, to begin with. And I went to the drug clinic today and got
a schedule of AA meetings. I'm supposed to go to at least three or
four meetings a week and get a sponsor. The Minnesota folks recommended I see an alcohol/drug counselor or a shrink every week, too,
but I'm not going to do that unless I think I'm getting in trouble."

"Shouldn't you be doing everything they say?" Matthew asked, a
faint worry line creasing his forehead.

"You wouldn't be so quick to recommend it if you'd been through
treatment," Allison said, shuddering a little. "I don't like counselors.
I don't like having people prying and prying and not satisfied until
they make you cry."

"Sounds like Pearl," Matthew said with a smile.

"I hope not! At least, not if I'm going to get to know her."

"Oh, you are, honey, I promise. Nah, she's not so bad. She just
reminds me sometimes of my grade school principal. And she was a
teacher." He laughed. "And she'll get in anyone's face – been in mine
more times than I can remember, including at dinner this evening.
But she has a really good heart under all that crisp stuff. And a lot of
wisdom."

"Matthew – should we talk about – things? I mean – about us?"

"Sure, if you want to. Honey, you're gonna poke a hole in that pillow if you keep picking at it like that." Allison put the pillow down on
the couch. "It's like I said on the phone, Allie: I love you and I want
to see where that goes, if you love me."

Her heart was beating double-time, she was sure of it! "I do love
you! I want to be with you! How are we going to work that out,
though, with Will and my – problems?"

Matthew sat quietly for a moment, looking at her. "How would we
do it if we didn't have problems? If we were like John and Carolyn?
I reckon they just did things together and talked a lot and came to
the conclusion that the Lord meant them to be married. Can't we do
that?"

Allison sighed. "I don't know. We're not going to see each other
all that often if I'm at meetings four nights a week and you go to bed
with the birds."

"Well, honey, I get up with the birds, too. That's what it means
to be a farmer. If you have four nights at meetings, that leaves three

187

nights free, doesn't it? We can have dinner, go to movies, take long walks, do things you think would be fun... I bet we can find ways to be together and not get in trouble. You can come to the house and hang out with my family and get to know them. They'll love you, I know they will."

"Will isn't going to love me."

"Allie, did they teach you in Minnesota to look at the bad side of everything?"

"No! I just – you know he –"

Matthew came over to the couch and raised her to her feet, back into his arms. "I know. We're just gonna have to work through it. Because I have missed you so much that I'm never doing that again."

Twenty-Nine

IF WILL HAD BEEN A PRAYING MAN, HE WOULD HAVE prayed for a blizzard Sunday night. No such luck. The Monday morning sun was threatening to melt the insides of his eyeballs and burn the faint hairs from his arms as he waited for the bus at the end of the driveway. He might have prayed, then, for the bus to break down before it got there, but too late – here it came. Will shouldered his backpack and climbed up the steps with the enthusiasm of a killer walking the last mile.

Get your guts up, he warned himself. *Don't let 'em see you sweat. If they think you're scared, they'll be like sharks after chum.* He made his way toward the back of the bus, not making eye contact with anyone along the way, pretending he didn't hear any snickers or rude remarks. Travis and Kevin, sitting in the back seat, waved him over. *Huh. That's new.* He sat with Kevin and muttered a greeting.

"Glad to see you back, man!" Kevin said. "Cool haircut." He was referring to the strip shaved horizontally across the back of Will's scalp, where a healing wound still looked big and red and ugly.

"Thanks. You oughta get one just like it," Will managed. "It's gonna be the next big thing."

"I don't think so," Travis said. "Costs way too much. You okay?"

"Yeah, sure. Maybe a headache sometimes. The doctor said I can go back to school – but no phys ed."

"Lucky, lucky guy," Kevin said, meaning it. "Maybe for the whole year?"

"I'm not looking that far ahead. Just gotta make it through today. I got in-school suspension."

"Oh, crap," Travis moaned. "Been there, done that. You'll be bored out of your mind."

"Lots of homework and stuff to catch up on."

"Yeah, but –you about gotta take an oath if you have to leave to pee."

Kevin and Travis flanked Will all the way into the office, and he thanked them. The looks in the hall had been acid enough to remove several layers of skin, especially the ones from members of the football team. In the office, he signed in and received a pass from the starchy secretary, who made no secret of her contempt for him. With a sigh, he let himself back into the river of kids flowing up and down the hall and let it carry him to the classroom which would be his prison for the next five days.

The first thing Will noticed was the brown paper covering the window in the door from the inside. A neatly computer-printed sign said in 72-point font: IN-SCHOOL SUSPENSION.

Terrific. Advertize it. Mom would have said 'add insult to injury,' and this time she'd be right. He opened the door and stood there, getting his bearings.

Just inside the door, to his left, a grim green metal desk was bolted to the floor. A scarred wooden chair sat behind the desk, and a laptop computer was open on its scratched top. The room held probably a dozen old-fashioned school chairs with the attached, moveable desk-arms. There was a large metal wastebasket with no liner in the corner on the right side of the door. Old, torn window-shades, also in green, covered the upper halves of the two windows on the back wall. That was it, except for the man sitting in the desk chair.

The man snapped his fingers and held out his hand. Will approached and handed over his pass. "Ryersen, huh?" the man said in a voice which could have scoured the grease off a barbeque grill in one pass.

"Yeah." Will locked his knees so they wouldn't shake obviously. The man was taller than Will, broader than Will's probation officer, none of it fat, and all the lines in the face under his gray crew-cut suggested frowns, not smiles.

"You know who I am?"

"No."

"That's 'No, sir.' Got it?"

"Yes, sir." *Wow! Gotta be a marine or something.*

"My name is Replogle. You call me Mr. Replogle or sir. I know who you are, and I know what you done, and I don't like having your kind in here any more than you like being here. So you keep your head down and your mouth shut for the next five days. Got it?"

"Yes, sir."

"Take a seat and do your work. You get a break at ten, after classes are in session, to go to the can. You eat your lunch at noon. You get out at three. Any questions?"

"Sir, do I go to the cafeteria for lunch?"

"You bring it with you. Didn't they tell you that?"

"No, sir."

"Bring it tomorrow."

"What about today?"

"You gonna give me a hard time, boy? Today you're gonna get really hungry, and that'll teach you to remember to bring your lunch. Sit down – anywhere." Mr. Replogle turned his attention to the laptop.

Will chose a chair by the window, hoping he would see something outside that spoke of hope. He dumped his bag on the floor beside him and drew out his calculus book and workbook. He had a lot of work to make up, and he might as well use the time to do it. He didn't want to get in trouble for bad grades, along with everything else. He was able to immerse himself in the flow of mathematics for a long time, until the harsh voice broke his concentration:

"Go to the can. You got five minutes. If I have to come looking for you, you'll be sorry."

Will all but ran from the room to the boys' restroom, less because of an urgent need to relieve himself than because of a passionate desire to get out of that man's presence. He was grateful to be the only occupant of the restroom and lingered just a moment in the calm silence. On the way back to his cell, he took a long drink of water from the fountain. He hadn't brought a water-bottle with him, either. *I'll know better tomorrow.*

"You're late," Mr. Replogle said as Will walked back into the room.

"Sir? Really?"

"You calling me a liar? Thirty-seven seconds late."

"Thirty- sev – I'm sorry, Mr. Replogle. I don't have a watch. I'll be more careful."

"You better. Get back to work."

The day dragged on. Will grew hungrier and hungrier, especially as he watched and smelled Mr. Replogle eating a huge sub sandwich, a banana and – insult to injury again – a big bag of homemade chocolate chip cookies. The man had to hear Will's stomach growling, but he didn't offer to share his lunch or to let Will go to the cafeteria. By two-thirty, Will's head was aching badly, but he didn't figure it was smart to ask for a pass to see the nurse. He just closed his eyes with his head tilted so it looked like he was reading. Finally the last bell rang.

"Gather up your stuff," Mr. Replogle said. "Get outta here."

Will needed no second invitation. He fled the room, weighted down by his book bag and his headache and his heavy heart, but determined to escape his captor.

"How'd it go?" Matthew asked as Will joined him and Ed in the barn for the milking.

Will's job was to muck out the stalls while the cows were being milked, and he hated it. But somehow, today it seemed not so bad, even though the stench made his stomach queasy on top of the cookies and milk he had wolfed down after school. He managed a smile for his father.

"Not bad. Got a lot done. Before the end of the week I'll be all caught up."

"Good for you!" Ed said, coming over to clap him on the shoulder and take his pitchfork. "Why don't you set down over there by your daddy and let me do this?"

"But – I'm supposed to – "

"Son," Ed said, beginning to use the pitchfork with the offhanded ease of many years, "you look kinda seedy. It's okay if you take it easy tonight."

"Sure," Matthew agreed. "No need to push yourself. Tell us about school."

I don't think so! "Uh, Dad, I do have a headache. May I go ask

Carolyn for some aspirin or something?"

Concern flooded over Matthew's face. "Of course! Do you need me to walk you back to the house?"

"No, I'm okay. Thanks." He walked away quickly, before Matthew could change his mind and follow.

"Not his best day ever," Ed surmised.

"How could it be? It has to be embarrassing to go back, with all the talk."

"Ease up, son," Ed said quietly, and Matthew noticed he was clutching the handle on the lid to the milk tank as if he intended to rip out its rivets.

"Yeah. No violence. Do you have any idea what I want to do to those kids?"

"Same as me, prob'ly. But the Lord says turn the other cheek and forgive seventy times seven – you know what's in the Book."

"Ed, I love you like a brother, but don't do this to me, okay? I know I'm not looking much like Jesus these days – sure not feeling much like Him! I'm praying, but it isn't doing any good." Matthew hung his head in defeat.

"What you praying for, son?"

"Mostly to not kill anybody. For God to give those kids justice. For Will to be all right."

"You might ought to go see the pastor or talk to John," Ed suggested. "Get sorted out."

"You might could be right," Matthew agreed.

"You could be right," Allison nodded to the woman beside her. "I don't want to go through any of it again."

"So you have to recognize that only a power greater than yourself can restore you to sanity," the woman persisted. "You can't control it, or you never would have ended up in so much trouble. I mean, who volunteers to ruin their life?" She laughed and took a healthy slug of her coffee, grimacing at the taste.

"Awful, isn't it?" Allison laughed, carefully sipping at her own. Even with three creamers and four sugars, it tasted like used motor oil, complete with a rainbow slick floating on top. "I hear what you're saying, Lucy, but I'm just not ready to talk about God."

"In program, that's only 'God as you understand Him,'" Lucy

said. "Don't you believe in anything bigger than you? How about the power of the group?"

"That's what they said in rehab. Use the group. I guess that's what I've been doing. I mean, if everyone tells me the same thing, they're probably right, right?"

"I think so," Lucy said. "But over the years I've really come to believe in one big God. He's been so good to me – only miracles could have taken what I did to my life – my job, my husband, my kids, my parents – and turned it all around. Don't you want that, too?"

Allison laughed. "Who doesn't? I have to go. See you next week, Lucy."

Steering her little blue car toward home with one hand and finishing her terrible coffee with the other, Allison had to laugh to herself. At every AA meeting she met someone like Lucy, convinced the program was sent by God and would save her. Or He would save her, as the tall, skinny guy from the night before had proclaimed in sonorous tones more suited to her idea of church. Allison figured her own hard work and will-power would do the trick, even though they had tried in rehab to convince her she didn't have any will-power. What a crock! But – 'Try having will-power over diarrhea,' they'd said. 'Can you control that?'

I need to get some sleep, Matthew fretted, tossing until the covers were untucked from his narrow bed and twisted around him. Hating the sense of confinement, he wrestled his way out and stood on the rug by the bed to reorder the sheets and blankets. *It's going to be time to get up pretty soon, and I don't think I've slept more than ten or fifteen minutes, total. Lord, please, let me sleep without dreams.*

The dreams were sleep-stealers. Will bleeding on the emergency room cot, lying like a corpse on the ICU bed, the bloated, laughing face of Pete Coombs daring him to strike it – and when he was awake, the images were even more fine-tuned. He could imagine so clearly the feeling of bone giving under his knuckles and blood flowing hot over his hand...

I used to be afraid I'd abuse Will if I took him. Never occurred to me I'd want to kill somebody else for hurting him. Lord, what are You doing, letting all this bad stuff happen to my boy? Why didn't You stop it? If You want Will to follow You, why do You make it so hard for him

194

to love You?

Matthew flopped back into the bed and lay there rigid until the alarm went off, finding wrestling with God a full-contact sport, and not for the faint-hearted. *You do need help,* he acknowledged to his baggy-eyed reflection as he brushed his teeth. *Lots of help. Again.*

Thirty

THE WEEK PASSED. WILL AVOIDED CONFRONTA-
tions with the drill sergeant and encounters in the
restroom and caught up on all his homework. At home
he did a few chores and "rested" in his room, claiming headaches even when he didn't have one. He spoke with Tracy on
the phone twice, and even her mother was nice to him when
she answered. It should have been a peaceful time, but all Will
could see was the countdown to Monday, when he would have
to go back to his regular classes again.

"Look here," Pearl said to Will as he slumped at the kitchen table
after school toying with his snack instead of eating it, "this down-in-
the-mouth attitude is not going to help." She sat down opposite him
with the firmness of someone planning to stay as long as it took. "You
need to start thinking about how to deal with all this."

"You think I haven't?" he burst out. "It's *all* I think about! I'm going back to classes Monday and all those guys are going to be waiting
for me!"

"I'm sure they aren't going to do anything," Carolyn said from
her post at the sink, where she was peeling potatoes. "The principal
has surely talked to them. And they know that boy got suspended.
He still has another week to go, and no ball-games. Nobody else will
want to get into that kind of trouble."

Will ran his hand through his hair and shook his head. "You don't
get it. They're gonna be madder than ever because of what happened

to Pete. They're gonna blame me, and they're gonna find some way to make me pay."

"Oh, no," Carolyn said, "that can't be."

"Of course it can," Pearl snapped. "It's the way children are. You think a new baby is so nice and innocent, but that's not true; they're born with that fallen nature that makes us selfish and cruel, and it refines itself to be sharper and harder as they grow – unless they have godly instruction from their parents and then find the Lord. I'd guess offhand that none of these bullies is even pretending to walk with the Lord."

Will nodded. "I don't think so. But that just means they're dangerous, because there's nothing to say they shouldn't hurt somebody they don't like. And what am I supposed to do, Grandma? Pray for them?"

Pearl smiled at his sarcasm and nodded briskly. "Of course. I am. And work on some plan to confront your problem and resolve it."

"Maybe if you just told them the truth..." Carolyn ventured.

"Yeah. Maybe." Will gave up all pretense of eating and walked out of the room, leaving the clueless women behind him. Back in his room he sat at his desk and thought until his mind felt like a gerbil on a wheel, but no bright ideas came to him.

Talk to them. 'Hey, Pete, hey, Chance, how's the team doing? Good chance for the playoffs? Oh, and by the way, I'm not gay and I don't steal your lunch money and I sure don't want to be beat up again. See, my cast is still on. Want to sign it?' Right.

"I don't work Sunday," Allison told Matthew over the phone, "so we could get together Saturday night if you want to. I know you can't stay out real late, but – "

"That's a great idea! Dinner out? A movie?"

She pictured him standing barefoot on the kitchen floor, wrapping and unwrapping the phone-cord around his finger, smiling... *Oh, Matthew, if I could only tell you what I really want to do Saturday night!* "I thought maybe you'd come over and let me make dinner for you. And – and you could bring Will, if he'd come."

"Oh."

"Well, we don't have to!"

"No, you just took me by surprise, that's all. Let me ask Will if he

197

has any other plans, and if he'd be willing. I'll call you back, okay?"

Matthew made his way to Will's room and knocked on the closed door. "Will?"

"Come in."

Will was lying on the bed, an arm over his eyes, shoes obviously kicked off over the end of the bed to land in a heap.

"I was just on the phone with Allison," Matthew said, "and she's invited us to dinner tomorrow night."

"What?" Will removed his arm from his eyes to stare at his father. "Are you serious?"

"Yes, I am. She invited you, too." Matthew looked away, a faint flush rising up his neck to the tops of his ears. "I – uh – I wish you'd think about it."

Will was tempted to unload everything he had been storing up since that fatal moment at the fair, but he couldn't get past the look on his father's face: the flush, the sad eyes, the faint beginning of a smile at the corner of his mouth. *He loves her the way I love Tracy. He wants me to love her, too. How am I supposed to do that! How am I supposed to sit there eating dinner at her table, thinking about Mom?*

"I – " He was going to say, 'I can't,' but somehow it came out, "I'll go."

Matthew's smile broke over Will like a spotlight, flooding him with bright warmth and a strange feeling of – gratitude?

"Thank you," Matthew said. He couldn't seem to say any more, but the smile was enough for Will.

"Just one thing, Dad..."

"What?"

"Can she cook, or do I need to eat before I go?"

Matthew laughed, and Will joined him, probably the first laugh he had had since the beginning of the school year. It felt good, two good feelings in a minute, and he hoped he could remember it.

Getting there was definitely not half the fun. Neither of the Ryersen men was particularly socially experienced, and both of them suffered, without admitting it, some unmanly qualms about what to wear to dinner. Each of them was nervous about how the other would behave, and neither was going to talk about that, either.

"You both look nice," Pearl told them as they went through the kitchen on the way to the truck. She stopped Will for a moment, pulled his head down and brushed down a cowlick sticking up at the back of his head. "When all your hair grows back," she said, "that won't happen so much." She took Will by surprise as she licked her fingers and ran them over the recalcitrant hair.

"Ew! Quit it!"

Matthew laughed, but he ran his own hand over his hair. He and Will had the same growth pattern. "Let's go," he said. "It's rude to be late for dinner."

"God bless you," Pearl said, smiling at them impartially. "Have a good time."

As they drove, Matthew noticed Will rubbing the palms of his hands on his clean jeans. He understood how difficult it must be; his own palms were a bit sweaty, too. They sat in silence all the way to Lewiston, all the way to Allison's townhouse, where Matthew parked the truck on the street and locked it.

"Thank you for coming with me," Matthew said as they climbed the steps. "It means a lot to me."

"No problem," Will replied, affecting a casual sound his clenched hands and narrowed eyes belied.

Before Matthew could knock or ring the bell, the door flew open and Allison was taking both their hands, ushering them in, making welcoming noises and fluttering about like a hummingbird. She was dressed in pale blue jeans and a bright blue sweater, looking as young and pretty as a cheerleader and demonstrating much the same sort of enthusiasm. Matthew couldn't help it – he smiled at her and drew her into his arms.

"Slow down a minute, Allie. We're not leaving, are we, Will?"

"Uh – no."

"I'm just so glad you're both here! Dinner's almost ready; want to come into the kitchen with me while I finish up?"

Exchanging a look, they followed her and took seats at the break-fast bar. Nobody said anything for a moment, while Allison checked something in the oven. She turned back to them and began to assemble a salad from a host of ingredients laid out on the bar.

"Will," Allison said, "when I first met your father, when we first began to think maybe we liked each other, he had a really hard time making conversation. So I kind of got used to being the one to write the dialogue. I'm a really good talker, if you hadn't noticed."

Will snickered. He couldn't help it, apparently, because he blushed immediately. "Yeah. Well, he gets over it, doesn't he?"

"Yes, he does. Except for when he doesn't. And you? Maybe you're pretty quiet, too. So I just want you to tell me if I need to put a lot of energy into keeping things going, because I can – and I will – but it'd be nice if we could just get to know each other. And enjoy dinner."

Please, God, Matthew prayed. *Please let him go along.*

"I'd like to enjoy dinner," Will said with a straight face. "If you can cook."

"Will!"

"Relax, Matthew," Allison said, smiling. "I think that was a joke." She turned to look Will in the eye. "I *hope* that was a joke, because I wouldn't want to have to poison you." She grinned at the boy, who grinned back.

Thank You, God!

Matthew knew Allison's lasagna wasn't as good as Carolyn's, but it was good enough to bring Will back for seconds. And the apple pie for dessert, not as good as Pearl's, still went down easily under its load of melting vanilla ice cream lightly sprinkled with cinnamon.

The conversation had gone better than he had feared, too. Allison talked a little bit about the sick kids she was caring for and Will asked a couple of what seemed to be genuinely interested questions. He hadn't talked about himself, but he never did.

"I'd like to know about your mother, Will," Allison said, causing Matthew's heart to rise in his throat, along with his dinner.

"What about her?"

"Oh – I don't know – just anything you'd like to tell me. I mean, here you are, and I know you look so much like your dad that it's freaky, but what about her? What do you remember? Do you miss her?"

Oh, Allie, honey, you sure rush in where angels fear to tread!

But Will seemed to be taking it well. He looked Allison in the eye and sat up straight in his chair.

"Yeah, I miss her. A lot sometimes. She wasn't like you." The sharp edge in Will's voice brought Matthew up straighter in his chair, too, but Will continued with no apparent hostility. "She was a lot taller than you, and pretty skinny. I think her hair was brown, but she always had it bleached a kind of yellow blond. And her eyes were blue, but not like Dad's and mine – more – more – like the sky. She liked to wear red lipstick. I remember when I was really little – maybe three – she'd let me play in her make-up sometimes. She spanked me pretty good one time for drawing faces on the mirror with her lipstick and blue eye-shadow.

"She wasn't a very good cook – not like you and Carolyn – but she made really good buttered popcorn. We ate that a lot, 'specially when there wasn't much money. She and my stepdad used to take me to the park sometimes in Louisville to feed the ducks. She and Jesse, that's my stepdad, bought me a Star Wars lunch box for school."

Will stopped, his face unfocused as he looked back. Then he went on, "Do you know about my mom? I mean, after Jesse. She got bored with being a mom and a good wife, and she started drinking and fooling around. He finally got fed up and divorced her. Then things got – never mind." Will stood up and walked into the living room.

"Oh, my!" Allison said. "I had no idea – I'm sorry, Matthew, I didn't mean to – "

"And you didn't. He told you more in five minutes than he's told me the whole time we've been together. He's gonna hate himself a little bit for giving in and liking you, but I think this has been a great time." Matthew rose and leaned over the table to kiss Allison's forehead. "I think we better not push our luck, though. We'll go home now."

"Oh, no! I thought we could play cards or a board game or something."

"One step at a time, honey."

Matthew went into the living room. "Had enough for the first time? Ready to go?"

"Yeah. It was okay, though." As Allison came into the room, Will turned to her to say, "Thanks for dinner. It was good. And thanks for asking about my mom. Nobody ever does." With that, he stepped to the front door and ran down the steps, leaving the adults agape.

"Well!" Allison laughed. "Ryersen men never cease to amaze!" She snuggled up to Matthew and drew his arms around her waist. "Kiss me good-night?"

"Yes, ma'am." He complied. "Thank you. This was good. Really good. Maybe we'll do it again real soon."

The noise of the F-150 engine was the only sound in the truck. Neither of the Ryersen men seemed inclined to break the stand-off until Will took a deep breath and said, "She's nice. Good cook. Maybe you should marry her."

Matthew managed to keep from putting the truck into one of the twelve-foot-deep drainage ditches which lined so many Fulton County roads, but it was a near thing. "What!"

"I said – you heard what I said." Will slouched down in the seat and didn't look at his father. "I know you want to, and I know she wants to, so the only problem would be me, right?"

"Will, you're not a problem," Matthew said, glancing at the youth. "Both of us understand it's hard for you to let go of the idea of your mom and me, hard to imagine another woman in what you think should have been her place. You don't have to say what you think I want to hear. I love you whether you like Allison or not. If we end up together like we want, well, I guess you'll have to live with it. But you don't have to like it ever, if that's how you really feel. It won't change how I feel about either of you."

"Okay, but the thing is – I really did like her. And I kept think-ing about Tracy. How I would feel if somebody said I can't see Tracy because they don't like her. I mean, nobody has the right to tell some-body else who to love, do they?"

"No, they don't. Love's not like that, anyway. I mean, we don't get a whole lot of choice about who we love, I don't think. I can tell you to not love Tracy, but I can't make you not love her. You can tell your-self not to love her, for that matter, but even you can't make yourself stop it, now – can you?"

"No."

"On the other hand," Matthew went on, more slowly, feeling his way and not liking it, "God tells us to love everybody. And He doesn't say just the Tracys and Allisons of the world, either. He says everybody. Even the people we hate. Even the people who hurt us... Oh, s – "

"Whoa, Dad! Language!" Will laughed. But the laugh faded quickly. "You're thinking about those guys on the football team, aren't you? Having to love them?"

Matthew nodded, keeping his hands on the wheel and his eyes on the road. "Yeah."

"How – why are you supposed to do that?" Will's voice rose and quavered a little. "They hate me! Why should you or I love them?"

Matthew shook his head this time. "Because that's what Jesus says, and that's what Jesus did. They hurt Him, too – bad – and some of His last words were asking God to forgive them. I don't figure I'm quite like Jesus, though. It's a hard teaching."

"How'd we get on this?" Will asked. "All I said was it would be okay with me if you want to marry Allison."

"I don't know, son. Let's just – forget it for now. We're almost home, and I'm too tired to think about anything but how early milking's gonna come tomorrow morning."

From his room, Will could see the faint gleam of a night light in Ed's bathroom across the road, and he knew Ed and Pearl were both sleeping peacefully. The yard light gleamed on the little white fence and the battered old El Camino over there, everything just as it should be. Down the hall, John and Carolyn's room was dark and a sliver of light shone under Matthew's door. *Reading his Bible,* Will thought, *or maybe some poetry. He's a strange dad, a farmhand who reads poetry and dates nurses and carves mice in his spare time. I'm not like him at all – well, unless you count the poetry. And the way I look. And the way I try to avoid talking about certain things... Shoot! I don't want to turn into my father! Don't want to turn into my mother, either, though. Not top quality stuff either way.*

Undressing to his underwear, Will turned on the desk lamp and sat down to his school books. He really didn't have much homework, because the in-school suspension had given him hours each day to study and hadn't allowed anything else. It was just a habit to turn to his books to avoid thinking about other things.

Other things. Like what am I going to do Monday morning?

Will drew his knees up and wrapped his arms around them, shivering. He would have to walk down that hall to his locker, past all the jocks and their cheerleader girlfriends, under the hot eyes of all the underclassmen who knew what people were saying about him. He would have to pretend not to hear the snickers, the nasty comments, the whispered threats – and invitations. He would have to take his seat in classrooms where nobody except maybe Tracy wanted to sit next to him, where anybody on his way to the front of the room for any reason might punch him in the kidney or slap the back of his head or drop a hate note on his desk...

Suddenly Will leaned over and vomited Allison's good lasagna into the wastebasket by his desk. Trying to do it quietly was a good trick, and it went on for a long time. When the spasms finally stopped and he could breathe and wipe the tears and snot and sweat from his face with a dirty tee-shirt, Will could only think, *Just like my father. Exactly like him.*

Matthew propped the pillow behind his back against the hard headboard and opened his Bible to the Psalms. He was looking for a little wrath and judgment tonight, he thought, to remind him how God dealt with the bad guys. He found it right away, too, in Psalm 3, verse 7:

> **Arise, O LORD!**
> **Deliver me, O my God!**
> **Strike all my enemies on the jaw;**
> **Break the teeth of the wicked.**

That's it, Lord! Break their teeth and smash their jaws and let them see how it feels to be bullied. Let them see how it feels to be on the receiving end for a change!

Matthew gave a savage grin, imaging Pete Coombs with his broken jaw hanging agape and a handful of cracked-off teeth lying at his feet in a pool of blood. He felt his fists clench on the edges of the Bible and relished the tight skin over his knuckles.

And then he heard that Voice again, speaking other scripture:

> **Blessed are the meek, for they will inherit the earth...**
> **Blessed are the merciful, for they will be shown mercy...**
> **Blessed are the peacemakers...**

No, Lord, I don't want to hear that.

Please. Listen, Matthew:

> **Love your enemies, do good to those who hate you, bless**

those who curse you, pray for those who mistreat you. If someone strikes you on one cheek, turn to him the other also…

Matthew closed the Bible and put it back on the table. He slowly got out of bed and knelt on the rug beside it, bowing down until his forehead touched the floor. He prayed for forgiveness and prayed to be willing until his knees ached and his back ached and his heart ached from being unable to submit.

After stealthily cleaning out the wastebasket and brushing his teeth, Will crept back to his room and resumed his seat at the desk.

There is a way out. You know there is. Any time you quit being too chicken to take it.

He opened the desk drawer and fished out the knife from the back. As he had many times now, he held it to the light to let the shine reflect from the sharp blade. It was pretty, slender, small, with a curved handle to fit a man's hand, a point so fine it almost disappeared. He looked at the tender skin of his left forearm, where half a dozen tiny red dots or quarter-inch lines were fading to pink. His dad had been right that it didn't hurt to cut with this blade because it was so sharp, but he had been either too cowardly to make a serious cut or too smart to make a mark that might raise questions. So far, even when he didn't have long sleeves, no one had noticed these little marks.

Why would they? Nobody cares enough to look for them. Nobody looks at you at all any more. They don't see you.

Twisting the blade back and forth in the light, Will thought again about the evening. Allison was a nice person, and she lit up like a spotlight when she looked at his dad. And he looked at her the way Will wished somebody, anybody, would look at him, like she was the most important person in the whole world. He never saw his father that happy any other time.

What would it be like if they got married? Where would they live? They sure couldn't live in that little room of Matthew's! But her townhouse was too far for Matthew to drive to work at three o'clock in the morning, especially in the winter. And he had chores at night, too. No, they would have to find a place close by, unless his dad quit his job. But what would he do then? He wasn't dumb or anything, but farming was all he'd ever done, and he liked it.

Nurses make good money. Maybe if he didn't have to take care of me, his money and hers would be enough to buy a place of their own. I bet he'd like that, a place of his own. He doesn't talk much about losing his grandpa's place in Kentucky, but when he does he gets this sad look... If he was free of me, they could move to Kentucky. She can find a job anywhere, I bet. Maybe he could even buy back the old place, the MacKenzie place. Allison wouldn't care where they are, not as long as they're together.

The knife seemed to have a will of its own as it bent to the bend of Will's elbow, where a large blue vein pulsed with his increasing heartbeat. Just a poke, not a slice. Just enough to take the pressure off. Like that.

Thirty-One

MATTHEW SAT QUIETLY BETWEEN CAROLYN AND Ed in the third pew on the right, where the Abbott family always sat, and let the organ music fill him. Pearl didn't play often anymore, but when she did – heaven would probably sound like this, he figured, with a choir even better than the church choir backing up the music. He was already half-way to a prayer when the music stopped and Pastor Corrigan asked the congregation to join him in prayer.

Pearl came down from the platform, leaning heavily on the rail by the side steps, and took her place next to Ed. *There's still room in this pew,* Matthew thought, *room for Will and Allison both. Even room for little Longsuffering in one of those baby seat things if we'd squeeze up a bit. Lord, that's my heart's desire: Will and Allison saved and worshiping here with us. Since nothing is impossible for You, why not this one thing? I'd do anything to know they're safe in a relationship with You – anything!*

Miles had ended his prayer and stepped up to the wooden podium at the front of the platform, laying out his open Bible and some note cards he wouldn't use. "Today's sermon is titled, 'Be Careful What You Say.'"

Matthew snorted audibly, garnering an elbow in the ribs from Ed and a curious glance from Carolyn. *If you only knew,* he laughed to himself, shaking his head. *I'm startin' to feel like a steer in a cattle drive, headed toward the chute for sure. Okay, Lord, I'm listenin'.*

"What's your problem?" Will asked. "You been standing there with your mouth half-open and your eyes all glazed over like you're high or something, and I've asked you twice to hand me that plate in your hand."

Matthew blinked and looked at Will sheepishly. "I was just – thinking, I guess. Here. It probably dripped dry already, but give it a swipe." He handed the plate to Will and plunged his hands back into the sudsy dishwater. "Plenty more where that came from."

"Must be either really good thoughts or really bad ones," Will said, "to make you zone out like that. How come we have to do the Sunday dinner dishes all by ourselves? There's more today than any other meal all week!"

"Yep. I just figured we might give the ladies a break, since they did all the cooking. I'm not sure how much Carolyn should be standing and working now."

"Well, Ed could have helped." Will dried another plate and stacked it in the cupboard.

"Oh, come on. It's not that bad. I'm the one getting dishpan hands here. And besides, I thought we might talk."

"Talk?"

"Yeah, you know, I say something, you say something, back and forth..."

Will fielded the last plate and started on the pile of silverware laid out on a towel on the counter. He began to polish each piece with his towel, even though they were stainless steel and didn't need to be shined. "Nothing to talk about."

"You and I both know tomorrow's Monday. That's got to be on your mind, son."

"So? You aren't going to let me drop out of school, are you?"

"What! No. Of course not! Kid as smart as you needs to graduate well and go to college. Be more than a dumb farmhand like me."

"That's what I figured – you'd make me go on. So that's what I'll do tomorrow: get on the bus, go to class, try to stay out of trouble. No sweat."

Matthew looked directly at his son, noting the troubled gaze which didn't quite meet his and the faint tremor of the hands polishing the forks.

"How can I help?" he asked.

Will shook his head. "You can't. It's – it's just going to be what it is. Maybe Mr. Howard has had a talk with all those guys' parents and nobody will mess with me. Maybe."

"Maybe. Do you want me to go in with you and talk to Mr. Howard?"

"No! I mean, no. No thanks. That would just make it worse. You know, 'Sissy Ryersen has to hide behind his daddy.'"

"Oh." Matthew considered for a moment and then withdrew his hands from the dishwater and dried them. "I do know one thing to do, if you'll let me."

"What?"

"I'd like to pray for you."

Will backed up a couple of steps. "Now?"

Matthew smiled, remembering his own response to other people's prayers in the beginning. "Yeah, now, here, out loud. Nobody here but the three of us, and the folks in the other room won't interrupt. I promise nothing weird is going to happen, either."

"You can't say that," Will insisted, backing up another step. "I remember lots of weird stuff, like when Pastor Corrigan prayed over your knee, and when I heard that voice in Chicago that time – "

"Sometimes God comes close. He never does it to hurt us, Will. He wants to show how much He loves us. I know you have this idea He doesn't love you anymore, but it's not true. He loves you like crazy. And He tells us to pray. Will you let me, please?"

Will sighed and stood still, as if he knew his father was going to lay hands on him. "All right. Why not?"

Matthew came close to Will and put his hands on Will's shoulders, bending his head until their foreheads were almost touching. He closed his eyes and took a deep breath –

And the phone rang.

"I'll get it!" Will said and grabbed the receiver.

Allison grabbed the receiver. "Hello?"

"Allison, this is Alice."

Allison frowned at her reflection in the mirror over the couch. Why was Alice calling on Sunday afternoon, just to check up on her?

"Hey, Alice! If you want to know whether I'm sober or not, why don't you come on over and join me for some mint chocolate chip ice cream? That's my drug of choice these days. I have a meeting tonight, too, and you could come with me to be sure I'm going. Meetings are loads of fun."

"Allie, that isn't why I called."

Allison registered that Alice's voice was flat and serious, neither her usual good humor nor the suspicious, tight tone Allison had come to know before she went into treatment. "I'm sorry, Alice. What is it?"

"I just thought you should know before you come in to work tomorrow..."

A chill ran down Allison's back. "Am I fired?"

"No, no! No, it's – well, it's Benjie. They brought him in to the e.r. a couple of hours ago – shaken baby syndrome, Allie. He didn't make it. I'm so sorry."

Allison fell onto the couch. "No. He was supposed to be safe in foster care. This can't be right; the social worker promised!"

"I'm sorry. Would you like me to come over?"

"Thanks, but I'll be all right. I'll – just – go to my meeting..."

"Why don't you call Matthew if you don't want me? I know he'd come."

"I'm fine, Alice. Fine. Thanks for letting me know ahead of time. I'll see you in the morning." Allison disconnected the call with her finger but sat there holding the receiver until the incessant beeping and recorded hang-up message finally penetrated her shock. Carefully hanging up the receiver, she walked into the bathroom and checked the medicine cabinet. Nothing there but Band-Aids and aspirin. She went into the bedroom and checked the drawer of her nightstand. Nothing there but tissues and a nail file and a Gideon Bible she'd been given in rehab. In the kitchen she found soy sauce and mustard and chocolate syrup in the fridge, but no beer. The cupboards held cereal and canned soup and chocolate chip cookies, but no whiskey.

I'm safe. I can overdose on Hershey's syrup, but it won't make me fail the drug test and I don't have to confess it at a meeting. God grant me the serenity to accept the things I cannot change.

Giving up her peregrinations, Allison lay down on the bed and pulled the spread over herself. As she remembered Benjie, slow tears began to flow and she felt again the dull ache of empty womb and empty arms. *You must not be real after all. What kind of a god kills babies? How could you let this happen! He was so little and helpless! Why didn't you take care of him?*

The church basement was pretty much like all the other church basements in the area, slightly dark and worn, a bit low-ceilinged, fitted with ugly old masonite-topped long tables and brown metal folding chairs. It had vaguely unpleasant odors of mildew and ancient cigarette smoke, from the days when smoking had been allowed and AA meetings had resembled seedy politicians' secret meetings in smoky back rooms.

Tonight it was just vaguely depressing, the lighting poor and the coffee as bad as usual. Allison filled her cup anyway and added three creamers and four packets of sugar.

"Don't see how you can stand that!" said the man standing next to her. "I drink it just the way God made it." He gave her an engaging grin which featured deep dimples and tossed dark hair back from his forehead. "My name's Frank, by the way. You must be new here; I'd remember such a pretty girl."

"My name's Allison," she replied, giving him a provocative once-over. "We must not have met, because I'd remember a jerk who tried to hit on the new girl." Leaving him gawking, she found a seat on the far side of the table.

A tall, slender woman with close-cut gray hair took the seat to Allison's right. "Hi, I'm Carol. Nice job with Frank over there."

"I'm Allison. Does he do that with all the women?"

Carol laughed and took a swig of the Pepsi she was carrying. "Yep, pretty much. Even the older ones like me. He won't be messing with you again anytime soon, though."

"Good. I'm not in a mood to be messed with." Allison sipped her coffee and wiped a smidgeon of lipstick from the rim of the cup.

The chairman called the meeting to order, and Allison relaxed into the safe and comfortable routine of AA meetings. This one was a discussion meeting, and the topic was Step Two, which the chairman read: "Came to believe that a power greater than ourselves could restore us to sanity." As they went around the table, each person introduced himself or herself by first name, followed by, "...and I'm an alcoholic" or "...an alcoholic and addict." The whole group would enthusiastically respond, "Hi!" and the person's name. Allison tried to pay attention to the comments people were making.

They seemed to fall into two categories: some people focused on 'sanity,' and whether they were insane or not; some focused on the concept of a 'higher power.' The latter group seemed to be the majority tonight, and the majority of them ended up saying, "...whom I choose to call God..."

Carol was nudging her. "Oh. Sorry. Uh – my name's Allison, and I'm an alcoholic."

"Hi, Allison," they chorused.

"I – uh – I'm still pretty new at this, but I guess I have been insane. It's insane to think you can drink like a fish and not get in trouble at work or with your family. It's insane to think nobody notices. It's insane to know you're losing control but to think this time will be different. I get that part now. But this 'higher power' thing – God? I think that's a bunch of crap. What kind of a god would let us get so screwed up in the first place? Either he wouldn't have any power, or he'd be the meanest son – I mean, jerk – in the world. So I guess the only power greater than myself that I'm going to trust is the group. I thought about drinking this afternoon, but I thought about having to come here and tell you what I did – so I didn't do it. That's all."

"Keep coming back!" they chorused loudly.

Carol patted her shoulder. "Good job!"

The end of the meeting followed soon, and everyone stood in a circle, holding hands while they recited The Lord's Prayer. Allison didn't speak, because she didn't believe it, but she bowed her head, respectful of those who did. Halfway through the prayer, she had to open her eyes and look around the circle, because the hair was standing up on her arms and something seemed to be going on in the room.

Nobody else seemed to notice anything; they hugged and chatted and cleaned up the room. Carol came back and gave Allison her phone number "just in case."

It must have been just me, Allison thought to herself on the drive home. *Just one more proof of insanity.*

Thirty-Two

WHEN WILL GOT ON THE BUS, HE WAS RELIEVED to see Travis and Kevin motioning to him from the last seat. That dilemma was covered, at least. Kevin rose to let Will sit in the middle, squashing in on the aisle to present a barrier.

"Thanks," Will said, hunching his shoulders together.

"We got your back," Trav said.

When the bus decanted them into the stream of students going into the building, Kevin and Travis stayed on either side of Will, or one beside and one behind, all the way to his locker and into his homeroom class. They were with him in calculus and English classes, and they ate lunch with him at the losers' table, even though they could have sat somewhere else. At the end of the day, they marched him out to the bus and rode in their sentinel positions all the way to his stop.

This procedure was repeated Tuesday, Wednesday and Thursday. But on Thursday afternoon, Kevin twisted his ankle in phys ed and was taken to the hospital. He called Will that night, apologizing because, "Man, I can't hardly crutch to the bathroom. My mom's gonna let me stay home tomorrow, and then she'll drive me to school next week. I'm sorry, Will."

"Hey, it's not your fault. Well, maybe your fault for being a clumsy dork, but it's okay. Trav can be my bodyguard. I haven't even seen those guys except at a distance."

As he ended the phone conversation, Will wondered what Friday would bring. He was pretty sure they were only keeping their distance while watching for an opportunity. If his only ally was Travis, that wouldn't stop them. Trav was a good friend but probably a poor fighter. He was short and skinny and nice. Pete and Chance would eat his lunch for sure.

"You need to eat more than that," Pearl said, nodding at the small pile of hamburger, tomato and macaroni casserole on Will's plate. "You, too, Matthew."

"Yes, ma'am," they said in unison, bringing smiles to everyone's faces. But neither took another spoonful.

Will didn't know whether his dad just didn't like the stuff or was having some kind of problem; he knew for himself that his gut was too knotted up to swallow much. He forced down a couple of bites and watched Matthew do the same.

"I don't know why I bother," Carolyn sighed. "I could just hand you each half a glass of milk and a cookie and be done with it. Will, what's the matter with you?"

He turned red. "Nothing. Just not hungry." He tried to make himself take another bite, but it just didn't happen. "I got homework; may I please be excused?"

"No dessert?" Carolyn asked.

"No, thanks. Maybe later." He scooped up his dishes and darted into the kitchen, then up the stairs.

"That boy is scared," Pearl said. "I had Ed Lewis in school, and I've half a mind to give him a call."

John laughed and said, "You'll scare him to death, Pearl. Maybe it's worth a try..."

"No," Matthew said. "I offered to talk with Mr. Howard and Will pretty much begged me not to. He thinks it'll be worse if we interfere any more. He may be right."

"So we don't do anything?" Carolyn asked. "Just let him get beat up again?"

"It's been four days," Ed said, "and nothing's happened. Maybe they give up."

John shook his head. "I wish I could agree with you, Ed, but I think they're just biding their time. We need to keep praying for Will's safety, and for the Lord to reach the hearts of those boys and

214

turn them around. If anything else happens, I don't see any choice but to go to the police."

Friday morning Will sat in the rear seat of the bus with Travis, who took the aisle position. They walked into school together but separated at Trav's homeroom. "See ya at lunch," Travis said.

Will entered his own homeroom as quietly as he could, easing his way to his seat in the back row. Tracy came bubbling in with Susan and some other girls and came to sit beside him.

"How's it going?" she asked.

Will allowed himself a deep breath of the baby shampoo and roses scent that was Tracy these days before answering, "Fine."

"You hear about Kevin?"

"Yeah. Guess he'll be back Monday," Will said, keeping part of his attention toward the front of the room, where Pete Coombs was now seated. Mrs. Mulroney turned toward the board to write some gem of wisdom and Pete turned toward Will and Tracy. "Jerk," Will muttered.

"What?"

"Nothing. I like your hair."

"Thank you!" Tracy blushed lightly, making her even more beautiful, making Will's tongue cleave to the roof of his mouth.

Fortunately, the bell rang and scotched any further conversation before Will could make a complete fool of himself. He and Tracy waited in the back until Pete had left before going to their first period classes.

In the lunchroom, Will and Travis sat with Tracy, and the jocks ignored them, except for the fulminating glares Pete sent Will's way from time to time. Chance was in great form, telling stories that captivated his group of jocks and cheerleaders. His handsome face shone with laughter and self-admiration. Will wished he would have a heart attack and drop dead face first into his tater tots.

That hopeless wish must have showed on Will's face, because Chance made a detour on the way out of the lunchroom.

"Hey, Ryersen."

"What do you want, Chance?" Travis asked.

"I'm not talking to you, sissy-boy. I'm talking to the fag, here."

Tracy stood up and glared up at Chance. "You shut up, you big

215

bully. Go away!"

"Still hiding behind the little woman, huh?" Chance taunted. "Well, that's cool for now. But she can't cover you twenty-four/seven. So just remember, it's coming."

Will stood up, which put him eye-to-eye with Chance. "Thank you for the warning," he said softly. "I appreciate it very much." He picked up his tray and walked across the cafeteria to the trash bins as if he couldn't feel daggers at his back.

"What's with you, man?" Travis asked, his voice cracking only a little. "Why are you so down on Will? I know he never did anything to you – or any of you guys."

"We don't like his kind in our school," Chance said. "Can't see why you do, either, unless you're the same kind. Is that it?"

"You'd better get away from here," Tracy snarled. "I may have an accident with this tray any minute!"

Chance laughed an easy laugh and pivoted on his heel. "Later," he called over his shoulder as he followed Will's path to the trash bins.

"I wish I were a football player," Tracy said to Travis. "I'd kick his – well, you know."

"I do," Trav agreed. "And I wish I was, too. I can't even kick my little brother's you-know."

"If I knew which one of those trouble-makers is making all these hang-up calls, I'd call his mother and give her what-for!" Pearl said to Carolyn as she dropped the receiver back into its cradle for the umpteenth time. She pursed her lips until all the little wrinkles stood out as she flounced back into her chair.

"Let's not tell Matthew and Will and the others," Carolyn said, joining Pearl at the table. They were snapping the last of the beans to freeze, and the big enamel basins brimmed with produce, the green smell growing as the raw ends of the snapped beans were exposed. Carolyn inhaled with pleasure and popped a raw bean into her mouth. "I love these!"

"Well, if you have to have cravings, I guess raw vegetables are better than pickles and ice cream," Pearl smiled. Then her frown returned, aging her quickly. "I'm still praying, and so far nothing has happened at school, but how long will that last?"

"I don't know. I don't understand the whole bullying thing. When

I think of our baby growing up to go through something like this, I can hardly stand it. I don't remember kids being so mean when we were in school." Carolyn ferried her basin of snapped beans to the stove and dumped them into a kettle of boiling water to blanch them.

"Oh, I think there have always been bullies. Look at Cain and Abel. Well, no, don't look at them, because that certainly didn't turn out well! I do remember certain children when I was teaching – but most of them were obvious misfits, skinny little runts or boys who loved piano lessons – you know. Will isn't like that. Here, take those beans out!"

Carolyn quickly scooped the beans into a colander in ice water to stop the cooking process and dumped the second basin of raw beans into the boiling water. "I love the way they get so bright green!" She took the chilled beans out of the ice water and set the colander to drain in the sink. "No, Will's tall and strong, and he has presence. Not like a football star, but he's no wimpy, strange kid. Just quiet." She moved the second batch of beans from boiling to ice and then set the second colander in the other half of the sink to drain.

"I think we'll have these all in bags before supper," Pearl said, clearing away the bean scraps. "A freezer is a wonderful thing! I remember when we cooled milk in the springhouse and later bought huge blocks of ice from the ice man for the icebox. It came packed in sawdust; he cut it from the river during the winter and stored it in an underground pit full of sawdust from the mill. Now, don't bother making any remarks about my age," she added, a twinkle in her dark eyes.

"It must be wonderful to remember so many changes," Carolyn said, spreading the drained beans on towels to dry. "I wonder what our children will remember when they get to be old – uh, older."

"I wish I could be around to find out! The world has its terrible aspects, but it still never ceases to amaze me."

"Will only has this year to go, then he'll graduate and be out of Lewiston High School. Maybe he'll go to college and fit in better there. Maybe he'll be one of the ones to invent something to amaze all of us." Carolyn smiled to herself and patted the side of her abdomen, where little Longsuffering was doing push-ups. "Maybe this baby girl will shop on the moon."

"Heaven forbid!" Pearl was about to say more when the phone

rang again.

"I'll get this one," Carolyn said, forestalling Pearl, moving to the phone. "Hello? No, I'm sorry, he's not available right now. Who? Oh. Yes, I'll give him your message."

"A real conversation this time," Pearl said.

"Yes. It was the guidance counselor from school, Mrs. Yancy. She wants Will to stop by her office tomorrow during home room to talk about the ACT tests. I guess he has to take those to get into college."

"Good. He'll do well, and he can get a scholarship out of here."

"Pearl! Surely you don't want him to go away!"

"Surely I do. That boy has no more interest in being a farmer than – than I do. He needs to go somewhere to find out who and what he is."

"What'd you do, man?" Travis asked as they rode the bus home.

"Nothing. She wanted to talk to me about taking the ACT. Said I should have taken it last year, but I can still do it next month."

"Yeah. Kevin and me took it last year, but you said you didn't want to. How come your dad didn't make you?"

"I didn't tell him."

"You gonna tell him this time?"

"Nah. I'll just do it. Mrs. Yancy said I don't have anything to lose if I don't want to go to college, but I have to have it if I do want to go, even to Northwest State."

"Yeah, a community college isn't bad – cheaper than four-year schools, and a lot of the credits transfer if you want to go for a four-year degree."

"How'd you get so smart about colleges all of a sudden?" Will asked, grinning and elbowing Travis in the ribs.

"I been looking schools up on line. My dad and mom expect me to go, and I guess I want to. I know I'll have a job with my dad, on the farm and in the trucking business, but he says I'll need a degree to take over for him – someday. I think I'm gonna apply to Ohio State; they have a great ag program."

"You want to be a farmer?"

"Sure. I been training for it all my life. And I like my dad's trucking business, the whole business end of things. I think I'll study accounting and business so I can run things for him. I don't 'specially want to ride a tractor all the time – but that's okay, too. What about you?"

"I don't know. I sure don't want to be a farmer! No offense; it just isn't me."

"You ever think about it? What you want to be, I mean."

"Not much. Guess it's about time, though." *If I live long enough to figure it out.*

"Hey, Will! You ought to apply to Ohio State, too! Then we could room together. It's a huge school, so I know they'd have something you'd like to study. Kevin's probably going to go there, too; his dad's an alum. His mom, too, I think."

"Yeah, sure, Trav. I could do that." *Like I'll get good enough scores to win a scholarship. Right. No way Matthew's going to be able to pay for it. Maybe I better go to refrigerator school or something.*

"Your blood pressure's up a little," Dr. Dana told Carolyn, "and you've gained a little more than I would have liked."

"That doesn't make sense," John protested. "Mostly all she eats are fruit and vegetables."

"Is that true?" the doctor asked.

"Carolyn squirmed a little in her chair. "Well, of course not. I do seem to crave raw vegetables, and I figured that's healthy. I don't salt them, either."

The doctor pursed her lips and tapped her fingertips together a few times. "Hm. Are you eating salty things like chips or even popcorn? Do you salt your food?"

"No, not really. I salt when I cook, but not a lot."

"Are you having swelling in your hands and feet?"

"Maybe just a little, at the end of the day. I can still get my rings on and off."

"That's a good thing," Dr. Dana said. "I asked you to come in again now, even though it isn't time for your next regular appointment, because there were some things with your blood work that I didn't like. One of them is an imbalance in your electrolytes, another is a low red blood count. I want to switch you to a different prenatal vitamin and add an iron supplement. Now these are horse pills you may find hard to swallow, and they will upset your stomach if you don't take them with food."

"Is this serious?" John asked, forcing his voice to remain calm while his heart threatened to beat out of his chest.

"Not right now," Dr. Dana soothed. "We have a ways to go, though, and I want to keep on top of things. No sudden emergencies in the middle of the night, agreed?"

John and Carolyn nodded furiously.

"So," the doctor continued, "fill the prescription and take these new pills, put away your salt shaker for the duration, rest every afternoon with your feet up, don't eat salty foods like peanuts, chips, popcorn, pickles – anything like that. And try to avoid stress. Let somebody else do the worrying in your house for the next few months, okay?" She gave them the big, luminous smile which so reassured her patients. "This little girl is doing fine, and we're going to bring her to the home stretch just that way. See you in October!"

In the car on the way home, Carolyn looked over at John as he clenched the wheel. His mouth was set in a hard line, and a familiar twitch had appeared in the muscle of his jaw. She put her hand on his knee.

"It's all right, John. Nothing to be alarmed about. I trust Dr. Dana, and she didn't look the least bit upset. It's just something to deal with, not to worry about."

"Don't *you* worry! You heard what she said about avoiding stress!"

"I'm *fine*, John. Really. The only person stressing out is you. Please, honey, let's just trust God together and figure out a substitute for salt on my steak."

John tried to relax his jaw. He tried to ease his grip on the wheel. He tried to sound positive and hopeful as he agreed with his wife. He knew he wasn't a very good liar, but he tried. *God help me! Help me to be calm and strong for her sake. Help me to trust You to take care of her and our baby. Forgive me for this fear – I know it's not from You!*

"Remember the verse, 'The Lord has not given us a spirit of fear, but of power, and of love, and of a strong mind,'" Carolyn said, as if she had been reading John's mind.

"Right. No fear." *'I will fear no evil, for Thou art with me...' Lord, I do believe; help Thou my unbelief!*

"I think lemon juice may be a substitute for salt," Carolyn was saying.

"Sounds – great," he agreed, hoping it was true. He was feeling obliged to fast from salt with her, and he really wasn't looking forward to it. What had happened to the good old days, when all a father had to do was drive his wife to the hospital and sit in the waiting room until it was time to hand out cigars?

"I don't understand!" Allison said to Alice. "Why wouldn't there be a funeral for Benjie?"

Alice sighed and tried to still Allison's frustrated pacing. "I don't know, Allie. I guess there isn't money in the county budget for funerals. And probably nobody to come..."

"I'd come! And what about Benjie's mother? I know she didn't do a good job, but I think she loved him." Tears began to flow down Allison's cheeks as she thought of Benjie's mother. She was thinking at the same time of her own babies, with no funerals and no graves to visit and no one to mourn their passing except their mother.

"Stop it!" Alice commanded as she stood up and put her arms around the tiny woman pacing in front of her. "Just stop! You can't do this, Allie. Here, blow your nose." She handed Allison a handful of tissues. "I know it makes you sad, but you can't do this to yourself. It's bad for the job and it's bad for your sobriety."

Allison blew, a decidedly un-princess-like honk, and dropped the tissues into the wastebasket under the desk. "You're right. All I need is for somebody from personnel to come checking up on me and find me in a mess. They'll be sure I'm using." She straightened the front of her scrub top, smoothing down Pooh Bear and Piglet, and took another tissue to wipe any residual mascara from under her eyes. "Do I pass muster?"

"You do. Now go do vitals on those kids."

As Allison charted the vital signs of seven children between five and sixteen, all of whom were recovering well from the minor surgeries or pneumonias which had put them on her ward, she continued to think about Benjie. Where was he now, and who was taking care of him? Did babies go to heaven, if there was a heaven? Did they go to hell because they didn't "have Jesus in their hearts" like the preachers said?

How could You do that to a baby? What kind of God are You, anyway? Why don't You pick on somebody Your own size!

Thirty-Three

L EWISTON HIGH SCHOOL LOST THE LAST TWO FOOT-
ball games in September and the first one in October.
   Pete Coombs blamed his poor October showing on lack of
practice, Will Ryersen's fault.

On the second Monday in October, Will found the football con-
tingent waiting for him by his locker after school. He walked away
and made it safely to the bus, but he knew the armistice, if that was
what it had been, was over.

Dr. Hanna prescribed medication for John's heartburn and Dr.
Dana prescribed short walks for both John and Carolyn. Carolyn's
blood pressure and blood counts were normal, and all three gave a
huge sigh of relief. Walking in the cool, clear October air, holding
hands the way they had when they were dating, John and Carolyn
floated in peace and trust.

Pearl was knitting a pink baby jumper with matching bonnet and
booties.

Matthew also felt a peace he hadn't felt in a long time. The problems with Will seemed to have gone away, and he was hopeful about
his relationship with Allison, although he had to keep shoving down
a notion that she was keeping something important from him.

Allison attended three meetings per week whether she wanted to or not and checked in with the HR department once a week. She was already accustomed to having the HR nurse appear, cup in hand, at unexpected moments. She made it a point to keep well-hydrated so that she could provide the required specimen at will.

She managed to stuff down her memories of Benjie, and she didn't tell anyone how often he visited her in dreams. They'd think she was crazy, and she didn't need that! She thought about telling Matthew everything, but she didn't want to spoil their infrequent time together with sad things. What if he didn't understand? After all, kids weren't at the top of his list the way they were for hers.

Thirty-Four

WILL HANDED OVER FORTY-NINE DOLLARS AND fifty cents in cash in exchange for his ACT papers and walked into the Lewiston High School in-school detention room, the test site, where he traded his papers for a test booklet and waited for the word to begin. He was surrounded by a couple of dozen other high school kids, male and female, all different races and types, some from Lewiston and many not, all looking less nervous than Will felt.

I gotta be nuts to be doing this! I don't have a chance of a good score! I bet these guys have studied with those tutors I heard about and know everything down pat. What's the use? Maybe if I leave right now they'll give me my money back. Fifty bucks would buy a lot of other stuff. I don't want to tell Kevin and Trav I flunked, or Tracy. At least I didn't tell anyone at home I'm here...

The test proctor, Will's English teacher Mrs. Bender, gave the go-ahead, and all the young faces bent to their work. Will stared at the first page for a while without even really seeing it, sweat forming on his hands and forehead, negative self-talk still running through his head: *I can't. I was stupid to think I could...* He gripped the number two pencil so hard it snapped in half, drawing glares from surrounding students. Mrs. Bender stalked toward him and held out her hand for the two halves. Will nearly gaped in surprise as she handed him another pencil – and smiled!

No, came another voice, one he hadn't heard in a long time, *no, you don't have to listen to that. You are smart enough to take this test and pass it well. Just do it. You can. You can.*

When he finally handed in all his work, Will found himself so tired he could hardly walk through the huge old building and across the parking lot to the truck. Once inside, he leaned on the steering wheel for a while trying to gain enough strength to drive home. His hand was shaking from all that writing, and his stomach ached with hunger.

Burger King, he thought, *Taco Bell. McDonald's. Pizza Hut. Yeah!*

With enough energy generated by the thought of fast food, Will managed to start the truck and find his way to McDonald's. He stoked his furnace all the way home, pausing his thoughts long enough to think about what he would say when he got to the house; he had told everyone he was spending the day with Kevin, but they would ask what they had done together.

It just might be easier not to lie, Will thought briefly, but he smothered that foolish idea before it could grow.

"So what did you and Kevin do all day?" Pearl asked.

"Uh – you know – just messed around. He still can't walk much without his ankle hurting, so we – uh – played video games and stuff."

"Really."

"Yes, ma'am." Will didn't look her in the eye.

"I see."

Busted. I don't know how she knows, but she does. Rats!

"Grandma?"

"Yes?"

"Can I tell you something?" Will looked at her then, squirming like a worm on a hook, and she looked back at him with fierce black eyes. He cringed.

"Go ahead," Pearl said. "Let's sit down in the living room while you do."

Pearl sat in Carolyn's chair and Will tentatively sat opposite her in John's chair. He was never comfortable there, but it seemed the right place. "I lied."

"I know."

"I mean, it isn't anything bad..."

"Lying is a sin, Will. Don't minimize what you do. Why did you feel the need to lie to me in the first place?"

Man, she's fierce! "I – I just didn't want anyone to know what I was doing, in case it doesn't work out."

"What were you doing that you thought would upset people?"

"Nothing! I mean – well, see, the guidance counselor at school, she thought I should take this test called the ACT – "

"I know what it is. I suggested you take it last year, remember?"

Will hung his head. "Yes, ma'am, I remember. I didn't see why I should, back then. I mean, I didn't think about college. But this year I like my classes, and I got to thinking... Anyway, Mrs. Yancy said I should do it, and Travis and Kevin said I should do it, and I had enough money saved to pay for it – so – "

"So you've spent your Saturday taking the ACT, and you weren't going to tell any of us about it."

"Yes, ma'am."

"You thought we would be upset with you for testing?"

"No, ma'am. I mean – I don't know! I didn't want to have to tell you I flunked."

Pearl shook her head, and a small smile escaped her control. "Do you think you – 'flunked'?"

"I don't know. It was long. It wasn't as hard as I thought it would be, but maybe I just didn't get how hard it was. I just figured if I flunk I don't have to be – you know – humiliated, because I –uh – I had the scores sent to Kevin's house. I didn't mean to lie, exactly, just to kinda keep it a secret."

Pearl stood up, in stages, and walked the few feet over to Will, putting her hands on his shoulders. She had shrunk with age; sitting down, he could almost meet her eye-to-eye. Will looked into her wrinkled face and found the lines all formed by her smile this time.

"You don't ever have to worry about disappointing us with your schoolwork, Will. You have been a good student, and we all know how smart you are. You work hard, even when other things in your life are going badly, and we're all proud of you. There's no shame in trying and not doing well."

Will was appalled to feel his eyes filling with tears.

"Stand up," Pearl ordered, and he complied.

"Now, then," she said and put her arms around him, drawing him into a hug.

Will could hardly believe it was happening! He felt something melting inside as he returned the embrace and rested his cheek on top of her head. Pearl didn't like to hug – everybody knew it – but here she was hugging him as if she never planned to let go!

"I love you," Pearl said into Will's chest, "and Jesus does, too. You are good enough. You are worth everything, which is exactly what Jesus gave for you. Don't give up on yourself, boy; the best is yet to come."

And then it was over, Pearl turning away and pretending to adjust her hair, apparently as embarrassed by her behavior as Will was. She started to walk out of the room, then turned back:

"And you still owe your father and the rest of your family nothing but the truth."

He nodded helplessly as the old woman trundled out of the room.

"Sure you won't come with us this morning?" Matthew had asked.

It seemed almost like a ritual to Will: every week Matthew asked, he refused, Matthew said –

"Maybe next week."

And Will answered, "Maybe," because he didn't like to see the disappointment on everyone's faces.

And when they came home, they would talk about the sermon at the dinner table to make sure Will got the message whether he wanted it or not. And one of them, usually Carolyn, would remark in passing that she had seen Tracy.

This week they had gone through the ritual again, and Will was alone in the house, rattling around like a single dried pea in a pod. The silence weighed a ton on his shoulders, so he went to his room and turned the radio to his favorite hard rock station, letting AC/DC's "Hells Bells" roar around him and pound in his chest. He tried a few dance moves, but even without confirmation in the mirror on the back of the closet door, he knew they were lame.

He went to his back pack, which leaned against the desk, and opened the "secret" compartment on the inside of the flap, withdrawing a legal-sized white envelope addressed to Matthew Ryersen at Kevin's address. Kevin had brought it to him Friday, but he hadn't had the nerve to open it yet.

So do it, stupid. Just rip off the end and haul it out and get it over with. Like pulling off a Band-Aid. Do it!

With a here-goes-nothing shrug, Will drew out the paper and read it quickly. Then again. Then a third time. It couldn't be. There had to be some other Will Ryersen – *Yeah, right. It's you. And you did it.*

The end-zone dance Will was doing now was pure joy on the hoof. He waved the paper over his head again and again, whooping and hollering like the idiot he knew he was, but unable to stop. It was only nine-thirty, according to his alarm clock, and he wouldn't be able to tell anybody for the next three hours. He thought he might explode before that!

He remembered time passing this slowly in juvie, but never on the outside. Will tried to sleep, but the adrenaline was still coursing through his veins, making it impossible even to lie down, much less fall asleep. He tried to read, but the words didn't seem to mean anything. *I did it. I did it! Now I can – what? What do I want to do with my life if I really get a choice?*

As the cars pulled up to the house, Will came tearing down the steps as if something were on fire.

"What in the world – ?" Carolyn said.

Before anyone could say anything else, Will ripped open the passenger door and shouted, "I did it!"

Matthew climbed quickly out of the back seat, prepared for something terrible, but he was arrested mid-step by the unmistakable delight on his son's face as the boy grabbed him in a bear-hug, chanting, "I did it! I did it!"

John got out more slowly and smiled at the wild boy and his taken-aback father. "What did you do?" he asked.

"What's going on?" Pearl asked as she and Ed converged on them from the El Camino.

"We don't know yet," John said, "because Will hasn't settled down enough to tell us. It seems to be something good, though, so let's go inside and find out about it."

All trailed in behind John and Carolyn, all by now grinning in spite of themselves because no one could recall ever having seen Will so happy and excited, not even when they got the new truck. Finally everyone was seated at the dining room table and the ham and scalloped potatoes and succotash had been passed. The prayer had been said, calmly, without hurrying through, and even Will had managed an 'amen.'

"Now," said John, "what's going on, Will? It looks too good to keep to yourself."

With the moment of revelation upon him, Will suddenly felt shy and stupid. Why did he think it would matter that much to anybody else, anyway?

"Go ahead, boy," Pearl said. "Suspense isn't good for this old heart." She winked at him.

Taking a deep breath, Will said, "Mrs. Yancy, the guidance counselor, wanted me to take a thing called the ACT, a test for getting into college. Kevin and Trav took it last year, and I know Tracy took it, too, so I thought – why not? A couple of weeks ago, that Saturday I told you I was spending the day with Kevin? I went to the school and took the test. It was long, and it was hard, and I figured I flunked. I had them send the report to Kevin's house so you wouldn't know and I wouldn't be humiliated – "

"You lied about it?" Matthew said.

Will looked down at his plate and nodded. "Yeah, kinda."

"Will!" Pearl snapped.

He sighed. "Yes, ma'am." He made eye-contact with Matthew, pleading for understanding. "Yes, sir, I did lie. I'm sorry. I was so afraid I couldn't do it – couldn't pass like the other guys did – and I didn't want any of you-all to be ashamed of me." He hung his head.

"You-all," Carolyn noted. "He's gone Kentucky on us, Matthew, just like you do. Will, honey, we would never be ashamed of you for trying to do a hard thing and not managing it."

"Looks to me," Ed said, "like you done better than you thought. Can't imagine you'd be jumping around the yard yelling like that if you flunked it. So how'd you do?"

Will's eyes were filled with wonder and his smile stretched ear to ear as he looked at his father and said, "I got a thirty-two, Dad. That's – that's a really high score. Like thirty-six is as high as it goes."

All around the table faces beamed and hands clapped and voices exclaimed congratulations, but for Will only one opinion mattered – and Matthew hadn't moved or said a thing.

He's not impressed. He doesn't care. All he cares about is that I lied.

Just before Will could bolt from the table, Matthew stood up and walked around the table to him, dragging him up from his chair into a hug. "I – am – so proud of you, son! That's fantastic! You sure didn't get it from me."

The heat swept over Will from toes to head and he thought little bubbles were fizzing in his veins. *Proud of me! He never said that before. But I lied...*

"I'm sorry," Matthew was saying, and Will forced himself to pay attention. "I'm sorry you felt like you couldn't trust me enough to tell me the truth. I wish I knew what to do to earn that trust. Please forgive me."

"Dad – I – sure. It's – "

"Sit down and eat your dinner before it's cold," Pearl instructed, and they both resumed their chairs at once. "Now, then, Will, have you decided what you want to do with this amazing score?"

"Do with it?"

"I think she means applying to colleges," John said, smiling at Pearl, who returned a flinty look at being interpreted.

"Oh. No, I – I never figured I'd be able to go, because it costs too much."

"You need to understand," Pearl said, "that a score like that, with your good grades, will make you eligible for scholarships and will just about guarantee admission to quite a few schools. Maybe not Harvard or Stanford, but good schools, nonetheless."

"Sure beats being a farmer, don't you think?" Ed teased, well aware of Will's lack of enthusiasm for the farm.

"I guess so, for me. But I don't know what else I – "

"And you don't have to decide today," Carolyn said, settling the matter. "Just eat and be glad; that's enough for now."

"Matthew," John said, changing the subject, "if you don't mind, I'd like you to bring in the corn over on the Harris acres. It'll take you into the night, I think, but we have a lot to get in, not just there, and it's supposed to rain Tuesday, Wednesday and Thursday. If things get wet and it cools down like it's been doing at night, we're going to have corn rotting in the ear."

"No problem. I'll just pack a lunch and work as late as I need to."

"That works," Ed said. "I'll finish off across the road here, and college boy can help me with the milking."

Matthew enjoyed riding the combine over the ripe cornfields, especially on such a beautiful late October day. The cab was warm, the sun was clear, the sky was beautifully blue and the birds flew up before the monster machine as if they were orchestrated.

Lord, thank You for all this beauty! Thank You for being a God of second chances and bringing me to this family, this farm, this time of my life. Thank You for Will, and for this wonderful opportunity opening up for him! I knew he was smart, but he must be a genius!

Hours passed, and the sun grew orange as it sank toward the horizon.

Time for dinner. I guess I can just eat while I drive. Not going to get this done before dark, though.

Will managed to do some homework and help with the milking, even though he still felt a crazy disconnect, as if his feet weren't quite touching the ground. Ed teased him about grinning like a loon, and Carolyn and Pearl couldn't stop patting him every time he came in range. After supper, he decided to call Tracy, the one person he most wanted to tell now.

"Hi," she said. "What's up?"

"You aren't going to believe it!" Will replied. "Say, can I come over? I want to tell you this in person."

"Oh – well – I guess so. Let me ask my mom; hang on."

Will waited, tapping his foot and tapping his fingernails on the counter and sighing with impatience, until finally he heard her voice again, bubbly and glad.

"Mom says it's okay for you to come over. She even said I can go for a ride with you if we don't stay out late."

"I'm on my way," he promised, then remembered his dad had the truck up at the Harris fields. *Rats.* "Hey, John, can I borrow your truck? Dad has ours, and I want to go see Tracy."

"Sure," John said easily. "I don't need to go anywhere."

"Thanks! I'll be careful." He snatched the keys and ran.

"Hot date," John said to Carolyn, smiling.

"What is it?" Tracy asked before Will was even through the door. "What? What?"

Laughing, he said, "You aren't going to believe it, but – well – "

"Will, you're blushing!" Tracy teased.

"Could we just ride? I don't want to tell your mom or anything..."

Moments later they were driving down a country road, watching the moon and stars come out in the clear October sky. Tracy had brought a sweater, a dark green that brought up the green in her eyes, and she snuggled into it waiting for the heater to kick in.

"It's not that cold," Will joked. "But I can hold your hand if it's chilly."

"Maybe that would be a good idea," she said softly, moving her left hand to seek his right. "Now can you tell me what's happened?"

"Let's get out and walk in the moonlight," Will said. "If you're cold I can put my arm around you."

He parked the truck in a farmer's turnaround at the edge of a corn-field and left the keys in the ignition. As they walked hand in hand down the county road, Will realized they were near the Harris place. "My dad's over there harvesting corn," he said, nodding his head in the general direction of the fields.

"It must be nice," Tracy said, "being able to work outside like that. Peaceful. Is that what you're going to do, Will?"

"I thought I might have to, because there's no money for college, and I didn't figure I'm that smart, but – "

"But what?"

"I didn't tell you before, because I was so sure it wouldn't work out – but I took the ACT a couple of weeks ago – "

Tracy's squeal of joy could probably be heard in Williams County as she threw her arms around Will, jumping up and down. He hugged her back, a moment of pure bliss – she was there, she cared, he had finally done something right.

Then Tracy pulled back and said, "You took the ACT and you didn't tell me? Will, how could you!"

"I didn't want to have to tell you I screwed it up."

"Oh, but I could have prayed for you."

"Yeah, I guess you're right. But somebody must have, because –

Tracy, I got a thirty-two!"

Tracy stopped dead in her tracks and swung Will around to face her. "A thirty-two! I only got a twenty-seven, and even Kevin only got a twenty-eight! You're brilliant!" She threw her arms around him again and administered a hug which removed testing from his mind immediately.

Remembering that Tracy was a nice girl, Will disentangled himself gently long before he wanted to and smiled down at her. "Thanks. I guess I was dumb to handle it that way. But who would have thought I'd pass?"

They resumed walking, Will's arm around her now, the green of her sweater almost black in the moonlight. Off in the distance to their right, on the other side of the road, he saw the headlight of his father's combine.

"Have you thought about college?" Tracy asked. "I mean, now you can get scholarships."

"That's what Pearl said. I think – I think maybe I'd like to go... But I don't have any idea what I want to study. I mean, what *do* I want to be when I grow up? Trav and Kevin, it's all about the farm. But not me. And it's not like it's my dad's farm, anyway, you know?"

"Well, let's pray about it and ask the Lord to show you the way."

"Uh – maybe some other time, okay? No offense, but I just – "

"I know," Tracy sighed. "I am going to pray for you, though. If you don't like that – tough." She took the sting out by hugging him again, grinning all over her face.

He grinned back at her, tightening his embrace. "Tracy..."

"What?"

There's only one thing I want to do right now..."

She apparently could read his mind, because she stood on tiptoe and raised her mouth to his in a gentle kiss, their first, and now he knew he had died and gone to heaven.

But angel kisses heated up just as fast as the other kind, and Will forced himself to back off. "I – maybe we better walk some more, okay?"

"Sure."

She sounds disappointed! Man!

They joined hands and took a few meandering steps down the road before they heard the sound of an engine coming, moving them quickly onto the verge, where Will put himself in front of Tracy, just in case.

"You're so gallant," she teased. "My white knight!"

He couldn't help himself; despite the oncoming car he just had to draw her into his arms for one more quick kiss, a kiss that should have been over in seconds but had a mind of its own, leaving them locked together in the sweep of the headlights as the car rushed past.

"I'm sorry," Will said, having gone from ecstatic to miserable in moments. "I hope that wasn't anyone we know. I hope it wasn't anyone who knows your dad!"

"Don't be silly. My dad's friends wouldn't be out here on a Sunday night. In fact, besides us, I wonder who would be."

"More than one person, I guess," Will said, "because now there's one coming from the other way."

Matthew was nearing his turn by the road when he saw a car fly by and then, moments later, a car come flying from the other direction.

"Durn fools," he muttered. "Probably kids, driving like that on a curvy road in the dark."

Then he noticed the car screech to a stop and three men pile out of it. They seemed to hesitate by the car for a moment, then moved forward as one. At that point Matthew noticed two other figures standing at the far edge of the road. One was small, either a woman or a child. He couldn't hear anything over the mild roar of the John Deere, but he didn't like the way the three moved in on the two, especially when the taller of the duo placed himself between the smaller one and the oncoming men.

"Tracy, stay behind me," Will said, trying to sound much calmer than he felt. "If they start something, run to the truck and lock yourself in and drive outa here."

"I won't leave you!" she said.

"Aw," one of the three said, sarcasm evident in his tone, "isn't that sweet? You stick around, girlie, and we'll have some fun for you when we finish with sissy-boy here."

Will had to try. "Billy, you don't have anything to do with any of this. Why don't you just go get in the car? Pete and Chance want to beat the crap out of me, but it's not your fight."

"The heck it isn't! We lost the last three games because of you, and Pete's still not in shape for this week because he had to sit out all his practices. You screwed all of us, Ryersen, you and your hick dad."

Surprised at how much anger the crack about his father could raise in him, Will struggled for control. He could feel the adrenaline coursing through him, flushing his face, tightening his gut, pumping his arms and legs, settling like a red haze in his head, but he forced himself to draw a deep breath and try again.

"I'm sorry about the team. But Tracy doesn't have anything to do with it, and you'll get in big trouble if anything happens to her. Let her take my truck and get out of here."

"What do you think, Chance?" Pete asked, leering at Tracy.

"If she's too stupid to stop hanging out with a faggot, then maybe watching us beat him to a pulp will wise her up to who the real men are." Chance smiled his best chick-magnet smile at the trembling girl as he said, "You know, Tracy, I could be persuaded to give up Jenny Peterson for you. You'd like being my girlfriend; I'm the most popular guy in school. And I have plenty of money to take you out. Go out with me, and you won't have to call walking down a country road in the middle of the night a date."

"I wouldn't walk out of a burning building with you," Tracy snarled, her voice shaking but still game. "Go home, guys. This is no good. You're going to get in the same trouble again."

Chance laughed, and it was nasty. "Not to worry. You're gonna be our insurance, Tracy. See, if either one of you tattles to Daddy, or anybody else, something really unfortunate will happen to you." He came closer, so that Tracy could see him clearly in the moonlight. "You know what I'm talking about, don't you, babe? Do I look like I'm kidding?"

"You son – " Will took a step which closed the gap between him and Chance and drew back his fist, but Billy stepped in from the side and grabbed his arms.

"It's tempting," Chance said as Will struggled to get free, "but I think Pete gets the first shot."

Before Will could say or do anything else, Pete's huge fist slammed into his face, splitting his lip so the blood flowed freely down his chin, snapping his head back so sharply it ricocheted off Billy's sternum.

Pete drew his fist back again.

Matthew was almost to the edge of the road. He saw the man grab the other man, saw the second man back off and the third man take the first swing. And at the same moment the John Deere's headlight drew close enough to illuminate the players in the drama – Will and Tracy and the football players!

Matthew leaped from the cab and took off running, clearing the drainage ditch like an Olympic broad-jumper and thundering across the road, roaring, "Stop!"

The boys were startled and Pete's fist was arrested in mid-swing as they turned in alarm to see who was coming.

"Uh-oh," Billy muttered, letting go of Will. "Let's get out of here!"

"Don't be stupid," Chance said. "Three of us, one of him, no problem. The fag here isn't going to give us any trouble, are you, fag?"

Matthew skidded to a stop between his son and the others and looked them over, clenching his fists and getting ready for the fight. "What do you think you're doing?" he asked, his voice a scary metallic sound Will had never heard before.

"We were just cleaning up the road," Chance said smoothly. "Don't like to see trash along our lovely Fulton County highways, right, guys?"

"You hurt bad, Will?" Matthew asked without turning around.

"No."

"Then that's it, boys. Go home. I'll be in touch with your parents in a little while. Nobody is going to beat on my son three-to-one, especially not a bunch of punks like you. I've met your father, Chance, and I can't believe he'll be happy about this."

"Chance?" Billy said, almost whimpering.

"Shut up, Billy. Pete, you still want your shot? If you do, let's take daddy first, then sonny-boy. He doesn't like three-to-one, so let's let him try three-to-two."

Matthew sighed and tried to remember whether he had ever even been in a fight. Not that he could recall. *Lord, help us!*

"Dad," Will said, his voice kind of mushy around his rapidly swelling lip, "what are we going to do?"

The three football players laughed hysterically, and Pete stepped up to Matthew. "Okay, old man, here's for the suspension that cost us three games!" He swung from his toes and his fist cracked into Matthew's cheekbone, driving him to the ground.

Will watched with horror as his father fell backward, landing on his tailbone in the gravel at the edge of the road. An immediate purple goose egg rose on his cheek and he sat there dazed for a moment before scrambling to his feet. Pete immediately followed up with another punch, this time to the gut, and Matthew fell again, gasping for breath and then vomiting. The other two boys were moving in like hyenas on fallen prey, and Will knew he should do something to stop them...

Tracy was screaming, over and over, and he didn't know how to stop her. He wanted to do something, anything, but he could only stand there frozen, the pain in his lip throbbing and the terror in his chest paralyzing him.

Dad, get up! Do something!

He watched his father wipe the vomit from his mouth and stand up, clearly wobbling, clenching his fists. He raised his hands...

"That's it!" Chance said. "Fight back like a man! I know you can't be as much of a sissy as your son."

That's it, Dad, fight! I'll help...

Matthew drew back his fist as Pete came at him the third time and – dropped it. Pete's punch connected with Matthew's jaw with the sound of a wrecking ball, and Matthew fell again.

"Get up!" Pete yelled, but Matthew stayed down.

"Dad, get up!" Will cried.

"Stay out of it, sissy-boy," Chance said casually, as if he were just refereeing a kids' ballgame. "Get up, Daddy. Pete's not finished thanking you for ruining his season. You're not being much fun, you know, so let's see you take your best shot. Just one, so we know you have some guts."

Matthew sat up, but he didn't stand. "No," he said. "I'm not going to fight you, and neither are you, Will. This kind of anger is wrong, boys, and I'm not going to let it rule me."

"What's he talking about?" Billy asked.

"I'm talking about forgiving people who hurt you, son. I'm thinking about how Jesus handled it when they beat Him and flogged Him and crucified Him. If He could take all that and still ask God to forgive the people who hurt Him, then I guess I can, too."

"A Jesus freak!" Pete laughed. "What are you, a Quaker? Get up, old man, and fight."

"No," Matthew said again, "I won't."

"Then we're gonna beat the crap out of you," Pete threatened.

"I guess so," Matthew said, arms crossed over his aching stomach.

Will watched in horror as the three closed in on Matthew. Time was hanging suspended like a crystal, and it shattered when Pete's army boot smashed into Matthew's jaw, followed by Billy's kick to his kidneys and, finally, Chance's kick to his head. Blood was beginning to flow from Matthew's scalp and face and his grunts and muffled outcries of pain increased as the three continued to kick him.

It was happening so fast! Tracy had stopped screaming and had her face buried in Will's back, so the sounds of heavy blows and resulting agony were perfectly clear in the still night air.

I have to do something! I can't let them kill him – I can't! But his feet seemed glued to the ground and his hands hung leaden at his sides.

"Had enough?" Chance asked, breathing heavily from the exertion. "Get up and give us one good punch and we'll let you go."

Matthew struggled to a sitting position again and spoke, blood spraying from his lips. "No. I forgive you, Chance. I forgive you, Pete. And I forgive you, Billy. God, please have mercy on these boys."

They swarmed in again, and Matthew went down under a barrage of fists and boots. Pete turned away from his assault and made a move toward Will –

"Tracy, come on!" Will grabbed her hand and ran for the truck, practically dragging her behind him. He flung her into the cab and ran to the other side, leaping inside and hitting the locks. With hands shaking and heart pounding like a jackhammer in his chest, he started the truck and peeled out.

"You can't just leave him!" Tracy said.

"I – I – I can't help him! It's no use if he won't fight! I'll take you home and you can call the sheriff's office like he said. Don't tell your dad!"

"But, Will, they'll wonder – "

"Use the phone in your room! Tell them we went for a ride and now you have some homework to finish. You can't tell them anything! You know what'll happen if you do!"

Will halted the truck by the porch and Tracy ran up the steps without looking back at him.

And now you can go home, hardly hurt at all, to wait and see whether those goons killed your father. Sissy isn't bad enough. Coward!

But it wouldn't have done any good. I couldn't fight all three of them by myself! I can't even fight Pete! It's not my fault; I wasn't looking for trouble.

You are such a loser. No one had better ever put their faith in you.

"Wipe your shoes on the grass," Chance instructed, leading by example.

"Man, that felt good!" Pete exclaimed as they got into the car and drove off.

"Is he dead?" Billy asked. Unlike the other two, he was green and trembling, although he wasn't ready to admit he hadn't enjoyed it as much as they had.

"No," Chance said, "he's not dead. But you can bet he's not gonna mess with us anymore, and neither is sissy-boy. People have to learn you don't mess with us and get away with it."

"Will's gonna call the sheriff," Pete said. "And he's gonna say who did it."

"No, he's not going to say," Chance contradicted. "He isn't going to risk anything happening to Tracy. We go home, we go to school tomorrow, we act normal – and nobody knows any different. We spent tonight at your house, Pete, playing video games. I won."

The pool of blood spreading around the crumpled body on the edge of the road shone black in the moonlight.

Thirty-Five

THE WAITING ROOM OUTSIDE THE SURGERY SUITES looked just like all the other waiting rooms they had sat in over the last few years, and the free coffee tasted just as bad as it did on every other floor in the hospital. John and Carolyn sat close together, his arm around her shoulders and her hands protectively clasping her belly, sheltering little Longsuffering within from the dangers without, while Pearl and Ed sat stiffly upright on hard molded-plastic chairs, sentinels, and Will stood jigging his leg by the window, boring visual holes into the parking lot.

"It's been two hours," Carolyn said.

Nobody responded; what was there to say? They had prayed together, and now most of them were praying privately, Will guessed. He wished he could...

The double doors swooshed open and two men entered the room, both in bloody scrubs, paper hats and paper booties. They all knew Dr. Hanna, their family physician, a heavy-boned, solid man with iron gray hair and bushy gray eyebrows, but the taller, thinner man was an unknown.

"They're all family," Nate Hanna said to his companion. "Talk to all of 'em. Kid over there is his son."

"I'm Dr. Lefley," the taller man said, "and I've just operated on

Matthew. He's holding his own, but I want to explain what's going on before you see him."

Will turned from the window to stare at the doctor. Was that his father's blood all over him?

"Matthew was severely beaten and lost a great deal of blood. We've given him three units so far, and we may have to give more. He appears to have been punched and stomped repeatedly, all over his body. He has six broken ribs, one of which punctured his left lung. We've reinflated that. He has a broken jaw, broken bones all over the right side of his face, and a hairline skull fracture. Both kidneys are severely bruised and bleeding, and I'm still not sure he doesn't have a laceration in his liver somewhere, although I couldn't find it. This means we may have to go back in if the bleeding doesn't stop."

Dr. Lefley paused, as if waiting for questions, but there were none. Everyone just stared at him, frozen, eyes huge and mouths open.

"In addition, of course," the doctor continued, "he's a mass of bruises all over, head to foot. I'm detailing all this for you because you need to be prepared for how awful he looks. Both eyes are swollen shut and his face is probably unrecognizable. I suspect he's going to need plastic surgery on that cheekbone/occiput area.

"But I want you to remember: it looks worse than it is. He's probably going to be just fine."

"Probably?" Carolyn whispered.

The doctor sighed. "Probably. I can't make any guarantees. We have him sedated and on a ventilator right now, to let him rest and start healing. In a day or so we'll get him breathing on his own. We're monitoring his brain for excessive swelling and giving him meds to minimize that."

"Thank you for your work, Dr. Lefley," Pearl said, rising and coming over to shake the doctor's hand. "I trust we will be kept informed of every change."

Dr. Hanna gave a gruff laugh as he looked at his colleague's face. "She's not kidding, Tom. This family won't go home and ignore him – or you." He turned to them and said, "We have him in ICU, and that means only two people back there at a time, ten minutes an hour, but I'm going to take all of you back there at once now so we get it over with and you can go home to bed. I don't want any loud noise or fainting or anything else that gets me in trouble for breaking the rules – got it?"

They nodded in unison and followed after Dr. Hanna like duck-lings as Dr. Lefley stood there shaking his head.

I don't want to see! Will thought, frantically trying to think of a way out of it; but no solution came, and there they were, crowding into the cubicle directly in front of the nurses' station, staring at the thing on the bed.

The ventilator whooshed and clicked, some kind of monitor gave a steady series of beeps, and there were tubes down his throat, through his nose, in both arms – and one snaking out from under the sheet near the bottom of the bed into a plastic collection bag which was filling with blood. Every visible inch was either bandaged or grossly swollen and purple. The thing bore only rudimentary resemblance to a human being.

The only sound in counterpoint to the machines was a soft whimper from Carolyn, who moved forward to place her hand on Matthew's foot, the only part which didn't seem damaged. "Oh, Matthew," she said, then bowed her head and wept quietly.

Pearl marched up to the head of the bed, spine never straighter, and bent over next to what was probably Matthew's ear. "Do not die," she said loudly. "God isn't finished with you. Ask Him to heal you and do – not – die."

"Pearl," Nate Hanna said gently, "he can't hear you."

She turned to face the apostate and mowed him down with a flinty glare. "Of course he can hear me. Even people in deep comas hear. Remember that if you're talking in front of him and don't say anything negative. I mean it, Nate."

"Yes, ma'am," he replied, his smile uneasy and his hands making a surrender gesture in the air.

"Will," John said, "come on up here," but Will was already run-ning away down the hall.

Thirty-Six

IT SEEMED OBSCENE THAT THE MOON WAS STILL SHIN-
ing, although it was much lower down the sky now, that
the stars were so crisp and clear, even against the lights of
Lewiston, when everything had changed. Will huddled on the
stone bench outside the hospital and tried to empty his mind
of the hideous figure on the bed upstairs. He thought maybe he
should be crying, but he felt dry as stone.

*He's going to die, and I killed him. I should have fought for him. I
should have run to the Harris house and called the cops. I should have
found the tire iron in the truck and bashed Pete's head in before he could
hurt him like that! If I hadn't been there, it wouldn't have happened.
They didn't know he was over in that field. If I hadn't come to Lewiston
High, they never would have started anything and he'd never have been
involved. If I hadn't come here, he and Allison would be married now
and making a pretty little baby.*

"You're going to freeze, sitting out here all alone," came a voice
from behind him. He turned to see Allison standing there.

"What are you doing here?"

"I know somebody who knows somebody... Anyway, they know
I – care for your dad, and they called me."

"Have you seen him?"

"Yes, I was just there. He looks terrible, doesn't he?"

"He doesn't even look like himself!" Will felt something rippling
inside him and clutched his arms even tighter around himself.

"In a couple of days the swelling will go down," Allison said, sitting beside Will on the bench, "and he'll look like Matthew again. I think he's going to be all right, Will. He's stable, no particular signs of swelling in his brain, no big bleeding – I think he'll be fine."

"You'd know, wouldn't you?" Will asked softly.

"Yes, I would. I'm a very good nurse, Will, and I'd know." She tentatively put one hand on Will's shoulder, prepared for him to reject her violently.

Instead, he turned to her and buried his face in her shoulder, tears he hadn't been able to feel before suddenly gushing forth like water from the rock.

"It's all my fault!" he sobbed.

"No," Allison returned, hugging him with all her might, "it is *not* your fault. Whoever did this – they're vicious, subhuman beings and deserve to be punished. There's no excuse for battering a man like that – he didn't even have any money, did he?"

"Money?" Will sat up and wiped his nose on his sleeve, half-laughing. "Money! He never has any money! No, it was pure hate."

Allison patted his arm and asked, "What do you mean, it's your fault?"

Oh, no! "Just – just – I – if I'd been there – you know, to help him – "

"Then they could have beaten you, too. Heaven only knows how many men there were, but somebody said there were at least two of them, and they had weapons of some kind."

Nobody knows! The only other people who could tell them are Tracy and I, and we're not talking. I can't; I have to at least keep her safe.

"Yeah," he said, "you're right. Hey, thanks for – uh –"

"You're welcome. I think your family is on their way down now to take you home to bed. Get some sleep, okay? I'll watch over him tonight, I promise. If he needs you, I promise I'll call right away."

"Thanks," Will said again. "You know, I see why my dad l-loves you. You're a nice lady. Take good care of him. I'm going to the car." He ran off toward the parking lot, the Ryersen flush across his ears and face hidden by the dark.

At home, they all went to bed, whether to sleep or not. Will shrugged off Carolyn's mothering and urged her to take care of the baby because he couldn't bear to receive tenderness he knew he didn't deserve. In his room he lay still on the bed and listened to the voice inside his head which told him what a guilty loser he was, not trying to stop it this time because he knew it was true.

On the bus the next morning, Kevin and Travis grabbed him right away and bundled him into the seat between them. "Man, we heard about your dad," Trav said. "How is he?"

"I don't know. I saw him last night, and he looks awful. The – men – hurt him real bad, but I think he's going to live."

"You mean he could die?!" Kevin asked, eyes wide.

"Yeah. But I don't think he will."

"What happened?" Trav asked.

"I – don't know for sure. It seems like somebody beat him up really bad. Maybe a couple of guys."

"I heard he was out at the Harris place," Kevin said. "Why would anybody go out there to beat him up?"

"I. Don't. Know." Will said. "How'd you hear all this, anyway?"

"My dad's an EMT, remember," Travis said, "and we have the scanner and all. He's one of the guys who took your dad to the hospital. He said it was awful!"

"Shut up, Trav," Kevin said. "Yeah, by now pretty much everyone will know something, Will. You know how gossip goes. Don't worry about it. I'm sorry about your dad, and we'll all be praying for him. Mom said to let us know if you need anything."

Will nodded and kept his head down.

A similar scenario played out at school, where teachers and principal and more students than he would have expected expressed sympathy and sought details with poorly concealed avidity. Will kept his head down and kept moving between classes. At one point he saw Chance and Pete and Billy near his locker, and they gave him long, hard stares to remind him to be silent.

He walked up to them with bravado he wasn't feeling and said quietly, "Don't worry, I'm not going to make any trouble. Just stay away from Tracy."

Two weeks went by. Sheriff's deputies came to the house twice to talk to the family, trying to find information about Matthew's attackers, but were finally convinced nobody knew anything about motive or who had done it. Tracy and Will clung to each other in bleak despair, unable to talk, unable to move past it. Matthew underwent plastic surgery on his face and retreated into the safety of pain medication. He told the deputies he couldn't remember anything, which the doctor confirmed could certainly be the case. The rain washed the blood off the road and Ed finished bringing in the corn.

November came, and Matthew came home, recognizably himself, although so thin and frail Will thought the light might shine right through him. He spent a lot of time sleeping, getting up to walk around a little and to eat the soft things he could get past his broken jaw, but he was clearly not himself.

"I don't know what to do!" Carolyn burst out one evening as John was helping her fold some laundry. "There's something – I don't know what's going on, but I know there's more than just Matthew being sick."

"Honey, it'll be all right. I think a man's sense of himself must be shaken by being battered like that. We're supposed to be so tough. I've been trying to think how I'd feel, trying to talk to him about it, but he just shuts me off, too. But you have the baby to think about, and I don't want you getting upset."

"Well, I'm afraid you're too late for that!" She piled folded towels into the laundry basket for John to carry upstairs. "And I'm worried about Will, too."

"I know. Here, give me those tee-shirts and things. I'd rather not pair socks."

"Finicky, aren't you?" she teased. "What about Will?"

"He's shut down again. He avoids his father."

"Do you think he could be – well – ashamed of Matthew? Because he was hurt so badly? I mean, if he thought his father was supposed to be Superman or something..."

"I hadn't thought of that. I guess more prayer is called for."

In the morning, after the chores were done and breakfast over, John took Matthew's breakfast to him on a tray. They were still doing this to save Matthew trips up and down the stairs, although Dr. Hanna said there was no reason he shouldn't be getting back to normal.

"Come in," Matthew called to John's knock on his door.

"Breakfast!" John announced, apostle of the obvious.

Matthew pushed himself up in the bed and took the tray, with its little folding legs, from John. "Thanks." He seemed to be waiting for John to leave, but John pulled over the desk chair and sat down.

"You're welcome. I sure hope you eat everything on that tray, because the womenfolk are fussing a lot about how skinny you are."

"Yeah. I got dressed yesterday to go to the doctor and my jeans fell off without being unzipped. It just still hurts to eat – my jaw – "

"I think you can swallow everything on that tray without chewing, so no excuses, okay?"

"Sure. Oh, goody. Oatmeal."

They grinned at each other, although Matthew's grin was still restrained, and he tucked into oatmeal and soft-scrambled eggs and applesauce as if they were gourmet fare. "You still here for a reason?" Matthew asked, observing John's settled-in look.

"Yep. I've been worrying about you and Will, and I figured enough time's gone by without your saying anything that I'd better just ask. What's going on, Matthew?"

Matthew nearly choked on a bite of egg but managed to wash it down with orange juice. "Would you please ask the dear ladies in the kitchen if I could start having coffee again anytime soon? I don't know why they think I can't handle it – or maybe it's a punishment?"

"You need punishment?" John asked, only half-joking. "Was all this your fault?"

Matthew smiled again and shook his head, "No. That much I do remember: I didn't start anything." He looked away and thought for a moment. "John, I need to tell somebody some things, but I can't unless I have your word you won't tell anyone, even Carolyn."

"That's asking a lot."

"I know, so if you don't want to hear it, I'll – well, I guess I'll talk to Miles. Pastors have to be confidential, don't they?"

"Yes, they do. Okay... You're not going to tell me you killed anybody or stole anything, are you?"

"No!" Matthew laughed.

"Then I'll respect your terms. Go ahead."

Matthew lifted the half-empty tray and John put it on the desk. "I do know who did it," Matthew said, "and I know why. But I'm not going to admit that to anyone but you, and I'm not going to tell you who they were. There's a reason for that."

"I hope it's a good one," John said, anger in his eyes.

"A funny thing happened when they came at me..." Matthew paused, his eyes seeming to focus on something far away. "The first punch knocked me down, and it hurt like the devil. I got up and got ready to cold-cock the guy – as if I could – but when I pulled back my fist – I couldn't do it."

"You couldn't hit him?"

"Yeah. I'd been reading in the Bible what Jesus said about how to treat people who hate you and persecute you, about how He forgave the people who hurt Him and killed Him, and it all came roaring back inside my head. If Jesus could take all that and not lash out – and He could have smashed His enemies with a word! – well, then, who was I to go after those kids in anger?"

"Kids? It was kids?"

Matthew paled. "No! Never mind; I didn't say that!"

"Okay, relax. So you decided to respond in love instead of in anger."

"Yeah, I did. And the funny thing is, I *was* angry; I was ready to kill the guy. And then I wasn't. I felt sorry for him. Sorry for all of them. They egged me on to fight, but I told them I wouldn't because of Jesus and I – "

"You what?"

"I forgave them. I asked God to forgive them."

"Wow. And then?"

"And then they kicked the crap out of me," Matthew laughed.

When Matthew went home from the hospital, it released Allison from her vigil at his bedside and gave her no excuse to avoid AA meetings anymore. No one had said anything, but the hospital HR people had the right to ask her to produce signed slips indicating when and where she had been to meetings; she didn't want to get into any trouble at work. Besides, she kind of missed parts of it, like talking with Carol and some of the other women. It was amazing how similar people's stories were, even though their lives were so different.

Focusing on Matthew had allowed Allison to ignore the pain over Benjie's death, but this particular Tuesday his cute little face seemed to be before her everywhere she went.

"You all right?" Leslie asked as they passed in the hall.

"Fine. Why?"

"You look kind of upset, and you were going to walk by me without even saying hello."

"Oh. Sorry – a lot on my mind."

"Is it Matthew?" Leslie asked, aware, as they all were in pediatrics, of Allison's boyfriend and his terrible injuries.

"He's fine. I mean, he's getting there, anyway. No, just something else. I have to go – changing a dressing in seven." She hustled away from Leslie, but the image of Benjie remained behind her eyes.

Finally, after work, after dinner, after trying to read a paperback novel and being unable to remember the name of the Regency heroine from one page to the next, Allison heaved a sigh and went to brush her teeth in preparation for going to the meeting at St. Michael's.

The speaker was an old man with a skinny, long, wattled neck and beer belly that made him look like a turkey. He wore patently false teeth, which he took out after a few sentences, declaring they pinched, which left his speech more of a nasal mush than Allison cared to listen to. She closed her eyes and replayed the images of Benjie in his sling on her chest and Matthew lying battered in the hospital bed, opening his eyes for the first time to see her.

Suddenly she heard the old man say, "So I told God, 'Kill me or save me, but I'm tired of screwing around with you' – and here I am."

Yeah. God – if you're there – kill me or save me, because I'm tired of you screwing around with me.

The group rose and held hands around the table for The Lord's Prayer. Allison joined in this time and noticed again the hair rising up on her arms and the back of her neck. Everyone said 'amen' in unison, then the ritual chant: "It works if you work it – keep coming back!"

It's like a football huddle, she told herself as she dumped her coffee and folded a few chairs. *We're all a bunch of players and cheerleaders at the same time. 'It works if you work it!' How many clichés are there in AA – a thousand? 'One day at a time.' 'Today is the only day you have.' 'Nothing so bad a drink can't make it worse.' Oh, yeah?*

"Want to go for coffee?" Carol asked, coming up behind.

"Oh! Uh – no thanks. Maybe some other time." *I have to get out of here before I suffocate!*

"Sure. Call me if you need anything. You still have my number, right? And just remember to ask Him for help to stay sober in the morning and thank Him for keeping you sober today when you go to bed."

"Right. See ya, Carol." *I can't breathe!* She ran up the stairs and all the way to her car, diving inside as if it were a hyperbaric chamber to saturate her with oxygen.

St. Michael's was an old Catholic church on the far side of Lewiston from Allison's home, lots of soaring gray stone arches and pointy spires and stained glass windows. It was huge and imposing and suggested a God-on-high presiding over mere mortals so far beneath Him.

The hospital chapel, on the other hand, was a really small room with no windows, only a fake stained-glass window in abstract pale blues, greens and rose. It had four little pews and its tiny altar under the fake window was just a plain oak table with a two-foot-high brass cross on it. Allison could see it all in her head and was only mildly surprised to find herself standing in the aisle there a few minutes later.

I've been here before. It feels safe, anyway, and I can breathe in here.

She sank down on the right front pew and closed her eyes. It was peaceful there. No pictures played through her mind, no condemning voice whispered in her ear, nobody asked her to do anything or believe anything or help anybody. Allison idly picked up a Gideon Bible which was lying on the pew and riffled the pages. It wasn't like she'd never read any of it before; she'd grown up in a family that went to church fairly often and had a Bible in her nightstand.

I remember reading some stories in there one day when I was home sick from school. But I don't remember Mom or Dad ever reading it or saying anything about it... I do remember Matthew saying something about it's not just a book of stories, it's the actual words of God – but how could that be? Men wrote it.

She closed her eyes and opened the book at random, a sort of test, she supposed. If it opened to something that really applied to her life, then maybe... *Maybe what? Maybe I'll believe it? Ha!*

1 John 1, verse 8, "If we claim to be without sin, we deceive ourselves and the truth is not in us." *Huh. Well, I guess I don't claim to be without sin, not after three abortions and all those guys.*

Verse 9, "If we confess our sins, he is faithful and just and will forgive us our sins and purify us from all unrighteousness." *Confess?*

To whom? Purify how? There's no getting over things like I've done, and how could anyone forgive them?

Closing the book gently, she laid it down on the maroon plush of the seat and shoved it farther from her. The little room seemed to have lost its serenity, and something was sucking all the air out of it. Allison tried to draw a deep breath and panicked when she couldn't, running out of the room and across the lobby, through the double doors into the parking lot. The sky was murky with clouds, the air heavy with impending rain – or maybe even snow. Allison climbed back into the little blue car and drove home as fast as she dared. No comfort anywhere. No safety anywhere. A drink would feel so good!

The answering machine was blinking as Allison came into the living room, tossing her coat carelessly onto the couch. Hoping it was Matthew, who called almost every day, she punched the button:

"Hi, this is Carol. Listen, I don't want to seem like a nag or anything, but I was worried about you tonight and now you're not home yet and – well, I just want you to know you can call me any time, day or night, or three o'clock in the morning – call me *before* you take that first drink, Allison, and let me help you. I mean it. Well – okay – that's it, I guess. Have a good night. Bye!"

Why doesn't she just leave me alone! I don't want her help! I don't need it. I don't need anything but Matthew and work and... and a drink. I can go to Max's Bar; they're still open. Or just go to Kroger and buy a bottle of wine or a case of beer...

A case *of beer? That sure sounds like a planned binge, because you can't begin to drink that much at one time!*

Do I really want to ruin everything? Because that will be it: Matthew, job, Alice, roof over my head – But what more do I deserve? I couldn't save Benjie, I murdered my babies, I'm no good for Matthew.

"I think this is what they call 'stinkin' thinkin'," Allison said to herself slowly. "Maybe I am the same as all those other people at meetings. Maybe I do need help."

She grabbed her purse and scrabbled through old gum wrappers and grocery receipts and ATM receipts and shopping lists until she found the slip of paper she was looking for.

"Carol, this is Allison, and I want a drink."

"Let me in," Carol said through the door. "You'll be glad you did."

"Go home," Allison insisted. "I'm sorry I called and bothered you; I'm fine."

"I'm not going," Carol said. "Your choices are to let me in or to have me stand here yelling through the door until I humiliate you in front of all your neighbors."

The door opened inward, apparently all by itself, and Carol pushed forward with her elbow, both hands being full of huge Styrofoam cups with lids sprouting spoonstraw-handles through special openings. She found Allison standing behind the door, her face as sullen as a two-year-old's right before the tantrum.

"Atta girl!" Carol said, holding out one of the cups. "Here, this is good for whatever ails you."

Allison was somewhat over two; she couldn't be bribed. "What do you want?"

"Well," Carol said, moving to the couch and plunking down in the middle, placing the cup she had offered Allison on the coffee table next to the blue and white giraffe, "I want to help you to not take the drink you're thinking about." She took a drag on the spoon/straw and her face nearly melted into bliss. "Oh, that's so good! I really wish you'd try it, because I know you're gonna love it!"

"What is it?"

"It's a super-thick, double-chocolate Snickers shake from the Fridgey-Freeze. My remedy of choice for chocolate deprivation or craving a drink. Or both."

Maybe she was closer to two than she realized, because in spite of herself Allison moved to the table and took up the drink. Sitting in the easy chair, she tasted and swooned. "Oh, my – that's maybe the best thing I ever tasted!"

"Told you so."

Allison was tempted to make a smart-alecky retort, but her mouth was full again.

"Seriously," Carol said, although she was smiling at the look of bliss on Allison's face, "sometimes craving a drink really does come from low blood sugar. That's why the AA old-timers tell the newbies always to carry candy. But for women, it's gotta be chocolate."

"Thanks. I don't think that's it, though, at least not this time."

"You want to talk about it? Sometimes that helps to sort it out – whatever 'it' is."

"You've heard my story, where I work and how I ended up in treatment and now on work probation."

"Yes. Work not going well?"

"No, work's going fine. But there was this baby – I took care of him, and he was doing so well, and they sent him to a foster home because his mother was neglectful – and the foster parents – I don't know. They did something, or they didn't do something, and he – died."

Allison put the drink back on the table and swiped at her eyes with the sleeve of her shirt. Every tear she blotted away was replaced by another one, until the stream down her cheeks was too much for her sleeve. Carol saw a box of tissues across the room and brought it back to Allison.

"He was special to you, huh?"

Allison nodded, blowing her nose. "You know about the abortions, right, and that I can't have any kids?" Carol nodded. "And I even had the idea I could adopt Benjie, or Matthew and I could, because I know he wants to marry me, and his son has come around to the idea..." Her shoulders shook with renewed weeping, and Carol just let it happen. At last Allison seemed to be over the worst of it and began mopping up.

"Do you blame yourself for the little guy's death?" Carol asked.

"What!"

"Do you think you could have changed things?"

"If I had spoken up about wanting to adopt him, maybe they would have given him to me instead of to that foster home. If I had visited him, I would have seen whatever was going on in time to stop it!"

"Really?" Carol raised an eyebrow at Allison. "You have that much power?"

"Maybe!"

Carol shook her head. "Even if you had asked for the baby, they would have put him in foster care while they were inspecting you and your home and making you give them some plan about how you'd care for him and such. Even if you had visited, you might have missed whatever the problem was. Sorry, girl, but you just aren't God, and you just can't control everything. In fact, you can't control much, can you?"

"You sound like my counselor in treatment," Allison said. "'All you can control is *your* attitude and *your* behavior.'"

"Sounds like a smart counselor."

"She was, but nobody likes to hear that. I don't care if I never hear the word 'powerless' again in my whole life!" She picked up the shake and slurped down several big mouthfuls.

"Pretty mad about it, aren't you?"

"You're darn' right I am! It's not fair!"

"Nope. See, though, here's where things like the Serenity Prayer come into play, Allison. I accept what I can't change. I let it go. I believe there's a power greater than me who is in charge when I don't have the faintest idea what's going on, and he or she or it knows what it's doing. When I surrender my will and my life to that power, then I don't have to worry about things. He has it covered."

"You go from he to she to it – what're you talking about, really? What kind of 'power' lets babies die and drunks run over people and –"

"Not everybody in AA believes in the same thing – you know that. And it's not my job to try to sell you or anybody on my own belief system. Your 'higher power' is whatever you choose to make it. After a lot of years in program, I've figured out my higher power is the traditional God of Christianity. That's probably true for most of the folks in program in the Bible-belt, at least from what I hear at meetings. But I know some people who believe in karma and a few who believe in their own inner spirit and some who believe in 'the universe,' and then quite a few who believe in the power of the group – you know, like a group conscience: if most of the people in the room say this is true or the right thing to do, then that's what they'll do."

"But you believe in God – capital G."

"Yes."

Allison made a slurping noise in the bottom of her cup and looked surprised enough that Carol laughed. "I didn't realize I drank the whole thing so fast!"

"So what, as long as you didn't get brain freeze. May I answer your question about what kind of a power lets babies die?"

Allison shrugged. "Why not?"

"Okay. Seriously, I don't think God kills babies or sends drunks driving so they can hit somebody. I think sometimes stuff just happens."

"You mean God couldn't stop it?"

"He could…"

"Then He's still some kind of a monster, if He could stop it but He doesn't."

"I can see why it seems that way. You know anything about the Bible?"

"Some."

"The story of how it all began?"

"You mean Adam and Eve and all?"

"Yeah. The story of creation. When God made the world and the universe and then made man, everything was perfect. There was no such thing as sin or evil and no one was ever supposed to die. Then Adam and Eve broke the rules – sinned, if you will – and everything was changed forever. Now the world is far from perfect, and people do terrible things – sin – and everything dies. That isn't God's fault. It's the consequences of man's attitude – 'I want to be like God' – and man's behavior – 'I will do whatever I want to do.' We brought it on ourselves. It's like any loving parent letting his child face the consequences of her behavior. Forget your lunch for the umpteenth time – go hungry at school; eat too much candy – get sick; break curfew – get grounded. That's how we learn to do the right thing and to take responsibility for ourselves. If our parents love us, they let us learn from our mistakes."

"Being grounded is a lot different from babies dying!"

"Come on, Allison," Carol said, exasperation coloring her voice, "you know what I'm saying."

"All right. I do." She studied her perfectly oval little fingernails for a moment before looking up at Carol. "But I don't – how do I – oh, I don't even know what the question is!"

"Honey, it's all about the first three Steps, and the summary is: 'I can't, God can, I think I'll let Him.'"

"How does anyone actually do that?"

"Do you believe you're powerless over alcohol – and other stuff?"

"Yes. I guess..."

"Do you believe in *something* greater than you are?"

Allison sat there a long time, thinking, remembering her times in the chapel in treatment and in the hospital, the way the hair stood up on her arms and the back of her neck when they prayed at meetings, the sense of Something there... "Yes. I guess I do."

"Then are you willing to turn your life and your will over to Him?"

"What if I do?"

"Then the program says He'll 'restore you to sanity' and help you live 'a life of sane and happy usefulness.'"

"Happy?"

"Sure. What's the point in a life of screwed-up, miserable usefulness?"

They found themselves laughing together, and Allison felt something loosening, like opening one's belt after a heavy meal and finally being able to draw a deep breath again. "Oh, yeah, I want that," she said.

"All you have to do is ask," Carol said. "Now I'm going home to my kids and leave you alone to have a long conversation with your higher power. Call me anytime!"

Thirty-Seven

FOOTBALL SEASON WAS FINALLY OVER, AND THE Lewiston High School fans were trying to put it behind them, focusing on basketball now, and their hopes for another winning season. Chance Rupp, triple threat, was practicing his foul shots by the hour, occupying a small corner of his mind with how to strike again at Will and his crazy father. He replayed that October night endlessly, the amazing high of hearing the cries of pain and the melon-thunk of boots smacking into human flesh. He held Will responsible for the woes of the football team, the six and four season which should have been ten for ten. If he didn't get into OSU because his season had been poor, maybe he'd have to kill Will Ryersen.

Matthew had to admit to himself that he was glad to see December. He finally felt like himself again, and he wanted nothing more than to get on with his life. The house was filled again with that low-level buzz the holidays usually generated, and he cheerfully carried boxes of ornaments down from the attic, went with Ed and Will to choose a tree from the tree-farm in adjoining Henry County while recounting to Will the story of his chain-saw accident there the year David died, dutifully tasted new Christmas cookie recipes and pronounced all of them winners.

"Would you like to invite Allison to Christmas dinner?" Carolyn asked.

"Really?"

"No, I'm just teasing. Of course, really! You said she doesn't have any family, and I hate to think of her being alone on Christmas."

"Are you sure you're up to it?" he asked, looking askance at her burgeoning middle.

"Up to one more plate on the table? I think so! For heaven's sake, Matthew, this baby isn't due until February. I'm fine."

Matthew blushed. "I didn't mean to – uh – "

"Never mind," Carolyn laughed. "Just ask her if you want to."

"Maybe," Tracy said, "maybe you need to talk to somebody."

"You mean, like a shrink?" Will asked, glaring at her and sliding away from her a bit on the leather couch they shared in Tracy's family room.

"Well... I don't know – somebody! You're so moody and miserable I feel like I can't do or say anything right, and you don't want to tell me what's going on, and – oh, I don't know!" She moved toward him.

"I don't need to talk to anybody. There isn't anything anyone can do." He moved away again.

"You can keep scooting over," Tracy laughed, "and I'm just going to trap you in the corner." She slid over and leaned in against Will, draping his arm around her shoulders.

"What if your mom comes in? She won't like to see us like this."

"Will, you dummy, if we're going together – well, she needs to get used to it." She nestled closer and his arm tightened around her of its own accord. "Now, listen to me: you need to get yourself straightened out. You need to apply for college, like yesterday! And I want my boyfriend to have a smile when he sees me, like he's glad to see me and wants to be with me."

Will colored and looked at his Converse shoes. "You know I want to be with you, Tracy. Come on. I'm just – I'm afraid, okay?"

Tracy drew back to stare at him. "Afraid! Of me?"

"No, afraid of – of what might happen next. You know those guys aren't giving up. What if one of them – or a bunch of them – comes after you because of me?"

Her eyes clouded, and the change pierced Will. She shouldn't have to be afraid. And if there were bullies, she should have someone to protect her, not someone who ran away and left the people he loved to be beaten half to death.

"I have to go," he told her. "I'll see you in school."

"Will! Come on! Will you at least *think* about talking to somebody?"

"Yeah, sure," he lied, heading for the door.

"I'm praying for you," Tracy said as he pulled on his jacket.

He smiled at her and kissed her on the forehead, quickly, so her mother wouldn't catch him. "Thanks."

He didn't look back to see whether she was standing in the doorway watching him.

"I don't want to intrude," Allison said.

"You're not. Carolyn asked me to invite you. You didn't have other plans, did you? I thought you told me you worked Thanksgiving and New Year's and got Christmas off this year."

"Well, that's true," Allison agreed, cuddling into the corner of the blue couch and snuggling the phone to her ear, imagining the combination to be Matthew sitting there with her.

"So you'll come?"

"If you're sure it won't be an imposition. I mean, Christmas is all about family, and your family is used to being together without strangers."

"Honey, look at 'my family.' Half of us aren't even related. The Corrigans might even be coming if the weather's bad. Her folks live in Pennsylvania somewhere, and his folks are in Cincinnati. Allie, everyone would love to get to know you better, and you'll have fun, I guarantee it. Please come. Even Will thinks it's a good idea."

"Will? A good idea?"

"He said so."

"The Corrigans – that's the guy from your church, right?"

"Pastor Miles, yeah."

Allison was quiet so long Matthew finally said, "Are you still there?"

"Oh! I'm sorry! Yes. I was just –uh – wondering – "

"What?"

"Well, I wonder if I could go to church with you some Sunday."

"What!"

"I know – stupid idea. Forget I said anything."

"No, wait a minute! I think it's a great idea! Can you come this Sunday?"

Allison tried to draw a deep breath and found her chest tight, her hands starting to sweat.

"You aren't working this weekend, are you?" Matthew asked. "Will and I can pick you up around eight-thirty. Please say yes."

What am I doing! "All right. Eight-thirty." *If You let me screw this up, I will never, ever forgive You!*

Will was finishing his calculus homework when his father knocked on the bedroom door and entered at Will's invitation. Will gestured for him to take a seat on the bed and waited anxiously for whatever was coming.

"How's it going?" Matthew asked, waving his hand vaguely at the cluttered desktop.

"Fine. I'm finished. What's up?"

"I –uh – need to ask a favor of you."

He's blushing. What's with that? "Sure."

"I was on the phone with Allison." Matthew paused, seemed to be gauging Will's response to that, then continued, "Carolyn has invited her to join us for Christmas. But you knew that, right?"

Will nodded.

"So I had kind of a hard time convincing her she wouldn't be an intruder, and I told her what you said. I hope that's all right."

"Sure." *It's fine, but why does my opinion matter? It's none of my business now.*

"She finally said yes."

"That's good."

"Yeah. Then she did a funny thing. I mean, odd-funny. She asked to go to church with us. I was really surprised!"

Okay... and...?

"I told her we'd pick her up around eight-thirty Sunday morning."

"We?"

"Well, I sort of told her you and me."

Okay, now I get why he's embarrassed. He's afraid I'll be mad and afraid I'll make a liar out of him to his girl. Dad, you're such a dork.

"I guess it won't kill me to go. It'll make Tracy happy, too."

All right, Dad. Big father/son moment scene now. Cue sappy music while father gives son big hug and son hugs back and – yeah, just like that.

Will allowed himself to linger in the embrace, savoring its warmth and love, even as the voice in his head reminded him how much he didn't deserve it.

Overnight the first real snow of the season began, leaving over an inch of fluffy, movie-set snow over everything, with more still coming down. Allison thought it was so pretty it looked fake, and she wondered whether it would close the roads into town, trapping the Abbotts at the farm. Matthew had told her once about that happening.

She stood in front of the full-length mirror appraising herself, wondering what was the proper thing to wear to church. Having tried most of the possible combinations in her closet, evidenced by the huge pile now on her bed, she had settled for a chestnut brown wool skirt whose hem kissed the tops of matching mid-heeled boots and a soft, long-sleeved white sweater with a cowl neck. It did seem to her that no more skin than absolutely unavoidable should be showing.

Fastening small gold studs in her ears, she grimaced at her hair, pulled back into a conservative bun at the nape of her neck, and debated again the appropriateness of the light application of mascara and pale lipstick.

Listen, God, I'm sorry if this isn't plain enough. If it's too much, I'll do better next time, I promise.

I'm insane. What next time? Why am I even doing this? God, why am I even doing this? Oh, nuts. Listen, they'll be here any minute, so grant me the serenity and all, okay? Thanks.

"You look nice," Matthew told her, helping her into her bright blue coat.

"I'm okay?"

"What do you mean, okay? You look great!" He escorted her down the slippery steps to the truck, where Will sat shotgun, watching their approach.

"I mean – am I going to look like an idiot or a sore thumb or something dressed like this?"

"Hey, Allison," Will said, hopping out to let her slide in to the middle of the seat, then climbing in after her.

"Hi, Will. I meant," she continued her conversation with Matthew as he got in and started the engine, "are my clothes appropriate for church?"

"Haven't you ever been to church?" Will asked.

"Not for a long time, since I was a little girl."

"Oh. Well, you look pretty, and people wear all kinds of stuff to church. Heck, in the summer a lot of the guys – even the old guys – wear shorts and sandals. With socks. The old guys," Will snickered.

Allison relaxed, comforted by both Will's comment and the non-chalant way he had delivered it. Her relaxation lasted all the way to the church parking lot, where she began to feel her whole body turn to ice.

I shouldn't have come! What will all those people think? They'll know I don't know what I'm doing, that I'm not one of them. Maybe they'll think I'm just there to try to get in good with the Abbotts. That would really stink! They'll hate me for messing with Matthew, trying to take him away from some nice church girl.

"It's okay," Will was saying as he gave her a hand out of the truck. "They don't bite, honest. Dad will look out for you, and he won't leave you alone."

"You're a nice guy, Will," she said, smiling at him. "Thank you for trying to make me feel at ease."

"Is it working?"

"Kinda."

"Well, then. Hey, Dad, I'm gonna go look for Tracy, okay? Meet you at the truck after church." He took off at a lope, leaving Matthew and Allison to follow more carefully across the parking lot and the salted but slightly icy sidewalk.

It wasn't the biggest church she had ever seen or entered, but it might have been the greatest concentration of church people she had ever seen in one place! The lobby – or whatever they called it – was seething with smiling men, women and children, all of them looking squeaky clean and homey as buttermilk. It also appeared that almost all of them knew and loved Matthew, for they came to shake his hand or hug him, expressing their pleasure that he had recovered and an-gling shamelessly for introduction to Allison.

"This is my girlfriend Allison West," he told them, pride and happiness evident from the tone of his voice to the grin on his face.

He's such a nice person. How could anyone ever want to hurt him? And all these people! They seem pretty nice, too. They sure are going out of their way to make me feel wanted. I wish this could last.

"We're down front," Matthew murmured, taking her elbow and leading her toward the third pew, where the Abbott family was waiting for them.

Everyone moved down two to make room. "Let me have the aisle," Allison whispered, and Matthew stepped in first, grinning.

"I remember how the first time feels," he whispered back, although the service hadn't started yet and no one else was whispering.

Allison was relieved as she looked around, subtly, she hoped, to see nothing strange or overwhelmingly churchy. The women were mostly dressed as she was, or wearing slacks, and mostly the older men wore suits, while the younger men wore sweaters or casual shirts. There were people of all ages, including toddlers racing around the aisles and babies in their mothers' or fathers' arms. She thought of Benjie and sighed.

A tall, stork-like man in a black suit, white shirt and bright red tie patterned with green Christmas bulbs came up the steps to the stand behind the (*Lectern? Pulpit?*) and plunked a large black Bible down in front of him. His dark hair was wavy and slightly in need of a trim, beginning to gray becomingly at the temples, and dark-rimmed glasses perched on the beak of his nose reinforced the impression of a scholarly stork.

"That's Pastor Miles," Matthew said.

After the pastor's warm welcome, a group of people swarmed out from behind the platform and took their places amidst microphones and musical instruments. *A band! I wonder what that's all about – a concert?*

Everyone stood; the pastor prayed and left the platform while the band and singers launched into one lively tune after another. Allison didn't know any of the songs, but she liked the rhythm and the enthusiastic way everyone in the audience was singing along. The words were flashed on big screens up by the ceiling on either side of the platform, so she was able to see the songs were all about Jesus, how wonderful He was, how great it was that He had come to be born as a human to save everyone from their sins.

That's what Carol was talking about. I can't believe You'd do that to Your own son!

When the singing was over, the pastor came back and called several children up on the platform. He was talking to them (but through his lapel microphone, so everyone could hear) about "advent" and the meaning of "the candles." As one child lit a pink candle which had already been burned, Allison noticed the arrangement of four colored candles around a big, fat white one on a small table next to the – whatever that thing was called where the pastor had put his Bible. Another child lit the second pink candle, also one which had been lit before, and finally, after a prayer, the third child lit a candle which was purple.

As the children went back to their parents, the pastor stepped up to the – thing – and began his sermon, all about "advent," the third Sunday – today – and how the theme was joy.

"I'm so glad you came!" Tracy whispered in Will's ear as the sermon began.

"Yeah," he answered quietly, preferring to focus on her hand holding his out of sight from their seats on the other side of Tracy's parents.

You ought to be ashamed of yourself, sitting here like you belong with the rest of these people. These are good, brave, strong Christians who love their God and love their families and stand by each other. What do you think you're doing here?

"Advent is a solemn time," Pastor Miles was saying, "because we realize not only the wonderful gift of Jesus' coming to live among us, as one of us, but also what that brief life as man would cost Him for our sakes. But it's also a joyful time, for exactly the same reason, that He gladly, lovingly paid that cost in full – for our sakes! And we know that for us who believe Jesus Christ is Lord, ask forgiveness for our sins and choose Him as our Lord and Savior, He is coming again to bring us to be with Him forever."

If a person can be forgiven. If he hasn't done something so bad it's unforgiveable. Oh, God, I wish –

What's the use of wishing. You already know it's too late for you. No one is ever going to forgive you for what you did to your father.

How can it be that simple? Allison wondered.

Please, Lord Jesus, let her hear You! Matthew prayed. He held her little hand and ran his thumb over and over her knuckles, almost without realizing what he was doing. It was easy today to feel the joy Miles was preaching, and he wanted more than anything to imagine a future in which he and Allison shared that joy into eternity.

Glancing at her out of the corner of his eye, Matthew thought he saw tears in Allison's eyes; but before he could fish out his bandana to give it to her, she blinked and they were gone, if they had really been there.

As they filed back down the aisle to the door, Matthew asked, "Did you like it?"

"I guess so," Allison said. "The music was great! And the guy – the pastor? – he said some interesting things. And," she grinned, looking more like herself and sounding that way, too, "the roof didn't fall in or anything, so I guess God isn't going to get me for being here."

Carolyn tapped her from behind and said, "Oh, no. He likes to have everyone home for Sunday dinner."

"What?"

"It's a half-joke," John said. "When the pastor preaches from the Bible, God's Word, we say we're getting fed. So 'home for Sunday dinner...'"

Allison laughed uneasily. "Okay. I get it."

Then they were reaching the door and being greeted by the pastor and his equally tall, stork-like wife, Penny. It was just a ritual moment, she told herself, but they were both so nice, without being pushy.

"Will you come home with us for dinner?" Carolyn asked in the lobby. "I have a huge roast, and there's plenty of everything else, too, including room at the table."

Wow, they're so friendly! "I don't want to intrude."

"You're not," John assured, smiling, echoed by Ed and Pearl.

"Tell her what's for dessert," Matthew said, smiling at her.

"What's – oh, a chocolate cheesecake I'm trying," Carolyn said.

Allison elbowed Matthew in the ribs, although carefully. "You don't play fair!"

"Nope. So stay, all right?"

"Thank you all. I will."

In the parking lot, they found Will waiting in the truck.

"Did you stay for the service?" Matthew asked, a slight frown creasing his forehead.

"Yeah, I stayed. Sat with Tracy and her folks." He crawled back in next to Allison but cleaved to the door and said nothing else all the way to the farm.

In the house, Will said to John, "I have a headache; may I be excused to go lie down?"

"Ask your father," John said automatically.

Will went into the kitchen to find Matthew, who was gathering things to help Allison set the table.

"Dad, I have a headache; may I go lie down?"

"Oh, I'm sorry!" Carolyn said, coming to him and rubbing his shoulder. "Do you want some aspirin?"

"I'll get some upstairs." He turned for the door and encountered Allison. Looking down a considerable distance into her bright blue eyes, he smiled a little. "Glad you can stay. Excuse me."

"Are you sure you're all right?" she asked. Then making a joke of it, she added, "You know, I'm a trained medical professional."

"Yeah, sure. No, it's just a headache. I'll be fine."

"Do you get headaches often since your injury?"

Come on, lady, back off! I don't even have a headache. "No. I'll be fine. I just need a rest." He pushed gently past her and escaped to his room.

Dinner was pleasant and Allison had never felt so welcome anywhere in her whole life. *No wonder Matthew lives here instead of getting his own place! These have to be the kindest people in the whole world! I wish my parents had been like John and Carolyn. If I married Matthew, this would be my family, too. God, is that unfair, to want to marry him even though I can't give him children? Is it too selfish?*

"Where'd you go?" Matthew asked, touching her arm.

"I'm sorry!" Allison blushed a little at the interested gazes pinning her from all sides. "I was just thinking of something."

"What?" Matthew asked.

Why not? "I was thinking I've never met nicer people in my whole life. You are all such a wonderful family! You're really lucky to have each other."

"Thank you," John said, echoed by the others.

Pearl, however, fixed Allison with 'the look,' which led Matthew to mutter, "Uh-oh" under his breath.

"Actually," Pearl said crisply, "we aren't 'lucky' at all. Luck has nothing to do with it. We are blessed. God in His goodness and grace has given us to each other. No luck, no coincidence – God's plan all the way."

"Oh."

"Say, 'Yes, ma'am,'" Matthew prompted under his breath.

"I heard that," Pearl said, fixing 'the look' on Matthew.

"Yes, ma'am," he said, grinning at her and forcing a reluctant smile to her lips.

"I'm sorry," Allison said. "I – uh – I've always said 'lucky.' I didn't mean any offense."

"And none taken," Pearl said. "But now that you are beginning to have a relationship with the Lord, you will want to acknowledge Him in everything. It's only polite."

Beginning to have a relationship? Is that what it is? Lord? "I'll try to remember," she told Pearl, who smiled at her and nodded.

Thirty-Eight

"PLEASE INVITE ALLISON AGAIN TO JOIN US FOR Christmas," Carolyn said to Matthew as they worked together on untangling the Christmas tree lights. Ed and Will would be bringing the tree any minute, and the decorations already waited in their boxes all over the living room.

"I will. I think she'll come. Hey, can I ask you something?"

"Of course. What is it?"

Matthew felt the Ryersen flush creeping up his neck and frying the tips of his ears as he tried to look at her straight on and failed. "Well, it's just – you're a woman – "

Carolyn couldn't help laughing. "Yes, I am."

"I mean – when John asked you to marry him – "

"Oh, I see where this is going!"

"Well – did he – did he have the ring already when he asked you, or did you get to pick it out? What would a girl rather do?"

"He actually had one in his pocket," Carolyn said, "and it's been on my finger ever since." She waggled her left hand at Matthew, smiling softly as she remembered. "He came for dinner and we went for a walk afterwards. He took my hand and told me he knew he'd never love another woman the way he loved me, that he believed it was God's plan for us to be together and he'd be so happy if I would marry him. Then he pulled out the ring and said, 'So will you marry me?'"

"What happened then?"

"Why, I burst into tears and grabbed the ring and dropped it in the grass in the back yard. It took us half an hour to find it, crawling around on our hands and knees in the twilight – not terribly romantic," she laughed, "but I did manage to say yes in there somewhere."

"Do you think it matters if it isn't a very big ring?"

"Oh, Matthew, I don't think it matters at all. Allison loves you; and since she's found this new relationship with the Lord, there's nothing to stand in the way of your getting married. Are you going to get her a ring for Christmas?"

"I think so. I just – I want to do it right, you know, and I want to be sure Will's okay with it, too."

"Guess you'd better ask him, then," Carolyn said, laying the untangled lights across the seat of the couch. "Which can happen any minute, because here they are."

Matthew waited until after dinner, when everything on the farm was battened down for the night and Will had long since retired to his room, to bring up the subject of Allison.

"I want to ask you something," he said, sitting in Will's desk chair while Will reclined on the bed, legs hanging over the edge like afterthoughts.

"Yeah?"

"Your opinion matters to me in this," Matthew said. "More than anyone else's. I want to ask Allison to marry me. But not if you don't want me to. If you need me to not do it, then I won't, son, because I want you to be happy."

Will sat up on the edge of the bed and stared at his father. "You're kidding, right?"

"No! Why would I be kidding? This is one of the biggest decisions in my whole life – and in yours."

"I get that. I mean, why would you even bother asking? You love her, she loves you, you know she'll say yes – so why not just go for it?"

"I guess because I need your blessing."

"My bl – Dad, you don't need permission from a seventeen-year-old to get married."

"No, I don't. I need your blessing."

Will shook his head, eyeing his father suspiciously. "So... how do I do that? Is this some Bible thing? I remember Jacob blessing his sons, but not a son blessing his father."

"I don't think it's in the Bible, at least, I don't know, but I mean I need to know you're okay with it, not mad about it anymore, really able to be glad for me – for us."

"Okay. If that's what you want: yeah, Dad, I think it's a great idea for you to ask Allison to marry you. I think it'll be great if she says yes, and I hope you guys will be really happy."

Matthew took in his son's flat demeanor, slumped shoulders, and sighed, going to the bed and sitting beside the youth, putting an arm around his shoulders, feeling more bone than had been evident there a month before.

"Thank you, Will. I hope you really mean it. And I promise marrying Allie doesn't mean caring less about you. I love you, and I will always love you – "

It was impossible not to notice the flinch of Will's shoulders, his drawing away and turning his face so his father couldn't see it.

"Thanks, Dad," Will said, no sarcasm evident. He stood up and crossed the room to his desk. "You go for it. Now I better do some homework, okay?" He sat at the desk and opened a book, picking up a pen and turning a page.

Matthew left quietly.

"You're sweating," Ed said.

"Yeah," Matthew agreed, wiping his face with a blue bandana, then wiping his palms. He shoved the bandana into his pants pocket, where it pushed against the ring box, making the sweat break out on his forehead again. "Let's get these logs in for the fireplace and get on with it."

"Carolyn outdone herself for dinner this year," Ed remarked, stacking a number of small logs in Matthew's arms before hoisting up some for himself. "Best pie I had in – oh, mebbe in days."

"You never met a pie you didn't like," Matthew teased, balancing his load as he knocked snow off his shoes at the back door.

"Ain't that the truth! Here, let me get the door."

They wiped their feet again on the old rag rug Carolyn kept on the enclosed back porch for that purpose and went straight through to the living room to dump their logs in the big basket beside the fireplace.

The room was warm and glowed in the soft light of candles and oil lamps, reflecting on the shiny ornaments filling the tall spruce tree, welcoming all comers home, whether it was home to them or not. A huge pile of presents sat under the tree, and all the people Matthew loved best were concentrated in that one room.

"Let me hang up your coats," Allison offered, taking both and going through the kitchen to the back porch as if she had lived there for years.

"Such a nice girl," Pearl observed, smiling a little, obviously feeling mellow on this special occasion.

"Yes, ma'am," Matthew answered, unaware how much his face betrayed.

"Time for presents," John said as Allison returned to her seat next to Pearl on the couch. "Will, you're the youngest here, so you can hand 'em out."

With no apparent enthusiasm, Will slouched over to the pile and began to distribute the gifts, saying nothing as he handed out each one and made a pile of his own on the other side of Pearl on the couch. Matthew settled at Allison's feet and rested his hand on her ankle as they accumulated a number of packages each.

"All right," Carolyn directed as Will finished his stint as elf, "now we can open them! Let's do one at a time, in a circle, so we can see everything. Pearl, let's start with you, then Will..."

Some things were annual and predictable: warm socks for each of the men, plaid flannel shirts for Matthew, Ed and Will, blue and green this year, an apron for Pearl, her favorite bath salts for Carolyn. Others were more individual: a soft, quilted pink robe for Carolyn and a gift certificate for a massage at the new place in Lewiston; sheet music – Mozart and Paganini – for Pearl; the collected poems of Theodore Roethke for Matthew from Will. A whole new pile had been started for the baby, full of tiny pink things which made Matthew and John sweat for another reason.

Allison was delighting in a bright blue cashmere scarf, hand-knitted blue mittens, a huge new coffee mug – blue, also, but covered with tiny pink flowers and saying on the front, "Think Spring!" Several other items filled her pile as she opened a box and drew out a soft pink sweater with a cowl neck.

"Oh, Matthew, thank you! This is beautiful!"

"You're welcome."

"You're blushing," she said with a grin.

"Never mind! Here, open this one," he shoved another box at her.

This box had not been professionally wrapped, and it was heavy. She hefted it onto her lap and carefully tore off the wrinkly Santa paper. "What could it be – so heavy?"

"Well, open it!"

"Okay, okay! Let me see – oh, Matthew!" Her eyes filled with tears even as her mouth was smiling and her hands were caressing whatever was in the box. She drew it out and held it up for all to see: a burgundy leather-bound Bible that looked at least half as big as she was. "I love it! My very own Bible! With everything in it, not just the New Testament and Psalms!"

"Yeah," Matthew said, gruffness in his voice disguising the joy he felt, "now you can return that other one to the Gideons." He paused a moment, cleared his throat and forced himself to say, "You missed something."

"What?"

"On the front."

"What on the front? It says Holy Bible and – oh."

"What?" Carolyn asked. "What's wrong?"

Allison's tears spilled over. "It says 'Allison West... Ryersen'," she sobbed. "Oh, Matthew!"

He rolled onto his knees and fumbled the ring box out of his pocket. Now or never!

"Allie, I love you so much. Will you marry me?"

Even Will found a smile for the occasion as Matthew took out the small diamond and offered it – and Allison nodded her consent. The ring fit perfectly, and so did the embrace he gave her.

"A wedding," Carolyn sighed.

"About time," Pearl said, sniffling just a little. "Welcome to the family, dear girl. You will be happy here."

"Congratulations, you old son of a gun," Ed enthused, dragging Matthew to his feet and into a hug, pounding on his shoulder. "I agree with Pearl – about time!"

The women clustered, admiring the ring and immediately beginning to talk dates, while John came over to Matthew and hugged him, also. Matthew knew he was grinning like a fool, but his heart was so light he feared it would escape and fly away like an untethered kite.

She said yes! She loves me enough to marry me! Thank You, Lord! Oh, Lord, there's Will all by himself, looking miserable again. Please, please help him out of that pit.

He walked the few steps to Will and squatted down in front of him. "Hey."

"Hey, Dad."

"You okay?"

"Sure. Just – Hey, congratulations. I told you she'd say yes."

"Nobody likes a smart-alec," Matthew teased. "Do you want to go over and say anything to Allie before the women carry her away to the kitchen to find wedding cake recipes or something? It's okay if you don't..."

"Sure, why not?" Will stood slowly, sighing, and made his way to the cluster of women. "Hey, Allison, congratulations."

Allison stepped away from the others to look closely at Will. "Thank you, Will. Can we talk someplace for a minute?"

"I guess. Let's go in the dining room." He ushered her out under everyone's questioning eyes and offered her a seat at the table.

"Will you join me?"

He sat down across from her, avoiding eye contact.

"Will? Can you look at me?"

He raised his eyes.

"I need to know how you feel about this. Did your father talk it over with you before he asked me?"

"Yeah, he did. I told him it's cool. I told him you'd say yes."

"That obvious, am I? Don't snicker!"

"Sorry. Yeah, it's pretty obvious about both of you. And it's good, really. You'll be good for my dad. He needs – somebody."

"Will, I understand going into this that I'm not your mom, and I'm never going to replace your mom – and you will always be number one to your dad. I get that, and I won't try to cross those lines, ever. If you think I am, I want you to tell me right away. I like you, and I trust we're going to be able to be friends. I don't want to mess that up, but you have to let me know."

Will nodded. "Friends. Sure. Thanks."

"So you'll tell me if I'm out of line?"

"Yes, ma'am, I will," he told her with the ghost of a smile. "I want

273

my dad to be happy, and you're what makes him happy. I won't get in the way of that."

Allison got up and walked around the table to put her arms around Will's shoulders, hugging him even though she felt his retreat, kissing the top of his head before she left him to sit there alone and ran back to the shelter of Matthew's arms, praying to her new-found God that Will would come around and share their joy, not just endure it.

Thirty-Nine

"WHAT DO YOU WANT FOR YOUR BIRTHDAY?" Allison asked, startling Will out of his meditation on alternate escape routes from the second floor at school.

"Huh? Oh – I don't know."

"Spread your hands a little," Pearl prodded, indicating the slack forming in the skein of pink yarn he was holding taut so she could wind it into a ball. "Something for your dorm room at college, maybe. Or a really good dictionary. Not quite that tight."

Will sighed, finding the magic tension for the yarn, wishing he could adjust his own tension level so easily. "Yeah, sure."

"Yeah, sure, what?" Allison laughed. "C'mon, Will!"

He sighed again. "Dictionary. Really good calculator. Sheets and towels? Shoot!" He shook his head, almost laughing. "Sounds like I'm the one getting married."

"Well, it is kind of like setting up housekeeping," Carolyn said. "Once you make up your mind, anyway. Have you decided where to go yet? He applied to four schools," she confided in Allison, "and they all accepted him. We're so proud!"

Please don't. Please let me be.

"I know," Allison said. "It's great! What do you think, Will?"

I think you should stop trying to include me in the girl-talk and get back to the wedding. "I don't know. Kevin's going to OSU, but Pearl says Cincinnati's really good. Too bad I'm not a music major."

"Indeed," Pearl said, not looking up from the stitches she was casting on.

"Defiance gets my vote," Carolyn said. "It's more expensive, because it's a private school, but it's commuting distance, and you won't have to leave us."

I don't want to leave you, either, but I have to get out of here – go someplace I don't see my dad every day and have to think about what a coward I am.

"I guess you'll figure it out," Allison said, tossing down the needles and bit of yarn she had been pretending with. "All I care about is that you'll still be home in June for the wedding. Promise me you won't find some excuse to skip that!"

"Nah, I'll be there. Giving away the groom is too funny to miss."

"So, back to your birthday," Carolyn said. "Any requests for dinner? I'd be willing to go all out; you only turn eighteen once in a lifetime."

"Whatever you feel like cooking is fine with me," Will said. "Cake. Dad likes birthday cake."

"Chocolate, of course," Allison said.

"Food talk makes me hungry," Carolyn said. I'm going to see whether there's any ice cream to put with those chocolate chip cookies." She stood awkwardly, finding her balance, alarming Will with her girth and the sudden grimace which came over her features.

"Hey! You okay?"

"Of course. Just a cramp from sitting in one position too long. Baby girl here is getting crowded – puts pressure on everything inside."

"Ew!" Will cried. "Too much information!"

Carolyn lumbered off to the kitchen and Pearl finished casting on a long line of stitches. Will wondered whether he could safely excuse himself now and escape the hen party. He had no appetite for either cookies and ice cream or female conversation.

"Just sit tight," Pearl said, and he figured she was reading his mind again.

"Yes, ma'am."

From the kitchen came a sudden sharp exclamation of surprise and the sound of water hitting the linoleum. Everyone jerked to attention, and Will saw his chance. "I'll go see what happened," he said, already halfway there.

Carolyn was standing in the middle of the kitchen floor in the middle of a puddle, and there was a faint, strange smell in the room.

Will skidded to a halt.

"Oh," she said, "hi, Will. Would you send Allison in here and go call John?"

"What's wrong!"

"Nothing, really. My water broke, and that means I'll have to go to the hospital. The baby's decided to come a little early. Guess I don't get any ice cream tonight."

"Allison, come here!" Will yelled, reluctant to leave Carolyn alone. "I – I'll get a mop," he said, gesturing vaguely, absently noting the pounding of his heart in his chest. "Are you sure about the baby? Should you sit down? Isn't it bad to come early?"

"Will. Hush. Yes, it's early, but not terribly early, just a few weeks. Allison can help me and John will take me to the hospital. Then the doctor will meet us there. I haven't had any real contractions yet, so there's no hurry. Now you call John for me, honey, and don't worry. We'll be fine."

Will and Allison bumped in passing through the swinging door, and he heard a new tone, the nurse tone, in Allison's voice as she questioned Carolyn.

"Baby coming?" Pearl asked.

"How'd you know?"

"Age and experience," she smiled. "I think John and the others went to the grange meeting over at the township hall. We'll call him there, though I don't know whether they'll answer the phone at night." She rose, putting down her knitting, and trundled off to the kitchen, Will trailing behind.

"I don't think it's going to be much longer," Dr. Dana encouraged as Carolyn gave a deep cleansing breath at the end of a contraction. "She'll be here soon. Any urge to push yet?"

"No," Carolyn answered. "What time is it?"

"It's almost midnight," John said, surreptitiously rubbing his hand, which was beginning to feel as if the bones had been pulverized. "She's going to be a tomorrow baby, like David. Here, sweetheart, grab on!" he said as another contraction gripped her, this one sooner and harder than the last.

Please, God. Please, God! Let her live. Let the baby live. Let them be all right, please, God, please...

"Do you want to cut the cord?" Dr. Dana asked John as she wrapped the slimy little body in a pink blanket and laid her on Carolyn's chest.

Staring at his daughter through tear-filled eyes, he shook his head, unable to speak. The baby was perfect. Carolyn was perfect. He was so in love with them and so terrified he couldn't form a thought, much less a sentence.

"Isn't she wonderful!" Carolyn said, stroking the tiny back. "Our daughter."

"I love you both so much," he managed before laying his head on the edge of her pillow and weeping out loud.

Ed, with his usual calm, had gone home to bed at ten o'clock, and Allison had left soon after. But Pearl had remained with Matthew and Will to wait for news. She had fallen asleep around midnight right there on the couch and Will had covered her with an afghan.

"Can she sleep like that, sitting up?" he whispered to his father.

"Looks like it," Matthew said.

"Do you think Carolyn's all right?"

"That's about the twenty-fifth time you've asked me that," Matthew replied, no evidence of impatience in his voice or on his face, "and I can only say I don't know. But I think they'll be fine. We're praying for them – "

Well, you are, anyway...

" – and I trust God that He has it all under control. So we'll just – answer the phone!"

Will, younger and faster than his father, made it to the receiver first. "Yeah?"

"Hello to you, too," came John's chuckle. "We have a beautiful little daughter, and she and Carolyn are both fine. Is your dad there?"

Will handed the phone to Matthew, shaking his head, a goofy grin spreading across his face for the first time in longer than Matthew could remember.

They're all right! Thank You, God!

"Johanna Grace," he heard Matthew say, "and we'll call her Gracie."

Forty

"HAVE A NICE BIRTHDAY?" DAN ASKED.

"Yeah, sure," Will replied, staring at the desk between them. He noted the stack of manila file folders, all with names on them, his on top.

"This is the big one – old enough to vote, old enough to join the army – and old enough to get off juvenile probation." Dan smiled at Will, who didn't notice because he was thinking about the file folders. "When a client reaches eighteen, we have some choices," Dan continued. "We can kick him or we can keep him 'til he's twenty-one or we can transfer him to an adult p.o."

"Mm-hmm," Will murmured absently.

"So I figure a bad guy like you – adult p.o. for sure."

"Mm-hmm."

"Will!"

"What!"

"You're not paying attention here. What's going on?"

"Nothing! I'm just – nothing." Will silently cursed the Ryersen flush creeping into his ears. "I'm sorry, Dan. I was distracted. What did you say?"

"Tracy, huh?" Dan teased. "That's okay. I was saying now that you're eighteen, there are three choices for me: keep you, transfer you to adult probation or let you go. And since you've turned into a pretty good client and passed all the drug tests and stuff, I'm going to let you go."

"Let me go."

"Yeah. You know – no more probation, no more having to check in, no more peeing in a cup – free at last."

"Oh."

Dan frowned. "You don't seem very pleased about it. I don't expect to see you doing a happy dance or anything, but I thought maybe you'd at least smile a little. Something wrong?"

"No! I am happy! It's just going to seem strange not coming here every week or two."

Like, weird, but I think I'll miss you.

"You'll be so busy getting ready for college and doing the senior skip with your buddies you aren't going to remember my name in a couple of weeks." Dan stood up and reached his hand across the desk. "I've enjoyed getting to know you, Will, and I'm proud of you. Keep up the good work. And let me hear from you once in a while, okay?"

Will also stood, realizing, *This is it. A handshake and out the door. I'm done here forever.* "Thanks. You put up with a lot from me, and I never said it, but I appreciate it."

Their handshake was warm and strong and left Will cold and uncertain when it was over. He headed out the door for the last time, not looking where he was going, and almost walked into Chance Rupp coming out of his father's office next door.

"Watch where you're going, Ryersen," Chance said, pushing past.

"What are you doing here?" Will asked.

Chance turned back and gave Will a contemptuous stare. "I'm visiting my dad. What are you doing here?" He went on down the hall and out the front door while Will stood there.

Is that what happened? Did he somehow read my file! Then he knows everything.

When the baby cried, everyone jumped to pick her up and soothe her. "You know," Pearl said, "that child is never going to learn to go to sleep on her own or to amuse herself, the way you all spoil her."

"That'd be easier to take if you wasn't holding her and playing with her when you said it," Ed responded. "Lemme hold her a while now."

"Nonsense," Pearl responded, "she's perfectly content where she is."

That much was true. It was also true, of course, that Gracie was living up to her name by being a placid, snuggly baby who rarely cried
280

unless her food supply was denied too long and smiled and cooed for anyone who gave her a glance or a kind word. It was also true that having a baby in the house had brought new life into the family in more ways than one. Even Will would smile for Gracie and held long conversations with her about the finer points of calculus or the soliloquies of Hamlet. Matthew had rapidly learned to carry her as if it were second nature, to burp her, to change her tiny diapers, unless they were really nasty, which was clearly women's work, and to sing her to sleep. Only Allison held herself a little aloof.

"I know it's hard," Matthew had said to her one evening as he drove her home, "but I think it would get easier if you'd just give in and hold her."

"You don't know anything about it!" she had snapped, bursting into tears.

Now he tried again, taking the pink bundle from Pearl and walking over to Carolyn's chair, where Allison was temporarily ensconced. "Here, honey, hold her for a minute. She's clean and dry and fed – won't stay that way."

Allison looked into the four-month-old face, round cheeks and big round eyes and little wisps of strawberry blond hair waving around the edges, and wondered whether her babies would have looked like this. Her eyes filled with tears, but she took Gracie into her arms for the first time in weeks. "Hey, baby. How are you, pretty girl?"

Gracie smiled up at Allison and made the little noise Will said resembled a pigeon cooing.

God grant me the serenity to accept the things I cannot change. Oh, she's so beautiful, Lord, and so perfect and healthy! Thank you for her life and her health. Please take care of her, don't let her be like Benjie.

"When we get married," Matthew said, sitting on the arm of the chair and leaning into Allison, "since Will's too big for a crib, maybe we could adopt a littler one. Maybe a girl. I used to have a fantasy – "

"Not in front of the baby!"

"Not that kind of fantasy. Seriously. I could see this little bitty girl with your hair and eyes, running around the front yard in a little ruffled dress – well, I'm just sayin' we could..."

"Will," Allison asked across the room, "would you like a little bitty baby sister?"

"Whatever. Sure. Why not?" He came over and snatched Gracie

from Allison's unprepared grasp. "Here we go, Baby Grace. Let's go look at the pretty flowers." He disappeared with the baby out the front door.

"She doesn't have a coat on!" Allison said, getting to her feet.

"It's all right," Carolyn said. "It's eighty degrees out, and Will won't let her get cold. He likes to walk around the yard and the barn with her and tell her all the things she's seeing. I don't know that she understands any of it, but she seems to enjoy the ride."

"He'd be good with a baby sister," Matthew told Allison.

"You're right. I never thought I'd be able to say this, but – well, I know God can give me the strength to do it if we want to. I'll think about it, anyway."

The phone rang and John, who was closest, answered it. He came into the living room looking for Will. "He has a call."

Called in from the back yard, Will cradled Gracie in one arm and picked up the receiver in the other. John and Carolyn went into the living room to give him some privacy.

"Ryersen," the harsh male voice said, "this is just a reminder. Keep your mouth shut and Tracy doesn't get hurt. Talk to anybody – *any-body* – and you won't like what gets done to her. And watch your own back, homo, because you know now dear old dad doesn't care enough to fight for you."

Will hung up the phone and dropped into a kitchen chair, clutching Gracie close to him with both arms until she began to squirm from being held too tight. Loosening his grip a little, he buried his face in the sparse curls on top of her head and asked, "Oh, Gracie, why does this keep happening? Why can't they just forget all this? Why can't they leave me alone?" He let his tears drop onto her head and breathed in the sweet, clean scent of baby. Why couldn't life ever be easy? He was so tired.

The blue and white cap and gown of Lewiston High School draped precariously across the desk, the flimsy rayon threatening to slide onto the floor into a mass of permanent wrinkles. They seemed to dare Will to move them, put them out of the way to ignore them.

It's all over. School's over. Tomorrow night we graduate and then it's off into the big wide world. I thought I wanted that, but now that it's here – I'm scared.

282

Of course you're scared. You're afraid of everything. You don't even have the guts to do the one thing you know will get you out of this life.

"Dinner!" Carolyn's voice floated up the stairs. Will heard his father leave his room and go down the stairs, other voices greeting below. He sat on the bed.

"Will!" Matthew bellowed. "Dinner's ready!"

"Coming," he called, still sitting there.

In a few moments, he heard someone climbing the stairs and looked up to find Pearl, red-faced and puffing, standing erect as an angel of God in his doorway.

"What's the matter with you?" she asked. "Are you ill?"

"No, ma'am. I'm coming. Sorry you thought you had to come and get me."

"I'm too old and arthriticky to be climbing up all those stairs," she chided. "But I was worried about you. We have hamburgers and home-made fries for dinner, and I know you like those. It's rude to keep us waiting."

"I'm sorry, Grandma," he said, hanging his head like a six-year-old.

The old woman came into the room and patted her boy. He looked at her and saw tears in her eyes. "I love you, you know, and I'm praying for the Lord to heal your heart, Will." She sniffed and wiped the end of her nose with a blindingly white little wisp of a handkerchief. "Now come down to dinner, please."

"Hey, Will!" Ed called up the stairs. "You got a phone call!"

"I'll get it in John's room," Will told Pearl. "You go on down, and I'll be there in a minute."

Sitting carefully on the quilt-covered bed, Will picked up the receiver.

Let it be Tracy. Let it be Kevin. Please!

"This is Chance, faggot. Listen up: I don't want to see your pansy face at graduation tomorrow night ruining everything for everybody else. You just tell daddy you have a tummy-ache and stay home. If you don't, you aren't going to like what we have planned to let everybody know what you are."

"Chance – " Will cleared his throat and continued, "Chance, this isn't cool. You got no right to do this, and it's not fair. I never did anything to you or Pete or anybody. And I'm not gay! I know you must have read my file in Dan's office, and that's illegal. Plus, what you saw in there is what happened to me, not what I did to somebody else. You and your goons need to stop this crap and let me and my family get on with our lives."

"You don't get it, do you, faggot? You don't belong with the rest of us. Now do as you're told, or we mess up graduation for you and for Tracy. I've got a party she can come to, and we'll show her a real good time."

"Stop it! You can't – "

"Oh, yes, I can. You know I can. By the way, how's that little baby in your house doing? I saw you out in the yard with her the other day. Little girl, right? I'm surprised they let you anywhere near her, perv, and it sure would be a shame if something happened to her. So get smart and get out."

The line went dead.

Will found every bite sticking in his throat and gave up almost immediately. "I don't feel so good," he said. "Please may I be excused?"

"You don't look so good," Ed said. "Kinda like bad cheese."

"You are pale," Allison chimed in. "Why don't you go up and lie down? Do you need anything?"

"No, thanks. I'll just lie down. I'll sleep, okay?"

He lay on the bed and tried to not think, but of course it didn't work that way. The voice in his head told him the truth over and over again: *Loser. Coward. Selfish. Stupid. When the chips are down, you run away like a baby. No one can ever trust you. Failure. Hopeless. Better off dead, so you don't hurt anybody else. Better off dead.*

"Tracy," Will whispered. "And Gracie. They can't hurt Gracie because of me! I would be better off dead. Then nobody else will get hurt."

He finally got up and went over to the desk. The wood-carving knife was still there in the back of the drawer, and he drew it out again. By now he was well aware what it could do and how easy it was to use.

Do it. Stop being a sissy-boy fooling around with little bitty cuts. You know how to do it – or are you too chicken to finally do something right?

The other voice reminded Will, *If we confess our sins, he is faithful and just and will forgive us our sins...*

That might be true for some people, but it isn't true for you. You abandoned your father, the man who gave you life, who took you in when you had no place else to go, who learned to love you and rescued you from Chicago, who prays for you... You left him to die at the side of the road because you were too cowardly to stay and fight for him. He has Allison now; he doesn't even need you. Nobody needs you, and nobody wants you. Get it over with.

Through tear-blurred eyes, Will contemplated the knife. It would hardly hurt. If he did it right, it wouldn't take too long. He didn't need to leave a note, because they all knew what a loser he was and what he'd done.

He thought about doing it in the bathtub, but the idea of being found naked was repellant somehow. *The wastebasket. I can hang my arm into the wastebasket to catch the blood. Okay.*

Rolling up his sleeves, Will scooted the chair close to the desk, so that when he passed out from blood loss he would fall forward instead of onto the floor, which would upset the wastebasket. He took the knife in his right hand and positioned the wastebasket on his left, testing to be sure he would have the right angle to have it catch the flow.

That's right. Do it.

"I'm sorry, Daddy." He made a fist to bring up the veins and with one quick slash ran the blade down from elbow to wrist.

The bright red flow was immediate and fast. He had hit what he aimed for. Dropping the knife onto the desk, he positioned his arm and listened to the rapid patter of drops into the metal wastebasket.

TO BE CONTINUED...

(Turn the page for a sneak peek.)

Ryersen Trilogy Book Three

Prologue

"Remember that you are dust, and to dust you shall return," the pastor's voice intoned, carried through the crowded cemetery on the light early May breeze. Over a hundred people crowded around the raw grave, many standing on grass so green it couldn't be distinguished from the artificial turf attempting to hide the edges of the hole. Overhead, the sky was lightly covered by a scrim of wispy gray clouds, leftovers from the early morning rain, and all the trees around the edges of the cemetery were dressed in fresh greens for the occasion.

"I didn't think he'd come," one elderly woman said to another sotto voce, clasping her black pocketbook against her black spring coat.

"Who is it?" the other woman asked, straining to see where the first one pointed. She wore black, also, but her pocketbook was a patchwork of colors and her sensible shoes were red, the only color competing with the beauty of May except for one bright blue coat in the front row with the family.

"It's that boy – you know. The one who used to live with the Abbotts."

"Oh. Him." The second woman considered for a moment. "I thought he died."

Chapter 1

ALLISON RYERSEN TURNED HER TEAR-STAINED eyes away from the grave to gaze up the sloping road, past all the serious gray funeral home vehicles, past the dozens of cars with little white-and-purple flags fluttering from their hoods, to the gray sky and grassy hill beneath it. Everything was blurry, because she couldn't seem to stop the tears from falling slowly, no matter how many times she wiped her eyes on Matthew's blue bandana. Blinking to clear her vision a little, she stared at the figure standing just below the crest of the hill, in the middle of the road. As she looked, the clouds parted for a moment and wide beams of watery sunlight fell on the man, gilding his hair and face and clothing like a Renaissance painting.

Allison gasped, and the sound was not lost on her husband, who put his arm around her and whispered, "What's the matter?"

"Look!" she said, pointing. "It's Will!"

Matthew's arm was suddenly gripping her so hard it hurt. "Will," he whispered.

"Go get him," Allison whispered back. "Bring him down."

Matthew seemed to hesitate, so she shoved him just a little, the way one might shove a recalcitrant horse or an encroaching Great Dane. At that nudging, he took off with a ground-covering stride toward the tall figure still standing unmoving in the road. Allison watched them meet, not touching, standing there like statues until she thought she couldn't stand it. Why didn't one of them give in and hug the other! Why didn't one of them say something?

"Let us pray," Pastor Corrigan said, drawing Allison's attention back to the burial service.

***

Will. He's not a boy any more. Oh, Lord, let me know what to say to him. Help me to build a bridge.

Matthew stopped about ten feet from his son, unsure how close he was allowed to go.

"Hello, son."

Slate-blue eyes met slate-blue eyes. "Hey, Dad."

"I'm glad you could make it. Come on down and join us, won't you? Allison would like to see you, and I know everyone else will, too."

"Thanks. I wasn't sure I'd be welcome after all this time."

Matthew's eyes filled with tears he didn't try to hide. "You've been welcome back since the day you left, Will. I've missed you so much – "

"Dad, you have to know it wasn't – I didn't stay away just because of you. There was just so much – my fault – " Now Will's eyes were tearing also, but he seemed to feel more shame, because he turned away, as if to go again.

Oh, no, not this time! I can't take ten more years of this!

Matthew closed the space between them and took Will's arm, turning him around so they were face to face, eye to eye, in fact, as there was not a hairsbreadth of difference in height between them.

"Will, it doesn't matter to me why you left, why you stayed away, even why you came back. You're here, and even today – maybe especially today – nothing matters more to me. I need you, Will, right here with me. Please."

"Dad! Come on – you can't – "

Matthew saw the embarrassment and consternation riding across Will's face on the Ryersen flush that rose up his neck and across his ears and cheekbones. It was like looking in a mirror, and he knew Will must know it, too. They were so alike, although Matthew's wheat-blond hair now had silver frosting, and wrinkles from constant exposure to sun and weather permanently wreathed his eyes. He understood, too, the feelings coursing through his son, because they were alike in that, also, quick to feel and quick to take on a burden of guilt. He liked to think time and experience and the loving corrections of his wife and family had tempered some of that...

Will was shaking his head. "Dad, I – I'm sorry. I should have come sooner. Maybe if I'd been here – " He began to cry in earnest, fumbling in his pocket for a handkerchief.

For a moment Matthew expected him to pull out a crumpled blue bandana, the standard handkerchief for an Abbott family male, and was surprised by the ironed, neatly folded, bright white square. Then he shook off that line of thought and did what he had been wanting to do from the beginning.

This is right. This is where you belong, Will.

Holding Will close in his arms was different now, Matthew realized. The frame was heavier, filled out with muscle, a man's body, not a boy's. The weeping was a man's weeping, too, painful and reluctant, soon to be over as a man's mind told him not to be unmanly. The hands which clutched at him were a man's hands, strong and broad. Even so, his mind recalled the small-for-his-age ten-year-old who had stifled his tears in a couch cushion rather than ask for comfort.

"I've got you, son," he murmured and held on.

***

"Amen," Pastor Corrigan said. "Please join us back at the church for a fellowship meal and some time to talk with the family."

People began to mill around immediately, some leaving, some moving forward to speak to the bereaved. Several were staring at the reunion taking place near the hill, but most were still unaware of Will's return. Allison couldn't take her eyes off the two, even as she responded to words of condolence here and there and tried to keep an eye on the rest of the family. At least they were finally in each other's arms where they belonged.

I feel like the watchdog nanny in Peter Pan, Allison teased herself, *herding the people I love together. I wish I could just run up there and – and what? Looks like they have it under control. Oh, God, thank You for bringing Will back! Would it be too much to ask that he would stay? We need him now.*

***

"Will you come to the church, then, and talk to folks?" Matthew asked as Will pulled away gently and blew his nose.

"I'd rather not. Those people coming up the hill are staring at me, and I'd just as soon not be the topic du jour in front of myself."

"Topic dew what?"

"Sorry, Dad. Today's gossip. Maybe I could just meet you at the house afterwards." He paused, a sudden look of confusion on his face. "I mean – which house?"

Matthew laughed. "It's okay. Come to John and Carolyn's, like always. The door's not locked; you can find yourself some lunch while you wait, because all the dear church ladies have been bringing casseroles and trays of stuff until the refrigerator's full."

"All right. I'll see you when you get back." Will turned away again and made his way to a sleek black car of some breed Matthew couldn't identify but would bet wasn't made in America.

"Will – "

"Yeah, Dad?"

"You really will be there, won't you?"

Will looked straight at his father. "Yes, sir, I really will. No running, I promise."

***

The fellowship hall was full of tables and chairs, with hardly any room for the well-padded to get between them. A huge buffet of what ten-year-old Gracie Abbott referred to as "funeral food" invited partakers with tantalizing aromas and colors. Several of the older church women presided over drinks and desserts tables, and some kids from the youth group were ferrying plates and drinks to those who were not quite up to braving the lines at the buffet. The air was humid and warm with the steamy scents of food and the breath of over a hundred people.

"Let's sit down," Allison said to Matthew and the others. "I know they have that table over there reserved for us."

"You make a great sheepdog," Matthew muttered into his wife's ear, affection and humor in his voice. "Guess we need one today."

***

Eric Showalter, the mayor of Lewiston, and his wife Anita sat with Dr. Nate Hanna, the Abbott family's physician for as long as anyone could remember, and the Harrises, a farm family active on the

Lewiston school board and athletic boosters' committee. Al Harris had also been an FFA advisor for many years, until long after his own sons had graduated.

"Been quite a time for the Abbotts," Al said. "Couldn't believe it."

"Really," Lynn Harris agreed. "What a shame!"

"Death comes to all of us," Eric intoned, only to grimace as his wife's bony elbow connected unerringly with his ribs. "What? It's true, isn't it?"

"Yes, but maybe you don't want to say it quite so loudly during a funeral meal!"

"Oh. Sorry, folks." Eric gave himself to his ham loaf and roast beef, lest he find himself eating shoe-leather again.

"Always have good food here at funerals," Al Harris said, changing the subject. "Eat up, Doc! You haven't touched a thing."

"Not hungry, I guess," Nate responded, his gruff voice even more gravelly than usual.

The Showalters and Harrises exchanged knowing looks. Everyone in and around Fulton County, Ohio, over the age of forty knew Nate Hanna had been hopelessly in love with Carolyn Seibenek Abbott since they were kids.

"Did you see who showed up?" Anita asked the table at large.

"Who? Where?" Eric asked, echoed by the Harrises.

"That boy. You know, Matthew Ryersen's son, the one who disappeared after those rumors went around – off to college, they said, but he never came back. Until today."

"Which rumors?" Lynn asked. "You mean about how he beat up his father? I heard Matthew almost died! And then I heard the boy committed suicide, but that couldn't be right if he went away to college."

"Well," Anita said, leaning in to speak in hushed tones, "the truth is, nobody knows what happened to Matthew. I don't believe for a minute that Will did it – "

"Oh, that's right," Lynn said. "Your daughter was dating him, wasn't she? So I'm sure you'd know everything!"

"No, no, they were just – ah – school friends," Anita said, obviously trying to distance her child from the unpleasant rumors. "But I do know he attempted suicide, didn't he, Nate?"

"Anita, for heaven's sake, you know if he had I couldn't discuss it! What's the matter with all of you – no hot topics already up for discussion, you have to dredge up stuff that happened ten years ago?"

"Don't be a crusty old thing," Anita teased. "I guess you can't say anything. I'm sorry for asking. Well, Tracy told me he tried to kill himself, but I never did learn why. Anyway, he did go away and never came back – until today."

"How'd you even know it's him?" Al asked.

"Oh, you can't miss it! He looks just like his father, only twenty years younger. Same eyes, same face, same hair, same body, even same gestures. It's remarkable, even after all that time apart. Did you see them hugging in the road?"

"I thought we wouldn't ever have to talk about that boy again," Eric complained. "He's gone and ought to stay gone."

"Can't deny the boy a chance to come home for the funeral," Al said. "He is family, sort of. Even if he's a bad guy, he probably has feelings."

"Excuse me," Nate said, gathering his untouched plate and cup and rising, "gotta get back to the office. Nice to see you all."

"Well, he was testy!" Anita said, watching the doctor's back as he hurried through the crowd.

***

Will parked the Toyota near the porch and climbed out to stand under a maple tree, surveying the landscape. It was remarkable how little had changed. The shutters on the house were dark green now instead of black, but the porch swing was the same and so were the flower beds, spring bulbs rioting already in the mild air. The maples and oaks were all still standing, though he could see where a large limb had been removed from the maple nearest the house. If he let himself, he could readily imagine it was May of 1999 instead of 2009, and Carolyn would call him any minute to come in for lunch.

Although tempted to walk around to the back door, he took himself in through the front, passing into the living room, where he paused again to look around.

John's and Carolyn's chairs still flanked the fireplace, with its figured tiles and carved mantel. The couch had a new slipcover, something with dark green stripes, but the plush green carpet looked as new and fresh as it had ten years before, and the bookshelves were still stuffed with volumes and the occasional treasure. The bust of

Christ his father had carved for John long before Will had come to the Abbotts still sat on the bookshelf, surveying the room. Will had never liked that statue; it was creepy, the way it looked like the man was being tortured. Who wanted to watch someone suffer? Shaking off the eerie feeling, Will went through the dining room into the kitchen.

Now, here was change! The room had been repainted some kind of peachy color, and the curtains which had been white with big red apples were now a different kind of white material with ruffles top and bottom. The old appliances were all gone, replaced by sleek stainless steel things; even the old porcelain sink had been swapped for a double sink in stainless. The cupboards were all new, some pale wood like birch, with glass fronts. Even the old setting hen and big apple cookie jars were gone. In their place sat a big clear glass jar like the old candy jars in general stores. And it was empty. That had never happened before.

Will put his hand on the cookie jar and tried to imagine – but he couldn't. In that one artifact, the truth had come home. Carolyn Abbott was dead.

About the Author

Photo courtesy of Mike Moore, New Beginnings Studio

Mary Mueller recently celebrated her seventieth birthday, an age she never expected to reach, by completing a concealed carry weapons class with her son and grandson. She has not yet taken up skydiving, (or pearl diving, for that matter), but she is working on the final book of the Ryersen Trilogy, co-writing the 2013 Easter drama for her church, and managing to keep a houseplant alive for over a month as of this writing!

Also by Mary Mueller

Stargazer: The Story of Mary

Stargazer is a first century masterpiece of the life of Mary, mother of Jesus. In retelling the biblical story, we follow Mary from a young girl, through her betrothal to Joseph, the birth of Christ, his childhood, his ministry, and his eventual crucifixion and resurrection. This heartwarming story will help you better understand the biblical story of Mary and the culture she lived in, as well as bring you to a new understanding of the humanity of Christ.

www.ingramcontent.com/pod-product-compliance
Lightning Source LLC
Chambersburg PA
CBHW020554260626
47157CB00003B/702